About the Author

Christine Merrill wanted to be a writer for as long as she can remember. During a stint as a stay-at-home-mother, she decided it was time to 'write that book.' She could set her own hours and would never have to wear pantyhose to work! It was a slow start but she slogged onward and seven years later, she got the thrill of seeing her first book hit the bookstores. Christine lives in Wisconsin with her family. Visit her website at: christine-merrill.com

D0237698

Regency Secrets

Regency Secrets:

Those Scandalous Stricklands

CHRISTINE MERRILL

MILLS & BOON

All rights reserved including the right of reproduction in whole or in part in any form. This edition is published by arrangement with Harlequin Enterprises ULC.

This is a work of fiction. Names, characters, places, locations and incidents are purely fictional and bear no relationship to any real life individuals, living or dead, or to any actual places, business establishments, locations, events or incidents. Any resemblance is entirely coincidental.

This book is sold subject to the condition that it shall not, by way of trade or otherwise, be lent, resold, hired out or otherwise circulated without the prior consent of the publisher in any form of binding or cover other than that in which it is published and without a similar condition including this condition being imposed on the subsequent purchaser.

® and TM are trademarks owned and used by the trademark owner and/or its licensee. Trademarks marked with ® are registered with the United Kingdom Patent Office and/or the Office for Harmonisation in the Internal Market and in other countries.

First Published in Great Britain 2022
By Mills & Boon, an imprint of HarperCollins*Publishers*
1 London Bridge Street, London, SE1 9GF

www.harpercollins.co.uk

HarperCollins*Publishers*
1st Floor, Watermarque Building,
Ringsend Road, Dublin 4, Ireland

REGENCY SECRETS: THOSE SCANDALOUS
STRICKLANDS © 2022 Harlequin Enterprises ULC.

A Kiss Away from Scandal © 2018 Christine Merrill
How Not to Marry an Earl © 2018 Christine Merrill

ISBN: 978-0-263-30564-7

MIX
Paper from
responsible sources
FSC **FSC™ C007454**
www.fsc.org

This book is produced from independently certified FSC™ paper to ensure responsible forest management.

For more information visit: www.harpercollins.co.uk/green

Printed and Bound in Spain using 100% Renewable electricity at CPI Black Print, Barcelona

A KISS AWAY
FROM SCANDAL

To Clara Bloczynski: there can be only one.

Chapter One

'I have a problem.'

In Gregory Drake's experience, most conversations began with exactly those words. But that was to be expected, given the unusual nature of his profession.

Gregory fixed things.

Not in the usual sense. Watchmakers fixed watches. Tinkers mended kettles. But Gregory was not a tradesman as much as a student of human nature. He fixed lives. When members of the upper classes were confronted with a situation that was difficult, embarrassing, or simply tedious, they came to him.

He made their problems go away. Quickly, quietly and without another word.

It was why he was welcome in the reading rooms at Boodle's and White's and most of the other clubs in London. He could claim membership in none of them. But he was so often found in attendance at them, sharing hushed conversations with important people, that no one dared to ask the reason for his presence. Though society might see him as an underling, even its most august members kept a respectful distance from him, not wanting to embarrass their friends. More importantly, they did not want to annoy the fellow who could be counted on to rescue them when trouble arose.

Today, Gregory stretched his legs towards the fireplace to warm the January chill from his bones. Then he looked expectantly to the man in the opposite chair. 'Does your problem involve a woman?' Until his recent marriage, James Leggett had been a well-known rake who courted scandal almost as actively as he chased the females that embroiled him in it.

At this, Leggett laughed. 'It involves several women. But none in the way you probably expect, given my reputation.'

'If not an *affaire de coeur*, then what could it be?'

'It concerns my wife's family,' Leggett said, with a sigh. 'Lovely ladies, all. But there are far too many of them for one man to handle.'

'That is why you are speaking to me,' Gregory said, with an understanding nod.

'The branches of the Strickland family tree are so full of women that it is all but dead. My darling Faith has two sisters and a grandmother.'

'The Dowager Countess of Comstock,' Gregory supplied, to prove he was well aware of the circumstances. 'The Earl had no brothers and all three of his sons are dead. But, I understand the Crown has found an heir to the earldom. There is a cousin of some sort, several times removed and living in America.'

Leggett nodded. 'This leaves the ladies in a somewhat precarious position.'

In a just society, it would not. In Gregory's opinion, men should be required by law to make provision for the future of female relatives and property should be divided equitably amongst all siblings, regardless of sex. But no one gave a damn for the opinion of a fellow without inherited wealth, nor did it make sense to argue reform with a man who had benefitted from the current system. Instead, he described the situation at hand. 'The last Earl left them a pittance and the ladies fear that the new one will take even that away from them.'

'It is not as if they will starve in the streets,' Leggett said quickly. 'I will provide for them, if no one else shall. But they are worried. The heir has called for an audit of the entail to be completed before he arrives.'

Suddenly everything became clear. 'I take it there might be some problems in the accounting?'

'The Countess is a delightful woman,' Leggett said with a smile. 'Charming and sweet-tempered, but a trifle foolish. She could not resist keeping up the appearance of wealth where it no longer existed.'

'She has been selling off the family jewels,' Gregory said. Women of titled men sometimes grew so used to the baubles they wore that they thought of them as personal property and not things meant by law to be passed down the generations, from one peer to the next.

'Nothing as dire as that. It seems she's pillaged furniture, paintings and assorted bric-a-brac.' Leggett held his hands wide to indicate the variety in the theft. 'It is all quite random. The only record of the sales exists in her faulty memory.'

'You need someone to search the Lombard merchants for the missing items.'

'With a dray and draught horses if necessary. God knows how much is missing. Buy it all back at my expense,' Leggett said, closing his eyes in resignation. 'And finish before the arrival of the new Comstock. There are rumours of rough seas between here and Philadelphia, but weather will not forestall discovery once his man of business arrives. With two sisters yet to be married, my wife is terrified that any scandal will spoil their reputation.'

'I have contacts in the industry that might help me with retrieval,' Gregory assured him. 'You are not the first to come to me with such a problem. Once I am on the case, it will be sorted in no time.'

'But in the past, you did not have to contend with the Strickland sisters.' Leggett gave him a rueful grimace.

Gregory countered with what he hoped was a reassuring smile. 'If they are named for the three theological virtues, how much trouble can they be?'

'How much trouble? As much as they can manage, I suspect.' There was something in the quirk of his lips that was not quite a smile. It spoke of bitter experience. Then, his face gentled. 'My Faith is a continual delight, of course. But she has a will of iron.'

'The shield and bulwark of the family?'

'Rather,' Leggett replied. 'She is the eldest and used to running things. I am removing her from the equation, for my pleasure and her piece of mind. A month in Italy will leave you free to do the work she would take on herself, if I allowed her to.'

'That is probably for the best,' Gregory said cautiously. 'And the other two?'

'Charity is the youngest,' Leggett said.

'A sweet child, I am sure.'

'She is no child. She is fully nineteen and cold comfort, at best.' Leggett glanced about him to be sure no one heard his candid assessment. 'A whey-faced girl with a mind as sharp as a razor and a tongue to match. She will be a great help, if you can persuade her to put down her books and leave the library. But she has the brain of a chess master and, if she decides to work against you, your battle is lost before it has begun.'

Gregory nodded, already thinking of ways to win the favour of Charity. 'And the third?'

'The *enfant perdu*, in the military sense, of course.'

'A lost child?' Gregory waited in silence for an explanation as Leggett sipped his drink.

'Are you familiar with the military concept of a forlorn hope? Those soldiers willing to risk certain death and lead a charge, straight into the enemy cannons?'

'They seek great reward.'

'Weighed against almost certain failure,' Leggett confirmed. 'That describes Hope Strickland. She is a girl with a plan. A rather stupid plan, in my opinion. But it is hers and she cannot be dissuaded.'

'And what would that be?'

'She means to wed the new Earl as soon as the fellow's shoes touch British soil. She thinks his marrying into the family will soften the blow of learning that the Dowager has been pinching his property.'

'Such a connection would be expedient,' Gregory said.

'It would save us the trouble of finding a husband for Charity,' Leggett agreed. 'She has spurned Faith's offer to share our home and refuses to put herself in the way of gentlemen who might court her. But if Hope snags the Earl, Charity could remain in the Comstock Manor library as though nothing had changed.'

It sounded almost like he was describing a piece of furniture that was valuable, but too heavy to move.

'All the same,' Leggett continued, 'a man should have some say in choosing his own wife.'

'And you know nothing about him,' Gregory added. 'He might already be married.'

Leggett nodded. 'Or he might be too young to marry. Or old and without the vigour for it. Also, he will have to be even-tempered enough to forgive the pilfering and inclined to care more for family than the money that this new title is bringing him.'

'He might not be the sort of man a gently bred girl should marry at all,' Gregory said.

'He could be a drooling idiot, for all we know: a villain, a cad, a deviant or a toss pot. I cannot let Hope marry into misery just to maintain the status quo for her little sister.' Now, Leggett had the worried look that so many of Gregory's clients got when faced with an insolvable problem.

'Women get ideas,' Gregory said in his most reassuring tone. 'Especially when they are thinking of the family and not themselves.'

'My wife was guilty of similar foolishness. When I discovered her, she was about to marry for money over love.' Leggett smiled. 'I managed to set that to rights. But I cannot marry all of them to save them from themselves.' Then he looked at Gregory in a way that hinted that the finding of lost objects would not be the hardest part of his job.

'You do not think that I...' Gregory paused. 'You do not expect me to find them husbands.' He prided himself on his ability to rise to a challenge, but matchmaking was not within his purview.

'Lord, no. We are all agreed that Charity is a lost cause. But Hope is more than pretty enough and will have no trouble finding a husband if she can be persuaded to look for one. I do not want the Season to slip away, or offers to be refused, as she waits like a princess in a tower for a rescue that may never come.'

'You wish me to make enquiries into the heir?'

'Any information would be helpful,' Leggett said. 'Should you find that there is a wife and ten little Stricklands in America, make Hope aware of them so she will abandon her scheme.'

'And if I do not?'

'I would not object to your taking a certain creative licence with the truth,' Leggett said, as optimistic in his own way as Miss Strickland was in hers.

'You wish me to lie to her?' Gregory put it plainly. Though he was not a gentleman by birth, he held his honour as dear, often more dearly than the men who hired him did. If he was to break his word with lies, he had no intention of hiding those untruths under elegant euphemisms like *creative licence*.

Leggett sighed. 'I merely want her to set her sights on the men right in front of her. Do what is necessary to persuade her. I will leave the details of it to you.'

'Thank you.' That left him plenty of room to manoeuvre before resorting to falsehood.

'And you will have ample opportunity to come up with something, since you will be forced to work directly with her. It is Miss Hope Strickland who holds the list of items you must retrieve.' Now Leggett was smiling in satisfaction as if he had made the matter easier and not more complicated.

Gregory began cautiously, not wanting to contradict the man trying to hire him. 'In my experience, the less the family is involved with these matters, the quicker they are handled.'

'I did not claim it would be easy,' Leggett reminded him. And there was that smug smile again, as if it gave him pleasure to see another man suffer what he had endured at the delicate hands of the Strickland sisters and their dotty grandmother. 'I will give you double your usual fee, since, if I am honest, I have brought you two problems, not one.'

More money on the table before he'd even opened his mouth to ask for it. Gregory already knew he could find the missing heirlooms. How hard could it be to prevent a marriage that was unlikely to occur, even without his intervention?

He looked at Leggett's smile and hesitated a moment longer.

'Triple, then. I am eager to depart for the Continent and wish to be sure that the matter will be settled to my satisfaction.'

The offer was too good to refuse, even if he'd wanted to. 'Consider it done.'

'Thank you. Miss Hope Strickland, Miss Charity and the Dowager are in London for the Season at the Comstock town house in Harley Street. I will tell them to expect your visit.'

'Very good.' There was likely to be nothing good about it. Other than the pay, of course. That was enough to reinforce the smile Gregory gave his new employer.

'And I trust this matter will stay between us?' Leggett said, in the slightly embarrassed tone of someone not used to admitting he had difficulties, much less asking for help with them.

'I shall be the soul of discretion,' Gregory replied. When one made one's living mopping up after the gentry, keeping secrets was part of the job description.

Chapter Two

'Good evening, my lord.' Hope Strickland stood in front of a mirror in the hall of the Comstock town house, examining her smile for traces of insincerity before deciding that it was as near to perfect as she could manage.

Then, she curtsied, analysing the results. She was not inexperienced with the niceties due a peer, but that did not mean she should not practise. First impressions were the most important ones. There could be no flaw in hers.

Not that it was likely to matter. The odds of success were almost nil. But if there was any chance at all to impress the next Earl of Comstock, she meant to try.

Now that Faith had married, Hope was left as oldest. It was her job to carry on as best she could and take care of the family that remained. It was clear, from their scattershot behaviour, that Charity and Grandmama needed all the help they could get.

She dipped again. The bend in her knees was not

quite deep enough and her eyes could not seem to hold the fine line between deference and flirtation.

'Are you still at that?' Charity was standing in the doorway, arms folded in disapproval.

'It pays to be prepared,' Hope replied, straightening the curl on the left side of her face that could never seem to follow its mates into a proper coiffure.

'Prepared to bow and scrape for the stranger coming to take our house out from under us?' Charity said.

Hope bit back the urge to announce that it was her sister who needed to mind her manners. Instead, she said, 'It is his house. We are but guests in it.'

'Family, you mean,' Charity responded.

'It would be nice to think so.' Hope turned away from the mirror to face Charity. 'I prefer to take a more realistic view of the situation. Though we share a surname, he has never met us before. He will not think of us as family unless we work hard to make him do so. When he arrives, we should greet him with warm welcomes and friendly smiles.'

'You don't wish to befriend him. You want to marry him. What are your plans if that does not happen? If you mean to be prepared, it should be against all eventualities.' Charity was far too logical for her own good. But that was no surprise. It had always been her nature to find the weakness in any plan and jab mercilessly at it until her opponent relented.

'If the Earl is not impressed with me, we shall have to make decent matches while we are in town. Then we will set up our own households and not con-

cern ourselves with him or his property.' She put a
subtle emphasis on the word *we,* hoping that her sister would acknowledge the seriousness of the situation and do her share to fix it. Hope had no real fear
of failure for herself. But they had always known
that things would not be as easy for Charity. And as
she usually did, Charity was making matters worse
with her refusal to even look for a husband.

'We must also thank Mr Leggett for his generosity in making a Season possible,' Hope added. She
touched her skirt to remind her sister of the elegant
wardrobes they'd purchased since coming to town.
Before their sister had married, it had felt as if they'd
been trimming, re-trimming and altering the same
tired gowns for ages. But now, everything in their
cupboards was fresh and new.

But you could not tell it from looking at Charity,
who was wearing a gown that was two years old and
could best be described as serviceable. It had done
well enough for hiding in the manor library, but it
was totally wrong for London. Her sister had noticed her silent criticism and responded, 'There will
be time for me to play dress up later. Right now, I
have other plans.'

Hope gave her a firm but encouraging smile. 'Of
course you do. But it will be rather hard to carry
them out while rusticating in the country.'

'For you, perhaps. I was doing quite well right
where I was. The sooner you allow me to return to
Berkshire the easier it will be on all of us.' While
Hope had jumped at the chance to come to town,

Charity had done nothing but complain since the moment they'd arrived.

'You speak of my need for alternate plans,' Hope said, smiling to hide her frustration. 'Do you have any of your own? When the Earl arrives, you cannot simply dig in your heels and refuse to vacate the manor. If he asks you to go, you will have to leave.'

Charity smiled. 'I do not need a second plan. The first one is near to fruition and I will be long gone before he ever sets foot in the house. If you would only allow me to return to the country…'

And there it was, again. The solution her little sister was continually hinting at, but refused to reveal. It did not sound as though she meant to reason with the new owner—as if there was a man on the planet who wished to be reasoned with by a girl just out of the schoolroom. But if not that, then what could it be? 'This plan of yours…' Hope hinted. 'I assume it does not include marriage? Because to achieve that, you might consider accepting some of the invitations you receive.'

Then, a worrisome thought struck her. 'Promise me you do not mean to dishonour yourself. We are not as desperate for money as all that.'

Charity laughed harshly. 'My dear sister, you may lie to yourself about your own future, but please do not lie about mine. She stepped forward and took Hope by the shoulders, turning her so they stood reflected, side by side in the mirror. 'No man will have me for a mistress. I am not pretty enough. I fully intend to marry, when the time is right. But it will take more than a new gown and a perfect curtsy for me to catch a husband. I will need a dowry.' She reached up and adjusted her spectacles, as if assessing her own appearance. 'A substantial one, I should think. It will take more money than average to compensate for both appearance and manner.'

'Do not say that about yourself,' Hope said hurriedly. But it was true. It was one thing to be a plain girl and quite another to be an intelligent one who could not manage to keep her opinions to herself. 'I am sure, once the Earl comes…'

'You will marry him, and he will look kindly on your beloved but eccentric, spinster sister?' Charity patted her shoulder. 'You are normally a very sensible girl, Hope. That is why it pains me to see you delude yourself.'

'I just want to see you happy,' Hope said. It was not as much a want as a responsibility. Now that Faith was gone, someone had to look out for the family and neither Charity nor Grandmama had the sense to take charge.

'I am happy,' Charity said softly. 'It may surprise you to hear it, but it is true. Do not concern yourself with my future. Think of your own. I hear Grandmother has got vouchers for Almack's. You must go and dance every dance, even without the presence of the Earl.'

'Of course,' Hope said, then gave her sister a pointed look. 'And you will come with me.'

'Perhaps,' Charity agreed, oblivious to the order she had been given. Then she kissed Hope on the cheek and turned to go up the stairs to her room. 'If I am not busy with something more important.'

Hope sighed. It was better than a flat refusal. Knowing Charity, by Wednesday there would be some excuse that would prevent her from coming out with them. But it did not matter. Just as her sister had suggested, Hope would go and dance until her feet ached. She would be as charming as she possibly could and see to it that every gentleman in London had met and been dazzled by Miss Strickland.

There was no point in being a wallflower. The new Earl of Comstock could have his pick of any girl in England. He would not look twice at a girl who was not courted by others.

She turned back to the mirror, and flashed a smile that would blind a duke at twenty paces. Then, the curtsy. 'Good evening, my lord.' This time, she dipped deeper and felt an embarrassing tremble in her front knee. She was nearly one and twenty, but hardly infirm. She could do better. She must do better.

She tried again. 'Good evening, my lord.'

'I should think good morning would be more appropriate. It is not yet eleven.'

She stumbled at the sound of a voice behind her and raised her eyes to see the reflection of the stranger who had entered the room as she practised.

It was he.

It had to be. Who else but the Earl of Comstock would be wandering around the house unintroduced, as if he owned it? In a sense, he did.

'And I have no title.'

'As of yet,' she said. There was no longer a need to practise her smile. When she looked at him, it came naturally. Who would not be happy in the presence of such a handsome man? Though she had never been one to dote on the male form, his was perfectly proportioned, neither too tall nor too short, with slim hips and broad shoulders on which rested the head of a Roman God. His blond hair was cut *à la* Brutus, curling faintly at the fringe that framed a noble brow, unmarked by signs of worry. His grey eyes were intelligent, his smile sympathetic.

Praise God, she had been delivered just the man she'd prayed would come: young, handsome and, judging by the twinkle that shone in those beautiful eyes as he looked at her, single. But not for long, if she had her way.

He tilted his head. 'You are correct. I have no title, as of yet. Nor am I likely to get one. But they are sometimes awarded to men whose service merits them and I am not yet thirty. With time and effort, anything is possible, Miss Strickland.'

She steadied herself from the shock and turned to face him with as much grace as possible, struggling to maintain the expression she'd been practising in the mirror. 'Then you are not my cousin from America?'

'The future Earl of Comstock?' His smile softened. 'Unfortunately, no.' He bowed from the waist. 'Gregory Drake, at your service, Miss Strickland. I was told you'd be expecting me.'

She could feel her smile faltering and struggled against the impolite response, *who?*

More importantly, *how?* She glanced to the front door which had not opened to admit anyone, much less this interloper. Then, she made an effort to compose herself. 'I fear you were incorrectly informed. I was not told there would be a guest this morning. You have caught me unprepared.'

He followed her eyes, read the meaning and gave a deferential dip of his head. 'I beg your pardon, Miss Strickland. I was retained by your brother-in-law to help with certain difficulties your family is experiencing. Since the matter is one that requires discretion, I entered through the rear to avoid calling attention.'

'The tradesman's entrance.' Of course he had. If Mr Leggett had hired him, why should he not begin there?

He nodded, solemnly.

A torrent of unladylike words filled her mind about trumped-up nobodies with delusions of a grand future who had the gall to tease her with them. And worse yet, who had the nerve to look like the answer to a maiden's prayers. He had no right to be so handsome, yet so inappropriate.

Then, the rant changed to encompass her sister's husband, who had hired this…this…person. She ended with a scold for Grandmama, who probably knew the whole story and had neglected to tell her any of it, just as she had with the difficulties surrounding an audit. The Dowager probably thought it amusing to throw the two of them together so Hope might make a fool of herself.

When she was sure that her actual words would leave her mouth with a minimum of bile, she said, 'So Mr Leggett has sent you to save us from ourselves.'

Her control was not perfect. She still sounded ungrateful, but she had a right to be angry. She had been behaving like an idiot when he'd entered. It likely confirmed what he already thought of the family: that they were a houseful of silly women, incapable of caring for themselves.

Of course, that was what she often thought, when faced with the latest exploit of her sister or her grandmother. She did not deny that they had problems, but how could a stranger possibly understand them the way she did?

She forced another smile. It was not the warm one she was saving for the Earl. The one she gave to Mr Drake was sufficient for solicitors and shopkeepers. 'How much has Mr Leggett told you about our difficulty?'

'Everything, I suspect. You seek the return of certain items before an impending inventory.' If he thought her rude, he did not show it. His manner reflected hers. He was professionally pleasant, but revealed no trace of his true thoughts or feelings.

So, he suspected he knew everything. That proved how little he actually knew. Even Mr Leggett did not know the worst of it for Hope had not wished to ruin Faith's honeymoon with what she had recently discovered. But Mr Drake should at least understand that none of it was Hope's fault. To prove her lack of culpability, she said aloud the words that had been echoing in her mind since she had learned the extent of their troubles. 'Grandmama should not have sold things that did not belong to her. Nor should she have kept our financial difficulties a secret for so long.'

He offered another sympathetic nod. 'But what could you have done, had you known?'

Very little. Faith had been the one in charge of the family budget and her decisions had seemed sensible enough. Economies had been taken in diet and dress. Rooms had been shut and staff had been released. How much less would they have had without Grandmama's judicious thefts refilling the accounts?

The fact that there had been no other solution did not make her feel any better, now that reckoning had arrived. 'The past does not matter. It is the future that I am worried about. There will be a scandal, if the truth comes out.'

'I am here to see that it never does,' he said. 'I have helped more than a few families with similar problems. Taking desperate measures when there is a shortage of funds is not at all unusual.'

'I assume Mr Leggett means to buy back the lost items?' It was a generous plan from a man who had no idea the depth of the problem.

'He said you had a list.'

'After a fashion,' she said, giving nothing away. By the look on Mr Drake's face, he expected her to turn over the details of her family's darkest secrets without as much as a by your leave. She had no reason to trust this stranger who appeared out of nowhere with far too much information and no introduction, verbal or written. For all she knew, he was an agent of the new Earl and they were already discovered.

He gave another encouraging smile. 'If you share it with me, then I will go about my business and leave you to yours. The matter will be settled without another thought from you.'

She could not help a derisive snort. It would serve him right if she told him the truth and then sent him on his way with no other help. 'Very well, then.' She turned from him and walked down the hall to the morning room. He could follow or not. It did not really matter.

She heard the measured steps of his boots follow down the corridor and into the room. When she withdrew the crumpled paper from the little writing desk in the corner, she turned to find him still a respectful few steps behind her. She handed him the list. 'There you go. Settle our troubles, if you still think you can.'

She watched his handsome brow furrow as he read down the column. 'Blue painting. Candlesticks. Third Earl's inkwell.' He glanced up at her, clearly surprised. 'That is all the detail you have? Nothing to tell me if the candlesticks were gold or silver?' The furrows grew even deeper. 'And I cannot make out this line at all.'

'Neither can I,' she said, trying to contain the

malicious glee as he was brought into her suffering. 'My grandmother is a woman of many words, but we can seldom get the ones we need out of her. It took some effort to get this much detail, for she kept no records of the things she sold and the places she took them. And I am quite certain there are items missing from this account.' Only one of them had any significance. But it was not a story she wished to tell, just yet. 'I will question her further, but I do not know how much more she will admit.'

'It is fortunate that dealers keep better records than their clients,' he said. 'It might take some persuading for them to give the information up. There are laws against dealing in entailed merchandise.'

'I am well aware of the fact.' Her grandmother was as guilty or more so than the people she'd bartered with. They might be receivers of stolen goods, but she was the actual thief.

'But if they do not remember her?' The look on his face changed to resignation. 'Would you recognise these items, if you saw them again?'

'Most of them, I think,' she said. 'I have lived in the house since I was ten. They should at least be familiar, should I find them in a shop window.'

He sighed. 'Then it would be best if you come with me, to retrieve them.'

'You are suggesting that I accompany a strange man to unseemly parts of London to retrieve stolen goods.'

'I am not a stranger, as such,' he reminded her. His

smile returned, though it was somewhat the worse for wear. 'I was sent by your brother-in-law to help you.'

'I have only your word for that,' she replied.

'How else would I know of your problems, if not for him?'

'You might have guessed them.' More likely, it was just as he said. He had been sent to help. But for some reason, his good looks and perfect manners annoyed her. It gave her a dark and unladylike pleasure to see him struggle.

His composure slipped for only a moment. Then he dug a hand into his coat pocket and came out with a paper. He held it out to her. 'If it is not as I say, how do you suppose I came by this?'

It was a letter of credit, signed by Mr Leggett, promising to honour any and all bills without question. The sight of it left her light-headed. He could not know what he was promising. Since Faith and her husband had already left for their honeymoon, it was too late to tell him.

He mistook the reason for her silence and said, 'If it helps, think of me as a servant who will be accompanying you as you set matters right. I will be there to assure your safety, handle the transactions and carry the packages.'

It did not help at all. The idea of him walking a pace behind her like some liveried footman was an abomination. He was too well spoken for a servant and not stern enough for a schoolmaster. If she stretched her imagination to the breaking point, she could see him as a solicitor, but there was a sparkle in his eye better suited to a criminal than a man of law. And no vicar would have that knowing smile.

He was simply too handsome to be going about town with. Should she be seen with him there would be gossip that had nothing to do with the Stricklands' financial troubles. And while it was quite all right for the new Earl to see her as sought after, she could not have him thinking that she was being actively courted by Gregory Drake.

'If you fear for your reputation, remember that it will be equally damaged if news of the missing items becomes public.'

'Unless the new Earl can be persuaded to com-passionate silence,' she said, wishing she could go back to her practising and pretend this meeting had never occurred.

Mr Drake tucked his letter back into his coat, along with her incomplete list. 'What do you know of your grandfather's heir, thus far?'

It was an annoying question, since the answer was obvious. They'd had no contact with the man, other than the request for an audit of the entail to be com-pleted before his arrival, and that had come through a solicitor. It did not bode well. But she put on a false smile to appease her interrogator. 'I know that he is family and familial bonds are strong. I am sure Mr Strickland will understand the difficulties faced by women who are forced to fend for themselves.'

'We must hope so, for I doubt he has any special affection for this country,' Mr Drake said, pulling another piece of paper from his opposite pocket. 'Mr

Leggett has also hired me to find what I could about the gentleman you are expecting.' He scanned his notes. 'It appears that his grandfather fought bravely in their revolution against this country. More recently, Mr Strickland's elder brother, Edward, was impressed into the British Navy. Miles Strickland became heir upon Edward's untimely death in battle.'

This was what came of optimism. Hope had allowed herself to believe, just once, that with a little effort on her part, things might turn out for the best. And this was how the Lord rewarded her. She swallowed her nerves. 'If our country has treated him so unfairly, perhaps he will refuse the title and remain in America.'

'It is too late to hope for that, I think,' Mr Drake announced. 'Even now, the schooner *Mary Beth* is on its way from Philadelphia to Bristol. If he booked passage on it, as he planned, he may arrive at any time.'

'We are not at fault for a war on the other side of the world, or the doings of the Royal Navy,' Hope said, feeling her vision of the future crumbling like a sandcastle at high tide.

'But there is still the matter of the missing entail,' Mr Drake replied, speaking slowly, as if to a child. 'It is best that we make sure he has no other reasons to be unhappy with you. Give me a day to examine your list in detail. If it is convenient, I will call for you tomorrow at ten and we will begin the process of making things right.'

She wanted to argue that it was not convenient at

all. He could take the list and go to perdition for all she cared. They were doomed. All doomed. What good would it do her to start a search that she was sure they could never finish?

But Mr Leggett must have chosen this fellow for his skills in retrieval. Perhaps he could find a way to make things marginally better. If he needed her help, then surely her help was required. The sooner it was begun, the sooner it would be over. And she could not depend on rough winter crossings to delay the Earl indefinitely. The house needed to be in something approaching order when he arrived at it. She forced another smile for Mr Drake. 'If this is to be settled, I do not see that I have any choice in the matter. I will accompany you as long as certain conditions are met.'

'And they are?' he said, with an expectant tip of his head.

'For the sake of modesty, I will remain veiled in your presence. We will speak no more than is necessary and under no circumstances will you call me by name while in the presence of others.'

If he was insulted there was no sign of it. His smile was as distant and unwavering as ever. 'Of course, Miss Strickland.'

'Then I will expect you at ten o'clock tomorrow.'

'Until then.' He offered a bow worthy of a true gentleman, then spoiled it by turning towards the back of the house.

She sighed. 'You are standing next to a door, Mr Drake. Please, use it.'

'As you wish, Miss Strickland. He turned and let himself out of the front door and into the street.

Hope moved to the window and watched him walk down Harley Street, sure she could not truly breathe until he was out of sight. Mr Leggett meant well, as did Mr Drake. Even if it did not make things better, their interference could not possibly make things worse. But had it been necessary to tell her about the Earl of Comstock's antipathy for England? It was almost as if Mr Drake took as much pleasure in seeing her disappointment as she had in his.

'My, what a charming fellow.' Grandmother stood behind her, looking out the window at their departing visitor.

'He was not charming,' Hope said, wondering if her grandmother had formed her opinion based on the way the man's coat hugged his shoulders as he walked. 'And how would you know, either way? You did not speak to him, did you?'

Grandmother peered past her at the retreating figure. 'Only briefly, when he arrived. He is the fellow James hired to help us with the entail.'

'You knew.' Hope could not help her shrill tone at the discovery that, once again, she had been denied important information and left in an awkward situation to fend for herself.

'Did I forget to mention it?' She looked at Hope with the widened eyes of one who thought that age and good intentions made up for outright lies. 'I did not want to trouble you. But when he arrived looking so young and handsome, I assumed the two of you would not want an old chaperon spoiling a perfectly lovely chat.'

Just as she had suspected. 'You sent a strange man to speak to me without as much as a footman to explain.' She probably assumed that if she threw the two of them together they would stick like lodestones, just as Faith and James had. 'I cannot solve our problems by marrying the first person who walks through the door, you know.'

Her normally cheerful grandmother arched a sceptical eyebrow. 'You are a fine one to say such a thing. That is your plan, is it not? To marry the new Earl?'

'That is entirely different,' Hope replied. At least she knew the Earl's family. Lord only knew what sort of dubious pedigree Mr Drake might have.

'It is not the worst idea,' the Dowager admitted. 'But as I tried to explain to your sister Faith, choosing a husband for financial expediency is never as satisfying as a union based on mutual affection.' She stared down the street in the direction Mr Drake had disappeared. 'Or, at least, temporary passion. That fellow was quite handsome, I thought.'

It was annoyingly true. His hair was the colour of winter wheat and, though she'd often thought grey eyes seemed cold, his were warm and inquisitive, especially when paired with that slightly sardonic smile. 'I did not notice his looks,' she lied.

'Are you ill?' Her grandmother reached out to touch her forehead.

Hope shook off the hand. 'Merely circumspect.

My parents would have thought it most unchristian of me to evaluate a man on appearance alone.'

The older woman gave a disapproving tut. 'When we encouraged your father to read for the church, we had no idea he would take the whole thing so seriously.'

Both her parents had been more than serious on the subject of morality. They'd been paragons of it, and died together, nursing their village through an epidemic. Then, Hope and her sisters had come to live with their grandparents and a whole new and comparatively decadent world had been opened to them. 'They would have wanted me to marry sensibly,' Hope replied. 'There is nothing sensible about Mr Drake.'

'A flirtation, then,' her grandmother suggested, with no thought at all to Hope's reputation. But then, as she frequently reminded them all, things had been different when she was a girl.

'Young ladies do not engage in flirtations,' Hope reminded her. They especially did not do it with employees of their families and she did not think Mr Drake was helping them out of the goodness of his heart.

'I am not suggesting that you dishonour yourself,' the Dowager added with a flutter of her lashes. 'But it would not hurt you to smile when you see a handsome man. It would not ruin you to laugh with him. The world will not end if you let him steal a kiss.'

'Actually, it might,' Hope said. 'Suppose someone learned of it? I would be shunned from polite society and Mr Drake would not be welcome in the homes of the men who employ him.'

The Dowager sighed. 'Young people nowadays have no spirit at all.'

'Gentlemen do not marry girls who have too much spirit,' Hope replied.

'All the more reason *not* to marry a gentleman,' she supplied. 'Of course, it is possible that the new Earl will not be one. He is American, after all. Lord knows what barbaric habits he has developed.'

'He is probably married,' Hope said, glumly. It would be just her luck if he turned out to be a married man who hated the English.

'Then, perhaps you should look elsewhere. As I reminded you before, Mr Drake is a very handsome man.'

Hope offered a weak smile in response. At times like this, she was never sure if her grandmother was joking, addled by age or simply lost to all propriety. But she had lived with the Dowager far too long to be surprised.

'Mr Drake has no interest in me, beyond the task set for him by Mr Leggett. There will be no lingering glances, no stolen kisses and definitely no marriage. We will find what missing items we can, he will collect his payment and that will be the end of it.'

'If you say so, my dear.' The Dowager shook her head in disappointment. 'But in my opinion, you are wasting an opportunity.'

'I certainly hope so,' Hope replied with an adamant nod of her head.

Chapter Three

So far, the Strickland family was everything Leggett had promised they would be: intelligent, maddening and beautiful. Though of those attributes, the best the Dowager Countess could seem to manage was two out of three.

Judging by her granddaughter, she had been stunning thirty-odd years ago, and was still a handsome woman. But from the dearth of information she'd provided about the problems she'd caused, it was clear the Earl had not married her for her mind. When Gregory had tried to question her upon arriving at the town house, she had deliberately changed the subject, wanting to know more about him than he had cared to share while revealing nothing at all about the shops she had frequented or the things she'd sold to them.

Then, there was Miss Hope Strickland, who was currently sitting beside him in a rented carriage on their way to a pawnshop. She was simmering like a soup kettle with the desire to finish her part in the search as quickly as possible so she might never lay eyes on him again.

And a very pretty kettle of soup she was. Chestnut hair, large brown eyes and a pert nose accented the sort of soft, curvy body a man longed to hold. But the set of her beautiful shoulders and the straight line of her eminently kissable lips had assured him of the unlikelihood that anything would happen between them. She was the granddaughter of an earl and had heard the common 'Mister' before his name and dismissed him out of hand.

Likewise, he had noted her grandfather's rank before even meeting her and had come to the same conclusion. He was not the sort of fellow who dallied with female clients, especially when there were titles involved. When one was a living example of what might happen when such niceties were ignored, one did not take them lightly.

At the moment, Miss Hope sat beside him silent, cloaked and veiled, as if his very presence brought a risk of contagion. Her desire for anonymity made perfect sense. But there was something annoying in the way she had demanded it, as if she had not trusted him to protect her unless ordered to do so. It left him with the urge to strip off one of her gloves and touch her bare hand, just to see if she melted from upper-class perfection to a wailing puddle of mediocrity. Or at least tug on the curl that had been bouncing at the side of her face yesterday. This morning, it had been held in place by not just one but two hair pins, as if she was punishing it for being unruly.

Hope Strickland was the sort of woman who liked both people and things to be orderly, proper and predictable. He would likely be a great disappointment to her. Hopefully, they could manage to put their differences aside while working together. Until the matter of the entail was settled, they would be near to inseparable.

He glanced towards her and away again, hoping she had not noticed his interest. It felt as if, somewhere deep inside his head, an alarm bell was ringing. They should not be alone together. It was dangerous to her reputation and to his…

Something.

He wasn't sure exactly why, but he knew in his bones that he shouldn't be alone with her and it had nothing to do with society's expectations of virtuous young ladies. He had no worries about self-control, either hers or his own. But the silence in the cab was wearing on his nerves. It made him want to converse, even though she had made it quite clear she did not want to speak to him.

He should never have requested her help. It was not as if he had to find the exact items again. He merely needed a good approximation. The American Stricklands had not spent the long years away pining for the candlesticks they meant to retrieve today. One set would be much like another to the new Earl, as long as he did not note an absence of light in the dining room.

But what the devil did the Dowager mean by an 'oddment'? It was the only word he had deciphered in the line of scribbling near the bottom of the list. And how was he to decide which 'blue painting' was the correct one? Only a member of the family could guide him through the inadequate descriptions provided to him and Miss Hope Strickland was the only one willing to help.

But since she had done so begrudgingly, he had a perverse desire to see her discommoded. That was why he had chosen the worst shop on the list as their first stop. There would be almost no chance at success for it traded in the saddest of merchandise, not the sort of things likely to be found in one of England's greatest houses. While he knew that there were better hunting grounds ahead, she would leave the shop coated in the miasma of despair that seemed to hang about the financial misfortune of others.

The carriage stopped in front of a plain door in St Giles, marked with the traditional three balls that indicated its business. He exited, offering a hand to Miss Strickland to help her to the street, while keeping a wary eye out for the cutpurses and beggars that would appear to harass the gentry.

To his surprise, she did not shrink back in terror at the riff-raff that surrounded them. But neither did she offer thanks for his assistance. Instead, she sailed imperiously past him to stand expectantly at the door, waiting for him to open it.

It was only common courtesy that he do so, but for some reason, it rankled. All the same, he opened and she passed through. And at last he was rewarded with the response he'd expected, the utter confusion of a gently bred lady who had never before shopped for someone else's cast-offs.

She paused in the entryway as if afraid to go further. He could tell by the subtle shifting of her bonnet that her eyes were darting around the room, stunned to immobility by the cases of brass buttons and mismatched earbobs, and racks upon racks of shabby coats and fashionless gowns.

He shut the door and stepped past her. A quick scan of the room proved that none of the finer items would be found here, but he had no intention of leaving without making an enquiry, lest Miss Strickland realise he'd only come here to torture her. He rang the bell on the counter to summon the proprietor.

The man who stepped out from behind the curtained back room was every bit as fearsome as he'd hoped, a gaunt scarecrow of a fellow with one eye that did not seem to want to follow the other. It gave the impression that he could watch both his customers at the same time. At the sight of him, the girl who had been so quick to treat Gregory as her lackey now faded one step behind him, trying to disappear into his shadow.

It made him smile more broadly than he might have as he greeted the pawnbroker. 'Good morning, my fine fellow. I am seeking candlesticks. Not just any candlesticks, mind you. I want the sort the posh types pawn when they can't pay their gambling debts.'

The man answered with a nod and a toothless grin, then pointed wordlessly into the corner at a small display of plate.

Gregory glanced at it for only a moment, before choosing the gaudiest pair and walking back towards the counter. He felt a sharp tug on his sleeve and looked back at Miss Strickland.

'Those are not ours,' she whispered.

'I thought you could not describe what we were looking for,' he countered.

'I cannot. But I am sure that I have never seen those in my life.'

'Neither has Miles Strickland. He has never seen England, much less these candlesticks.'

'That does not make them right,' she countered. 'Ignorance is no substitute for truth.'

Perhaps not. But in Gregory's opinion, it made for a pretty fine excuse and had worked well in the past. 'It is not as if we will be lying to him. He will expect to find candlesticks and we are leaving him some. He will never know the difference.'

'But I will,' she said.

Hadn't Leggett said something about the sisters being the daughters of a vicar? If so, their ingrained morality was proving deeply inconvenient. 'Your sister's husband is not paying me enough to turn the town upside down for things that are likely lost for ever.'

'If all that was needed was to grab the first things that came to hand, I could have done it myself.' Noting the wary way she had watched the proprietor, he doubted that was the case. But she had no trouble standing up to Gregory, for he saw a faint flash of irritation in the brown eyes glittering behind her veil. 'I do not know what he is paying you, but I am sure Mr Leggett did not hire you to do the job halfway. If the funds were insufficient, you should have negotiated for more when he hired you.'

For a sheltered young lady she was surprisingly perceptive. She was annoying as well. But his fee had been tripled to account for that.

He gave her a subservient smile. 'Very well, then. I shall try harder.'

He turned back to the shopkeeper. 'You have a very small collection for an item that is one of the first to be sold, when the gentry's pockets are to let. Are there any others in the shop?'

The man favoured them with his wall-eyed gaze for a moment and Gregory set a coin on the counter. 'For the inconvenience of opening your stockroom to us, good sir.'

The man pocketed the coin and stepped back, pulling the curtain to the side to let them pass.

The little room at the back of the shop was cluttered, as he expected it to be, but not without organisation. The shelves were full of more dented bird cages, tarnished teakettles and chipped vases than could be sold in a lifetime. Beneath them were an equally large number of chests, full of silver flatware and... Lo and behold, candlesticks.

He threw back the lid and lit a nearby candle to supplement the meagre light streaming from a grimy window on the back wall. Then he gestured Miss Strickland closer. 'Here you are. If the items are to be found in this shop, you are the only one who might tell. Look for yourself.'

He had expected a shudder of distaste and the demand that he sort through the chest and display the contents to her. Instead, all her reservations fell away. She pushed back the veil and dropped to her knees on the floor beside it, digging without hesitation through the pile of dented flambeaus and sconces.

Suddenly, she sighed in surprise and turned to him with a dented pewter stick clutched in her hands. She offered it to him and reached up to push back her bonnet. Then she smoothed her hair out of the way, leaving a streak of tarnish on her soft, white brow. 'Does it match?'

He frowned in confusion and leaned forward to look closer. The decoration she held was designed to imitate a Corinthian column, the top a square of ornate tracery. On her forehead was a small V-shaped scar with a break that matched a gap in the decoration.

'Someone hit you with this?' He hefted the weight of it in his hands and felt the anger rise in his gorge at the brutality of the late Earl, her grandfather.

She nodded. Then, oddly, she smiled. 'My sister, Charity.' Her hand dived back into the chest and pulled out the mate, which was bent at the base. 'In response, I threw this one at her. But I missed and it hit the dining-room wall. There is still a crack in the plaster where it landed.'

He felt momentarily weak as the rage left him again. 'That is good to know. I would hate to think that either of you had a skull thick enough to cause such damage to it.' But if they had, it ought not to have surprised him. Hope Strickland was proving to be the most hard-headed woman he'd ever met. He doubted her sister was any different.

She was still smiling. 'Then, Faith came and pulled both our plaits until we cried. I had forgotten all about that.' She was looking fondly at the candlesticks, as if meeting old friends. She frowned. 'And now, we will have to give them to a complete stranger, just because he shares our name.'

Her dark mood disappeared as quickly as it had come. She looked back up at him, so fresh and unguarded that he felt a lump rising in his throat. 'But I remember this. It is why just any candlestick would not do. Perhaps the new Earl would not know the difference, but it would not be the same to me.'

'I understand.' He stared at the smudge on her forehead in fascination. He wanted to wipe it away, smoothing a finger over that small, white vee in wonder. A flaw should make her uglier, not more fascinating. Was it raised, he wondered, or smooth? A single touch, under the guise of cleaning away the grime, would tell him.

He cleared his mind, cleared his throat and pulled a handkerchief from his pocket, offering it to her. 'You have…' he touched his own forehead '…here.'

She gave him a misty smile and a shrug of embarrassment before wiping away the dirt and returning his linen to him.

He was no less intrigued once it was gone. Perhaps it was her reaction to the injury that drew him to her. He'd been in such childhood scraps himself, but did not remember any of them as fondly as she did hers.

Of course, he'd had no brother to strike him. He did not often think of that, either. But suddenly there was a strange emptiness in him, as if he was hungry, but could not decide for what.

It was probably tea. The single slice of toast he'd had for breakfast had burned away hours ago. He needed sustenance to fill his belly and clear his mind. The sooner they left this store and returned Miss Strickland to her town house, the sooner he could remedy the hunger. He held out one hand for the heirlooms and another to help her to her feet. 'Come. Let us pay for the return of these. Perhaps, tomorrow we can find your painting.'

They went back to the carriage and rode in silence back to Harley Street, where he handed her down to the waiting footman and carried the brown-paper bundle containing the candlesticks into the house for her.

The smugness he felt at today's success did not do him credit. He had been confident of his ability to deliver a satisfactory solution to Leggett's problem. But he had not expected to find a reasonable duplicate on the very first day, much less an actual item.

Despite his employer's warnings that the entire family was nothing but trouble, Hope Strickland might actually be the key to completion.

There was still the matter of her plans for the unsuspecting American. But since they had resulted from her lack of confidence that the entail could be made complete, today's success might have loosened her grip on them.

It had been quite gratifying to see the look on her face when they had found the candlesticks. Since he had caught her practising her smiles in a mirror, he'd doubted that any of the ones she'd given him were born of sincerity. In his experience, the ruling class was good at appearing to be things they weren't: kind, friendly and happy, for instance.

But her grin when she'd pulled the family silver out of that chest had been positively impish. The youthful mischief in her expression was a million miles away from the aloof mask she'd worn for the rest of their time together.

When she'd looked up at him, bathing him in an aura of true happiness, he'd had to remind himself that his reward for taking the job was not actually the smile of a beautiful young lady. He was doing this for money.

The proper Miss Strickland had seemed disgusted by the idea when she had talked of his fee. In her world, women might sell themselves to the highest bidder for a loveless marriage without turning a hair, but men were expected to do things for country, gallantry or sport. They never did anything as common as earning a living.

But as she'd talked of her childhood, she had forgotten what he was and looked at him as if he were an equal. Better yet, she had seen him as a man. There had been surprise on her face and perhaps a little awe in his ability to help her so easily. He had been flattered. He was smiling at her now, as he set the package on the dining-room table.

She looked up at him, as she removed her bonnet, and gave a slight toss of her head to free the last strand of her hair from the ribbon. Then, she smiled back at him with a puzzled expression that proved her earlier lapse was forgotten. 'Thank you for your help, Mr Drake. The day was more productive than I expected. But now I must go and change for dinner.'

It took a moment to recognise the reason for her statement. He meant nothing to her. In fact, she seemed a little surprised that it had been necessary to dismiss him. When servants were finished being useful, they were expected to disappear until the next time they were needed.

Instead, he had been standing there like an idiot, as if he thought they had a reason to converse socially. It was the same feeling that had come over him in the carriage and he must gain control of it immediately. He forced a polite nod in response and said, 'Of course, Miss Strickland. If it is convenient, I will return tomorrow and we will try another shop.'

Her already relaxed expression seemed to become

even more placid. She gave a contented sigh, secure in the knowledge that they understood each other. 'That will be fine, Mr Drake. And now, if you will excuse me?'

He bowed and she turned and left him to find his own way out.

He stood for a moment, staring after her, annoyed with her and with himself. When contemplating his place in society, he was not normally given to envy or dissatisfaction. By dint of his own effort, he had gained wealth and comfort and was smart enough not to be burdened by the sort of problems that led people to hire him. He was more than happy.

But today that did not feel like enough.

'Mr Drake.'

He jumped at the sound of his name. The girl who had spoken it was staring at him from the doorway. Leggett had said that she was but nineteen years old, yet there was something about the look in her spectacled eyes that made her seem much older. The illusion was encouraged by the rather old-fashioned way she wore her straight brown hair and the utilitarian cut of her gown.

'Miss Charity, I presume,' he said, bowing deeply.

She nodded. 'We have not been introduced. But then, you had not been introduced to my sister when you barged in on her yesterday.'

Apparently, there were no secrets in the Strickland family, especially not as they related to the harassing of strangers. He nodded in acknowledgement. 'Your grandmother led me to believe I was expected.'

She gave him a dubious smile.

He held out his open hands and shrugged. 'I gave her my card and she told me to find your sister in the hall. She assured me that Miss Strickland would know exactly what it was that needed doing. She made no offer of introduction. I assumed none was necessary.'

Miss Charity's expression grew only slightly less doubtful. 'If I were you, I would be very careful in following when the Dowager is the one in front. She veers wide of the truth when it suits her.'

'Why would it suit her to…?'

'Lie?' The girl finished his question with the same strange, knowing smile. 'Because in recent years, the truth has been quite unpleasant. She prefers to live in the past where things were easier.'

'But what does any of that have to do with me?'

'She would like my sister to be as happy as she was, in her youth. To achieve that, she must find a man for Hope.' Charity paused for a moment. 'Or men. I am unsure how many of the stories she tells are true, but they are always very colourful.'

'I see.' In truth, he did not. 'What does that have to do with me?'

Miss Charity looked over her glasses at him. 'You are male, are you not?'

'Of course. But what…?' And then, the truth came clear. 'You cannot mean—'

'I would not take it personally,' Charity interrupted. 'My sister has been uninclined to search for a husband outside of the one outlandish candidate she waits for. If Grandmother chose to throw a handsome man into her afternoon without warning, it was more of a call to awaken the senses rather than an actual attempt to mate the pair of you.'

At the clinical way she described it, he could see why Leggett had not hesitated in tripling his fee. 'That is a comfort, I suppose.'

'But you are not here to settle my sister's future,' she said, watching him more closely than he liked. 'How goes the search for the missing entail?'

'I do not anticipate any problems with it.' He kept his tone polite, professional and opaque.

She gave a shake of her head. 'The whole enterprise is unnecessary, of course.'

'You think so?' he said, surprised. Unlike the rest of the family, she seemed unaffected by the impending audit.

She gave a slight nod. 'If my plan comes to fruition, we need not worry about staying in the heir's good graces. But since you have been hired to complete the inventory to satisfy the rest of the family, feel free to grab items at random that fit the bill. What will some American know if every bell and button in the house is not just as my grandfather left it?'

'I suggested much the same,' he said. 'But your sister requires greater accuracy than that.'

'Hope appreciates order and is no good at dissembling,' Charity replied. 'She refuses to believe that the rest of us can get away with an adjustment of the truth because she knows she cannot.'

'Such honesty is a thing to be prized,' he said. 'You make it sound like weakness of character.'

'You do not have to live with it,' Charity said. 'At least, not yet.'

He stared at her, waiting for clarification, but none was offered. Perhaps she'd intended it as a joke. He had been told she was a rather odd girl.

'And how do you get along with my sister?' she added, which did not help his peace of mind at all.

'She has been most helpful in establishing the provenance of the item we have found. I appreciate her assistance and anticipate no difficulties in our working together.' He gave her what he hoped was his most distant and professional smile.

'I see,' she said in a way that made him want to demand an explanation of exactly what it was she saw. 'I am sure she will say much the same of you.'

'I am glad to know it,' he said, feeling strangely unsettled by the compliment.

'And is the restoration of the entail your only job for our family?' Charity's searching look had returned, prying at his composure as if looking for a crack.

There was no way she could have known the full scope of his mission. 'What would make you think I was here for another reason?'

'Because I know Mr Leggett,' she said. 'Before he met my sister, he was a rake who did not care at all for propriety, much less love. But now?' She clasped her hands and gave a mocking flutter of her eyelashes. 'He wants everyone to be as happy as he is.'

'That is commendable of him,' Gregory responded.

'Forward is what I would call it,' Charity replied. 'He is right to think that Hope should not wait needlessly for the coming of the Earl. She will find that for herself if we leave her alone.'

'Of course,' he said.

'But it would be just like a man to try subterfuge once he realises reason will not work. A distracting flirtation, for example…'

'What the devil are you implying?' He regretted the curse immediately, but the words had been so blunt that he'd forgotten he was talking to a young lady. 'I was not sent here to take advantage of your sister.'

'You are a problem solver, are you not, Mr Drake? Why would you not think of the most direct solution?'

'Because I am a gentleman,' he said. And because he knew from experience just what ruin such a thing might cause.

She touched a finger to her chin. 'You claim to be a gentleman. But I can find nothing of your past, or your parentage.'

'If it does not matter to Mr Leggett, why should it matter to you?'

'Because he does not know this family as well as I do,' Charity replied. 'And because, if I am honest, he is not as intelligent as I am. If he had thought through the implications of leaving a stranger to ferry his sister-in-law around London, you'd have already had this conversation with him.'

Gregory had not got as far in life as he had without remaining calm when faced with bigoted questions from the gentry. Normally, he would have spoken of his extensive résumé and presented references from other men of stature who had been satisfied with his performance.

But today, it did not seem to be enough. Only the whole truth would do. 'You could find nothing of my parentage because I do not know it myself. I have been told that my mother was from a good family, but died in childbirth. My father was less so. He seduced her, then abandoned her to her fate. When she died, her family was faced with the problem of an infant whose very existence was a blot on the family honour and the good name of a lost and presumably beloved daughter. They provided for my care and education anonymously, but have never shown an interest in the child I was or the man I have become.'

'I see,' said Miss Charity.

Her assessment annoyed him. 'If you truly do, then you will know that your sister's reputation is perfectly safe with me. Since I cannot prove my honour with a pedigree, I have done it with my behaviour. I have no intention of being the man my father was and leaving a lover dead or disgraced, or a son abandoned to the care of strangers and left to field such questions as the ones you are asking me.' He stared back at her with the same unflinching intensity she had been using on him.

It did not seem to bother her in the least. At last,

she sighed in what he hoped was satisfaction. 'Very well, then. You are honourable by choice. That is probably a better reason than those who claim their good name is enough to swear on. My apologies for pressing you to reveal so much of your past. But despite what the family sometimes thinks, I do love my sisters and will not stand by and let them be hurt.'

He answered with a respectful nod.

'And no matter what Mr Leggett may have asked of you, do not interfere too strenuously in Hope's future. It will sort itself once I make her aware of certain facts.'

He gave no response to this at all. Since she was not his employer, what she wanted did not signify.

She pushed her spectacles up her nose, which seemed to magnify her already large hazel eyes, and fixed him with a gaze that would have been quelling had it come from a man. 'And most important of all, you must not meddle in my affairs, no matter what my sister may wish of you. Keep Hope occupied with restoring the entail. Come to me when you reach the inevitable impasse and I will help you. But until then, do not bother me with it, for I am occupied with more important matters.'

'And what are these matters, Miss Charity?' he said and followed it with his most winning smile.

She touched the side of her nose and winked. 'All in good time, Mr Drake. But I assure you, they have nothing to do with husband-hunting at Almack's.' She glanced at the door. 'Do not let me keep you from your own business.'

And thus, he was dismissed for the second time that day. He bowed to her, as he had to her sister. 'Nor do I wish to keep you from yours, whatever it may be. Good day, Miss Charity.'

'Until tomorrow, Mr Drake.'

Chapter Four

As she waited for Mr Drake's return the next morning, Hope paused to admire the candlesticks which had been polished and displayed on the dining-room sideboard. They belonged in the manor, not in London. But this would have to do until she could arrange for them to be transported.

'So, you actually found something.' Charity stood in the doorway, arms folded across her chest. 'When I heard of your plans to go treasure hunting, I assumed Mr Leggett was wasting his money.'

'On the contrary,' Hope said, running an idle finger along the length of the pewter. 'Mr Drake is very diligent. I have the utmost confidence in him.'

'Grandmother said you did not like him,' Charity said.

'I do not claim to,' Hope answered. 'But I do like these candlesticks. It is nice to see them back in the family.'

'And it was very nice of Mr Leggett to find such

a handsome man to retrieve them,' Charity said with a sly smile.

'I had not noticed,' Hope lied.

'Then you are either blind or deliberately obtuse,' Charity said.

'Hmm,' said Hope, turning to the window to watch for the arrival of his coach.

'Of course, he is little better than a servant,' Charity added.

'It is unworthy of you to say such a thing,' Hope said. 'Our own father was a servant to the Lord and Mother was the daughter of Comstock's man of business. If Papa did not have a problem…' She turned back to continue the lecture and saw Charity grinning at her agitation. 'You were baiting me.'

Charity shrugged. 'I just wanted to see if you remembered our origins. Mr Drake thinks you terribly proud.'

'When did you speak to Mr Drake?' More importantly, why had they been discussing her? And had he really formed such a poor opinion of her in only two meetings?

'I might have run into him as he left yesterday morning,' Charity answered.

'You mean you were lurking in the hall, waiting to catch a glimpse of him,' Hope replied. 'You are too young for him, if that is your line of thinking.' Her little sister had shown no real interest in men thus far, which made her sudden curiosity about Mr Drake all the more alarming.

'I am nineteen,' Charity replied. 'Some would say

I am just the right age for marriage and at nearly twenty-one you are dangerously near to becoming a spinster.'

'You are still not right for Mr Drake,' Hope said, exasperated. Then she added, 'We do not even know if he is married.'

'Do you wish for me to ask him?'

'Certainly not.' Sometimes, it was convenient to have such a nosy sister, who would satisfy her curiosity without Hope having to admit she had ever wondered. 'It is not our concern whether or not he has a wife.' She sounded as disapproving as she was able, knowing that Charity could rarely resist the forbidden. Then she added, 'He is a total stranger to us.'

'As is the new Earl of Comstock,' her sister reminded her.

'There is no comparison between the two. We know nothing about Mr Drake, his finances or his family. If he is single, we do not even know if he wishes to marry. But the Earl will have no choice in the matter. He must produce an heir and might welcome a helpmate already familiar with the holdings he has inherited. In turn, he will offer security,' Hope reminded her, ticking off the logical reasons she'd used to convince herself of the plan.

'So, you will sacrifice yourself to maintain the status quo.'

'It is hardly a sacrifice to marry a peer,' she said, even though it sometimes felt like it.

'It is always a burden to alter your life for the good

of another,' Charity said. 'If you are doing so for my sake, it is not necessary.'

'If you don't mean to help yourself, then I must. You will not find a husband hiding in someone else's library.'

'I will be fine, with or without a husband,' Charity said. 'We might be fine together, if you will let go of the foolish idea that it is necessary to marry to be safe.'

'You do not understand…' Hope said.

'I understand more than you know. I simply do not care.'

'That is quite clear from your appearance,' Hope snapped. 'We are in London, not Berkshire. You might be required to receive visitors while I am gone. Please return to your room and do not come down again until you are wearing a new gown and a hair ribbon.'

Charity glanced in the mirror above the fireplace and then away again, unbothered by her sister's hectoring. 'The man I marry will have to love my imperfections, for I have no intention of changing my dress or my manner just to please him.'

'Then you do not know as much as you think,' Hope said. 'It is up to us to make ourselves desirable. It is not in the nature of men to compromise.'

'If a woman has enough money, they will do it quick enough,' Charity said with a nod.

'Since we are currently without funds that is not a consideration.' Not for the first time, Hope wondered if there wasn't a strain of madness running through the family. Sometimes she felt more like a keeper than a sister.

'Perhaps I shall sell some of Grandmother's jewellery,' Charity said. 'There are more than enough diamonds in her parure to spare one or two stones.'

'No!' Hope balled her hands into fists, trying to keep from tearing at her own hair. 'There will be no more pilfering from the entail. If that is the wonderful plan you keep hinting at, it is even more foolish than mine.'

'So you admit that your plan is foolish,' Charity announced, taking nothing else from the conversation.

'No!'

'Miss Strickland. Miss Charity.' Mr Drake had arrived unannounced, yet again, and was standing in the doorway, witnessing the whole embarrassing scene.

Hope pushed past her sister and grabbed him by the arm, trying to turn him towards the door. 'We need to be going. Now, Mr Drake.'

'Of course, Miss Strickland.' He pulled free of her grasp and stepped ahead of her to open doors and ready the carriage.

The bustle of the next few moments, putting on coat and bonnet, allowed her time to recover from her mortification. It was bad enough that he had caught her arguing with her sister and even worse that she'd laid hands on his person and tried to drag him from the room. If he had arrived a few minutes earlier, he'd have heard a discourse on his appearance, talents and marriageability.

Or had he heard? She had no idea how long he had been standing there, watching them fight. She stared across the carriage at him, searching his face for any trace of awareness.

As usual, his perfect face was effortlessly composed. There was no sign of clenching in that finely planed jawline. No indication that his lips, which were both firm and full, had a smile hiding in the corners. And though his eyes were alert, like a hawk scanning the distance for prey, there was no indication that the mind behind them was ruminating on a scrap of overheard conversation.

As her sister had said, he really was uncommonly handsome. It was not as if Hope hadn't noticed the fact yesterday. But now that she had a reason to study his face, it was rather like staring too long into the sun. Her cheeks felt hot and the image of him seemed to be embedded in her thoughts.

It was probably what came of staring. Ladies did not stare, even at people they wanted to look at. It was not Hope's habit to do so. Perhaps it would be better to drop her eyes and peer at him through her lashes.

But that sounded rather like flirting. She did not mean to do that, either. It was good that she was veiled, so that he did not witness her, blushing over nothing and unsure where to rest her eyes. It did no good to look lower, at the immaculate shirt front visible beneath his coat, or at his strong hands, resting casually in his lap as if waiting for the moment when they would steady her departure from the carriage.

It was growing stuffy under the veil. That was likely why she could not seem to catch her breath. Though she could not think of a rule against it, holding one's breath until it came out in sighs was probably as rude as staring. But now that her breathing had fallen from its normal rhythm, she could not seem to find it again. The first was too shallow, the next so deep that it sucked the veil into her mouth, which ended in a sputtering cough and the need to rip her bonnet away and gasp for fresh air.

Mr Drake glanced in her direction, surprised. It was clear he had not been thinking of her at all until she had called such mortifying attention to herself.

She cleared her throat and patted her chest lightly as if trying to clear her lungs. 'A bit of lint. From the veil, I think.'

He nodded in sympathy. 'You needn't wear it in the carriage, if it makes you uncomfortable. The shades are down and there will be more than enough time to put it in place when we arrive at a shop.'

'Thank you,' she said, still not sure if she wished to give up her disguise just yet.

'And, in case you have been wondering, your sister exaggerates. I did not find you overly proud on our first two meetings. Your behaviour towards me was well within the social norms.'

She had been right to worry. He had heard everything. Now, she was absolutely sure she was blushing at him. 'I apologise for the behaviour you witnessed as you arrived, Mr Drake. And for seizing your arm and forcing you from the house, as well. And for

Charity's lies,' she added, for that was what they had been.

'It is I who owe you the apology,' he reminded her. 'While I did not intend to eavesdrop, that was the result of not announcing myself sooner.' He offered a shrug and another smile. 'And though I do not know from experience, I am given to understand that it is the job of younger siblings to be as aggravating as possible.'

'You have none of your own, then?' It was not her place to ask, although he had opened the subject himself, so perhaps it was not too very rude.

He shook his head. 'No brothers or sisters at all. And so that Charity does not need to quiz me tomorrow, you can assure her that I am not married, as yet, but fully intend to do so, should I find the right woman.'

'You heard everything, then.'

He nodded.

'You must think us all quite horrid,' she said. 'My grandmother was a lax guardian, at best. Since she could not be bothered to teach her, it has been left to me to be a good example to my younger sister and to instruct her in ladylike behaviour. But I have had little success.'

'Perhaps if you refrained from throwing candlesticks at her,' he said.

'It only happened the one time,' she assured him, trying not to think of all the childhood stories Charity might tell him that would sound even worse. He might never have known of them had she been able to keep her mouth shut on the previous day. 'We were rambunctious children when we arrived at the manor. At first, we did not understand the value of the items we played with. When we were old enough, Faith and I were sent away to school for a time.'

'And Charity?' he asked.

She sighed. 'She said that, if we were not going to Eton, or some other place that would prepare us for university, it was not worth leaving the house. Her manners are abominable, of course. But she is too antisocial to bother with throwing candlesticks. And she is prodigiously smart.'

'That is a comfort, I suppose,' he said.

'But it pains me that she did not go to Miss Penny-worth's Academy to learn deportment. It improved my character immeasurably.'

He smiled and touched his arm, wincing in pain. 'As I can tell from the way we took our leave of the town house.'

She readied another horrified apology. 'That was most unlike me.'

'It was nothing,' he said in a soft voice that immediately put her at her ease. 'Since you take your manners so seriously, it is unfair of me to tease you over them.'

She would have been better off to remain silent. Now, he thought her both overly proud and humourless. But either of those was better than being as nosy as her sister had been. 'On the contrary, I do not fault you for any response you might give to the conversation you heard or my behaviour towards you. What you witnessed should never have taken place. As I told Charity, it is not our business to wonder about your personal life.'

'I took it as a compliment,' he replied, still smiling. 'A total lack of interest can be rather dehumanising.'

She remembered the look he had given her in parting on the previous day, as if he had expected something more from her than an awkward good-bye. Had she been the one to treat him as less than a man? It was not as if she hadn't been curious about him. It was just that ladies were not supposed to express it openly. But if he was willing to make light of the situation, then so should she. She gave him a friendly nod, hoping that it did not look as forced and awkward as it felt. 'If it makes you feel better, I will ask you at least one impertinent question a day until we have completed out task.'

'I will look forward to it, Miss Strickland,' he said, nodding back. Then he touched his hat brim to remind her to replace her bonnet and veil. 'As I mentioned before we parted yesterday, today we will be searching for the blue painting. I have several dealers in mind, specialising in fine art. I am sure your grandmother must have visited one of them.'

The paintings in the first gallery they visited would have been more at home in a museum than gracing the walls of Comstock Manor. The owner was obviously familiar with Mr Drake, plying him with offers of tea or sherry while Hope perused artwork. She allowed herself a few moments of guilty pleasure, wishing that she had the nerve to lie and claim even the smallest of the landscapes, for any of them were likely to be prettier than the painting they were truly seeking. Then she turned back to her companion and gave a silent shake of her head.

He rose and thanked the gallery owner, then led her back to the carriage.

The next place was similar. Mr Drake was still treated with familiarity, but there were no offers of refreshment. Though the art was not quite as impressive, it was still of a higher quality than Hope had seen at home. Again, she shook her head. And, again, they moved on.

With each successive shop they moved further from Bond Street until they stopped at a shop nearly as dreary as the one that had contained the candlesticks. The ragged collection of paintings stacked along the walls no longer hid Old Masters. A few were no better than girls' school watercolours. But the shopkeeper followed close behind them, assuring them that the frames were worth ten bob at least.

Mr Drake shook his head. 'The frames are not important. We are seeking an oil painting. Something with blue in it, I think, to match the paper on the drawing-room walls.'

The proprietors of the earlier shops would have been horrified at the idea of matching art to the wall colour. But it must not have been an unusual request here, for the dealer announced that he kept the paintings sorted by colour. Then he led them to a dark and crowded corner of the shop where heavy gilt frames were stacked in precarious piles.

Mr Drake glanced at her expectantly. 'Did your grandmother say anything about the size of the painting?'

She shook her head. 'I doubt it was a miniature. But it could not have been very large, or I'd have noticed a blank spot on the wall.'

'We shall start in the middle, then.'

'Why?'

'Because they will be easier to lift,' he said, heaving a pile of paintings down from a high shelf with a grunt. They slid to the floor, raising a cloud of dust.

Hope tipped them forward, one by one, to look at the canvases. As she did so, he turned towards another shelf, pulling down more paintings, just as heavy and just as dirty.

The collected art was random, the only common denominator being colour. There were landscapes by moonlight, seascapes, a still life of berries, studies of birds, and portraits of blue-clad men and women in velvets, satins and…

She stared at the painting in front of her for only a moment, before averting her eyes in shock. Then she glanced back to be sure of its subject before calling to Mr Drake.

'I have found the painting.'

'Excellent. Let me summon the proprietor.'

She gave an embarrassed shake of her head, and pointed to the door. 'I…cannot…' She slipped her hands under the veil and put them over her eyes, sure for one mad second that if she could not see, she could not be seen by the two men in the room.

Once they'd looked at the painting, they would look at her and draw the inevitable comparison.

'Are you ill?' he said, taking her arm solicitously. 'It is uncommonly stuffy here. Lord knows what ill things might be breeding on these pictures.' He tugged gently on her arm to bring it down from her face. 'You may wait in the carriage while I settle on a price with Mr Barnstable. If you are not feeling…'

He glanced down at the painting.

'Ah. Yes. I see. Please, allow me to escort you to the carriage. And I would not advise lifting your veil until you are out in the street.'

To his credit, Gregory led the girl out of the shop and into the safety of the carriage without as much as a twitch of his lips. After her prim apologies in the carriage earlier, he could imagine how she felt about the painting they had just found.

Tempting though it was to comment on them, she would not appreciate his admiration of the artist or his amusement at the subject. It would take an amazing amount of self-control on his part to sit in the carriage with her and look her directly in the eye, without bursting into ribald laughter.

Once he was back in the shop and well out of her sight, he reverted to his true expression and grinned, hurrying back to the painting for another private viewing before calling to the shopkeeper, 'Oy, Barnstable! I've found the one I want.'

The old man joined him, smirking down at the picture before jerking his thumb in the direction of the waiting carriage. 'Thought you said the missus was looking for something to hang in the drawing room.'

'We will find something anon. I am buying this one for me.'

The man nodded in approval. 'Just as well. Ain't what I'd call blue, either.'

'Mostly pink,' he agreed.

'Especially the tits,' said Barnstable.

'The scarf is blue,' Gregory said with a shrug.

'Looks more like a hanky to me. Don't cover much, do it?'

It certainly didn't. The cloth the subject was holding at her hip was barely large enough to conceal the most intimate part of her anatomy. Other than that, she wore nothing but a sly smile. Her magnificent bosom was clearly on display, as was the round of her belly, the curve of her shoulder, the hollow of her waist.

'The artist was truly gifted,' Gregory added. There was no mistaking the identity of the subject. But that was only because patches and powder had been out of style for a generation. If the woman's hair had been its natural brown, he'd have assumed it was Hope Strickland and not her grandmother. The eyes and the shape of the face were the same and the come-hither smile identical to the one he had seen Hope practising in the mirror.

If the family resemblance continued below the neck to include what was hidden under his companion's fashionable morning gown, she would not need practised smiles and rehearsed curtsies. She had but to unbutton her bodice and she could have her choice of any man in England.

'Thirty quid,' Barnstable said, still staring at the painting.

'Twenty,' Gregory countered, unable to look away.

'Twenty-five. And I'll wrap it up tight so the missus don't see what you bought.'

With the deal settled and a holland cover tied over the canvas, Gregory returned to the carriage. Miss Stickland, who had pulled the shades and removed her bonnet again, was resting against the squabs, her eyes closed.

He took his place across from her and signalled the driver with a tap of his cane and they set off for the town house.

'You have it?' she asked, not opening her eyes.

'It is tied on top of the carriage. And very well wrapped. No one need know the subject but ourselves.'

She opened her eyes suddenly and stared at him as if she'd hoped to catch him leering at her.

He had anticipated her fears and made sure to meet her gaze with his most distantly professional expression. 'If it helps to remember the fact, I was chosen by Mr Leggett for my discretion. No one shall ever hear about what we discovered today.'

'If only my grandmother could make the same promise,' she said with a sigh.

'Things were quite different, a generation ago.'

'So I have been told,' she replied. 'At least, that is

the excuse that Grandmama gives, each time something like this comes to light.'

'Have there been many such incidents?'

'None as bad as this,' she admitted. 'There is usually no one to notice but my sisters and myself.'

'I am no one,' Gregory replied.

It was a foolish thing to say. Even more so if he had done it expecting her to deny the fact and reassure him that, in the universe she inhabited, he had any kind of personal worth. Instead, his announcement was greeted with silence that remained unbroken until they reached their destination.

When they arrived at the town house, Gregory supervised the entrance of the painting himself, carrying it, still draped, past the footmen and setting it on the floor of the main salon by the fireplace. Then he waited as Hope called for her grandmother and an explanation.

The Dowager entered the room and gave the pair of them a curious look.

'We have found the painting you sold,' Hope said, frowning at her in disapproval. 'But now, what are we to do with it?'

He walked to the painting and, being careful not to look down at the canvas, pulled a corner of the holland cloth that covered it. When this did not result in a response, he pulled the rest away.

At the sight of it, the older woman clasped her hands over her bosom with a sigh of delight. 'I have not seen this in ages. Wherever did you find it?'

'Where you left it, Grandmama. At an art dealer in Seven Dials.'

'I?' She laughed. 'I would have not parted with this for the world. How often does one have such a vivid reminder of the joys of youth? I can remember the days I posed for this.' She wrapped a hand behind her neck, arching her back until her breasts pointed towards the ceiling. Then she looked back at them and dropped the pose with a chuckle. 'My arm fell asleep. It was most fatiguing. But you must admit, the results were worth the effort.'

'We did not bring this here for a reminiscence of your sordid past,' her granddaughter said with a huff. 'We have brought it home to you to complete the entail. Now where are we to put it so that no one sees?'

'The entail?' The Dowager laughed. 'My dear, this does not belong to the earldom. This was a gift from me to your grandfather. It was his pride and joy until he lost it in a card game to one of my admirers. We had quite the row over that, at the time. But that was many years ago. I have not thought of it for ages.'

'You said you sold a blue painting,' Hope said, pointing at the drape in the painting. 'We were searching for it when we found this.'

The Dowager focused in the present for only a moment. 'Oh, that. The painting I sold is nothing like this, I assure you.'

'You remember it?' Hope said, exasperated. 'Then perhaps you can give us a better description than, *blue*. Is it of a blue sea? A blue sky? A blue dress?'

'Was that what you thought I meant?' Her grandmother laughed. 'It is not a painting of something blue. It is a portrait of the Blue Earl.'

'And which one was that?' interrupted Gregory, intrigued.

The Dowager's brow furrowed. 'The third or fourth, I should think. He was sickly pale and quite ugly, with grey skin and ice-blue lips. Something in the blood, they thought. He did not live to marry. It is just as well. God knows what his children might have looked like. The title fell to a cousin and there have been no further problems.'

'You sold a portrait of a Comstock?' Hope said, amazed.

'The ugliest one,' the Dowager said, defensively. 'I do not think we have to count him. He did not last much longer than the time it took to complete his likeness. Your grandfather kept the thing behind a door in the portrait gallery because he could not stand to look at it.'

'But the new Earl will most assuredly notice when the succession of his ancestors jumps from three to five,' Hope said. 'How could you think that it would go unremarked?'

'You did not notice, did you?'

Gregory held up a hand, trying to return the conversation to the salient information. 'Was the painting labelled in any way?'

'There is a brass plaque at the bottom,' the Dowager answered.

'And his costume?'

'Jacobean. A rust-coloured leather doublet that

makes his skin look truly ghastly.' She thought for a moment. 'His hair was thinning as well. Thank the Lord your grandfather came from another branch of the family tree. I loved him dearly, but I do not think I could have stood waking next to him if he'd looked like the Blue Earl.'

As he committed the details to memory, the Dowager went to the bell pull and summoned a pair of footmen, directing them to put the painting in her 'boudoir', an apt description of the sort of bedroom inhabited by a woman who would pose for such a picture. It was a credit to the loyalty of the servants in the Comstock household that they did not seem phased by any of it.

Hope Strickland watched the activity, her fists pressed against her temples as if it required physical strength to hold on to her sanity. Once the door had closed, she turned to him, angry and defensive. 'The Strickland family is one of the oldest in Britain.'

'I am aware of that,' he said, though he had no idea what difference it would make to the situation.

'We are not like *her*.' She pointed in the direction that her grandmother had gone.

'Of course not,' he said. The poor girl seemed to think it was possible to divorce herself from the woman who had given her her looks, if not her temperament. The Dowager might not have been born a Strickland, but to deny her as family was an act devoid of logic.

'If you insist on agreeing with me, you should do a better job of hiding your true feelings,' she snapped.

'I have no idea what you are talking about,' he said, giving her his most impassive smile. Then he spoiled everything by saying, 'But would it really be so bad to be like the Countess?'

'Perhaps in your family her behaviour is considered normal,' she said, her eyes narrowing.

'Perhaps it is,' he responded quietly. Since he could not name his parents, how could he know for sure? But it had been less than kind of her to point the matter out.

'Her frivolous nature is an affront to the memory of her sons, who devoted their lives to the good of others.'

'All the same, she seems most devoted to you,' he said, amazed that she could so easily dismiss the love that he'd longed for during his own, lonely childhood.

'If she truly cared for us, she would behave as the rest of the family did,' Miss Strickland replied, unimpressed. 'My father was a vicar who gave his life helping others. As did my mother.'

'It must have been very difficult for you,' he said, wondering if that was why she was so enamoured of self-sacrifice.

'Had he lived, my eldest uncle would have been a peer, committed to the well-being of his tenants and loyal to the Crown.'

'I am aware of that,' he said, wishing that she would let him forget the differences between them, even for a moment. It would serve her right if he pointed out that her uncle's demise made it impossible to know whether he had been a paragon or subject to the human frailties of an ordinary man.

'And the last of the three was at Talavera,' she finished. 'He died a hero.'

'Of course he did,' Gregory said, unable to contain his sarcasm any longer.

'What do you mean by that?' If he'd meant to insult her, he'd succeeded, for she sounded even angrier with him than she had been with the Dowager.

'I mean that it is a perfectly logical choice for a second son to go into the army when he is given the money for a commission.'

'But you could not afford one,' she finished, mocking him just as he had mocked her family.

'On the contrary. I had more than enough money to be an officer,' he snapped. 'But I do not like following orders.'

'Then it is most curious that you have put yourself at the beck and call of every gentleman in London,' she retorted.

She made him sound like a lackey, which was probably just how she thought of him. 'Let me clarify. I do not want to follow orders that will get me shot as a traitor, should I refuse them. More so, I do not want to follow orders that will get me killed when I obey. I am sure your uncle would be more humble than you are at his heroism, had he survived it. But he did not.'

'The men of my family were not afraid to give their lives in service to others,' she said in a soft, warning tone.

So she thought him a coward? Then let her. 'I do not wish to be a martyr for any cause, no matter how noble. My goal is to live to a ripe old age without leaving unacknowledged sons or impoverished daughters who must throw themselves on the first title that shows interest.'

'I doubt you will have to fear leaving a full house,' she bit back. 'You would have to marry before you get a widow and I cannot imagine a woman who would have you.'

'You cannot imagine?' He reached out and took her arm, forgetting his plan to keep his temper and his place. 'Perhaps it is because you are so sheltered you confuse prudishness for virtue.'

'There is nothing wrong with me,' she whispered. Perhaps it was true. Though when she shuddered at his touch it was with desire and not fear.

'There is nothing wrong with me, either,' he murmured in response. 'When I am ready to marry, it shall be to a woman who wants a man instead of a title. A woman who could appreciate this.' Then he closed the last of the distance between them and pulled her into a kiss.

Even as it was happening, what was left of his normally rational mind announced that it was a terrible idea. He had been goaded into an argument that had nothing to do with him and everything to do with her fear of seeing a body so like her own displayed as an object of desire.

But that was what she was.

It did not matter that she was an innocent, or that

she was so far above him in birth as to make a romance between them laughable. She was everything that had enticed his father, nine months before he was born. Had he known where it was, Gregory would have sworn on the grave of his mother never to make the same mistake. But now that the moment had come to resist temptation, he did not just choose the path to ruin, he raced down it without hesitation.

Perhaps there was a weakness in his blood, just like the Earl in the missing painting. The taste of Hope Strickland's mouth was like the boiled sweets he'd stolen as a child. She was all the more delicious because she was forbidden. The body that was crushed to his would be pillow soft and silk smooth under her gown, the most delightful resting place for a man both inside and out.

He felt her gasp against his lips as her mouth opened and he took advantage of it, slipping his tongue between them, filling her mouth. Her lashes fluttered against his cheek like the wings of a moth and her soft moan of alarm changed almost immediately to one of pleasure.

If he'd thought to prove some point, to assert some sort of dominance over her, he'd succeeded. It was time to let her go. His conscience laughed at the very idea. He had not done this to win an argument. He'd done it because it was what he'd wanted, from the first moment he'd seen her. Nor did he wish to stop, now that it had begun. He would not be finished with her until her body had revealed its last secret to him. With such a woman, the exploration might take a lifetime.

A lifetime?

This was madness. In a week, he would be working for someone else and she would go back to practising smiles for a cousin who might never arrive. He pulled away, trying to free himself before he was trapped for ever. But it was already too late. He was panting as if he'd run a mile. His body stirred as if they were tethered by some invisible bond and he could use it to draw her back into his arms, where she belonged.

They stood for a long, silent moment, a pace apart, staring at each other. He waited for an angry response, a stinging slap, a shriek of outrage. Or perhaps a scream of violation.

Instead, she stared at him with wide, confused eyes, her lips still parted as if the kiss had not ended. Perhaps she was still too shocked to put him in his place. Or perhaps she wanted more.

It did not matter what she wanted. The kiss had been a risky mistake that would grow even more dangerous if it was repeated. For all he knew, his father still bragged about the memory of seducing a beautiful woman. But his mother had not understood that she would lose her life as well as her reputation. If Hope Strickland could not call a halt to what was happening between them, it was up to him. Once again, he must do his job and rescue a member of a noble family from themselves.

This time the service would not just be gratis, it would come at great personal expense to his pride.

He allowed himself a last moment of melancholy

pleasure. Then he looked at her and wiped his mouth with his hand as if to rid himself of the taste of her lips. 'But no matter what my future might hold, I will not be wasting any more time on you than is absolutely necessary.'

'I…don't understand,' she whispered, touching her lips with her fingers.

'What is there to understand? You are a tiresome little girl who must brag about her dead relatives because she cannot tolerate the perfectly human mistakes made by the living ones. I would not spend five minutes in your company if I was not paid to do so. And I certainly will not be kissing you again.'

'Did Mr Leggett pay you to kiss me?' she said, her brows furrowing in confusion.

'Do not be ridiculous.'

'Then you did that on your own?'

'And I will not do it again,' he repeated, waiting for the rejection to register on her face.

'Then you had best go,' she said, still staring at him as her fingertip traced the curve of her lower lip.

He stared back, watching the slow movement of it along the edge of that soft, wet mouth. Then he forced his eyes away and pushed past her, towards the door and freedom.

Chapter Five

It had been one of the most embarrassing and confusing days of her life. It was one thing to hire a discreet agent to help with the family's financial difficulties and quite another thing to let him see the matriarch unadorned and unashamed, even if it was in oil and not flesh.

The painting never should have existed. But since it did, her grandmother could have spared her some embarrassment by being ashamed, or at the very least modest. And he never would have seen it if they had not been looking for another painting which should have been hanging in its proper place in the family gallery, back in Berkshire.

The whole incident had been mortifying. But if she was honest, Hope had to admit that it had been made even more so by her own behaviour. If she had been as composed as Faith or as oblivious as Charity, Grandmama's painting might not have bothered her. She would not have become agitated or shrill. She would not have started spouting off about family honour to the point where she seemed vain and condescending.

But then Gregory Drake would not have kissed her.

And what was she to make of that kiss and the things he'd said afterwards? He'd implied that there was something wrong with it. Or perhaps that there was something wrong with her.

Perhaps there was. She had no right to be complaining about something her grandmother had done to please her husband, only to follow it by kissing a man who had not even asked to dance with her, much less wed her. And she had opened her mouth while she'd done it, which did not seem like the sort of kiss a nice girl would give, even after marriage.

Even worse, she had enjoyed it. All of her anger and frustration had disappeared at the first touch of his lips, replaced by something warm and delicious. If she had any criticisms at all, it was that it had ended too soon.

Then, he had announced that he wanted nothing more to do with her. He had stormed out of the house without saying goodbye. But in the middle of the afternoon, a large flat package had arrived containing the painting of the Blue Earl who was every bit as hideous as Grandmama had said. There was a letter attached, addressed to her.

Dear Miss Strickland,
With the Dowager Countess's more complete
description, I was able to locate the appro-

*priate painting with ease. I had but to return
to the shop we already visited and request the
ugliest portrait available.*

*I was led immediately to the Fourth Earl
of Comstock.*

Despite herself, she had smiled. Then she'd continued reading.

*After the events of this afternoon, I think it
is best that I continue the search for the missing items on the list without your help.*

*My behaviour towards you in the salon of
your home was inexcusable. When I was hired
by your family, there was an expectation that I
would treat you with respect. In both my words
and actions I have failed abominably.*

*Please be assured that, should I decide to
resign from the assignment, I will not be telling Mr Leggett the whole truth of my reason
for doing so. I will say that it is too difficult, or
too inconvenient for me to finish. Both might
be true. But the matter of this afternoon is between us and us alone.*

*Should I decide to continue, I will solicit the
Dowager's help with the remaining items. It is
possible that she will be more truthful to a person outside the family than she has been to you.*

The truth of that had stung almost worse than Mr
Drake's earlier rejection. Was she really as bad as

he had claimed this afternoon, so judgemental that her own grandmother did not want to speak to her?

She'd returned to the letter.

As I left today, I said that I would not waste my time on you. I regret these words more than any others I spoke for they imply that you were in some way at fault for what happened between us.

Any guilt or blame for today must rest completely on my shoulders. I am sorry that I proved to be the unworthy companion that you suspected I was and I give my word that I will not inflict my presence on you in the future.
Sincerely,
Gregory Drake

Now, as she dressed to go out for the evening, she was just beginning to accept the truth.

He had abandoned her.

She had suspected that it was happening as he had stormed out of the salon. She had convinced herself that perhaps things were not as bad as they seemed. As usual, she had been wrong. He was gone and the thought of it left her utterly bereft.

Their efforts to complete the entail would not be enough to solve her problems. But until the Earl arrived from America, it felt good to be doing something. It felt especially good to be doing that something with Mr Drake, who made the search feel more like a treasure hunt and less like a hard slog towards inevitable failure.

And then he had kissed her.

He had carefully avoided any mention of the kiss in the letter, which was currently tucked beneath the lining of the jewel case sitting on the vanity table in front of her. Even if someone bothered to search for it, they would not really know what had happened. But that meant neither would she. He did not explain why he had kissed her. He did not tell her if he'd felt anything other than embarrassment afterwards. And he had hinted that her feelings about it should be something between outrage, insult and disappointment.

As her maid, Polly, wrapped the stays around her body, Hope glanced in the direction of the hidden note, wishing it had been a *billet doux* instead of an apology. She would likely be married without ever receiving one, while Grandmama probably had boxes of them. She sighed.

Then, at the prodding of the maid behind her, she took a few deep breaths to prevent being laced into an uncomfortably tight corset. Some girls did not even need one. But Hope had the same sort of physique that had been so flagrantly displayed in the picture that Mr Drake should never have seen. As with so many gifts from her grandmother, she could never decide if it was a blessing or a curse. She took another deep, overheated breath and the maid loosened the lacings again before knotting them and dropping petticoat and ball gown over her head.

Hope took her seat at the dressing table and Polly began to undo the curling papers and arrange her hair. When she looked up at her reflection in the mirror, she saw Charity standing in the doorway, leaning against the frame.

'You should be dressing,' Hope said, attempting a disapproving nod that was cut short by Polly's tugs on her curls and the caution to be still. 'Lord Ellingham's ball is this evening and we will be leaving as soon as we have finished with my hair.'

'Correction,' Charity said. 'You and Grandmother will be going. I will be staying here. I am right in the middle of a most interesting passage in one of the Comstock journals I found here and I cannot be interrupted.'

'We did not bring you to London so you could tuck yourself away in a different library,' Hope said, approving the finished coiffure and dismissing her maid. 'You are supposed to be looking for a husband. You cannot do that if you do not leave the house.'

'As I have said before,' Charity answered, 'no one will want me without money. It is better that we spend this Season focused on your prospects.' Then she smiled, as if changing the subject, though her tone remained exactly the same. 'Did you have an interesting day with Mr Drake?'

Hope could not contain her blush. 'Did Grandmama show you the painting?'

'She showed me both of them,' Charity said. 'But I assume you are asking about the one she sat for. Or laid for, rather.' She threw one hand behind her head and rested the other between her legs.

'You should not have looked,' Hope said, shaking her head.

Charity shrugged. 'Everyone else did. Even Mr Drake.'

Hope winced at the memory and felt her cheeks grow hot.

Of course Charity noticed. 'And what did he think of the picture?'

'He was too polite to give his opinion,' Hope said.

'Is he always so gentlemanly?' Charity was staring at her as if she had already guessed the answer to the question. When she had that look in her eye, there was little point in trying to evade it. The interrogation would be relentless until she learned what she wanted.

Hope surrendered. 'He kissed me.'

There was no pause of surprise before the next question. 'Where?'

'On the lips,' she said, annoyed at the satisfied sigh that accompanied the words.

Charity responded with a huff of irritation. 'Where were you standing when it happened?'

'In the salon. Grandmama had just taken the painting upstairs and we were alone.'

Her sister leaned forward, her smug superiority momentarily forgotten in perfectly girlish curiosity. 'Did you like it?'

Hope bit her lip. 'Proper young ladies do not ask such questions, nor do they answer them.'

'I will take that as a yes,' Charity said with a satisfied nod.

'I should not have,' Hope said quickly. 'It happened so fast that I did not know how to stop it. But it ended quickly as well.' Which still felt strangely disappointing. 'It should never have happened at all,' she said firmly. 'And when it did, it was wrong to take pleasure in it.'

'Do not be ridiculous. Kissing is usually considered pleasant, or people would not bother to do it. You can hardly control a visceral response,' Charity said and slowly closed her eyes. 'And he does seem to be the sort of man who could evoke feelings.'

'Yes,' Hope admitted. Perhaps it was his fault, after all, for being too handsome to resist. 'But I am still not sure why it happened. He did not seem very happy afterward.'

'Considering his past, I expect he was not,' Charity said, acting just as she always did, as if she knew more than everyone in the room.

Hope sighed. 'Go ahead. Tell me what it was about his past that would make him unhappy to have kissed me.'

'I will if you tell me what it was that set him off.'

Was there any part of the day that had not been mortifying? And must Charity tease out every last secret? 'I was overwrought,' Hope said at last, shaking her head. 'After seeing the painting and Grandmama's reaction to it. It was humiliating. She could not contain her pride, even in front of Mr Drake. What must he think of us?'

'So you went on a sanctimonious rant about our honourable family heritage,' Charity retorted, making a face.

'Between her pilfering and her lewd paintings, Grandmama does not do a very good job of protecting our family reputation.'

'And you felt the need to explain it all to a natural son whose family would not claim him and who is now being paid to clean the Strickland linen,' she said, then stared at Hope, waiting for her to understand.

Hope had not thought it was possible to be more embarrassed by what had happened, but apparently, she was wrong. 'I had no idea he would think my words pertained to him. He must have thought me the most arrogant woman in the world.'

'It is worse than that,' Charity added, her smile even wider.

'Of course it is,' Hope said in a faint voice. It was as if, because she had enjoyed a kiss, God meant to punish her by spoiling every other moment in the day.

'Of the parents, his mother was the proud lady and his father the underling who seduced and abandoned her. I suspect he was appalled to find he was acting out a tradition from his own family, right there in the salon.'

'He will never want to see me again.' That was what the letter had said and what he had meant by it being all his fault.

'If he is attracted to you, what he wants to do

might be quite different from what he actually does,' Charity announced.

'He is not attracted,' Hope corrected. 'He said that he would not have spent a moment with me had he not been paid to do so.'

'That is quite possibly true,' Charity said. 'If he had not been hired by Mr Leggett, there is a good chance you would never have met. But now that you have, the fact that he is employed by the family makes no difference. It does not make him less than human. And it certainly does not make him any less of a human male.'

He was definitely that. Hope could not help the little tremble of excitement she felt when she thought of the strong hands that had grabbed her and pulled her into his arms.

When the cloud of fantasy cleared, she looked up to see Charity was staring at her as if she was an idiot. 'He kissed you because you are a beautiful woman and he *wanted* to kiss you,' she said, explaining it as if it should be obvious. 'His passions were likely inflamed by the presence of the picture which bears a striking resemblance to you. There were also the ideas I might have put in his head…'

'You told him to kiss me?' said Hope, horrified.

'I told him not to,' Charity said with a dismissive wave. 'Rather, I told him not to seduce you. Telling a person not to do a thing is often the same as urging him on.'

'Why would you do such a horrible thing?'

Charity grinned. 'Because when as fine a masculine specimen as Gregory Drake enters the house, someone ought to get a kiss from him.'

'And you decided it should be me?'

'You are the most insufferably proper girl in London,' Charity said. 'And I hope your tiny fall from grace will make you stop treating Grandmother and me like a pair of unrepentant sinners.'

'You must not tell Grandmama,' Hope said hurriedly.

'Of course not,' Charity agreed. 'Though I suspect she will applaud the incident, just as I do. But now that it has happened, we must decide for ourselves what you are to do about this.'

'We?' Hope said, shocked at her sister's audacity. 'You have done far too much already. From now on, any decisions will be mine alone.'

'And Mr Drake's,' Charity added.

'He has made his decision already,' Hope said, trying not to sound sorry for herself. 'He wrote to me to apologise and says our outings have proved too dangerous to my reputation and he will have nothing to do with me from now on.'

'I see,' said Charity.

But that sounded suspiciously like she had been rejected. It would be better if the parting was a sensible, mutual decision. 'And I do not plan on doing anything with him, either,' she added.

'Of course not,' Charity said with a definitive nod and a smile that belied it.

'I may not ever see him again,' Hope added. 'And

it is probably for the best. I cannot kiss him again, even if he should want to. It would not be right.'

'Because you are going to marry the heir,' Charity said with a resigned sigh.

'That is still the most logical thing to do,' Hope said. 'Then it will not matter as much if Mr Drake leaves us, or if the entail is incomplete. I will explain everything once we are married and ask for forgiveness.'

'Must you always try to think three moves ahead?' Charity asked. 'You are not particularly good at chess.'

'My skills are more than adequate. They might actually appear so if I was not always playing against you,' Hope explained as patiently as she was able. 'And while you are quite good at outsmarting me, I am still the elder. I need to think of others as I plan my actions. I cannot just fall in love, willy-nilly, with the first man that walks through the door.'

'Unless he has a title,' Charity finished for her, turning towards the door. 'Enjoy the ball, Sister dear. And try not to make too many conquests while you are there. It would be cruel to Mr Drake.'

'He does not matter.' Hope rushed to the door and leaned out into the hall, shouting at her sister's retreating back. 'And I do not matter to him.'

Chapter Six

Despite Charity's advice that she enjoy herself, Hope did not expect the evening's party to be much better than tedious. As the weeks of the Season crawled by without the arrival of her cousin, she'd come to view the events she attended with a kind of distant dread. She had to be on guard at all times, not wanting to have too much fun or enjoy herself so completely that she forgot her *raison d'être*. She must not lose her heart or her head, or cause a similar reaction from any of the gentlemen present.

If it seemed to be happening with Mr Drake, it was simply a sign that she had not been cautious enough. This was a reminder to be ever vigilant.

It was exactly the opposite of the advice she received from her grandmother, who sat opposite her in the family coach. 'Above all things, make merry, my dear. You are only young once. Now that Mr Leggett is providing for us, it is finally possible for me to give you the Season you deserve.' Her grandmother was wearing the faintly worried look she got sometimes when the matter of money came up.

'There was nothing wrong with the opportunities you provided for me in Berkshire,' Hope said to reassure her. 'The house party at Christmas was delightful.'

'That was for Faith's engagement,' the Dowager replied. 'If Mr Leggett had not invited himself to it, there would have been not one eligible man in attendance. And if not for him, Faith might have married that dreary Mr Fosberry.'

'He was not so bad,' Hope lied. Then added, 'But I am glad she married Mr Leggett instead.'

'Without a proper come out, with new gowns and a ball, Cyril was the only offer she got, and she had to trap him into it,' her grandmother added. 'Perhaps, when she and Mr Leggett return from Italy, we might persuade him to throw a ball for you.'

'I am quite content to wait until we can celebrate the arrival of our American cousin,' Hope claimed, smiling to hide any bitterness she felt. A year ago, she had wanted nothing more than a party swarming with eligible bachelors. Then there was no money for it. Now, there was no need. Either the Earl would marry her, or they would all have to settle for spinsterhood and rustication.

'Do not wait for anyone,' her grandmother insisted, patting her hand. 'Dance every dance. Find a balcony or a terrace, or at least the shade of a potted palm, and be alone with someone, just as all the other couples do. And if you break some young fellow's heart, be sure it is not before giving him a reason to remember you fondly.'

'You are not supposed to suggest such things,' Hope reminded her. 'You are to tell me to guard my virtue like a precious jewel.'

Her grandmother made a puffing noise in response and then grinned. 'Jewels are of no value if they are never put to their intended use.'

'Your metaphor is weak. Jewels are just as valuable if they remain in the lockbox,' Hope remarked. 'At least when they are there, one can be sure that they have not been lost.' She had resisted the temptation to substitute the word *sold*. If Grandmama had understood that, they would not be in the trouble they were in now.

The Dowager finally seemed to sense her thoughts. When she turned to look again, the older woman's expression was still loving, but faintly wounded. 'I know you do not approve of me, my darling. Perhaps I am a trifle too rackety to raise young ladies. But I was quite good at raising sons. They are easier, you see.' As they drove moonlight and shadow flickered over her face and her expression seemed to change the happy and rather foolish woman Hope expected into someone else who was much older, wiser and sadder.

Hope turned her hand to close it over her grandmother's. 'You have done well with us, Grandmama. It is I who am not as grateful as I should be. I promise, I shall dance every dance and have as much fun as I am able, without breaking any hearts at all.'

One broken heart a day was more than enough.

* * *

Hope had been looking forward to the Ellinghams' ball for reasons that both Charity and their grandmother would have considered sorely misguided. If it went in the manner of all the other balls she had attended this Season it was likely to be an entire evening where nothing of interest happened at all. Tonight, that suited her well.

She stood in the doorway to the ballroom revelling in the utter predictability that awaited her. There was no need to make polite introductions for there was no one here she had not seen a dozen times before. She could perform even the most complicated of dances without missing a step. Even the conversations would not vary from those she had had several times this year. She would not have to think about the entail, the Earl or Mr Drake for four long hours.

It would be heaven.

In the past week, she'd had far too much to think about and too many strange new feelings. With each new day, her life seemed to get more complicated, not less. Perhaps, now that she had driven Mr Drake away, things could go back to the way she had planned. Why could she not find comfort in the thought?

'Hello, Ellingham. Lovely evening.'

'Hello, Drake. As always, it is a pleasure.'

Hope clutched the door frame, afraid to turn towards the men talking in the entryway just behind her. There was no need. One was her host. Though the other had been a stranger a week ago, she knew the sound of his voice as well as she knew her own.

Why was he here? Had he followed her? It seemed unlikely since he'd wanted nothing to do with her just a few hours ago. Perhaps he had more than one employer. If so, she had no right to enquire as to his presence here. It was possible that he would not even want to acknowledge her should they meet.

She definitely did not want to see him. At least, not until she could manage to compose herself. She could feel the colour rising in her cheeks already. It would not matter whether they spoke or not. The whole room had but to look at her face to know that there was something between them.

Run!

She was not sure where she meant to go, but she could not stay where she was. In a moment, he could step forward and be at her side. She looked frantically around, spied a corridor to her left, darted down it, grabbed the first door handle she saw and slipped into the unlocked room, shutting the door behind her again with a soft click.

The music and chatter of the ballroom faded to a distant murmur. She was safe, isolated from the crowd and the one man she could not bear to see. But where was she hiding?

She turned slowly to examine the room. Apparently, she had chosen Lord Ellingham's study as her bolt hole. It was unoccupied and likely to remain so, for the only light came from the embers of the banked fire.

If she stayed here for just a few minutes, Mr Drake would disappear into the crowd. While she waited, she could prepare a proper response in case they met. She could practise it in the mirror, just as she did for the Earl.

The thought made her smile. It was a shame she did not have Mr Drake's composure. Other than those few moments in the salon, he had been unflappable. He had threatened to quit the job, but she doubted he would. There were still three items left on the list the Dowager had given her. She could not imagine that he would give up before he thought the job had been completed, no matter how awkward the interaction between them had been.

Or perhaps there were only two items.

She stared at the desk in front of her and the inkwell sitting on top of it. She had seen it hundreds of times in the same spot on her grandfather's desk in his study at the manor.

Hope's palms itched with the urge to grab it and run. Why should she not? It belonged in her family home, not in the house of some bargain hunter who graced his desk with castoffs from the Lombard merchants. Even better, she would be able to show Mr Drake that she was not totally reliant on his help. The quicker she could reclaim the items on the list, the sooner they could be truly free of each other.

As it had this afternoon, the idea of his departure raised a strange mix of feelings in her, both anticipation and dread. It was another sign that he should go. She had never been so confused by the presence of a man in her life. Who knew one kiss could cause such disruption?

If she hoped to leave the room at all this evening, she must not think of the kiss. There were more important things, right in front of her. She moved closer to the desk to get a better look at her prize. It was exactly as she remembered it: a graceful well of rock crystal, set upon a gold filigree base.

She held her reticule against the side, pleased to see that it was just big enough. She uttered a brief prayer for forgiveness for the theft and swept the thing off the desk and into her purse. She hurried back to the door, opened it slowly and glanced both ways up and down the hall to make sure she would not be seen escaping. Then she stepped out of the room and walked briskly back towards the ballroom.

'Miss Strickland.'

She froze in her tracks. 'Mr Drake?' How had she not noticed him in her brief search of the corridor? She turned slowly to the sound of his voice, with a smile that she was sure was nowhere near as convincing as the one she had while practising in her own home.

He was standing in an alcove, outside in the hall, and just out of sight of the study door. No. He was not standing. He was lounging, his posture as casual as that of any other young buck at this party. His dress rivalled theirs as well: immaculate blue coat, buff breeches, snowy linen and a cravat that was not just white, but *blanc d'innocence virginale.* It crossed at the front, not even tied, the creases and folds at his throat in perfect and crisp alignment as if he held them there by dint of his own considerable will.

'I did not expect to see you here this evening,' she said. Her voice was embarrassingly breathless.

'I assumed as much, from the way you ran into a private room to avoid me.' So this was no chance meeting. He had been waiting in the hall to catch her doing something she should not.

Or perhaps he had been waiting for his chance to do exactly what she had just done. He had come to retrieve the inkwell. Her smile relaxed as she imagined his surprise to find her one step ahead of him. She opened her fan and gave it a coy flutter. 'My dear Mr Drake, you are mistaken. I was not avoiding you. I was doing what you have obviously come to do for yourself. Now that it has been taken care of, there is no reason for you to remain.'

He gave a surprised laugh. 'You are dismissing me?'

Thank God, he understood. And she should thank God as well that their relationship had returned to being dull and professional instead of dangerously exciting. 'Yes,' she said, pointing towards the front door with her fan. 'You may go.'

He raised a hand to his face, cupping his chin and drawing a single finger across his lips as if to seal in the laughter that seemed to be happening somewhere deep inside him, for his shoulders shook and his eyes sparkled like sunlight dancing on choppy water. When he had regained control of himself sufficiently to speak, the hand fell away. 'Or, I could stay.'

'I do not think that will be wise,' she whispered. 'What if someone sees us speaking?'

'I do not know,' he whispered back. 'Perhaps they will think you are flirting with me.' Then he raised his voice to a normal tone. 'It will be much less intimate if we do not whisper. Even less so if we return to the ballroom, where the rest of the guests are gathered.'

'The rest of the guests?' Perhaps he misspoke, for that almost seemed to imply that he belonged there.

'I am sorry,' he said with mock surprise. 'I assumed you were invited as well. I must compliment Ellingham for the novelty of hiring a young lady to guard his door. Was I expected to bring the card he sent? I left it at home for my valet said it quite spoiled the line of my suit.'

'You have a valet?' It had been an exceptionally stupid question, but it was too late to call it back.

'Since my skills do not extend to pressing coats and starching linen, I thought it sensible to hire one.' His eyes hardened, ever so slightly and his smile chilled. 'I also have a butler, a housekeeper, a cook and as many footmen and maids as they deem necessary to effectively run my house.'

'Oh,' she said, softly. She had not given any thought at all to Mr Drake's living arrangements. Nor had it occurred to her that he had friends who might welcome his company. She had certainly not expected to find that they had any in common. She was as bad as Charity claimed if she assumed he appeared like a djinni, then disappeared again, existing only to serve her.

Before she could frame the apology that he so richly deserved, he was speaking again. 'But you must forgive me, Miss Strickland. Since we have met tonight, I have talked of nothing but myself. How are you, Miss Strickland? And how did you come to be sneaking out of Lord Ellingham's study? Most importantly, why is your reticule leaking ink?'

'Oh, dear Lord.' In her rush to reclaim the family property, she had ignored the purpose of the item she took. 'I forgot to empty it.'

He was staring at her. It was clear the explanation was not sufficient. 'It's the inkwell. The Comstock inkwell,' she added, for clarity. 'Grandmama sold it. Lord Ellingham must have found it in the shop and bought it. I was retrieving it from the study.'

'With Lord Ellingham's permission, of course.'

That would have been the sensible thing to do. She could have written him a letter tomorrow, requesting the chance to purchase it back. Instead, she had decided, on a moment, to take it now. 'No,' she admitted.

'You stole Lord Ellingham's inkwell.' He was staring at her now as if he could not quite believe the words he'd just spoken.

'I did,' she said, horrified.

He held out his hand, resigned. 'Give me your reticule.'

He had been here to enjoy an evening with friends and she had embroiled him in a burglary. 'You should not have to…'

'Give it to me,' he said firmly.

She held it out and he took it from her, pinching the strings between two fingers of one white gloved hand. 'Now go to the retiring room and get yourself cleaned up. You have ink on your hands.'

'Oh, dear.' Her own gloves were likely ruined, just as the reticule was.

'We will speak later,' he said.

Actually, she rather hoped they would not.

Chapter Seven

When Gregory had been offered triple his fee to deal with Hope Strickland, he should have taken the warning and run, as far and as fast as his legs could manage. After finding the blighted painting of the Blue Earl and shipping it to the Comstock town house along with his apology, he had sat down to write a letter to Leggett in Italy, tendering his resignation.

One of his favourite things about the job he had made for himself was the lack of awkward attachments once the task was finished. He had been left with casual friendships, of course. But there was no scorekeeping, guilt, recrimination, or even embarrassed gratitude attached to the things he had done for them. Once the bill had been paid for a service, all behaved as if it had never happened.

But when one started kissing the employer's family, one should quit the employment. Even if it had been an accident. Even if it was not going to happen again. Even if…a hundred other excuses and conditions he had run through trying to explain what had happened this morning.

Even if he never saw Hope Strickland again, there was no way to forget what had happened this afternoon. Perhaps it was a sign of an inherited weakness of character. Perhaps it was only her extreme desirability. But the more aloof she became, the more he wanted to ruffle her feathers. The more untouchable she appeared, the more he'd wanted to tug on the one wayward curl that she could not seem to stop worrying at.

And the more covered she was? The more he wondered if the body underneath matched that of her worthy ancestress. Tonight's gown was nothing like the modest day dresses she wore to go about with him. The primrose net clung to her full hips and the décolletage was so deep that a man could lose his soul it.

And her reticule was covered with ink. What had she been thinking?

She had been trying to escape him, of course. And trying to prove that she could do the job he'd been hired for as effectively as he could, so she might never have to see him again. When talking to him had been unavoidable, she'd assumed that he must be working. Why else would Gregory Drake be associating with decent people in the evening?

The answer to that was that he knew many of them and counted most as friends. He was invited to so many balls and routs that it was surprising he had not already made an acquaintance with the Strickland sisters. It was also sensible, now that they were in the same place, that he made sure she had been introduced to all his eligible friends. That was well within the parameters for the other half of his job: setting her cap and mind for anyone who was not the Earl of Comstock.

It was also the last thing on earth he wanted to do. When he had seen her disappear into a darkened room, his first, unworthy impulse had been to follow her and lock the door behind them. It had taken several minutes of internal struggling to focus on the only thing that should come to mind when he saw her: his job.

Now that he had regained control of himself, he returned the inkwell to its proper place, taking the time to clean up the spilled ink. Then he wrapped the spoiled reticule in a handkerchief and handed it to a footman, giving instructions that it be returned to the Strickland carriage to await its owner.

Once finished, he proceeded to the ballroom where he'd meant to be all along. He helped himself to a glass of punch, which Ellingham House always served strong. He had a second glass for good measure. Then he joined the dance to do the thing he had promised himself he would never do again. He needed to talk with Hope Strickland.

It did not take him long to manoeuvre himself into a position where the only natural thing to do was to offer to partner her. She looked around frantically for a moment, hoping to find someone who she might claim to have promised a dance to. Then she gave up and accepted defeat, and his arm.

They danced in silence for a moment before he said, 'You do not have to be frightened of me, you know. There will be no embarrassing repetition of this morning's incident.'

Did she look disappointed? If so, the expression passed almost instantly. She stared at his hand. 'How do you keep your gloves so clean?'

'I beg your pardon?'

'I ruined mine. The maid in the ladies' retiring room could do nothing with them and found me a pair to borrow for the evening. But you...' His hand touched hers as they cast down the set and she stared at it in amazement.

'I was very careful,' he said, when they met again. At least, he always had been, before he'd met her. 'Your reticule is in your coach and your brother-in-law will be billed for my ruined handkerchief. Also, Ellingham's staff will be missing two table napkins tomorrow.' He shrugged. 'A lesser inconvenience than a missing inkwell, I think.'

'You returned it?' She frowned.

'Because it did not belong to you. That particular style was a popular gift to servants of the Crown in the middle of the last century. The engraving on the base indicated that it was given to Ellingham's grandfather.'

He hoped it was only embarrassment that caused the dramatic scarlet flush in her face. For a moment, he feared she was becoming ill. 'I am mortified,' she murmured. 'And sorry to you as well. I should never have proceeded without consulting you.'

That was perfectly true. But it pained him to see her suffer over the mistake. 'You were precipitous in your actions, but they were somewhat helpful. Now that I have seen an example of the thing I am seeking, I shall have no trouble finding it in the shops I frequent. It shall be delivered to your house tomorrow, by noon.'

'You are too kind, Mr Drake.' Perhaps it was because she'd been veiled for so much of their time together that he found it so affecting to look into her eyes. They were the warm brown of a good sherry and just as intoxicating.

He felt himself flushing under her gaze and hoped it could be blamed on the warmth of the ballroom. 'It is nothing, Miss Strickland. I am simply doing the job I have been hired to do.'

'And I seem to go out of my way to make it more difficult for you,' she said. 'This afternoon, when I spoke of my family, or bragged, rather...'

'You have a right to be proud of them,' he said. He should not have had the second glass of punch. He was straining to smile, revealing too much of the man behind the façade he'd created to deal with his employers.

'Charity told me of your past. I did not mean to draw an unfavourable comparison between your life and mine, and I am sorry if it seemed so.' She reached up with a free hand and brushed at the stray curl, which was no more out of place than the rest of the soft ringlets surrounding her face.

He stared at it for a moment, watching in fascination as it caressed her cheek and then bounced away again. 'If I took offence, I am the foolish one. And as for what happened next...'

'You promised that we would not speak of it,' she reminded him, though she seemed more surprised than scolding. Had the reminder of their kiss pleased her? The smile that danced across her lips was more playful than practised.

He smiled back. This time it felt as relaxed and natural as moving through the patterns of the dance with her. 'I merely wish to reiterate my apology.'

'It is accepted,' she said. 'But you must stop taking all the blame on yourself. I was horrid to you.' She touched the curl again—clearly it was a nervous habit. 'And this evening, I treated you as if you did not belong here. I would not have been surprised if you refused to speak to me ever again. And yet you still helped me.'

'I would not have bothered you, had you not needed my help,' he reminded her.

The dance had ended, but their conversation had not. Out of the corner of his eye he could see several fellows moving forward to take his place. Before they could arrive, he held out his hand to her again.

Without a thought, she took it and they lined up for the next set.

'It is good that you did help me,' she added. 'Tonight, I thought to show you that I could manage alone. But I did not do very well, did I? I did not even notice that the thing I took had someone else's name written upon it.'

'I have been dealing with such problems far longer than you have,' he reminded her. 'Checking for details is almost second nature, as is keeping my head clear and my gloves clean.' He stopped himself before he could say more. What had begun as reassuring a client was beginning to sound suspiciously like bragging about his abilities.

'What seems natural to you is just short of miraculous to others,' she said. Her gaze dropped to the floor for a moment. When her eyes met his again, he felt the same euphoric jolt as he'd got from Ellingham's punch.

'Of course, Grandmama's list is nothing compared to other problems I am facing. I will need an actual miracle to solve them,' she said.

He waited through another series of steps, but she made no effort to enlighten him.

'If there is something bothering you that Mr Leggett was not aware of, I am sure he would want you to tell me,' he offered.

When next they passed in the dance, she was biting her lip, as if trying to decide. Then, she shook her head. 'The only one who will be able to help with this matter is the new Earl of Comstock. It is why I am so eager to meet him.'

'Of course you are.' Because all the things he had done for her, and all he might do in the future, had no value when compared with a title.

The dance ended, and he escorted her to the edge of the floor. Once there, she gave him what she probably thought was a sympathetic smile. 'I mean no disparagement of your abilities. But this is a family matter.'

As if all the things he had done so far were not. 'Just how well do you know your esteemed cousin, Miss Strickland?'

'Better than you do, I should think.' She was bluffing, of course. She knew nothing at all.

Until Gregory received responses to the enquiries he'd made, he knew little beyond the fellow's name. So he bluffed as well. 'I wonder, do you want to know the truth about the man you are saving yourself for?'

'I am sure there is nothing that will surprise me,' she said. But now her smile was the one that looked strained.

'I do not think you do,' he answered, strangely satisfied to have riled her.

'If you know anything, speak,' she challenged. 'But I think it is far more likely that you are just trying to be difficult.'

'Do you doubt my word?' She had every right to, since he had nothing beyond vague hints to offer her, yet he could not help continuing. 'Your brother-in-law hired me because of my abilities. I can find things that no one else can. Candlesticks, for example. And paintings. And inconvenient truths.'

'Then reveal them,' she snapped as all her earlier goodwill evaporated. 'It is your job to do so.'

'What would your response be if you learned that the future Earl was full seven and seventy?' A hypothetical question was not precisely a lie.

He watched her trying to suppress a shudder before replying, 'We cannot all be young and handsome. It is unfair to judge a person with only a single detail to describe them.'

It only became a lie when he embroidered over the half-truth. 'Then I will add the gout that has delayed his crossing, the excesses that brought it on, the bad temper resulting from the continual pain and what has been described as a difficult nature by his friends and employees.'

The beautiful girl beside him swallowed and there was a long pause as she tried to choose a response that did not reveal her obvious disappointment. 'People exaggerate for any number of reasons. You cannot know any of this firsthand, therefore you have no way of proving them.'

Now was the point where a man of honour would admit that he had spoken falsehoods in anger. Instead, he blundered on, jealous at her defence of a man she had never met. 'I suppose you will still doubt when you meet his wife, who must be old enough to be your mother since she has presented him with four daughters and a son. All but the oldest are unmarried and will no doubt enjoy a London Season along with the opportunities that his title will bring. What they will not appreciate is competition on the marriage mart by a pair of distant cousins.'

'Married.' He had expected her to look disappointed. Perhaps there would be a few bitter tears that her plans would come to naught, the kind of small tantrum as one often saw from pampered creatures used to getting their own way. Then, she would turn her sharp tongue on him, blaming the messenger as she had done after they found her grandmother's portrait.

He would deserve it for the foul way he'd just treated her. Had he learned nothing from this afternoon? Had the truce they'd forged on the dance floor meant nothing at all?

But tonight's response was far worse than the stunned silence that had greeted him after their kiss. Nor was it the slight upset he had expected tonight. No minor shock could have caused the sudden pallor of her face, or the stricken look in her eyes. For a moment, he feared she might swoon right there in front of him. It did not seem as if she was going to cry. Rather, she seemed to be doing a brave job of holding it back, as if she knew that once the first tear escaped, there would be a flood that could not be staunched for several hours.

'I am sorry,' he said, ready to call back every word of the last few minutes if it could erase the pain he'd already caused her.

'No,' she said, firmly, placing a hand on his arm as if she were the one to offer comfort. 'I will be all right. It is far better to know the truth than to nurture false hopes.'

But had they been false? There was still a chance that things were just as she believed and a stranger was coming to rescue her from across the sea. Or it could be just as he predicted. How could he recant, if he did not know the truth himself?

She swallowed again, and he saw the supreme effort it was costing to maintain her smile, which was every bit as lovely and as false as the one she'd practised in the mirror. 'The family is fortunate that he has been blessed with a son. The succession is secure and we needn't worry about the future.'

'But you and your sister...' he began to say.

'It was kind of you to think we might be competition for our new cousins,' she said, patting him on the hand. 'But I doubt they will have anything to worry about on that front. As long as he is kind to Grandmama and allows her the dower house, Charity and I shall find a way to manage.'

'Do not worry.' There was only one thing to do that could make this right. Now that it had occurred to him, it seemed to be the most sensible thing in the world. It would justify his rash and uncontrollable behaviour, whenever he was around her. If this was where he had been heading, since the first moment he'd seen her, his life made sense again.

The middle of someone else's party was no place to make an offer of marriage. But he must say something to assure her that one was coming. He grasped the hand that covered his. 'You and your sister will want for nothing.'

'Of course not,' she said, as if she had not heard. Then she gave him another dazed and dazzling smile. 'And now, if you will excuse me... I am not well.'

Then, before he could say the words he needed to, her hand slipped from his and she walked away.

Hope sat in the darkened coach for hours, listening to the chuffing of the horses and the occasional jingle of their harnesses until, at last, the ball ended and she was driven to the front of the house to retrieve the Dowager. As she usually was after an evening in society, Grandmama was tired but happy. Her face was rosy and her every breath seemed to exhale in a sigh of contentment. 'I swear, that was the most delightful evening I've had in ages. The food was excellent and the musicians played not a single note out of tune.'

'I am glad you enjoyed it,' Hope said, unable to keep the bitterness from her voice. 'It may be the last one we have.'

'Do not be melodramatic, dear.' The old woman smiled at her and shook her head. 'You young people. Every problem is the end of the world to you.'

'It is the end,' Hope said, trying to make her understand. 'Mr Drake knows something of the heir coming from America. He is married.'

'Good for him,' came the cheerful reply.

'It means he will not want me, Grandmama,' Hope said urgently. 'His auditors will find the missing items and I will not be able to stop what happens next.'

'With Mr Drake's help, you shall have them all back in time, I'm sure.'

'But not the diamonds, Grandmama.' Could it be

she had actually forgotten them? 'He does not even know they are missing, much less where to look for them. What has become of the Comstock parure?'

The Dowager gave her a puzzled look. 'It is in the lock room at the manor. You know I do not like to wear it. It is too heavy.'

'You do not wear it so no one will notice that the stones are paste.'

Her grandmother glanced out the window at the passing scenery, acting as if she had not heard. 'The moon is exceptionally bright tonight. It is a shame we are not in the country for it would be a beautiful drive.'

'You must tell me what you did with the diamonds,' Hope urged. 'If I know where to look, maybe there is some way we can get them back before he arrives. But if I cannot influence the heir... If he doesn't want to make me his Countess... There is no way we can guarantee that the secret will be kept. What if he is angry? What if he wants the money for them?' She reached out and took her grandmother's hand, squeezing it in encouragement.

After what seemed like an eternity, the Dowager turned her head from the window to acknowledge that she had heard the questions put to her. 'Hope, darling, do not worry. It will all turn out for the best. These things usually do, you know. But I have nothing to tell you on the matter of the diamonds. Please do not ask me again.'

Chapter Eight

Mr Drake returned the next day, promptly at ten.

It was a relief to see him because Hope had awoken feeling something rather like optimism. Given the reality of circumstances, the feeling was totally misplaced. But she could not help the contents of her dreams, which had been illogically happy.

The same man who was now walking up to her front door had figured prominently in them. They had been dancing together at the ball. And as he had last night, he had told her the horrible news about the Earl. But then, just as her future seemed darkest, he had smiled at her and taken her hand, pulling her out of the set to the gasps of those around her.

'Do not be afraid. You shall want for nothing. I have a big house with servants and room for your sister.'

He had actually said most of those things last night. But he had not taken her in his arms and kissed her, as he did in the dream.

It had been a wonderful dream. But she was awake now. No matter how handsome he was, with the sun shining on the fringe of his gold hair, he was not going to stick one of his immaculate gloves into his pocket and produce the Comstock diamonds. They were doomed. All three of them.

At least, she suspected so. She knew what happened to thieves. But what happened to their granddaughters? And was the punishment any less for dowager countesses? It might simply be disgrace and public ostracism. That would be bad enough, but it was better than Newgate.

Mr Drake had reached the door and she opened it as he reached for the knocker, startling him. 'You were watching at the window,' he said with a surprised smile that she could not manage to return.

'Soonest started, soonest done,' she said, hurrying out to the carriage where a groom was pulling down the step for her.

'I am glad you are feeling better,' he said, his smile flattening to an upward quirk at the corners of his mouth, and offered a hand to help her up into her seat.

'I beg your pardon?'

'Last night. When you left me, you said you were ill.'

'Oh,' she said softly. She'd had no idea what excuses she had made for leaving. After he had finished destroying her hope for the future, the evening had devolved into a miserable blur.

'We both knew you were not sick,' he reminded her. 'I upset you with my talk of the heir.'

'It is all right,' she said quickly, feeling her stomach lurch as the carriage began to roll.

'No, it is not,' he said. 'Last night…' he started to say, then paused to wet his lips.

His hesitance was unusual for he was rarely at a loss for words. She raised her veil so they might talk face to face, since whatever he wished to say must be important.

'Last night, the things I said to you were not true.'

'You received conflicting information?' she said, surprised to feel more uneasy than relieved by the reversal of fortune.

'I lied,' he said with a resigned sigh. 'It was cruel of me to taunt you and I never would have done so had I known how it would upset you.'

'You lied,' she repeated. 'But why?'

Again, he paused. Again, he wet his lips before speaking. 'It bothered me that you seemed to prefer the help of the Earl to anything I might offer.'

'You were jealous.' Now she was not just surprised. She was amazed.

'Yes,' he said. Then he added, 'Professionally speaking, of course.'

'Of course,' she repeated.

'I do not know any more about Miles Strickland than I did on the first day. He might be exactly as you hope him to be, single and eager to help you.'

The prospect should have made her feel much better about the future. Instead she felt a vague disappointment. 'He might also be exactly as you described him,' she replied.

'But we will not know for sure until he arrives.' He reached a hand out and covered hers in a gesture of reassurance.

She stared down at it. It was a nice hand. She had never been conscious of male anatomy before, especially not the extremities. When she thought of them at all, she imagined her father's hands, which she could remember as pale and gentle, or her grandfather's, which were thin and knotted. When she attended balls, the hands of the men she danced with seemed to have no weight to them at all, barely grazing hers as they danced.

But Mr Drake's gloved hand was solid and strong. It did not tremble as it lifted her into carriages. It had been faintly possessive as it had led her through the dance at the ball and it had not hesitated when forced to take her reticule and return her stolen goods.

She had seen the bare skin briefly, when he had removed his gloves to root through the chest of candlesticks with her on the first day. They had been darkened by sun with a smattering of freckles across the knuckles. The nails had been clean and neatly trimmed, but there was something about them that made her suspect he was not afraid to get dirt under them, if a task required it.

All in all, she'd have described his hands as 'capable'. Much like the rest of him, really. He met problems without flinching and dealt with them. It was what he'd been hired to do. He was not helping her by choice. He was doing it for money. No matter what she had dreamed, she must not expect anything more than that from him.

He cleared his throat and she started suddenly, aware that she had been staring at him.

He pretended that he had not noticed and removed his hand to pull the list from his pocket. 'I thought today we might try to find the oddment.' He gave her an expectant look.

She nodded in agreement, eager to turn her mind to a problem that might have a solution.

He offered an expectant wiggle of his fingers, staring at her in a much more forthright way. 'I thought, perhaps, a description would be forthcoming by now.'

'It would if I had one to offer,' she replied. 'Grandmama is mum on the subject, but assures me I will know it when I see it.'

'Oddment implies that it is a remnant of something,' he mused. 'Or did she use the term in a more general manner? Could she have meant an oddity?'

'I really have no idea,' she said. 'And if I cannot tell you what it is, then I cannot even tell you where to begin to look.'

'Then, I will take the initiative.'

Despite herself, those words made her feel instantly better.

He thought for a moment. 'There are several shops I can recommend that sell things no one else has. Let us assume that, whatever this thing is, there is not another like it in the whole of London.' He looked at her sideways for a moment. 'You may find these places rather unpleasant. They are not the sort that one normally takes gently bred young ladies.'

'I find the whole experience rather unpleasant,' she said with a sigh. 'Why should this day be any different?'

He held up his hands in surrender. 'You have made that clear. Just know that I am not doing this in an effort to upset you, again. You have been warned.'

Would it disappoint him, she wondered, if the more horrible he made it sound the more tantalising it became? Sometimes it seemed that the most interesting experiences were things that gently bred ladies were not supposed to do. Like kissing, for instance. No matter what Charity thought she knew on such subjects, it could not have been as satisfying as practical experience.

The shops they visited today were a different sort of revelation. Who knew there was a store in London that had an entire cupboard full of stuffed owls and the largest spider she had ever seen, preserved under a bell jar? Or that there was another place specialising in music boxes and clocks that had complicated animations on the hourly chimes? At that place, there were some cases he flatly refused to allow her to look into, insisting that though the mechanisms were clever, they would shock her worse than her grandmother's painting had.

But since the Comstock heirlooms tended neither to taxidermy nor automatons, they could not help her.

None of the many fascinating things she saw were the Dowager's oddment.

But at the third shop, she felt a familiar rush of excitement. There were Roman coins and lapis scarabs, and fragments of Greek statues. There were so many fingers and ears and arms and legs that she wondered if it might be possible to put them together like a life-sized puzzle.

And suddenly, she knew what they were looking for. 'Excuse me.' She stepped forward to interrupt the conversation of the shopkeeper and Mr Drake. 'Excuse me, sir. But do you have any more Egyptian artefacts?'

'In the box.' He pointed towards the marble.

'Those are mostly Greek. The thing I am looking for will be in a wooden box. Ebony, I think. With a gold ankh inlaid on the cover.'

At his blank response, she traced the symbol in the dust on the counter. 'And it is held shut by leather bindings.'

The man grinned at her. 'I did not take you for a connoisseur, miss.' He reached behind the counter and brought out a thing she had never expected to see again.

She smiled and held her breath as she opened it, fearing that the contents might have disintegrated with age.

Mr Drake leaned over her shoulder to look as she raised the lid and recoiled in disgust. 'What the devil is it? And why would anyone want the thing back?'

'My great-grandfather did not stop at the Grand

Tour. He went all the way to Cairo!' she said with pride.

'And dismembered a mummy?' The look of revulsion on the handsome face at her shoulder was properly impressive.

'Do not be such a ninny.' She waved it in his face and watched him jump. 'It is not a real toe. It is a false one. Made of ebony with a gold nail.' She ran a finger along the bindings. 'It fit around the foot just so and strapped on with these.'

'There are still bones,' he said. 'I can hear them rattling.' His face was bloodless white and he was still backing up.

'I do not know how you could. You are almost out into the street. And those are not bones rattling, they are the metal tips of the laces. Now come back here and pay the man.'

'Put it away, you ghoul.' He shuddered. 'Or you will never see me again.'

For the first time in what felt like ages, she laughed as she had when she was a child. Why had she ever stopped? Was there some rule that young ladies did not succumb to mirth? Or had she created one just for herself? No matter. She must remember to break it more often. She rolled her eyes at Mr Drake and put the prosthetic back in the box, closing the lid. 'There. All better?'

'Somewhat,' he agreed, reaching for his purse. 'We are taking that directly back to the town house, for Leggett is not paying me enough to ride around London with that abomination in the carriage with me.'

* * *

Once they'd returned home, she took the box to the library and left it beside the sofa that was Charity's habitual place. 'She will be so amused to see it again,' she assured him with an evil grin. 'I used to chase her around the house with it, when we were small. She retaliated by hiding it under my pillow one night. I did not sleep for a week.'

He stared at her, disgusted. 'What sort of women are you?'

'Ones that were moved suddenly as small girls to a house with few playthings,' she said, patting the box with affection. 'Until we settled in and Grandmama bought us proper toys, we had a most exciting time rummaging through the family heirlooms.'

'Are there any others as ghastly as this?' he asked.

'None that you will be forced to retrieve. The last item on the list is a porcelain vase and it is really quite ordinary.'

'That is a great relief,' he said, with a half-smile.

'And now I understand Grandmother's cryptic description of it. She could not abide the thing. We agreed to have a funeral for it, if we could have a proper Egyptian one with a burning barge.'

'Egyptians have pyramids,' he supplied. 'You are confusing them with Vikings.'

'I know. But we wanted a fire,' she said. 'It was most disappointing. In the end, we settled for a hole in the ground and a tapered stack of stones on top.'

'You were allowed to bury it?' he said, surprised.

'Grandmama encouraged it. She said it came

from a grave and, as decent Christians, we should put it back in one. We recorded it in the family Bible so that future, less squeamish Comstocks could find it.'

'And then she dug it up,' he stated.

Hope shook her head in amazement. 'She hated the thing. She must have been quite desperate for money, if she chose to retrieve this.'

'Though it was not first on the list, I'll wager that this was the first thing she took,' he mused.

'How can you tell?'

'Because it was as good as gone already. No one would miss a thing that had been given a formal burial. Who was likely to go looking for it?'

'When the Earl's agents came to do the audit, I would have told them the family story and shown them the Bible,' she said, surprised.

'And they would likely have left well enough alone,' he concluded. Then he added, 'But I am glad she decided to include it in the list. It makes things so much easier when the people who hire me do not hold back important details.'

'Oh,' she said. He was probably referring to their conversation from the previous evening. She wished he would stop hinting about the matter since she doubted there was anything that could be done without the help of Comstock. She gave him the most innocent look she could muster. 'Are people often less than forthcoming?'

'By the time it is necessary to bring in an outsider to sort out the mess, you would think that there would be no energy left to cover things up.' He shook his head. 'But there is always some small hope that the situation, whatever it is, will resolve itself without my help.'

'Or they know that it cannot be fixed,' she replied. No matter how much money Mr Leggett had given him, he could not have enough to buy back the huge stones in the Comstock necklace.

'Or they are ashamed,' he added.

It certainly explained her grandmother's behaviour.

'They needn't be,' he said softly when she did not reply. 'They have no reason to be so. If the mistake was someone else's, then any guilt rests with that person and not the one trying to help.'

'Thank you.' Even this tiny bit of absolution was a comfort. How had Faith managed for so long, when she had been the only one to know of the family's troubles? The money her marriage had brought made things easier. Yet, after less than a month of trying to rescue the Dowager, Hope felt near to exhaustion.

'I think it is because they do not fully trust me,' he said. 'I am not *of them*. Had it been my father who was of noble birth and not my mother, I might have been an acknowledged member of a noble family. I would never have had an earldom, but at least I'd have been able to tell you my true name.' His steely-grey eyes softened with sadness.

Was that what he thought the problem was? That she did not think a bastard was worthy of her secret? 'That is not the problem at all,' she insisted. 'I think you are the most fascinating man I have ever met and I trust you with my life.'

'Then prove it to me,' he urged.

Before she could even think to speak, she had kissed him.

Chapter Nine

They were like an ember, dropped on to dry leaves. For the shortest of moments they were still two separate things and it might have been possible to stop what was happening. And then they were one and they were on fire.

His hands came up to cup her face and he returned her kisses, on the mouth, on the cheeks, and eyes and hair. Then he bit her earlobe and groaned. 'I will never let you regret this. I swear on my life.'

How could he even think that she might? It was too wonderful to be sorry over. She wrapped her arms around him, laid her head on one of his strong, wide shoulders and all the worries of her life seemed to melt away.

His hands came away from her face and she felt them behind her and the little jolts of movement as he stripped off his gloves and threw them to the floor. Then his bare fingers were stroking the back of her neck and twining gently in her curls. 'Some night, soon, I shall come to you and pull all the pins out of your glorious hair. Then, I shall make you tease every inch of my body with it.' His lips returned to hers again and his tongue slipped into her mouth.

It was as it had been the last time. Only it was even better. Charity was right. He had lied when he said he wanted nothing to do with her. If his words had not convinced her, the power of this kiss would have left no doubts. She tried to mimic his movements, to thrust her tongue back against his, and heard the gratified moan of response.

Then he was pulling her backwards and they half-sat, half-fell on to the library sofa in a tangle of arms and legs and bodies. She was on top of him, almost in his lap. Her skirts must have risen well past her knees for she could feel the fabric of his breeches moving against the bare skin above her garter.

She should at least pause to arrange her dress. But if she had cared at all about modesty, she should not have kissed him in the first place. Nor should she be squeezing a man's leg between her thighs as she was now. It felt good to have him there, to have any part of him pressing upward to a spot that was more sensitive than it had ever been before.

His hands were on the fastenings to her gown, undoing them, pushing it down her shoulders so he could mouth the naked skin of her throat and lick his way down to the top of her corset. He ran a finger along the upper edge and inside it. His kisses slowed and he murmured, 'When I am sure we can be alone, I will have you out of this. Then, I will take all the time I like with these. I will suckle you until you beg me.'

She wanted that. But what would she be begging for?

Her body seemed to know. She was suddenly aware of her own hips, rocking against his breeches, riding his extended leg in a way that sent a strange trembling through her body.

He did not push her away. Instead, he responded by clasping her bottom with both hands, urging her to continue and sucking her lip between his teeth.

The sensation of that bite travelled directly to the place she was so eagerly stimulating and she moaned in surprise. The feeling was wicked and wonderful, and she should put a stop to it immediately. But for some reason, it was quite impossible. It was as if she was no longer in control of her body.

She heard him chuckle against her mouth and he pulled away from her, staring into her eyes with a devilish grin. Then there was a rustling as he pushed her skirts up even higher, letting his hands roam freely over the bare skin of her hips and thighs.

She froze, shocked. 'What…' It was all she could manage to say. The rest of her thoughts were drowned in a gasp as he bent his knee and held her hips still so he could stroke her between the legs with the top of his thigh. She did not know what was happening to her. But by the look in his eyes, it was clear that he did. Now, he was urging her to move, pinching her to make her squirm against him. And suddenly, her breasts, still constrained by the corset, felt as if they were held in the firm grip of a man's hands.

Gregory Drake's hands. Skilful. Clever. Hers.

He held her as she bucked and rubbed against him like some wild animal in a frenzy. Then, the tension in her broke and an uncontrollable shudder raced through her, a spasm of newly discovered muscles, followed by a rush of ecstasy that went on and on, long after she'd stopped moving.

When she had recovered sufficiently to be aware of anything other than the tingling place between her legs, she noticed the hard, insistent bulge in the breeches she was resting against.

She looked up, frightened.

His smile was strained, but satisfied. 'I think we have had enough fun for the day. If you will excuse me, for a moment?' Carefully, he disentangled himself from her skirts and left the room.

She could not decide whether to be relieved or disappointed by his words. Had her behaviour given him a disgust of her? What had she been thinking to act that way at all? She took advantage of his absence to try to rearrange her clothing and compose herself. But her gown still hung loose about her shoulders for she could not reach the tiny buttons to close it again.

When he returned, his posture had changed to be almost serenely relaxed. It was only when he looked at her that she noticed the true difference. There was a possessiveness in his gaze, and a trace of smug satisfaction to his smile. 'Let me help you with your gown.' He came to sit behind her and did up the fastenings as quickly as any lady's maid.

Then he laid his hands on her shoulders. 'How are you feeling, Miss Strickland?'

She felt magnificent. She wanted to answer back with the same cream-fed cat's smile that he gave to her, pretending to him and to the world that she had some control over the emotions still rioting through her. Though his hands were now touching her quite innocently, she felt as the Dowager had looked in the painting, naked, shameless and wanting more of whatever it was that had just happened. 'How do I feel?' she said at last. 'I am not sure, Mr Drake.'

He turned her gently until they were sitting side by side on the sofa. It was really quite proper, except for the absence of a chaperon and the fact that he had been making love to her just moments ago.

She turned to him, suddenly worried. 'Was that what is meant by losing one's maidenhead?'

She must have said something foolish for he laughed, just once, before gaining control of himself and giving her a patient smile. 'There is much more to it than that, my dear Hope.'

She could not decide what she liked better, being called by her Christian name or being called dear.

'Technically, you are still innocent,' he added. 'You would not be asking that question if you were not.'

'Technically,' she repeated. She did not feel innocent. She felt like Jezebel and Bathsheba, all rolled into one.

'While what has been learned cannot be un-learned, we did not actually...' He paused, probably sensing her eagerness for more forbidden knowledge, and thought the better of giving it to her. 'There is no physical evidence of what we have done. Only the knowledge that certain touches will bring you great pleasure.'

'So, we might do that as often as we liked?' she said and knew immediately by the shocked expression on his face, that it has been exactly the wrong thing to say.

'That would not be wise,' he said, sucking on his lip as if the words tasted bitter. 'It becomes quite difficult to stop these things, once they are started.'

'But if we did stop,' she said, 'no other man could tell what we had done together.' Could that even be possible? She was sure that, if she looked in the mirror, the change would be plain on her face.

'No other man?' he said, surprised.

'Well... Yes. If I were to marry, would my husband still think I was a virgin?' she said, putting it plainly so he might understand.

'Yes, Miss Strickland, you are still a virgin.' He stood up suddenly, running his hands down the front of his clothes in one sharp swipe, as if it were possible to shake the last hour out of their lives along with the wrinkles in his coat.

'Mr Drake.' She held out a hand to him, hoping he would come back to her.

Instead, he walked to the place where he'd dropped his gloves, scooping them up in one brutal move. 'As always, Miss Strickland, your manners are impeccable. One must never call a gentleman by his first name, even after he has put his hand up one's skirt.'

'Gregory,' she corrected.

But it was too late for that. He was pulling on his gloves with short, sharp, angry tugs. 'There is only one item left on the list for me to find. I am confident that I can retrieve it without bothering you for your help, if you can provide a more detailed description. I will leave my direction with your butler so you might send me the information by post. Good day, Miss Strickland, and goodbye.'

Once outside, Gregory waved off the hired carriage so that he might walk home. Or rather stalk. He wanted to stamp the whole way back to Wimpole Street where he could stamp to the brandy bottle in the study and slam every door on the way.

Damn Hope Strickland. Damn all women, for that matter. Never in his life had he taken such risks with his own livelihood. It was not bad enough that he had flirted with a woman from a family that employed him, he had compromised the honour of an innocent.

Even worse, he'd done it in broad daylight in a public room where they might have been interrupted at any time. Her younger sister haunted that library like its resident ghost. It had been a miracle that they had been alone together there long enough for anything to happen. Had Charity appeared, he would have educated both sisters on things that neither should learn before marriage.

It would have been even more embarrassing to be found taking a hand to himself in a nearby retiring room. But considering the state he'd been in when she finished, a release had been necessary, if only to prevent him from bringing the interlude to a more mutually satisfying conclusion.

Of late, he'd spent far too much time polishing his sword after visits with Miss Strickland, trying to maintain the control that had been shattered today. He had not planned for what had happened. He had hoped to encourage her to be honest and reveal whatever it was that had troubled her so on the previous evening. He had wanted to be her confidant, nothing more than that. He had asked for her trust.

Instead of the truth, she had given him a kiss. More than a kiss. She would have given him whatever he wanted. She had been more than eager to follow wherever he led. And what a sweet creature she had been. She had thoroughly enjoyed what they had done and made it clear from her questions that she had never experienced such a thing before.

He should have thrown her down on the hearth rug and shown her what it meant to be ruined for other men. Then, when he'd made the offer that had been on the tip of his tongue since last night, she would not have ruined it all by asking how best to appear innocent for the next fellow.

How big a fool was he that he'd thought there was some deeper meaning in what they'd just done? He was not just willing to marry her, for the sake of honour. Damn him, he wanted to do it.

It had always been his plan to marry, but he had thought of it as a distant thing, a crowning accomplishment to his success. But what more was needed to satisfy him, or his future wife? He had a house and no one to share it with and more money than he could spend on his own.

If he had been waiting to fall in love? He was not sure he believed in that particular emotion. But he would not be so foolish as to deny the existence of desire, which he felt each time he saw Hope Strickland. That was more than enough to be going on with.

If passion died, there would still be the protectiveness he felt each time she gave a worried tug on her hair. It made him want to take her away and show her just how pleasant it might be to take care of a husband and children, compared to a lunatic family that merely acted like children.

After he'd pleasured her today, he had come strolling back into the room, cocksure of his chances when he made his offer. But by the time he had managed to do up her gown, she'd been thinking of the Earl again. Truth and gallantry was rewarded with a kick in the teeth.

Eventually, Comstock's heir would appear. Then, if the man was young and single, or even old and single, she would do what she had planned to do all along and throw herself at him.

At some point, he had forgotten that his primary job was to complete the entail. He had become so wrapped up in the idea of the troubled and beautiful Hope Strickland that he had been willing to break every rule he'd ever made for himself. He had violated the trust her family had put in him, lying and seducing, taking advantage of a woman never meant for him. He was becoming the man he had sworn he would never be.

Tomorrow he would grab the first vase he could find that might suit the Dowager's list. Then he would leave Miss Strickland to sort out her own future, just as her sister had suggested he do. He would write to Leggett immediately and inform him of his resignation. Never mind what such an abrupt end might mean to his reputation. It could be no worse than what might happen if he lost control again and took Hope to bed.

Once he was free and did not have to see her every day, he would recover his equilibrium. Momentary madness had made him irrational, and willing to abandon his dearest principles in quest of a woman he could never have.

His thoughts of marriage were nothing more than an attempt to salve a guilty conscience. If he had been in his right mind, he would have seen that his offer would have been met with a surprised *no*.

The whole escapade had been a result of man's basest emotions—pride, envy and lust—as if he could not resist committing deadly sins in the presence of a woman named for a virtue. It was not, nor could it ever be, more than a huge mistake. For how foolish would he have to be to fall in love with Hope Strickland?

Chapter Ten

Gregory Drake was gone again and Hope was still not sure what she had said to drive him away. In fact, she had understood very little about the last hour of her life, other than that it had made her happy and that, for a few moments at least, she had been convinced that her problems no longer existed. Everything was going to be all right because Gregory Drake would make it so.

He had called her Hope and she was sure she had not responded properly to that. By the scowl on his face as she had called him Mr Drake, he had wanted to hear his name on her lips. She should have realised it. But was that the sort of error that could make a man leave for ever?

He must have thought her terribly stupid for asking the questions that she had, but she had needed some clarity. What they had done seemed like the sort of thing that should result in a proposal and she could not exactly compound one transgression with another by demanding that he marry her.

Apparently, it had not been necessary for him to offer. She was sure that what had happened between them was improper. But it was also an easily kept secret. There was no physical evidence and he was not the sort of man who would tell anyone about it.

She, on the other hand, desperately needed a confidant. There was much she still didn't understand about what happened between men and women. A girl from a normal family would have been able to ask her mother, but she'd lost hers a decade before such questions had occurred to her. Barring that, she should ask Grandmama.

And what a disaster that would be. The last thing Hope needed was a story about what had happened on that same sofa, a generation ago. If she refused to keep her own life secret, how could Hope trust that she would not brag to the world that her granddaughter was following in her notorious footsteps?

Faith would explain things properly. Faith was married and married women knew things. Sometimes they whispered secrets to each other, just as unmarried girls did. But it was easy to tell by their knowing looks and sly smiles that what they said was to be shared only amongst the matrimonial sorority.

Faith could help. But Faith was in Italy and could do nothing for weeks. Hope needed someone now.

That left Charity. It vexed her that she should have to go to the youngest member of the family for advice. But though the Lord had failed to bless her little sister with beauty, he'd more than made up for the lack with intelligence. She'd learned more from books than any of them did from experience. She would know what had happened and what to do about it. She could tell Hope what must be said to bring back Mr Drake, beyond calling him Gregory in the letter he was expecting.

But where was Charity, if not in the library? It was past lunch and she was always here by now. But she had not been here when they arrived, nor had she greeted them from any of the rooms they'd passed on returning home. A quick check of the house proved she was not writing letters in the morning room, nor in the kitchen pestering the cook for an early tea.

It was most curious. Perhaps she was ill and had decided to remain in bed for the day. Hope walked up the stairs and knocked softly on her sister's door, calling her name. When there was no response, she knocked more loudly. When there was still no answer, she tested the handle and opened the unlocked door to find the room empty. A letter lay on the perfectly made bed, its edges aligned with the pillow in mathematical precision. Her name was printed across the top in Charity's hand, perfectly legible and devoid of any feminine affectations or flourishes.

Before she unfolded it, Hope had a horrifying premonition of what she would find inside.

Dear Sister,
While I would not go as far as to call our stay in London delightful, it has at least been interesting. While the town-house library is small,

*it has given me a chance to explore several
unexpected lines of enquiry that I will explain
to you should they be productive.*

*But no further action can be taken here.
Thus, I have decided to retire to the country
until further notice. Thank Mr Leggett again
for the money spent in trying to launch me.
His heart is in the right place, as is yours. As
I keep trying to explain to you, my time and
my future should be my own. It is better spent
in our own library in Berkshire.*

*Do not concern yourself with my safe trav-
els, as the journey is not a long one. I am taking the mail coach and I will likely be home
before you find this letter.*

*My regards to Grandmother and Mr Drake,
Charity*

As usual when dealing with her youngest sister,
Hope was torn between the desires to scream in
panic or scream in frustration. Charity had many
deficiencies of character, but the greatest was her
overconfidence in her own abilities. She rarely bothered with protecting her reputation, declaring that
no one would notice or care if she ruined herself.
In choosing public conveyance over the Comstock
carriage with a maid and livery, she was thumbing her nose at propriety and tweaking her sister's
nose as well.

Something had to be done. It was unlikely that
Charity needed rescuing. She was correct in that it

was a short trip. But if her luck had run out and she had embarrassed herself or the family, the damage would need to be repaired.

Even if she was lucky, she needed to be persuaded back to London as soon as possible. Someone had to explain to her that the manor was no longer her home. She could not simply retreat there whenever she had a mind to. While they had not spoken of it, the family plan had been to seek other lodgings once the Season was over.

Mr Drake had apologised for lying about their future, but there was a chance that he had guessed it correctly. There might be several young Stricklands on a ship right now who would be bringing maids or valets, clothing and furnishings, planning to occupy the bedrooms she and her sisters had been using. Even if the new Earl did not bar the door against their return, she and Charity might be expected to make way for the heir's own family. Someone needed to tell her little sister the news in a calm and reasonable tone that she would understand and accept.

Hope did not feel up to the task. She did not want to lead her wayward sister back into the fold. She wanted to strangle her. Grandmama would be useless in any attempt to rein in Charity's recklessness. She had declared years ago that there was no point in lecturing the girl since she was unlikely to listen and clever enough to evade any punishment that man could devise.

What was to be done? Hope tapped the folded letter against her leg in agitation, wishing she had any other answer than the first one that came to mind. Then, she went to the writing desk and composed a letter to Mr Drake that had nothing to do with missing vases.

'I do not know what you expect me to do about this,' Gregory said, staring down at the letter from her sister that Hope Strickland had handed him. It was easier to do that than to look at her. As always, she was beautiful. But today, there was a vulnerability in her huge dark eyes that made him long to kiss it away.

'Bring her back,' Hope replied.

He stared at her, waiting for her to elaborate. When she did not, he asked the reasonable question, 'Why did you not go to the Dowager with this problem? It is her responsibility to chaperon your sister, not mine.'

'She is not here, either,' Hope said, her mouth set in a frown of disapproval. 'When I went to search her out, the servants said she had gone out of the city to visit a sick cousin and would not be back for a day at least.' She threw her hands up in exasperation. 'She simply disappeared without saying a word to me on the subject.'

'And what would you have done, had she told you?' he asked, trying not to smile.

'I'd have told her to stay right where she was, of course. Or she might have taken Charity with her. If my sister refuses to find a husband, she should be encouraged to do good works and to develop some sort of natural, feminine feeling towards the rest of the family.'

'Like a proper spinster, you mean.'

'It would not hurt my sister to read to an invalid, on occasion, instead of thinking only of herself.'

'I see.' He cleared his throat in what he hoped was a sombre manner. But he could feel his lips twitching in amusement at the sight of the left-hand curl bouncing furiously in time to her agitation.

'But they do not give a fig for my opinions. They go off in opposite directions like hens in the garden and they leave me to decide what to do about it.'

He suspected they did not think she should be doing anything at all, other than waiting for their return. But clearly, Miss Hope Strickland felt that action was required. If Faith Strickland had been anything like her sister, he felt a deepening understanding of James Leggett.

'Your letter said to come at once. That you needed me urgently,' he reminded her. 'You offered me no clue as to what this was about.' And he had made an ass of himself. He had come running, foolish enough to think that she might be longing to repeat what they had done on the library sofa. As usual, it seemed his urgent need for her was quite different than what she felt when she thought of him.

'I do need you, urgently,' she said. And finally, she realised how she had sounded, for she stopped speaking and turned crimson with embarrassment. Her brown eyes seemed to grow even larger than usual, pleading as she stared back at him. 'I know you are angry with me from before. And whatever I did to offend you, I am sorry for it. Really, I am. But Mr Leggett hired you to help our family and I do not know how to handle this on my own.'

So she had no idea what she had done to him, any more than she understood that she must phrase professional enquiries differently from love letters. And now, she had no right to look so soft, so vulnerable and so helpless that he wanted to scoop her into his arms and make love to her on the spot. Especially if she meant to stand up afterwards and look for another, better man.

He cleared his throat again and tried to put the idea behind him. 'Leggett's instructions to me were quite plain. There was nothing in them about policing Miss Charity's behaviour.'

'You were hired to retrieve things that are missing. She is missing.'

'She is not an item,' he responded. 'And you know exactly where she is.' He was tempted to assure her that the odds were slim that the girl had been set upon by white slavers on the mail coach to Berkshire. But then he would likely have to explain what that meant to her. It would not make the situation any better to put ideas into her head.

'Now you are just being difficult.' She frowned and balled her firsts on her hips to show her displeasure with him. But the gesture only served to accent her curves and remind him of something he had enjoyed earlier that he would not be seeing again.

He took a deep breath to fortify his resolve and

looked her straight in the eye. 'I did not bring difficulty to your family, Miss Strickland. It was here long before I arrived.'

'But you are supposed to make it better,' she insisted. She was looking at him as though he could work miracles, again.

He fought the urge to play the gallant and come to her rescue. He was not required to do so. But how hard could it be to convince Charity to return to London? At the very least, he could try and fail. Either result would gain him an excuse to remain in Hope's company for a few more days, hoping that things between them might change.

More likely, it would end just as their last interaction had. She might seem devoted now, but all he was likely to get in reward was more heartache.

'I will pay you,' she blurted and he felt the euphoria deflate as their roles returned to the realm of the disappointingly understandable.

'*"I will pay you"* says the woman who has no money, without even enquiring as to my fee.' He shook his head. 'It explains much about how your family came to be in financial trouble.'

'I will find a way,' she said. 'Set your price and I will meet it. Anything you want, I will give it to you, if you will help me with my sister.'

His mind flew straight back to the place it should not go, full of innuendo and wild fantasy. He had half a mind to tell her what he truly wanted from her and announce that he was happy to discharge the duty now that they had settled on a price for it.

But chances were, she would not even understand what he was saying.

Instead, he let out an exasperated sigh and said, 'Never mind. I shall add it to Mr Leggett's bill. Show me where to find her and I will haul her home.'

'The manor house is in Berkshire,' she said. 'I will leave a note for Grandmama and tell the servants that we are returning the items we have found. We will take the Comstock carriage.'

'We?'

'It might seem strange for you to go alone,' she said.

'Not really,' he assured her, already imagining what could happen if he had another opportunity to be alone with her.

'It would not be proper for you to be alone in the house with Charity,' she said.

He stared at her, searching for some proof that she saw the irony in her words. She was looking at him with the same sanctimonious disapproval that she had used on the first day they'd met.

He threw up his hands in surrender. 'Very well. We will go to Comstock Manor. Together. Tomorrow.'

'But…'

He held up a hand. 'You sister is most likely safe, for the moment. Since she is in the place she wished to be, I doubt she will take flight before tomorrow afternoon. And I have no intention of setting off, alone in a carriage with an unmarried woman, at nightfall. No matter how innocent you might think it, there is not a person in London that will not assume an elopement if we tear off into the night together.'

She paused to consider, and blushed as she understood. Clearly, she had been thinking of him as a utility, rather than a warm-blooded man. Then she nodded in agreement. 'We will set off first thing tomorrow morning.'

'Very good,' he replied. They would have the whole thing settled by mid-afternoon and he would be back in London by nightfall, alone.

As usual, Hope's life seemed to be better the moment Gregory Drake arrived. It should not have been so. Her family was still horrible, the diamonds were still missing and the new Earl might appear at any moment. Still, she felt better.

There was also the fact that Mr Drake had been trying to escape her since the moment they had first kissed. She had insulted him multiple times and offended him in ways she could not fully understand. And yesterday, she might have, quite accidentally of course, sent him a note that implied she was languishing on a divan and awaiting his romantic attentions.

Yet he was going to help her. Whatever Mr Leggett was paying him could not possibly be enough. Though she could not help it, the fact that they would be trapped for hours in a carriage together gave her a thrill of joy. He had made it quite clear that he could handle retrieving the last item on their list without her help. When he had left the house yesterday afternoon, she might never have seen him again.

And yet? Here they were.

He'd arrived at her house this morning, at eight rather than ten, ready to set off for the manor. She noticed that he had not bothered to pack as much as a change of linen for the trip. It appeared he expected a return to London as soon as the matter was settled. Then he could go back to ignoring her, just as he'd been intending to.

Perhaps he wanted to return quickly, but that was not what she wanted, at all. She did not want to experience any more emergencies that required his help, nor did she intend to manufacture one. But it was horrible to think that he might slip away again with a bow, a smile and an invoice for services rendered.

It would be easier if she were anyone other than who she was. Charity or Grandmama would have not hesitated to do something outlandish enough to hold his attention. But Hope was supposed to be the proper one. So far, her attempts at being daring and reckless with Mr Drake had only seemed to make things worse. *Gregory*, she reminded herself, as the carriage rolled away from the town house and towards the edge of the city. Before the day was out, she must at least find an excuse to call him by his name.

She had not bothered with a veil today, for, with the family crest on the door of the carriage, it should not surprise people that she was inside. But she made sure that all the shades stayed down until they were well out of the city, so that no one would realise that she was travelling unchaperoned with a gentleman.

'You could have brought a maid,' Gregory said, as she finally pulled back the curtain to let in the light.

'There was no time,' she said firmly. If this was the last time she was to see him, she had not wanted Polly sitting between them to spoil things.

'You found time to choose hair ribbons to match your gown,' he said in a dry tone. 'And to pack a valise and write to your grandmother.'

'I did not want witnesses,' she said. 'For Charity's sake,' she added, struggling for an explanation that was not too ridiculous. 'I do not need the maids gossiping about her foolishness.'

'Of course not,' he said. 'They will gossip about yours instead.'

'That is probably true,' she replied, surrendering. 'It is about time, I think. Faith and I were the sensible ones in the family. Now that she is no longer watching me, it is much more difficult to behave than I thought it would be.'

He turned away suddenly, and she was sure it was to hide a smile. Then, without turning back, he said, 'I suspect it will be easier once the new Comstock has arrived and you no longer have to hare about London in a closed carriage with a stranger.'

'I am not sure what we are to each other, Mr Drake,' she replied. 'But we have not been strangers to each other for quite some time.'

'Only days,' he reminded her. 'It has been less than a week since we met.'

'And what has happened between us…' she said cautiously. 'Would you describe it as normal?'

'No,' he said, much more quickly than she'd hoped he would.

He saw the shocked expression on her face and corrected himself. 'I mean, the activities are normal enough. If we were married, for example. Or…' he hesitated again '…or if we were in love. But never in my life… Well, not with a proper young lady, at least. And certainly not a proper young lady who I have only known for days.'

'Oh.' There had been a strange, vibrating sensation deep inside her, when he had said the word 'love'. It was rather like how she imagined a target felt when struck by an arrow. Until this moment, she had never thought of Cupid as anything other than a myth. But today, if she had looked out the window and seen him with bow in hand, she would not have been a bit surprised.

Her half of their interaction was suddenly much clearer. She was in love with Gregory Drake.

'Oh,' she repeated, nodding in understanding. It explained why she felt better each time she saw him and worse each time he left. It was why she couldn't seem to stop doing foolish things like kissing him when he came near to her. And why, even now, a part of her brain was searching for something she could do to make him stay.

And whatever it was would have to be spectacular, for it appeared that the feelings she had were not reciprocated. He had described love and marriage as a hypothetical explanation. But there was nothing in his tone or face to make her think he intended testing the hypothesis any time soon.

'And you barely know me,' he added, as if this was important.

'While you know me quite well,' she added. 'Whatever Mr Leggett has not told you could be found in *Debrett's*.'

She had said something wrong again. His expression had changed from open confusion to the distant smile he wore while working for her. 'You seem to think that being able to trace someone's family tree for generations is the same as knowing an individual. It is not, Miss Strickland. In fact, it is another thing entirely.'

At least, this time, she did not need Charity to explain how foolish she had been. 'I must apologise again, Mr Drake. I did not mean to imply that a person without such heritage is any less valuable. It is just that…' She bit her lip. 'Everything that happens in my family has happened to others. My father, my uncles and my grandfather have all *done* things. Although I am not proud of their actions, even my grandmother and Charity have stories to tell. While I… Well, I am simply not very interesting.'

Now he looked startled, as if the fact had never occurred to him, then blurted without hesitation, 'On the contrary, Miss Strickland, I find you fascinating.'

'Really?' She tried not to be too encouraged.

'You tell stories of physical altercations with your

sisters that lead to dented pewter, cracked plaster and bloodshed.'

'All children are prone to mischief,' she said.

'You think a dismembered toe is a beloved childhood plaything.'

'Actually, it is a prosthetic,' she corrected.

'You steal inkwells from family friends.'

'Not usually. That was an aberration,' she said.

'And you kiss like an angel,' he concluded.

They both sat in silence for a moment, as if neither of them had expected such an open admission.

Then he went on as if it had not just happened. 'I have no such childhood stories to tell. Yours have been both entertaining and enlightening.'

She leaned forward. 'Now I can prove that we are definitely not strangers. I cannot think of another person outside my family that knows so much about me.' She frowned. 'But I still know very little about you. Would it be rude of me to enquire about your childhood? In the name of friendship, of course,' she added.

'In the name of friendship, I will speak of it,' he said, his natural smile returning. 'If you have spoken to your sister, you are aware that I never knew my parents.'

She nodded.

When she did not seem surprised, he went on. 'I was left on a farm in Essex without as much as a name to give me a clue to my past. The farmer chose Gregory from his father and Drake…' He paused.

'For Sir Francis Drake?' she questioned.

'For a male widgeon swimming in the duck pond.'
He paused again, as if waiting to see if she would
laugh.

'It does not matter where it came from. It suits
you well,' she said.

He nodded his thanks and continued. 'The farmer
and his wife took me in because they had no children of their own. And for the money that had been
provided for my care, of course. But they had no
real affection for me, nor I for them. When I was old
enough to do so, I was expected to work. I learned
to weed a garden, clean a kitchen and milk a cow. I
also learned that I had no desire to do any of them
again, even if my life depended on it.'

'But clearly you were educated,' she said, surprised.

'At the village school run by the vicar,' he answered.

She could remember seeing such children in the
schoolroom at the vicarage, struggling through les-
sons, just as her father had struggled to persuade
their fathers of the need for at least a smattering of
reading and mathematics.

'When I was old enough, a letter came from a
solicitor in London that said I was to go to a proper
school that would prepare me for university. I am
sure the farmer only allowed it because he would be
receiving no more money to keep me.'

'That is a blessing, I suppose,' she said, trying to
imagine what it would be like if her grandmother

and grandfather had viewed her not as family, but as something between a servant and a burden.

'It was difficult at first,' he admitted. 'The young gentlemen I met there had little patience for an ignorant country lad.' Then he smiled. 'Fortunately, I was strong for my age and a quick student.'

'What did you have an aptitude for?'

'Far too many things,' he said, with a laugh. 'But I had no real attraction for any of them. I considered law, the church and banking, only to reject them all.'

'And seeing how you reacted to the toe, I doubt you'd have made a good surgeon,' she added.

He winced. 'Nor an officer. I am not, by nature, a violent man.'

'And you do not like following orders,' she reminded him and received another nod.

'I lacked the patience to be a secretary or man of business, catering to every whim of some nobleman.'

'You sought independence,' she said.

'I wanted to come and go as I wished. To work or rest as the mood struck me. None of the professions I considered would allow for such freedom.'

'This explains what you did not want to do,' she agreed. 'But not how you chose what you did.'

'I matriculated from Cambridge without plans and with dwindling funds, so I went to London to seek my fortune. There, I happened upon an old school friend who was in need of a stiff drink and an understanding ear. It seems he had lost a considerable amount of money in a disreputable gaming hell and was afraid to tell his father. I offered to investigate the matter and found the faro table was rigged. When I returned his losses, he pressed a reward into my hand to guarantee my silence.'

'And you decided to make a job out of helping people?'

He shook his head. 'On the contrary, I refused to take his money. A friend does not expect payment when help is needed.' Then he smiled. 'But the men that saw me handle the matter at the gaming hell were strangers to me. One of them needed his younger brother rescued from an adventuress. Another needed an unwelcome houseguest removed. I helped them and they paid me to do it.'

'And they told others?'

He nodded. 'I have become quite popular. The income from other people's troubles has got me a rather nice house in Wimpole Street.'

'But that is just around the corner from our home.' She had imagined him maintaining simple bachelor's quarters somewhere, until he had mentioned his servants at the ball. She had never expected to find him living so close to the Comstock town house.

'It has been most convenient working for your family,' he said with a grin. 'I can help you in the morning and be home in time for tea. If any of your neighbours need my services, please be sure to recommend me to them.'

'Do you plan on continuing in your career for long?' It should not matter to her if his job allowed him enough income for a wife and family.

But the longer she was with him, the more curious she became.

'Money is no longer my motivation, if that is what you are wondering,' he said. 'I mean to work as long as the job interests me.' Then he gave her a probing look. 'Solving one last, enormous task would be a wonderful way to end my career.'

'You are speaking of my problem,' she said quietly. 'The one I told you that you cannot help with.'

'You trust me with your sister's reputation and your own. But you keep hinting at a thing so big that I cannot manage it. It is clear to me that it troubles you.' He frowned for a moment, as if he could not quite understand his own curiosity. 'I do not like seeing you upset. Will you ever tell me what it is so that I may fix it for you?'

'You have a great deal of confidence in your own abilities,' she said.

'Of course I do,' he replied. 'I have never failed.' Then he gave her another of his half puzzled, half worried looks. 'But it is more than that. I appreciate the confidence you have shown in me, thus far. I do not want a secret to stand in the way of it.'

His eyes were soft again, as they had been when he had asked for her trust in the sitting room. It made her feel warm and safe, and a little sad that she could not give him what he wanted. 'And I do not want to be the person to destroy your perfect record by asking the impossible,' she said. 'I really do not think there is anything you can do for me. When we return to London, you will complete the list we gave you. I cannot expect more than that.'

'A Herculean task.' The smile he gave her now was the breathtaking one that he had given her on the first day. 'What use is my reputation if I baulk at doing the impossible?'

She wanted to tell him, almost as much as he wanted to hear it. She had told him before that it was a problem that could only be shared with Comstock. No matter what his temperament or marital state, the Earl was head of the family and was the only one who could decide what was to be done about the diamonds.

But suppose Mr Drake became part of the family? There would be no reason not to share her burden with a man who was her husband, or at very least her betrothed.

'I would be able to show you what I am facing when we arrive at the manor.'

He leaned forward, ready to aid her.

She held up a finger in warning. 'I would, if I wished to. But you have made it plain that you wish to be out of my life as soon as you have found the last item on the list. This is the sort of secret I cannot reveal to a man who refused to bring a clean shirt on this trip because he did not want to be trapped in the same house with me overnight.'

'You know my reasons for avoiding you,' he said, sounding almost as prim as she'd felt before meeting him.

'It is because you are afraid of what will happen,'

she said, shaking her head. 'So am I. But unless we can overcome that fear, I cannot tell you what you want to know and you cannot help me.' Then, she summoned all the courage she had and smiled at him. 'If things change? Then we will see if you can perform miracles, Mr Drake. Or may I call you Gregory?'

Chapter Eleven

The house was both more and less than Gregory expected it to be. In the bones, it was the sort of grand English manor one could not help but stand in awe of. A conglomeration of styles, from Gothic to modern, it had been built and rebuilt until it stretched to forty rooms and was set on acres of park land with trout streams, rose gardens and herb knots.

But on closer examination, it was clearly in need of care. The slates on the roof were cracked, as were the paving stones at his feet. The gardens were not yet choked with weeds, but it was clear that the gardeners fought a losing battle in them.

Inside was no better. The staff was smaller than he would have expected for such a large house and many of the rooms they passed through were cold and dark, the furniture swathed in holland cloth. When he pulled the covers back, he was relieved to see that the appointments were in better condition than the things they had been retrieving.

But that raised the question that had been tickling at the back of his mind since they had located the candlesticks on the first day together. If she was short on funds, there were dozens of things that would have fetched more money than she had probably got. What had made the Dowager choose the items she had?

Hope Strickland walked him through the house, taking care to point out the bedchamber that would be allotted to him, should he stay the night, as well as the chambers that belonged to her and her sister. Was this intended as encouragement to act on his desires? Was she truly offering herself to him, should he be brave enough to accept her? Or was she a naïve girl who did not understand the consequences of her actions?

There was also the matter of the mysterious problem she would not explain. He wanted to help her. He wanted other things as well. To hear Hope Strickland call him by his name in a moment of passion, for instance.

There was a way to have that and his honour as well. He should settle the problem of Miss Charity, then catch the next mail coach back to London. Once there, he could wait for the return of the Dowager, or Leggett, or even the new Comstock so he might ask permission to offer for Miss Hope.

But in the time that took, she might change her mind about him. Literature was crowded with metaphors about striking hot irons and seeking forgiveness rather than permission. If he went to her room tonight and declared himself, by morning there would be only one course of action.

Had his father thought that, before bedding his mother, or had it always been his intention to leave her? And after the pain and isolation of his own childhood, what would possess him to risk the future of his wife and child by repeating his parents' mistake?

Now, Hope was looking at him with a smile that was both seductive and expectant. She knew what she wanted from him and was awaiting his answer.

He responded in the only way an honourable man could, with a blank look and an obtuse smile. 'This has been very informative. But now I think it best that you take me to your sister.'

The further they got from the bedrooms, the more the old proper Miss Strickland returned. Her spine stiffened and her smile disappeared. Her sweet lips pursed into a frown. By the time they'd reached the library, she was in high dudgeon and stormed into the room, hands on hips to confront her sister. 'Charity, how could you?'

Miss Charity barely looked up from the pile of dusty journals that surrounded her. 'Quite easily, I assure you. I walked to the George and got my ticket for the eight o'clock coach…'

'You walked all the way to the George! At night and unescorted? Are you mad?'

The argument carried on without him, for Gregory had stopped on the threshold, momentarily stunned by the room. In his experience, people kept their libraries on the sunny side of the house to make best use of the available light when reading. But this had to be the darkest room he'd ever seen. It was full noon outside, but the frost-blasted ivy climbing the windows and the velvet curtains surrounding them left the room as dark as a crypt.

'I see you have brought Mr Drake with you to scold me as well,' Charity said, ignoring her sister's questions. 'Come in, Mr Drake. And the answer to your question is that it is better for the books.'

He started at being addressed, for he had said nothing to indicate the direction of his thoughts.

He was trying to frame the best response to her statement when she clarified it for him. 'You were standing on the threshold, staring at the windows, and I assumed you must be wondering why the room is so dark. It is because it has been designed with the comfort of the books in mind and not the readers. Too much light cracks the bindings and fades the ink.'

'I see,' he said, stepping into the room and joining the pair of sisters.

'We did not come all this way to admire the architecture,' Hope snapped. 'We have come to take you home.'

'Back to London, you mean,' Charity replied. 'Must I remind you that the town house is not my home any more than the manor is? At the moment, as you have been pointing out each time you hector me, we do not have a home. Nor did I have any money for alternate transportation.'

'You could have taken the Comstock equipage.'

'And left you and Grandmother with nothing? You'd have refused to allow it.'

'Ladies,' Gregory Drake said softly, holding his hands palm out to signal a stop to the conversation.

They both turned to look at him, a matching fire in their very different brown eyes.

He spoke to Hope in his most diplomatic tone, as if she were any other client and not the woman he wished to marry. 'Miss Strickland, need I remind you that you brought me here in hopes that I would mediate for you? I cannot do that if you wish to speak for yourself.'

She opened her mouth ready to retort, then snapped it shut again and shot another hot glare at her sister before turning back to him. 'Reason with her. It is plain that I cannot.'

When she made no move to leave, he added a conciliatory smile. 'It might be easier if you took this opportunity to refresh yourself from our journey. Then we might all meet again and discuss the matter over supper.' He had hoped to be gone by then. But if he wanted to settle the matter quickly, he had best give her some reason to co-operate.

Her jaw gave another involuntary snap and clench. Then it relaxed as it occurred to her that he had just promised to stay the night. She cast a final glare at Charity, then smiled at him. 'I shall see you both at eight. In the dining room,' she added, staring at her sister and the empty tea tray sitting on the table beside her. Then she quit the room.

There was a moment's silence after the door latch clicked shut. Then Charity looked up at him with a stubborn smile. 'Now, I suppose you shall call me an impertinent child and threaten to drag me back to London to do penance at Almack's for my misbehaviour.'

'The thought had crossed my mind,' he said. He looked at the chair beside her, calculated its probable level of discomfort when compared with everything else wrong in the room and then leaned a hip against a nearby library table. 'Save me the time and tell me if it will be effective.'

'No,' she said, with another smile.

'Then I shall have to try a different tack. I shall reason with you, as I would a man.'

'A truly novel approach,' she said with a surprised nod.

'I understand that you could not have asked for the family carriage, because you were sure the answer would be no.'

'You have met my sister. Do you doubt it?'

'But by leaving suddenly, you gave her unnecessary worry. That was quite unfair of you.'

There was a flash of something like contrition on the girl's face, before she said, 'Her refusal would have been unfair as well.'

He ignored her defence and went on. 'Apparently, she had reason to be concerned about you. You were safe enough on the mail coach. But it is dangerous of you to walk the streets at dusk alone. You may think that you are protected from robbery and assault by a plain face and a quick mind. But you aren't much more than seven stone soaking wet and there is no woman alive who is ugly enough to avoid unwanted attention from a certain type of ruffian.'

'I admit to my mistake,' she said. 'But at the time, I saw no other solution.'

'Then you did not look very hard,' he countered. 'Should you think of doing such a thing again, you will contact me and I will give you the money to hire a post chaise so you and your maid might ride in comfort and safety.'

'And then you would tell my sister what I have done, so she could put a stop to it,' Charity retorted.

'Not necessarily,' he said. 'If you asked for my word on the matter I would keep it, as long as I did not think you were doing anything too foolish or dangerous.' He glanced around the room and shook his head. 'While I cannot fathom why someone would be eager to sit in this room, I do not think your presence here puts you in any immediate risk.'

'My sister feels I have an unnatural attachment to the house,' she said.

'And do you?'

She thought for a moment. 'Despite what Hope might think, I understand that I cannot live here for ever and that I need to make plans for the future. She believes that I should do so by attending balls and throwing myself in the way of any eligible man who looks twice at me. I believe that the key to my future is in one of the books of this library.'

He waited for her to elaborate. When it was clear

that she had no intention of doing so, he spoke. 'Then I see no reason why you cannot make your sister happy as well as yourself. If you wish to read the books, take a crate full of them back to London. When you are through with them, exchange them for another batch. Attend a few balls to placate your sister and spend the rest of the time in study.'

She looked surprised at the suggestion. Then she nodded. 'If that is all it takes to make her happy, I can abide by the conditions. Though there might still come a time when I need to return to the house.'

'When it does, you will approach me and I will arrange for your travel. Then we will both explain the trip to your sister.'

She looked surprised. 'That does seem to be a most rational solution.'

He held up a finger. 'I have but one condition.'

'Of course you do,' she said, crestfallen.

'We must put the plan into effect tomorrow. Or the day after, if that is how long it takes for you to gather your research. I promised your sister that I would bring you back to London and have no intention of breaking my word.'

Her eyes narrowed as she considered the plan.

'You agreed it was sensible just a moment ago,' he reminded her.

She sighed. 'Very well. We will return to London tomorrow with as many books as the coach can hold.' Her eyes narrowed again. 'If you can get Hope to agree to the plan as well.'

'I am sure she will,' he said. 'I can be very persuasive, when it is necessary.'

'I expect you can,' she said, giving him a different sort of look entirely. 'Now, if that is all…' She glanced back at her books, then at the door, clearly eager to go back to her studies.

'Not quite,' he said, wondering how best to phrase the questions he needed to ask. 'You said that I should come to you when I could get no further.'

'I was under the impression that the completion of the entail was going quite well without any help from me,' she said, still watching him.

'You also said that was not my only task.'

She smiled. 'You are having troubles with my sister.' She steepled her fingers and leaned forward. 'Please, tell me more.'

'Do I have your word that you will not share this conversation with her?' he asked.

Charity laughed. 'You are still treating me as if I were a gentleman. How novel. I assure you, Mr Drake, I will say nothing.'

Now he was left with how to ask the questions he wanted answered. 'I do not fully understand your sister.' He thought for a moment. 'And I would very much like to. In fact, I must be sure I understand her completely before I proceed.'

'Does this pertain to the task Mr Leggett set for you of putting her off marrying the heir?' She was staring at him intently.

'Yes.' He thought for a moment. 'Somewhat.' And at last, he confessed. 'But it is also a personal matter.'

Now Charity's smile widened. 'I see.'

He took a breath. 'I want to know the reason for her obsession with Miles Strickland.'

'Then why are you asking me?'

'Because she has been loath to tell me. And before things progress any further…' God, had he actually said that? He must hope that, of all the things Miss Charity understood, they did not include how near he and her sister were to the point of no return.

He took a breath and tried again. 'Is she seeking a man with a title? Is it the rank that is important to her? Is it the money?'

'You want to know if another sort of man might have hope of marrying my sister?'

She paused, as if waiting to see how much he was willing to admit. When he said nothing, she continued. 'She has, on at least one occasion, warned me against snobbery and suggests that I emulate our own parents' humble behaviour.'

'That is good to know,' he said, trying not to be too encouraged.

'Given our difficulties, neither of my sisters considered it possible to marry for love. Faith sought money, but Hope is more concerned with security. The new Earl is the only man she can think of who would give that to the whole family.'

'But if all three of you are both safe and financially secure?'

'And free from prosecution or censure for playing fast and loose with the entail,' Charity added.

'Of course,' he agreed.

'Then I should think she would be more concerned with her own happiness than my future,' Charity said. 'I have been awaiting that moment for as long as I can remember. And if you are wondering if I approve of you as a future brother-in-law...'

'I did not ask that,' he said hurriedly.

'The situation is purely hypothetical,' she reminded him. 'If she did not feel the need to marry Comstock, I see no reason that she might marry an untitled gentleman as Faith did. Or even someone in trade, should she have affection for him. A man such as yourself, for instance. And now, if you will excuse me, I have much reading to finish before supper.'

Chapter Twelve

After she had been banished from the library, Hope found a maid to prepare the room for Mr Drake. Then she set about replacing the items that they had found in London. The candlesticks went to their place at the very centre of the long dining table where they provided light on the days when only the family was home to eat and good silver was not necessary.

The inkwell went on the left corner of the desk, for her grandfather had been left-handed. But suppose Miles Strickland favoured his right? Hope stared at it for a second, pondering the need for a move, and decided it would remain where it was. Anything else looked wrong to her.

The portrait required the help of the two footmen still at the manor. While Grandfather might have thought it belonged behind a door, it annoyed her to see the succession out of order. This required moving Comstocks numbers five to eight further down the gallery and pounding a new nail for Grandfather at the end of the row.

Once this was done, there was the matter of the oddment to sort out. She could not remember where it had been when they had first discovered it. After, its primary home had been the nursery. But that would take an excessive amount of time to explain to a new generation of Stricklands who might find it strange. Eventually, she decided on a shelf in the small parlour. Since that room also held the family Bible, she took the time to update the listing, explaining that it was no longer buried in the back garden without providing any embarrassing details on the reason for the exhumation.

At last, she paid a visit to the lock room to retrieve the false parure, then returned to her bedroom, as had been suggested, and sat wondering how much time should be allowed for the dust to settle on the argument that must be taking place in the library.

Charity did not like being dictated to and flatly refused to be reasoned with. At any minute, she was likely to burst into Hope's room to inform her that she was under no obligation to listen to a stranger's opinion of where she should be spending her time.

The afternoon had passed in silence, which made Hope all the more nervous as she waited for the inevitable explosion. But as she'd requested, Charity had appeared at dinner, promptly at eight. They were hardly started on the soup course when she'd announced her intent to return to London as soon as she was able to collect her research sufficiently for travel.

Gregory Drake never ceased to amaze her. He had been able to do exactly what she'd asked of him in a single afternoon. And he'd had time afterwards to prepare for dinner. As usual, his suit and linen were immaculate. He had managed a shave and change of cravat, despite his refusal to pack for an extended stay. The man was not just a worker of miracles, he was a miracle himself. Once Charity retired to the library, as she always did after supper, the two of them could be alone and she could thank him.

He had ignored her hints in the hall, earlier. But it was not from a want of desire. What she had asked him to do was wrong. But for the first time in her life, she did not care.

There was still a part of her mind that knew it would be better for the family if she married Miles Strickland. But that part grew smaller by the minute. That same family that she'd wanted to help had been trying to talk her out of her plan for weeks. Nothing they'd said or done had persuaded her she was wrong.

And then Gregory Drake had kissed her. When he had lied about it at the ball, the idea that the Earl might be married had devastated her. But now, she prayed it was true. It had been much easier to plan for a life of sacrifice when she had not known what she would be giving up. Now, she could not imagine a future without Gregory in it.

If he refused to come to her, when they had retired

for the evening, she would have to go to him. If she could not manage to tempt him with her body, she would tempt him with the secret he was obsessed with learning. This time, there would be no sudden angry departures. She would not let him escape her arms until she had heard a promise of marriage.

But before her happy future could begin, she had to get rid of her little sister. On any other night, Hope would have had trouble getting Charity to put down her books for a meal. But tonight she arrived at the table empty handed and was unusually loquacious. Afterwards, instead of disappearing to the library, she insisted that they adjourn to the parlour and set up the chessboard.

When Hope remarked that she was too tired from the journey to manage such a game, Charity had encouraged her to go straight to bed and invited Mr Drake to play the white. He accepted and they played in silence, while Hope sat alone by the fire, pretending to read.

Hope was not sure what he had said to her sister, but it seemed Gregory had made a conquest. It was either that or Charity had guessed her intent and decided to play chaperon. And it seemed that Gregory had seized on the opportunity as a way to protect her from herself and avoid another encounter like the one they'd had in the town-house library.

Why did he not understand that, for the first time in her life, she did not want to do the right and proper thing? Nor did she want to be saved from herself by well-meaning family. By half past ten, when the last of her patience had failed, she announced that it was time for bed.

Gregory rose, only to have Charity seize him by the wrist. 'If you are tired, Hope, then you must quit complaining about it and go to sleep. Goodnight to you. Another game, Mr Drake? I insist we make it two out of three.'

There was nothing for it but to retire as she had announced she was going to. She left quietly, with her dignity intact. It remained so until she had reached her room. Once there she threw herself on the bed and pounded the pillow in a girlish tantrum she was far too old for.

She had been unsure of what was happening while in London. She had known that she liked it. But for the sake of her reputation, she had known that she should not do it again. Gregory had agreed and was making an effort to stay separate from her. But rather than be grateful for his consideration, she was angry.

And jealous. Insanely so. Jealous of her own little sister, who had been showing both good sense and good manners, all evening. And who was, right this minute, alone with a man who did not belong to her.

If this was love, then she wondered why people were so eager to experience it, for it was very confusing.

She needed to talk to Gregory. More than talk. If there was something that made it impossible for a woman to marry any other man, then perhaps it worked the same way for men. If they did it, there would be no question that they belonged together, for ever.

She called for a maid to help her out of her clothing and into a fresh nightgown. Then she dismissed the girl and sat quietly in the dark on the edge of her bed, with the door to the hall open a crack, listening. The house grew quiet, and quieter still. And then she heard footsteps in the hall, and the sound of the maid coming to her sister's room and leaving it again.

A little later, she heard masculine steps walking to the room that had been set aside for Gregory Drake. How long did it take a man to prepare for bed? She was not sure. She waited another fifteen minutes, listening for the faint chimes of the long-case clock in the hall and hoping for the sound of stockinged feet walking from his room to hers. When they did not come, she surrendered to her desires and crept down the hall to find him.

She paused at his door for a moment, unsure of what to do next. Did one knock before seducing a gentleman, or simply open the door? If he didn't want her, he would refuse. It would be embarrassing, but then, at least, she would know.

But he was not going to refuse her. She remembered the things he had whispered he could do to her and the things he wanted her to do to him. All that was waiting for her on the other side of the door.

She dropped her hand to the handle, worrying for just a moment that it might be locked, before feeling it turn easily. The door opened without a squeak and she thanked the Lord for the diligence of the servants in keeping the hinges oiled. Then she stepped through it and closed it quickly behind her.

The room was lit by a single bedside candle. He sat up in bed, his chest bare, the covers bunched at his waist. He had been reading. But now the book in his lap was forgotten. He stared at her as if waiting for an explanation.

For the moment, she had none. Her mouth had gone dry at the sight of all that smooth skin covering a fascinating array of muscles. She'd imagined what he must look like, under his clothes, but the reality was far more affecting than she'd imagined it would be.

'I thought you had gone to bed,' he said. His tone was matter of fact.

He had spoken to her many times. He'd even whispered honey into her ears. But until now, she had never noticed how beautiful his voice was, like the deep tolling of a bell in a valley.

'Hope?' Now he sounded concerned.

She wanted to tell him that there was no reason to worry. She was fine. In fact, she was better than she had ever been in her life, because she was with him. And something wonderful was about to happen. She was going to tell him exactly how she felt, if only she could manage to catch her breath.

Suddenly, she was on the floor, looking up at the ceiling. Gregory Drake was standing over her with a worried look on his face. Then he was crouching, his arm beneath her head, urging her to drink something from a flask in his hand.

She sputtered over her first sip of brandy.

'You fainted,' he said gently. 'Drink. When you are feeling a little better, I will ring for a maid. Or perhaps your sister.'

'No!' At last, she'd found her voice. Apparently, it startled him for she could feel the slight jerk of his arm. She smiled hopefully up at him and reached out to touch the hand that held the flask. 'You do not want Charity to come here, do you?'

'Charity? God, no.' Now, he was the one to look faint. 'I have seen quite enough of your sister for one night.' He took the flask away, raised it to his lips and took a long, fortifying drink before answering. 'And if you are expecting a liaison, I am the one who should be creeping into your room.' He smiled.

'Am I doing it wrong?' she asked, still not sure exactly what *it* was.

'The whole situation is wrong,' he replied. 'I should not even know the location of your room and there are a hundred reasons why I should send you back to it.'

He stared down at the unbuttoned neck of her nightgown. 'But, damn me, when I look at you I cannot seem to think of any of them.'

'I am glad,' she said, straining up to kiss him before he could clear his head. He tasted of brandy and his mouth was open wide in surprise.

There was a moment where he still resisted. But only a moment. Then, he took control, cupping the back of her neck and holding her mouth to his and possessing it. It was every bit as shocking as the first

kiss had been when she'd had the feeling that his
iron self-control had slipped, giving her a glimpse
of something wild and dangerous beneath it.

And so it seemed tonight. His other hand was
unbuttoning the rest of her nightgown, pushing the
fabric out of the way so he could reach her bare
breasts. She trembled as his fingers touched her nipples, stroking lightly over their tips before closing a
hand over one, warming it with his palm.

As his hand moved, the sensation rushed through
her body and she arched her back and clenched her
legs together. She struggled free of his kiss and
turned her head into his naked shoulder, licking
against the skin before grazing it with her teeth.

'You learn quickly,' he whispered, pushing her
away. 'Show me what you want.' She wanted what
he had promised her before, to be kissed until she
begged. He moved against her mouth and she kissed
the planes of his face, the sharp line of his jaw, the
cords of his throat and the muscles of his chest. Then
she felt the rough, flat nipple touch her lower lip. She
seized upon it, trying to take it into her mouth, cir-
cling it with her tongue and biting gently.

But he did not beg, he laughed. 'Very well.' Now
his mouth was on her breasts, repeating what she had
done. Had it felt this way for him? She could not beg
for it, because the sensation was beyond words. She
squirmed under him, then relaxed, letting her legs
open wide until he was laying between them.

As she moved, the sheet he'd wrapped about his
waist shifted lower and she was surprised to feel

nothing but bare skin rubbing against her thigh. Was it really possible that he had been lying in bed, wearing nothing at all?

She could not resist her curiosity and drew her knee up, then slid it down along his body, pushing the linen down with it. There was nothing but skin roughened by hair, as far as she could reach.

He seemed surprised by her explorations and grinned at her. Then he braced himself on his arms and slid back up her body, until they lay hip to hip.

She gasped.

He grinned and kissed her, teasing the inside of her mouth with his tongue, sliding in and out with a series of deep thrusts, as his manhood settled between her legs. 'Perhaps you would be more comfortable if we moved to the bed.' He kissed her breasts again, with long, slow pulls on her nipples.

'Here. Now. Please.' He was right. He had made her beg.

He paused again, surprised. 'Do you know what you are asking for?'

'No,' she admitted, on another gasp. 'Tell me.' She rubbed her leg against his again. He groaned and bucked once against her as she raised her hips to meet him.

His hands circled her waist to hold her still. Then he reached between them and stroked once between her legs, making her moan in surprise. 'I could pleasure you as we did in the drawing room, but I do not know that I will be able to stop at that.'

'Why?' she whispered.

'Because I would be forgoing a pleasure as great as the one you experience.' His hand moved lower and his fingers disappeared inside her. 'I will feel it when I take you as a man takes his wife, by spilling my seed inside you. There will be no turning back once we start and no time for regrets. Also, it will probably hurt.'

She had not expected there would be pain.

He dropped a gentle kiss on the open 'Oh' of her mouth. 'That is just the first time. After that, there will be nothing but pleasure, I swear on my life. But once that has been done, there can be no more secrets between us and no talk of marrying other men. You must tell me everything in your heart and your mind, and promise to love me, and only me, for the rest of your life.'

If simple desire had not been enough to convince her, his words were more than enough. Brief pain in exchange for someone to share her heart and soul with, not just for now but always. 'Yes,' she said, breathless and a little frightened. Then she tugged at the hem of her nightgown, pulling it up between them and over her head.

He released a hiss of breath from between his clenched teeth. 'Your body feels as I knew you would, like the reward of heaven itself.' His lips roved down her throat and returned to her breasts. He buried his face between them and worshipped them with his tongue, his teeth and his hands.

The contact left her light-headed, as if she was floating in the same paradise he had imagined. She reached up and swept her hair forward, draping it over his shoulders.

He lifted his head and smiled. Then he slid down her body to kiss her between the legs as he had on the mouth.

Her first response was to pull away in shock. But his hands on her waist pulled her back again. At the renewed contact, a jolt of pleasure lanced through her body. She stiffened and then relaxed again, allowing him to do as he wished with her. She was rewarded with another pulse, and another, until the throbbing between her legs overwhelmed her.

Her fingers dug into the rug beneath her and she closed her eyes and arched her back. His fingers were pushing inside her again, spreading her wetness, stretching her. Then she felt the full weight of his body on hers and the sudden pain of his first thrust.

And afterwards, stillness, as his fingers stroked her until the pleasure grew in her again. She grabbed his biceps, feeling the taut muscle bunching under her fingers as he began to move. Her body seemed to cling to the unfamiliar fullness inside, tightening on it to heighten the sensation as he withdrew, only to enter again.

She could hear his measured breaths against her temple as he struggled for calm, waiting for her. But she did not want him calm. She wanted to break though the reserve and know that he was as helpless for her as she was for him. She dared to open her eyes and look up into his. She whispered his name.

His stroke faltered, and returned, stronger than before.

This time she said it louder. 'Gregory.' She gave herself over to the rhythm he set, rocking in time with him, letting her hands roam over his body. Everything about him was strange and wonderful, flat where she was curved and hard where she was soft. And where it mattered most he fit like a piece of herself she had never known was missing.

He was whispering to her, demanding that she come with him, as if they were on some journey that he did not want to complete alone. His breaths were ragged now, his movements a shuddering syncopation that made her body tighten and pulse against his. Then she felt a change. He muttered what sounded like a prayer and surged forward. Her body clenched. They were shaking in a rush of pleasure that went on and on until they were both exhausted.

They collapsed, him on top of her and her flat on the floor, staring up at the ceiling. When his head rose, his cheeks were flushed and his blond hair fell forward on to his face.

She reached up to smooth it. 'This is the first time I have seen you discomposed,' she said, smiling.

'Because you have bewitched me,' he said, with a happy sigh.

'Me?' She could not help being pleased with herself.

'Since the first day,' he said. 'It has been a losing struggle to keep my head.'

'If this is what happens when you fail, perhaps you should not try so very hard,' she said.

He pulled out of her and she sighed at the loss. Then he rose and scooped her up, carrying her across the room.

'What are you doing?' she said, laughing.

'What I should have done, before,' he said, with a stern look. 'I am taking you to my bed, where you belong.' He tossed her on to the mattress, then stood over her, hands on hips like a sultan surveying his conquest.

She stared for a moment, admiring the body she had felt rather than seen. Then she shook her head, to remove the fantasies forming there, and sat up. 'We cannot.'

'No?' He looked both surprised and disappointed. It was quite flattering.

She smiled. 'You said there could be no more secrets between us. Before we go any further, I must tell you the whole of our troubles. Then we will see if you are truly as brilliant as you claim to be.'

Chapter Thirteen

As she led him down the hall towards the Countess's suite, Gregory walked behind her, admiring the view. She was barefoot and naked, except for her rumpled nightgown, open at the throat so it hung low and bared her shoulders. Her hair was tousled and her skin was flushed. She looked well and thoroughly loved.

She looked back at him, smiled and held a finger to her lips, reminding him of the need for silence as they passed her sister's room.

He did not want to be quiet. He wanted to shout for joy. And to call a 'thank you' to her sleeping sister. When Hope had left them alone to play chess he had wanted to retire as well. Considering how much trouble he had caused by being alone with one sister, he dared not risk the reputation of a second one, even if their interaction was completely innocent.

But the younger Strickland had detained him, demanding one more game. The moment her sister was out of earshot she pushed away from the board. 'Now we will wait. Twenty minutes should be enough.'

'For what?' he had asked.

'For my sister to become angry enough to do something rash,' she said, with a smile.

He frowned at her. 'I do not want your sister to do something rash. And I do not need your help in winning her, if that is what you think you are doing.'

She laughed. 'Perhaps you need no assistance. But my sister needs twenty minutes.'

At last, he had relented. 'Twenty minutes, or twenty days. It should not matter either way, because nothing is going to happen between us until I have spoken with your grandmother.' It was pure luck that had made him say *nothing,* rather than *nothing more.* Even though she did not seem to try, Miss Charity was far too good at ferreting out secrets.

She was good at judging her sister's character as well. Though Hope had always claimed to be the proper one, he'd seen no evidence of it tonight. But it was no longer as important to protect her innocence as it had been. Before they'd made love, he had got a promise of devotion from her. There would be no more talk of the Earl, because she had promised to love only him.

He was going to marry Hope Strickland. The acceptance of his official offer was a foregone conclusion. Even so, he would make one, on one knee with a ring worthy of a daughter of one of England's noblest families. Tradition was important to her. It should be so to him as well. After all, he was starting a family line of his own. She would be the first Mrs Drake. There would be children. Offspring. Progeny. Descendants.

He thought he had been happy before. But now, his throat closed with emotion at the thought of the future. There had been an emptiness in him for as long as he could remember. And now Hope Strickland had filled it.

Ahead of him, she had stopped. She stood at the Countess's open bedroom door, beckoning him to enter. When they were both inside, she shut it tightly and lit the candles on the bedside table from the one she'd carried. 'What I am about to show you might be hard to see in candlelight. But I think that was rather the point all along. A dark room hides a multitude of sins.'

He felt a sudden chill of foreboding. Had that been a reference to what they had just done, or was she speaking of something else?

She continued speaking, unaware. 'I removed these from the lock room this afternoon, while you were busy with Charity.' She pulled a velvet box from the dresser and spilled the contents on to the bed.

'The Comstock diamonds,' he said, surprised.

Now she was poking through some of the most famous jewels outside the royal family as if they were nothing but jumble.

'The full parure consists of a tiara, eardrops, two rings, a brooch. And, of course, the lavalier, which must be three carats at least. Grandmama rarely wears anything more than the smaller of the rings.

She has complained for as long as I can remember that the rest are too heavy for any occasion less than a visit to court.'

As he stared at the jewels, the reason for her secrecy came clear. To verify what he already knew, he picked up the necklace, weighted it in his hand for a moment, then blew on it, holding it up in the candlelight to check the surface for fog.

Then he set it down with a sigh. 'How long since the real stones were replaced with paste?'

'I have no idea,' she said, sitting on the edge of the bed and tucking her feet beneath her to keep them warm. 'It was hard enough getting Grandmama to describe the rest of the items she took. But when she did not mention them, I became suspicious and examined them.' She ran a fingernail along the surface of one of the larger stones. 'They are scratched. No true diamond would have such damage.'

'And you asked her what had become of them?'

'She flatly refuses to say a word about them, claiming she will explain it all to the new Comstock when he arrives.' She waved a hand at the jewellery beside her and laughed bitterly. 'What will she say to him that might matter? A theft of this magnitude cannot just be explained away.'

'You were planning to give yourself to the Earl,' he said, shocked, but not surprised.

She cocked her head to the side, looking up at him with a smile that had become wiser in the last hour. 'I did not think of it in that way. I was not planning to *give* anything but my hand. But that was not what he actually would have wanted from me.' She looked into his eyes and one part of him melted as another grew hard. 'I may have diminished my value somewhat, since meeting you.'

'You most certainly have not,' he said. 'You were worth more than a pile of cold stones when we began. And now? I would not trade a minute with you for all the jewels in England.'

'Thank you,' she said. 'But much as I like to hear them, your beautiful words will not solve my problem.' She patted the bed beside her, indicating that he should sit. 'I need your beautiful brain to do that. Or at least Mr Leggett's beautiful money. How much has he given you to sort our problems?'

'He said I could have what was needed,' Gregory said, collapsing prone on the bed next to where she sat. 'I was to spare no expense.'

'Ha.' She made a sound that was far too harsh to call a laugh and fell back to lay at his side. 'And how much have you spent so far?'

'Seventy-seven pounds, five shillings and sixpence,' he said.

'That is very precise,' she said, glumly.

'I have receipts,' he said. 'I would not be in demand if I were not so accurate. I will waive my fee to him, of course, since we are to be family.'

'Are we?' she said, rolling to face him.

'That will be up to his wife's younger sister.' He took her hand and kissed the knuckles. 'I plan to speak to your grandmother the moment we return to London and hope that I shall claim a connection to Mr Leggett before he has even come back from Italy.'

'Do you think he might give us a wedding gift of fifty thousand pounds?' She reached to the jewels at her side and perched the tiara awkwardly on her forehead. 'Or perhaps one hundred and fifty,' she said, with a regal wave of her hand. 'You are far better at guessing the value than I. But I guess that the diamonds must be worth at least that.'

'You are assuming we could buy them back,' he reminded her. 'I doubt the biggest stone remains uncut. There will be no equal to be found, even if we could afford it.'

'At least we still have the settings.' She sighed. 'Although, with the luck I've had, I would not be surprised to scratch the surface and find they are gilded tin.'

'But at least this restores my faith in your grandmother's sanity,' he said, staring up at the canopy above the Dowager's bed. 'I was wondering why she sold such rubbish to get by. If she had already run through the money for the diamonds, it makes more sense.' He stopped, confused. There was something wrong in that assumption as well, but he was too tired to see what it was.

'It would have made even more sense, in the eyes of the law, if she had sold things that actually belonged to her.' Hope gave a bitter laugh. 'The rest of the jewels in her jewel case are real and not entailed. When I asked her why she did not part with those, she told me that they were gifts from Grandfather and had sentimental value.'

'Of course,' he said weakly.

'And now you see why I thought it was hopeless to even tell you. With your help, we have been able to replace the least important items. But I doubt that the Earl will be impressed by our efforts once he learns what is still lost.'

'That is quite possibly true.' And now he could see why she had not wanted to tell him of the problem, for he could not think of a better solution than the one she had been considering.

'Have you heard anything more about his arrival? How long do we have before he learns what Grand-mama has done?'

'No,' he admitted. Strickland was already over-due. At best, they had a few weeks before the reckoning she had feared. Now that she'd told him the whole truth, it appeared she had been right all along. For a wrong of this magnitude, marriage would have been a reasonable way to heal the breach and reunite the two branches of the family. If it had been any other woman, he'd have brokered the match himself.

Instead, he'd made bold promises about solving any problem put to him. He'd lain with her and ru-ined the best chance she had for the security she craved. Now the only thing he could do to set things right was to produce a king's ransom in diamonds on short notice and out of thin air.

She poked him again. 'You have not fallen asleep, have you?'

'No. Merely thinking.'

'You had gone so quiet, I was beginning to wonder. Do you have a plan?'

'The beginnings of one.' He was lying to her again. He had no idea what to do, other than stall and pray. 'Is the jewel case here? I wish to examine it.'

She rose on one elbow and gave him an odd look, then pointed to it, sitting on the mattress, a few inches from his head.

'Silly of me,' he said with a shrug and reached for it. 'It seems I have eyes for nothing but you.' Now that he'd started lying he could not tell one truth in twenty.

'I don't know what good it will do,' she said. 'He will not be impressed by a nice package if the jewellery is false.'

'It might do no good at all, but I must be thorough. I will not leave any avenues unsearched or any clues unexamined.'

'You cannot possibly think there is anything to be done,' she said, smiling in surprise.

He smiled back at her and felt the energy surging in his blood at the sight of such a supremely beautiful, infinitely desirable woman staring at him as if she thought he could hang the moon. She had confidence in him. He must have it as well. 'I solve problems. If I turn away when presented with a challenge, then what good am I?'

'If you can retrieve the diamonds, then you are not a problem solver, Mr Gregory Drake. You are a worker of miracles.'

He took a deep breath and felt more than his courage begin to rise. 'If that is what you require of me, Miss Strickland, I shall endeavour to provide.'

'That is not all I want.' She sat up and stripped her nightgown over her head, then straightened the Comstock tiara in her chestnut hair and added the massive, paste pendant which swung to hang between her magnificent breasts. Then, naked and bejewelled and as bold as a pagan princess, she straddled him.

If her body was not enough to make him forget his impending doom, her next words were.

'Take me, Mr Drake. Repeatedly. Until dawn.'

'Consider it done, Miss Strickland.'

Chapter Fourteen

Hope had never been the one to break rules. If questioned, either of her sisters would have declared her the one least likely to disobey and most likely to tattle on those who did. But after last night, she had to admit that being good was not nearly as much fun as being bad.

Lying with a man before marriage was something that a nice girl should never do. But not only had she done it, she'd learned that there was more to it than just lying still. In fact, sometimes she had done no lying at all. One could do things that were very improper while sitting, or standing, or kneeling on a mattress and clinging tightly to the bedpost while the man behind her whispered unspeakable suggestions in her ear.

Worse yet, she had done those things in a bed that was not hers, with the pride of the Comstock entail thumping furiously against her naked breasts. It was almost a relief to know the stones were paste, for she would have been afraid to do the things she'd done while wearing nothing but a small fortune in diamonds.

And she would do it all again, the minute she could get Gregory Drake alone. It was a shame that the object of the trip had been to collect Charity and take her back to London. If her sister had not been here, Hope might have made up some spurious excuse about beginning the inventory of the house. Then they might spend the week together, alone.

Of course, there would be no hope of finding the diamonds if they stayed at the manor. She did not think it would be possible for Gregory to figure out where they had gone, but she would enjoy seeing him try.

She came down to the breakfast table to find Charity already seated, a book spread on the table between her cup and her plate. Normally, she would have lectured her sister about reading at the table, but it was far too nice a morning to fret over trivialities. She took the chocolate pot and toast rack from in front of her sister, who did not even bother to look up from her work, and served herself.

'Good morning, Charity,' she said. When her sister said nothing, she answered for her. 'Good morning to you, Hope. Did you sleep well?'

Charity held up a finger to indicate that she was almost done with the passage she was reading. Then she slipped a ribbon between the pages as a marker and closed the book. 'I can speak for myself, thank you. Good morning, Hope. Did you sleep we…?' She'd looked up, the word trailing off into empty air.

'Well, well, well.' She cleared her throat. 'I mean, did you sleep well?'

The question was innocent, but the look on her face was anything but.

'Yes,' Hope replied, suddenly afraid to say anything more.

'That is good to know. And how did Mr Drake sleep?' Charity asked, with an arch look.

'You will have to ask him that. Or don't. Please,' she said. As usual, Charity knew more than she should. Was there something in her face that gave it all away? Was there some sort of brand that had appeared on her forehead to signal to the world that she had forbidden knowledge?

'Do not worry so, Hope.' Her sister held her cup out to be refilled. 'You look exceptionally well rested this morning.'

'Oh.' It was some consolation to know that the patronesses at Almack's would not bar the door against a fallen woman, should she have reason to return there. But it did not make this moment any easier.

And now the morning would be even worse. The door to the breakfast room opened and Mr Drake entered. He offered a respectful bow to her and a smile to Charity. He looked as he always did, deliciously perfect. Even with no valet, his suit was freshly brushed and his cheeks clean shaven. The gloves peeking out of his coat pocket were immaculate. 'I have been speaking with the coachman. He will be ready to depart at our convenience.' He was much better at hiding the activities of the previous night than she. There was nothing in his face or his posture to indicate that he'd gone to sleep with the rising of the sun, or spent time in a bed other than his own.

Charity smiled back at him with none of the sly awareness that she had used on Hope and offered him a plate of buns and teapot. 'Thank you so much for your help in this matter. The box is almost prepared. It should not take more than a few minutes once we are ready. Shall we say, twenty minutes?'

The perfectly composed Gregory Drake choked on his toast. It took a sharp slap on the back from Charity and half a pot of tea before he was able to catch his breath and answer, 'There is no reason to rush. I will call for the carriage at one.'

'And I will arrange for the kitchen to prepare a hamper so we might take tea on the road. Country air always gives me an appetite.'

At this, the poor man went pale, as if the mention of hunger put him in mind of something that had nothing to do with food.

'That is an excellent idea,' Hope said, glaring at her sister. 'Now perhaps you would like to go back to your book. We do not wish to keep you from your studies.' The sooner they were free of Charity, the better. The family had long since accepted that the youngest sister was the smartest one. But it sometimes felt like they were mice in a cage, the victims of her insatiable curiosity rather than the beneficiaries.

Before her sister could retort, there was a commotion in the front hall. Hope could hear her grand-mother greeting the servants and calling for her luggage to be brought in from the carriage. Even more unexpected than that, the activity was accompanied by a flurry of high-pitched barking.

Then the Dowager appeared in the doorway. She was wearing a new travelling gown and had a small black and white dog tucked under her arm that yipped continually as he tried to wriggle free of her.

Gregory sprang to his feet in a show of respect, but the Dowager waved him back into his chair with her free arm. 'Please sit, Mr Drake. I am the one interrupting your breakfast. I have been in a rented carriage five long hours and my legs need a good stretch.'

She stared at her granddaughters. 'Of course, I would not have needed a post-chaise if the Comstock carriage had been available.'

'I am sorry, Grandmama,' Hope began. 'But Charity...'

'I read your note,' she said with a firm smile. 'I was impressed by your ability to single-handedly deal with an emergency that occurred during a time when I was not home to accompany you.' There was something in her eyes that said she had calculated the timeline to the minute and knew full well that the problem had been discovered long before they had set out and solved long before breakfast.

The dog let out another miserable whine and the Dowager signalled the footman hovering in the doorway. 'Take care of Pepper, Jenks. I am sure he would like to stretch his legs as well. One of them, at least. Once he is done, you are to bring him straight back into the house. He will be living here, now, and must get used to behaving inside.'

'Grandmama,' Hope said, with a warning tone. 'He cannot be coming to live here because we are not sure how long we will be staying.'

'Do not be ridiculous, Hope. Pepper can stay as long as he wishes.' Her grandmother smiled. 'He does not belong to me, you see.'

'You have no right to bring a strange dog into the place. Does it belong to your sick cousin?' Hope threw her hands in the air. 'I do not understand.' It was bad that Charity had returned, but now the whole family was back where they did not belong and had grown by one.

The Dowager stared at her as if she were being unforgivably dense. 'Have you not guessed what has happened? Did you not realise why I had gone to Bristol? The seas were rough. The poor fellow has not had a decent meal in weeks and kept down little of the food he did get. He needed time to recover before travelling on to London.'

'Your cousin is…' Hope raised her eyebrows. 'That cousin?'

'When I returned to London and found that you were both gone, I did not want to waste the time on a letter. The news is so amazing.'

There was a sound of distant barking and then the sudden yip of a dog that had attempted to chase something more inclined to fight than run.

The Dowager gave a worried look out the window. 'I hope Jenks has not let Pepper too near the stable cats. The Earl wanted someone to bring the little fellow to his new home and I volunteered. I am assured that he is normally a sweet-tempered creature. Pepper, that is, not the Earl.'

She smiled. 'But Miles is a sweet-tempered creature as well. The pair of them have been cooped up in a small cabin for weeks. A dog needs to feel grass under his feet and there did not seem to be enough of it in London to suit him.'

'Miles?' Hope had heard but one in ten of the torrent of words in her grandmother's rambling discourse. But she had understood enough to realise that they had run out of time. She could not seem to take a breath. It was as if all the air was pushed out of her lungs, leaving her nothing to respond with. 'You saw him?'

'I escorted him back to London, where he will be for some time.' She gave the girls a disapproving look. 'I should never have given you such free use of the carriage, for he should be riding in it when he goes to the palace. Although he said it was not necessary to stand on ceremony. At least not until the formalities have been dealt with. There is a need to prove his identity, beyond doubt. Then there will be a Letter of Patent to transfer lands and title.' The Dowager waved her hand. 'It is all very tedious. Especially for Pepper, who did not like the town house at all.'

'Never mind the dog.' Now that she could manage to get a word in, Hope had to struggle to keep from shouting. 'Tell me about the Earl.'

Her grandmother waggled a finger at her. 'You are not still thinking of him, are you? It is very shallow of you to throw Mr Drake aside before even meeting your cousin.'

She turned to Gregory with a somewhat sterner smile. 'The two of you will be marrying, of course. After what happened last night, I expect you will want to do so as soon as possible.'

'What happened?' Hope said, trying to sound as though she did not know the answer to the question.

Her grandmother frowned and shook her head. 'Lord save me from poor liars and silly young girls.'

Was there no way to hide the truth of her behaviour, even for a moment? Charity had been lying when she'd said that the change in her was not that noticeable. It explained why girls were taught to protect their innocence at all costs. But like many strict rules, obedience had been more important than understanding. Of all the things Gregory had taught her last night, why had he not explained that there could be no turning back because, once she returned to London, everyone would know exactly what she had done?

Worst of all, Grandmama was not her usual, flippant self. She was more stern than Hope had ever seen her and, rather than telling an amusing anecdote about her misspent youth, she was giving them both dark looks and talking of marriage as a *fait accompli*.

'Nothing of interest happened last night,' Hope

blurted. Gregory's mouth, which had opened to speak, closed with a frown.

She continued. 'Charity can assure you of that, for I retired early and the two of them stayed up until all hours, playing chess. And I am not throwing anyone over for my American cousin, who is probably too old for me and married.'

'Old and married?' Her grandmother released a silvery laugh. 'Whatever gave you such an idea?'

'You, Charity and everyone else in the family,' she replied. 'Perhaps I have finally accepted what the two of you have been telling me all along. It would be too great a miracle for him to be young and unmarried. It is far more likely that he is old and has a wife and several children.'

'Then miracles do happen,' her grandmother said, stepping forward to pat her on the shoulder. 'He is barely thirty and single. He has nothing but Pepper to claim as family. Even now, the Crown is impressing on him his responsibilities and the need for an heir.'

'But I would never assume a man was right for me without even meeting him,' Hope said, staring down into her plate and trying to contemplate the magnitude of the mistake she had made. 'He might be miserly and foul tempered,' she added. 'He might not care about our family at all.' He might not be the sort of man she could love as she'd thought she loved the silent Gregory Drake.

'On the contrary, he is the kindest gentleman in the world.' Her grandmother was near to simpering over the newly arrived Comstock, who was, apparently, exactly the man Hope had expected him to be. 'Miles greeted me as long-lost family and expressed his intent to see that there is a settlement in place for the repair of the dower house and my expenses. I took the liberty...' She spun to display her new gown.

'You went shopping with his money,' Hope said with a sigh.

'He encouraged me to do it. He is writing a letter this very afternoon to thank Mr Leggett for his help in settling the family. And he enquired after you and your little sister. He did not say as much, but I am sure he means to see the both of you are well settled.'

'He does?' Her plan might not have been wise, but it had not been hopeless at all. Instead, she had abandoned it and thrown herself away on a man who did not want her until she had all but forced herself upon him.

'I think he was asking about you girls with a particular reason in mind.' Her grandmother giggled again. 'It is too late for you, Hope. But perhaps Charity...'

'Do not involve me in your schemes,' Charity said, without looking up from her book. 'I have no intention of marrying a man I have not met. And any man I do want to marry will have to fit certain criteria before I consider him a suitable husband.'

'He is young, rich and an earl,' the Dowager said. 'How much more can you expect from him?'

'Stop!' Hope rose so quickly that her chair tipped backward, hitting the carpet with a thud that echoed her word. Her napkin, still clutched in her hand, waved like a flag of surrender as she pointed to the shocked faces around the table. 'Stop it this instant, both of you.' She turned to Charity. 'Not another word of this nonsense about standards so high that a peer will not suffice. If he offers, you will marry him and that will be that.' Then she turned to her grandmother. 'And not as much as a breath about it being *too late* for me.'

'But I assumed that you and Mr Drake...'

'You assumed incorrectly,' she said, glaring across the table at the man who had let her ruin herself. 'Mr Drake is nothing to me. And I am nothing to him. Once he has finished his job for our family, I never want to see him again.' She narrowed her eyes. 'If he were in any way decent, he would be gone already.' Then she threw her napkin to the ground and ran from the room.

Was he a fool or a coward? Gregory could not decide how to explain what had just happened to him. He'd sat in silence and let Hope do all the talking, amazed that she was so quick to deny him. After swearing there would be no one but him, it had taken one censorious glare from her grandmother to turn her mind and her future back to a marriage with her cousin.

Now that she was gone, the room fell silent. Charity returned to her book as if nothing had happened. The Dowager stepped forward and took an empty seat at the head of the table. At a glance in the direction of Jenks, the footman, a cup and plate appeared in front of her. Tea was poured and food offered.

She sipped, then looked over the rim of her cup at Gregory. 'Young man, I must know one thing before I decide what to do with you. You will answer in honesty. I will know if you do not.' She stared at him.

He nodded.

'Did you break her heart intentionally, or was it accidental?'

Charity looked up from her book. 'Grandmama, he—'

'I did not ask your opinion, girl.'

He gave her a brief nod of thanks, then turned to the Dowager. 'If I hurt her, it was without intent. Since we met…' How could he explain what had happened when he did not understand it himself? 'I have not been myself.'

'And who are you, when you are at home?' the old woman asked with the glare of a countess addressing someone of insignificance.

'Before I met your granddaughter, I thought myself a man of honour, good sense and moderation,' he admitted.

'And since?'

'I have been both better and worse than I ever thought I could be,' he said. 'I thought she had committed her heart to me. I had intended to speak to you about her future, as soon as we returned to London. But I had not thought it would be over breakfast.'

The Dowager relaxed and took another sip of tea. 'Your explanation is sufficient. I will tell neither

Mr Leggett nor Comstock what has happened, unless Hope requests it of me. You have one week to either settle the situation with my granddaughter, or settle the matter of the entail. If either is incomplete at the end of seven days, I expect you to disappear from our lives, just as quickly as you arrived. Is that understood?'

'Yes, your ladyship.' As he stood and left the table, he could already feel the clock ticking.

Chapter Fifteen

Hope sat on the edge of her bed, waiting for the clock to strike one so she could return to London. At all costs, she avoided her own reflection, afraid to see the change that everyone else had noticed in her own face. She had considered and rejected the idea of staying behind in the country to lick her wounds and sending Mr Drake back with Charity. Though it might be more pleasant to avoid confrontation, it did not change the fact that this house no longer belonged to her.

And there was still the matter of the missing diamonds. Mr Drake's promise of help was likely as fleeting as everything else about last night. That left her with explaining their loss to the new Earl of Comstock. She could not imagine he would have been as personable as Grandmama thought him had he known the truth.

There was a knock on the door.

'Go away,' she said. He did not have to say a word for her to be sure it was Gregory on the other side.

'We have to talk.'

'No, we don't,' she said. 'Never again.'

He opened without permission, came in and closed it behind him. 'Then I have to talk and you must listen.'

'If you mean to apologise, do not bother. I do not wish to hear it.' She kept her eyes focused on the floor, not daring to look at him.

'I am not sorry about last night, if that is what you are referring to,' he said. 'I refuse to apologise for the most wonderful night of my life.'

'If it was so wonderful, then why didn't you speak when my grandmother wondered about it?'

'You did not give me a chance,' he said, then dropped to his knees in front of her so that it was impossible for her to evade his gaze. 'Just as I had no chance to refuse you last night, or in the library in London.'

'Are you suggesting that this is all my fault?' she said, trying to pull away from him.

He reached out to grasp her hands before she could escape. 'There is no fault. No one is to blame because we did nothing wrong. We love each other.'

'Do we?' Had he ever said so, before this moment? Or had she simply assumed that he must love her to do the things he did.

'I thought it was understood,' he said, giving her the same narrow-eyed look she was giving him. 'But after what you said to your grandmother, it seems I was mistaken. You talk as though you would still prefer to wed an earl.'

'Not *an* earl,' she said, yanking her hands free. 'The Earl of Comstock.'

'Now that you know he is everything you dreamed he might be, I am no longer worthy of you,' he said, standing up again.

'That is not true,' she snapped, averting her eyes so she did not have to look into his. To do that was like staring into the sun, blinding and confusing. 'There is nothing wrong with you. It is me.' She did not have the words to explain what had changed in her, but something had.

'Perhaps it is you,' he said. 'Did you not understand that we would be obligated to marry, after what happened last night?'

'Obligated?' she said. That was what she had wanted. To make sure he had no choice. But now that it had happened, it was an empty victory.

'Yes,' he said. There was a faint softness in his voice. 'You might be carrying my child. I am not capable of doing what was done to me and abandoning a son or daughter, allowing them to be raised by strangers.'

She had not considered the possibility of a baby. But neither did she think that a child would be the first thing on his mind when making the offer she had hoped to hear. Now that she had fallen, what she had thought would be an act of love was nothing more than a duty. She stood up and walked past him to open her door. She pointed to the hall. 'You may think we have to marry, but I have no intention of forcing you to wed me. Nor can you force me to wed you.'

Now, he looked baffled. 'No one is being forced to do anything. If, after what has happened between us, you do not want me, I cannot make you. And if there is a child…'

'There will not be,' she said, terrified for the future. What child would want a mother bearing the mark of licentiousness that her sister and grandmother had spotted so easily? 'I will not be with child. I refuse to be. I will not have it. Or I will and I will give it to you, since that is all that you seem to care about. Now please leave me alone.'

'You think I do not care about you?' He laughed. 'Hope Strickland, I care more for you than I have ever cared for a woman in my life.' His hands reached out to her in supplication.

She could feel herself weakening and turned away. 'I care for you as well.' The words sounded false, even to her. They were far too weak to encompass her true feelings which ranged from love, to fear, to confusion and back to love again. 'I care for you. But that does not make it right.' She walked to the door and opened it, praying that he would understand and leave.

He shook his head, amazed. 'Very well, Miss Strickland, I suppose I must thank you for changing a lifetime's assumptions about the world and my place in it. I have wasted far too long trying to be a better man than the father I never knew. I thought he abandoned my mother to bear me and die. But perhaps she sent him away for no reason, just as you are doing to me. You have taught me that in matters of the heart women can be every bit as cruel as men.'

The four of them rode back to London in ominous silence. Or rather, three of them did. Charity disappeared into her book the moment she was seated, blissfully unaware of the tension inside the coach.

The Dowager was her usual self as she entered and sat down, smiling brilliantly and joking that she would enjoy playing chaperon for the young people. Still smiling, she took the seat next to Hope and gave Gregory a look that said if he as much as stretched a finger in Hope's direction, she would have him thrown from the coach and whipped by the driver.

Hope might as well not have been there at all. She was not just quiet; she hardly seemed to breathe. Nor did she move, staring straight ahead at her sister on the seat across from her for the whole trip.

Gregory tried to tell himself that it was better than the alternative. When a love affair ended, some women were prone to hysterical tears, or angry tirades. They went out of their way to make the parting as difficult as possible.

But not Hope Strickland. After hours of nothing, it would have been a relief to see any emotion at all. The woman sitting on the other side of the coach from him might have been a total stranger instead of the most passionate lover he'd ever known. It made him wonder if he had imagined the last week. He could see no sign on her face that she had been in any way moved by him.

It was not until they were alighting back in London that he could be sure she still remembered. He offered his hand to help her down and she hesitated as she took it. But it was not from fear or revulsion of him. There was something in her eyes that hinted at a fear of her own reaction. Her heart was not totally lost to him, if she had to fight the response to his touch.

But what did he feel when he looked at her? He looked after her as she moved across the pavement towards the town-house door. In a few steps, she might be out of his life, which would return to its comforting routine. Jobs would be started and completed. Clients would come and go. He would remain safe and unaffected.

Her rejection had hurt him, of course. But that was almost a novelty. He had been rejected by women before and had never experienced a pain like that caused by her denial during breakfast. He had gone to her room sure that a simple explanation would be enough to set things right. Surely a girl as proper as she was would see that a hasty marriage was the best protection for her honour. Instead, she had rejected him again. A part of him did not want to try a third time.

But then his thoughts had turned to his father again. He had always imagined a rake or a rogue who did not care about the pain he'd left behind when he left. But perhaps he was just a coward. Perhaps he had slunk away from the woman he'd loved and the family he might have had, because he'd not been brave enough to claim them.

He had formed his character with no other plan than to be different than someone he did not know at all. Perhaps that was why he'd fallen in love with the sort of girl who caused more trouble being good than any enthusiastic sinner ever had.

He hurried down the path until he was one pace ahead of her, blocking her way to the door. Then he smiled at her as he had when they were nothing more than client and employee. 'If it is convenient for you, I shall return tomorrow at our usual time.'

'Return?' she snapped. 'What makes you think I would wish to see you again?'

'We have one item left to retrieve,' he reminded her, pulling out the list that was still in his pocket. 'A Chinese vase.'

'You said you would locate it without my help.'

He shrugged. 'I was mistaken.'

'You are mistaken now.' Her voice was shrill as if the idea of seeing him again drove her one step closer to madness. 'I have no wish to see you, ever again.'

'I have no wish to force my attentions on you,' he said, as mildly as possible. 'But I have a job to complete. It will go faster, and I will be gone sooner, if I have your help.'

She paused for a moment, as if weighing temporary discomfort with eventual freedom. 'Very well. One day. If the search takes more than that, you must complete it on your own.'

'Excellent,' he said with another one of his professional smiles to put her off her guard. 'We will do our best to settle the matter tomorrow.'

* * *

When Hope returned to the house, her grand-mama was waiting just inside the door. 'Well?' the Dowager said, arms folded across her chest.

She stared expectantly back at the Dowager, wondering if, after all the stories she had heard about the foolishness of overly strict morality, she was about to receive a dressing down for her own fall from grace.

'You were speaking with Mr Drake,' the older woman said. 'Have you settled the problem between the two of you so I can book St George's for the wedding?'

'There is no problem between us,' Hope said, with a forced smile. 'He was employed by Mr Leggett to help us fix the problem you created. Tomorrow, we are going out to find the Chinese vase. Then his job will be finished and we will see no more of him.'

'What utter fustian,' her grandmother snapped. 'When I arrived at the manor, he was staring at you like a moonstruck idiot, unable to string two words together. And you looked like Eve, waiting for God's judgement with the apple still in her hand.'

Had it really been so noticeable? How was she to go about London with him? Or without him, for that matter? Was it something that would fade with time? Perhaps it could be washed away.

'Stop playing with your curls, Hope Strickland,' the Dowager snapped. 'If you are trying to look less guilty, you are making matters worse and not better. I'd blame your parents for dying before they could teach you to lie, but it did not seem to matter in Charity's case. She is younger than you and there are days when I cannot get a single truth out of her.'

'What am I to do?' she said at last, dropping the charade and pressing her palms to her face to hide the blush. 'I cannot see anyone looking like this. I certainly cannot meet the new Comstock. He will think me unchaste and want nothing to do with us.'

Grandmother shook her head in pity. 'Do not waste time worrying that men will want nothing to do with you. There are more than enough of them who prefer a girl with a glow in her cheeks and a twinkle in her eye. They are nothing to be afraid of. If you are walking out with the man who put it there, they will leave you alone.'

'I cannot spend the rest of my life in the company of Mr Drake,' she whispered.

'Well, not every moment. But once everyone is calling you Mrs Drake, it would be rather stupid of people to show surprise that he is bedding you.'

She turned back to her grandmother. 'For the last time, I am not going to marry Gregory Drake. He has not even asked me to.'

'He has not asked?' Surprisingly this seemed to bother the Dowager more than anything else. 'Then I shall have him dragged back here immediately to do right by you. And there will be none of this nonsense about punishing him for his hesitation by refusing.'

'That is not the problem at all,' Hope replied. 'He said it was his duty to marry me.'

'And so it is,' the Dowager said, with an exasperated shake of her head.

'But when I went to his room, I thought…'

'Did he invite you?' her grandmother said with a confused frown.

'He would never do something as dishonourable as that. Before we went to Berkshire he said that he did not think it wise for us to see each other again,' Hope explained.

'But then you insisted that he accompany you. And you went to his room when the household was asleep,' her grandmother said, her voice raising. 'You pestered the poor man until he succumbed, instead of giving him the chance to court you properly. And now you are complaining about the quality of his proposal.'

She had been so focused on her plan to marry Comstock that it had never occurred to her to flirt with him as Grandmama had suggested and allow things to develop slowly, as was proper. It was just as it had been at the ball, when she had resorted to theft, rather than asking permission. 'This is like the inkwell, only worse,' Hope said, closing her eyes in shame.

'My dear, I have no idea what you are going on about. But if it in any way resembles the current situation, please do not enlighten me. All I want to know from you now are your feelings towards Mr Drake.'

'I love him,' she said. But instead of making her happy, the words came out on a sob.

'Then stop torturing the poor man,' her grandmother said with a sigh. 'You say he is coming back tomorrow morning to see about finding the vase from the hall?'

Hope nodded.

She glanced at the clock on the wall. 'It is growing late and he has probably had quite enough of our family for the day. We will not try his patience further. But if he is planning to return, he has either forgiven you, or can be persuaded to do so. Do whatever is necessary to mend the breach between you. I will make myself available in the drawing room, tomorrow between two and seven, should he wish an interview to discuss your future. But as I informed Mr Drake at breakfast, I will not see you moping about the house for more than a week. After that time, if you have not found a husband for yourself, I will arrange a marriage for you, just to get you out of the house.'

Chapter Sixteen

When she was through being badgered by her grandmother, Hope escaped to her room to find that the inquisition was not yet over. Her sister was waiting for her in her bedroom. Charity had seated herself upon the bed, propped herself up with every pillow in the room and spread her dusty books all over the coverlet.

'You have a room of your own,' Hope reminded her.

'Neither of us has a room,' Charity said, barely looking up. 'Have you forgotten that the Earl has arrived?'

Hope closed her eyes for a moment to let a fresh wave of panic wash over her, before opening them to stare back at her sister. 'If he is not here tonight, there is no reason for us to share this space.'

'Grandmama says he claims to have no need of the town house.' Charity frowned. 'Perhaps he does not understand that Parliament is in session and he must take his seat in the House of Lords. It would be rather foolish of him to stay at a hotel until the Season is ended.'

'Do not worry,' Hope said, bitterly. 'I am sure he will be along to evict us once he has a better grasp of the situation.'

'You mean when he discovers that the diamonds are missing,' Charity said.

Hope pushed her sister's books out of the way and sat. 'Who told you that?'

Charity had finally stopped reading long enough to look at her, with her usual expression of patient superiority. 'No one had to tell me anything. I have been playing with the whole set from the moment I was out of the cradle,' Charity replied.

'You were doing what?'

Her little sister shrugged. 'You and Faith would not share your dolls with me. You said I was too young. So I stole Grandmama's jewel case to play at being grown up.'

'You wicked little thing,' Hope said, before remembering that it was never possible to change Charity's character with scolding.

'Grandmama caught me at it. It made her laugh to see me decked in tiara and bracelets. She made me promise to put them back in the box when I was done and set aside the things she did not want me to damage. But those were the pieces that Grandfather had given her and not the diamonds. She had not a thought for the pride of the Stricklands. Do you not find that strange?'

'I am long past finding Grandmama's behaviour strange,' Hope said.

'Well, I did. When I was old enough to understand, I went to the library...'

'*Quelle surprise.*'

Charity ignored the jab. 'I searched for a book that would explain how to tell real diamonds from false. And it was then I noticed the scratches on the stones. Real diamonds are hard and will only be scratched by other diamonds.'

'You knew they were paste and you did not see the problem with it?'

'If it did not bother Grandmama, then why would it bother me?'

'Because our grandmother, the woman who should be protecting us, is constantly doing things that put us in jeopardy. She steals things that do not belong to her and sells them without a thought to the consequences. If it did not bother her that the diamonds were false, it is because she was the one who took them.'

'Or perhaps it is because they were false when she received them, on her wedding day. And false for Great-Grandmother as well,' Charity said, unperturbed. 'Either she does not know that they are paste, or she has always known and has grown used to the idea. It does not matter, either way.'

'It matters immensely,' Hope snapped. 'It matters because we will be lying if we give false stones to Miles Comstock and present them as real.'

'We are not going to give him anything,' Charity

said. 'They are already his. And it is quite possible that his auditor will know even less about diamonds than we do. He will open the case to see that all the spaces are filled, write it in his ledger, then lock them away again.'

'But when they are worn, everyone will discover they are false,' Hope said, horrified.

'No one has noticed as yet,' Charity reminded her.

'Because our grandmother is such a persuasive liar,' Hope said with disgust.

'Or ignorant of the truth,' Charity reminded her. 'It is possible, you know.'

'But unlikely,' Hope said.

'You, on the other hand, will definitely know. You are also a terrible liar,' Charity declared. 'This is why you are convinced that disaster is imminent. Because, as you have proven in the past twenty-four hours, you are physically incapable of keeping a secret.'

'Even if I can persuade Mr Drake to make another offer, I will have to rusticate until the wedding,' she said, closing her eyes in resignation. 'I cannot face anyone in this condition.'

'Fallen from grace?' Charity threw her hand across her face and collapsed on the bed in a mock swoon. She sat up immediately, as composed as ever. 'Stop being so dramatic and look in the mirror.'

'I do not wish to,' Hope replied.

'You cannot avoid it indefinitely. Look at yourself.'

Hope allowed one more moment of hesitation, then turned suddenly, in case the expression was something elusive that might hide if she took the time to prepare her expression.

She stared into the mirror, then stepped closer for a better look. The family was right. Something had changed, but what? Her hair was styled in the same way it had been yesterday. Her gown was not new. She had never needed rouge or powder, nor did she need it today. And then she saw it.

As Charity had reminded her, when it came to words, she had never been good at dissembling. But that did not mean that she went about with a Friday face when things were difficult. Problems were no easier to bear if one kept a pleasant smile, but one was spared the inconvenience of nosy strangers wondering what the matter was.

But today, it seemed she could no longer control her expression. The frown of confusion staring back at her was too real, as was the look of surprise. She had expected to find a brand of infamy. Instead, it was as if her emotions had been laid bare for all to see.

'I should probably marry Mr Drake,' she said and watched the radiant smile that followed the announcement. Though strangers might not guess what she had been doing last night, there was no hiding the fact that she was in love.

'At least you are no longer talking about becoming the next Countess of Comstock. You would be the last girl in the world I'd choose if I needed someone to walk about London in a paste tiara.'

'That is probably true.' It was also strangely cheering to free herself of the plan. 'But I must still meet with Mr Strickland to explain about the diamonds.'

'Or you could return to Berkshire and avoid him,' her sister said. 'You never need meet Miles Strickland at all, you know. There is no law that says we have to associate with family, if we do not wish to.'

'That is true,' Hope said, turning back to face her sister. It had never occurred to her that it would be possible to avoid a meeting. But if she withdrew from society, he might not bother to seek her out.

'If he does not marry immediately, we might be long gone from both his houses before he even thinks to ask about the diamonds, much less look at them,' Charity added.

'It is not as if he will be wearing a necklace and earbobs to Parliament,' Hope said, feeling not just better about the future, but almost happy.

'Then it is settled,' Charity said with a nod. 'If you cannot keep mum about it, you will avoid Miles Strickland and give up on the idea of becoming his Countess. If you marry, it must be to a man who solves your problems instead of adding to them and who can protect you from your excessively virtuous nature. And I could not suggest a better husband for you than Gregory Drake.'

Gregory's smile faded once he was out of sight of the Comstock town house. The Dowager had promised a week to set things right. While Lady Comstock might not plead his case for him, he did not think she would be working actively against him during that time.

But though she had allowed him a sennight, Hope Strickland had given him but a single day. There had to be something he could do to stretch that, so her temper might cool sufficiently to hear his apology. Before he had understood the magnitude of her problem, he had convinced her of his ability to work miracles. If ever one was needed, it was today. It might take a handful of diamonds to earn him more time and the three-carat stone to set things right between them.

He began his search at the jeweller that had provided the leather case for the Comstock parure. After speaking to the proprietor, he went to another more dubious shop. From there, he went to a place so obscure that it had no name on the window and no number on the door. He left, satisfied, a short time later.

Next, there was the matter of the new Comstock. He'd had no real opinion of Miles Strickland when he'd still been at sea. But now that he was on land, Gregory had developed a genial hatred for him that had only grown with the Dowager's description of a prince among men. As long as Hope remained Miss Strickland, her cousin was a threat to their future happiness. Something would have to be done.

Gregory's agent at the dock confirmed that Miles Strickland, travelling alone except for his little dog, had arrived five days ago in Bristol, then, after travelling to London with the Dowager, his luggage had been directed to the Clarendon. It was near to supper and the food there was excellent. In Gregory's opinion, there could be no better time to investigate the competition for Hope's attentions.

When he arrived in the hotel's dining room, there were few empty chairs. He signalled for the assistance of the porter, scanning the diners already seated. In a far corner at a small, poorly lit table, he saw a man with shoulders so sloped that they did not just seem to bear the weight of the world, they looked as if someone had dropped that weight from a great height.

He gave a nod of his head in the direction of the fellow and held a coin where the porter could see it. 'Is that man an American?'

The servant nodded. 'Mr Strickland from Philadelphia.'

'And did he request that unfortunate spot, or did you force it on him?'

'He said he was not interested in company.'

'Well, we do not always get what we want, do we? Take me to him.'

As they approached, Gregory called out, 'Potts! Old fellow, I have not seen you since Cambridge. Lud, but this place is a crush tonight.' He dropped into the seat opposite the new Earl. 'You do not mind if we share a table, do you?'

From the front, Strickland looked as miserable as he had from the rear. Perhaps the Dowager had not exaggerated when she'd spoken of her visit to a sick cousin. His skin was sallow, probably the result of poor diet, hard travel and a passage spent cooped up below deck. From the poor fit of his suit, there appeared to have been a sudden loss of weight.

Fortunately for Gregory, Strickland had not yet acquired the aloof nature of a peer, nor did he realise that a man of his importance should never have been interrupted by rude strangers. A word to the staff and the scribbled title 'Comstock' on the hotel register would have been all the protection he needed. Instead, he was left blinking in surprise, as if unsure of what to do about the intrusion. Finally, he said in his strange, flattened accent, 'I am sorry. You are mistaken. I am not the man you are looking for.'

Gregory blinked back at him, feigning surprise. 'An American? Then you cannot be Potts, though you are the spitting image of him from the back, at least.' He glanced around the room, shaking his head. 'But this place is still packed to the rafters and you have one of the few empty seats. Would you mind terribly?'

'Not at all,' Strickland replied with a look that said he was not sure whether he minded, but did not see what he could do to stop it.

'Gregory Drake,' he said, offering a hand.

'Miles Strickland,' the Earl answered, taking it.

'You are clearly new to England, Mr Strickland. How do you find it?'

Comstock took a deep drink from the glass in front of him. 'Utterly mad, Mr Drake. I am not surprised that my country wanted no part of it, if it chooses its governors based on their last name rather than their abilities.'

'I assume this means you will not be staying with us long.'

Now Miles Strickland looked even more miserable and poured the last of the wine from his bottle before draining his glass in a single gulp. 'If I could find the money for it, I would be on the first boat back to Philadelphia.'

Gregory tried to contain his surprise. 'How fortunate that we should meet, Mr Strickland. You sound like a man who might be in need of my services.' He reached into his pocket and produced a card.

The Earl stared at it for a moment, puzzled. 'You describe yourself as a solver of problems. Is this a common thing in England? I am sure I have never heard of such in Massachusetts.'

'I am the only one that I know of,' Gregory said, trying not to brag.

Strickland gave a gloomy shrug. 'That is very interesting. But the problem that has befallen me is nothing a stranger can solve. Once you hear it, I doubt you will want to help me, even if you are able.'

'That is what they all say,' Gregory replied with a smile. Then he raised a hand to signal the porter. 'Let me buy us another bottle of this excellent wine. After a nice chop and a few more glasses, you shall tell me all about it.'

The meal came, then the bottle. And then things got interesting.

Chapter Seventeen

The next morning, Gregory arrived at the town house as he always did, on the stroke of ten. But he'd arisen earlier than usual to prepare for this visit than he had the others. The creases in his cravat were as sharp as the razor that had shaved him. He wore his best coat and new gloves and had spent more time adjusting the angle of his hat than a sailor spent with a sextant.

He was not a vain man. But if this turned out to be the last time he saw the woman he loved, he wanted her to remember him at his best. And if it was not the last time? Then everything about the day must be perfect.

Hope was waiting for him in the hall of the town house, as she always did. Had she taken care with her appearance as well? It seemed so. Her bonnet was new and matched a green-velvet coat that would be more appropriate on Bond Street than the neighbourhoods he had been taking her to visit. Even the errant curl was under control today, tucked safely under her bonnet.

'Are you ready to accompany me, Miss Strickland?' He offered his hand to her.

He felt her tremble as she accepted it. 'Yes, Mr Drake, I am ready. Let us finish this, shall we?' The arrogance that had coloured her voice on the day they'd met was gone, replaced with an unexpected gentleness. And had he really seen a sparkle in her eye as the veil had dropped to shield her face? It had looked almost like a tear.

She was sitting across from him in the carriage now. He could not tell whether she looked away from him, or gazed at his face as steadily as he was gazing at hers. It did not matter. He would not allow her to do either in silence. At this late date, each word he could wring from her would be deemed a step towards regaining her love.

'Did you sleep well, Miss Strickland?'

The veil on her bonnet rippled, as another shudder ran though her. It must have been embarrassment, for she whispered, 'You are not supposed to ask things like that, Mr Drake.'

She had not called him Gregory, but neither had she snapped at him. Things were going better than he'd expected they would. 'Would you have preferred that I asked how you find the weather?' He pulled up the shade and glanced out the window. 'It is a lovely day, is it not, Miss Strickland?'

There was a moment of silence, as if she could not decide how to answer the simplest question. Then, she said, 'I am sorry, Mr Drake. After all that has happened between us, I do not think I know how to make polite small talk with you.'

'What do you wish to do instead?' He had several suggestions, none of which were appropriate for broad daylight or a closed carriage, even with the shades drawn.

'I wish to apologise,' she whispered. 'It was very improper of me to come to your room in the manor. And I behaved even worse the next day, when Grandmama caught us there together. I have treated you abominably.' She expelled the words in a single rushed breath and they were barely loud enough to be heard over the rattling of the carriage wheels.

'Perhaps you have,' he agreed and heard a surprised gasp from behind the veil. 'But I cannot blame you. I should not have allowed anything to happen between us. While I am working, it is a point of pride on my part that I treat the families of the men who hire me with the utmost respect. With you, I have broken that rule.'

'I did not mind,' she whispered.

'I did,' he said. 'And if it were possible to go back to the day we met, things would be different.'

'But since we cannot, do you think it might be possible to start again, now?' Her voice was so quiet that he almost could not hear it.

'I would like that very much,' he said. 'But we must wait until the list is complete.'

'What difference will that make?' she asked.

'Once it is done, I will no longer be in the employ of your family. Then, if you still want to know me, we will meet at properly chaperoned social gatherings, as other ladies and gentlemen do. We might be friends.'

'Or more than friends,' she said, then gasped again as if she'd realised that it was not her place to make such a claim upon him.

He smiled at her to assure her she had not been too forward. 'We will start fresh. This afternoon, after we have found the vase.'

'I would like that,' she said. He could not see her smile, but he was sure it must be there.

'I am glad to hear that, Miss Strickland,' he said, falling back on professionalism to hide the pleasure he felt at her response. 'But first we will find your vase.' He pulled a piece of paper from his pocket. 'I have compiled a list of likely dealers in ceramics and fine porcelain that might have purchased it from your grandmother. Were you able to get a more exact description from her?'

'I do not need her word for the vase. I know perfectly well what it looks like,' she said. 'And I can also assure you that it was not in any of the shops we have already visited.'

'Do not worry. I have no intention of wasting your time with those places, Miss Strickland,' he said, turning to the second page of the list.

'In fact, I do not see why you cannot just grab the first vase we see, as long as it is about three feet tall and of a Chinese design,' she added.

'But that would be dishonest,' he reminded her, trying not to smile at her eagerness to be done. 'And you told me on the first day that such a casual approach would be insufficient.'

'That is true,' she said with a disappointed sigh.

'Do not worry, Miss Strickland,' he said, forcing his smile. 'I will take you to every last shop in London, or to China itself, if necessary. But we will return the correct vase to the correct place in the correct house.'

Once they arrived at the first stop, they fell back into the familiar pattern of their searches. Gregory made polite conversation with the shopkeeper while Hope examined the displays, searching for the vase. When she found nothing, she touched his arm, shook her head and they went back to the carriage.

They tried again. And again. In their past excursions it had taken no more than a few stops to find the missing item. But today, they progressed down the extensive list that Gregory had made, with no luck at all. After the progress they had made towards a truce, he did not want to see the afternoon spoiled by simple bad luck.

'I hope you do not think I am leading you in circles. I swear to you, I thought we would find something by now.'

'I am sure you are doing your best,' she assured him. 'Perhaps we will find it at the next shop.'

When they stopped again, he held his breath and uttered a silent prayer, for there was a huge Chinese vase sitting in a corner of the shop. She went to it immediately, running her hands over it with familiarity.

Gregory went to stand behind her, looking over

her shoulder. 'Is this it?' He could not keep the excitement from his voice, but she was too preoccupied to notice.

'The colour is right. The one I remember had the same pattern of flowers running up the side and the red dragon twining in and out of them.' She pointed down at the base. 'And I have tripped more than once over the cast-iron stand.'

She ran her fingers over the rim and shook her head. 'This is smooth,' she said. 'There should be cracks.'

'We are looking for a cracked vase?' He did his best to contain himself, but she turned and caught him stifling a laugh.

'And I suppose you are about to suggest that we break this one.' Her response was frustrated, but not angry, as if the humour of the situation was not lost on her.

'I will do so if it makes you laugh again,' he said softly. 'But I promised you we would find the right vase and I always keep my promises. Come. There are other places we can search.'

They visited three more shops and he found it harder to smile with each failure. If he wanted to assure her of his ability to care for her, he did not want to appear to be a failure. 'I am beginning to wonder if you are trying to destroy my perfect record,' he said, trying to make light of it.

'I have told you from the first that I did not believe you could not solve every problem,' she said.

She was speaking of the diamonds again, but since

last he'd seen her something had changed. It was as if she was resigned to their loss. He gave her an encouraging smile. 'Sometimes, there are solutions you have not even imagined yet.'

'If you are suggesting that I run away with you and avoid the issue, you needn't bother. No matter what happens, I will not leave my family when they need me most.'

Her declaration caught him off guard. She had been as eager to start again as he was. But then, it had been as if he'd walked towards an open gate, only to have if it swing shut in his face. As usual, the Stricklands were on one side and he was on the other. Neither a night of passion nor a proper daytime courtship was likely to change that. 'Of course not,' he said, still numb.

The coach was stopping at the last shop on his list and it was almost a relief. If he was to fail, let it be soon. Then he would give her his other piece of news and see if it was more disappointing to her or less. 'I do not really expect to find anything here,' he said with a shrug. 'We have not visited it before because I did not think there was a chance of finding anything of value. But I will not give up until I am sure all hope is gone.' And he was closer to that than he had ever expected to be.

Despite the cold in the February air, the shop's front door was propped open and smoke billowed out into the street. Once their eyes had adjusted to the dim light inside, they could see that the majority of it came from a tiny fireplace in the corner and the few smouldering lumps in the grate that were barely worthy of the name coal. The rest came from a long pipe the proprietor puffed, filled with the foulest tobacco in London.

'Hello, Tibbett,' Gregory said, holding a handkerchief to his nose, attempting to block the smell.

'Drake!' The man put down his pipe and the smoke wreathing his head cleared enough to reveal his jagged-toothed smile. 'What can I help you with today?'

'We're looking for a vase,' he said, smiling back. 'A posh one. Wide like a pot and so high.' He held out a hand.

'Don't have much call for that,' Mr Tibbett said, frowning and pointing. 'What I got is there, in the window.'

Gregory gestured to Hope to look for herself, though he had seen nothing close to the duplicate she had shown him earlier. But before she could reach the alcove that served as the display window, she stumbled over a heavy metal something that was being used as a stop to hold the front door open.

He was at her side to catch her before he'd even had time to think. That was how it had been on the first day and how it would always be. No matter what she said or did, today, tomorrow, or in the past, he loved her. He could not help but care.

She paid no attention to his touch, too focused on the thing at her feet to notice his help. She pulled free and crouched, hauling the doorstop away and letting the door swing shut with a bang behind her.

She swung her arm wide, nearly knocking off his hat as she held the thing aloft.

She struggled to carry it to the counter for the ornamental cast-iron stand must have weighed at least a stone. As Gregory watched in amazement, she set it in front of Mr Tibbett with a loud clunk. 'It is here. It must be for I have stubbed my toe on this so many times I would know it anywhere.' Apparently, she no longer needed his help. She pushed past Gregory, pulled up her veil and spoke directly to the proprietor. 'Sir, can you help us? There is a vase that belongs with this stand.' She held out her arms in an *O* shape to indicate the size. 'It is nearly waist-high and decorated with chrysanthemums and a dragon.'

'A big red snake, you mean,' he said.

'Rather like that,' she allowed. 'But I think, actually…'

'I have been meaning to throw the pieces away for ages. But the old lady what brung it promised she would return for it.'

'That is the one, I'm sure.'

'Pieces?' Gregory repeated, alarmed.

'I never would have taken a thing in that condition. But she insisted…'

'My grandmother can be most persuasive,' she agreed. 'And just as she promised, we have come to collect it and to pay you whatever was promised.'

'What condition were we speaking of, precisely?' he interrupted.

Since what he thought was obviously unimportant to her, she ignored Gregory's question, as did

Mr Tibbett. 'It's in the back room,' he said, gesturing them further into the shop. When Gregory stopped on the other side of the curtain that separated storage from shop he called, 'No, further than that. You'd best light a candle. I do not waste the money on them, since there is nothing of value there.'

'The thing we have spent all day searching for has no value,' Gregory repeated to her as Hope pushed past him again, reaching for a taper and going back to the stove to light it.

She walked past him yet again, light held aloft, trying to see to the backs of the dusty shelves. 'There it is,' she said at last, pointing towards the corner, at the pile of broken china.

'It was in one piece when it arrived,' Tibbett said a little defensively. 'But when I tried to move it…'

She waved his protestations away. 'Do not concern yourself, sir. It was broken long before it ever came to you. It was in the hall that we used for footraces when we were little girls. Someone bumped into it at least once a year.' She looked embarrassed. 'But I was the one who finally knocked it off the base. I glued it back together and crossed my fingers. Grandfather caught me at it, of course. But his punishment could not change what had happened.'

'I was told no such thing when I took it,' Tibbett said, his eyes narrowing. 'I'll still be wanting the original price for it,' he said.

'And I have no intention of wasting my client's money on something you were too lazy to chuck in the bin,' Drake replied with an equally steely gaze.

'Pay the gentleman, Mr Drake,' Hope said, stooping down to gather up the pieces of the last Comstock heirloom. 'I will put it back together again when we get back to the town house.'

'Forgive me for asking, Hope. But are you mad?'

Apparently, the answer was yes. At the sight of her precious vase, she could not even be bothered to lecture him about his rudeness. She was on her knees, ready to scoop the broken pottery into her spread skirts.

He seized her wrist to stop her and pulled her to her feet. 'If you are intent on having it, let me do that. You will cut your hands.'

She gave him a militant look as if ready to remind him that it was not his place to dictate to her like a lover or husband. He glared back to tell her that she could just as easily have ordered him to do what he'd offered to do, since, apparently he was nothing more than a dustman for the peerage.

Then he turned back to Tibbett. 'I'll pay the original price if you throw in a trunk to carry the pieces.'

'The pot, a crate and a sack,' Tibbett countered.

'Done,' Gregory said with a sigh. 'And the use of your coal scuttle and a brush, to sweep up the pieces. He opened his purse and counted out the bills the man requested and recorded the amount spent in the little notebook. Once that was finished, Gregory turned back to the pile of broken pottery, stooped down and began piling the bits into a sack. Then, he carried it to the carriage.

Hope was already waiting for him inside it.

As they set off for the town house, he spoke. 'You are not seriously planning to leave that mess for the new Comstock.'

'I will try to put it together again,' she said and appeared puzzled that he would even ask. 'It belongs to his estate. My great-great-great-grandfather…' She paused, counting on her fingers and trying to remember generations. 'At least, I think it was that many greats. The Fifth Earl. He was involved in the silk trade with the Orient. This was a gift from a Chinese princess. It is almost priceless.'

'If by that you mean without value, I wholeheartedly agree,' he said. If they had seen another vase just like it, the stories she had been told were likely rubbish, just like the vase.

'You think an antique porcelain vase from China has no value?'

'That used to be a Chinese vase,' he said, pointing at the pile of shards in the box at their feet. 'Now it is nothing.'

'It is simply damaged,' she said, gathering her skirts to be clear of the grime on the box at her feet. 'When I was a child, I was not as careful as I might have been. Accidents happen.'

'I do not doubt it,' he said. 'But then we clean up after them and move on with our lives. Rational people do not turn London upside down to find the contents of the dustbin after the junk has been carted away.'

'A little paste, a little patience and it will be good as new,' she said, with a smile that was almost as fragile as the porcelain had been. 'At least, it will be as good as expected. It is centuries old.'

Centuries old. Just like her family was. And there was the problem. She could not seem to separate the things from the people. 'Can you put flowers into it?' he asked, folding his arms.

'Why would I do such a thing?'

'Because that was its intended purpose.'

'I seriously doubt that,' she said. 'It is far too large for a bouquet.'

'What is it for then?' he urged.

She stared at it for some time, trying to figure out what its purpose might have been. 'I think it might have been a cistern. Or a very large chamber pot. Or perhaps it was meant to hold an ornamental fish.'

'Well, it is useless for any of those things now. It will never hold water again. But I can find you any number of new pots just as good,' he said. 'The one we looked at several shops ago was nearly the same.'

'But it will not be ours,' she reminded him.

'It was not yours in the first place,' he reminded her. 'Nor was it your grandmother's, when she sold it. And the new Earl would not know it from a hundred other similar vases I have seen in shops all around London. He would likely be grateful to have it re-placed so that at least one thing in his home does what he expects it to do.'

'You cannot possibly understand,' she said. 'We are attempting to maintain the history of the family.'

'Of course not,' he said with a grimace. 'Since I have no family to claim me, I am forced to live in a nice house with modern conveniences and undamaged goods. In turn, your cousin has come all the way from Philadelphia to live in a house full of useless and broken items, kept for the sake of posterity. Do you not see the madness of this plan? If you cannot, I suspect Comstock will notice it when he arrives at the manor.'

'You have no idea what the new Earl will or will not think,' Hope said, growing more annoyed by the minute.

'Haven't I?' Gregory said, trying to be patient, so she might find the truth on her own. 'I am not the one who has been building Miles Strickland into some kind of saviour who will fix all the problems of the family with a wave of his hand.'

'No, you haven't. You tried to make him into a villain because you were jealous,' she reminded him.

'I did,' he agreed. 'Nor did I tell you that the other half of the task put to me by Leggett was to disabuse you of the notion that marrying him would solve all problems. He even gave me permission to lie to you, just the way I did.'

'So you blame my brother-in-law for your bad character?' she said, shocked. 'Did he tell you to seduce me as well?'

'I blame no one but myself,' Gregory said, his face hardening. 'I refused his suggestion and planned to reason with you instead. But at the ball, I was willing to throw away my principles for one moment of your attention. Today is proof enough that reason would have been pointless. I will never be able to change the mind of a woman who chooses to ignore what is right under her nose.' He pointed down to the box at her feet, wishing that she could see it as he did.

'I have no idea what you mean,' she said, honestly puzzled.

'Have you never wondered why, when it came time to rob the entail, your grandmother chose the things that she did?'

'Because she was selfish and did not think of the future difficulties it would cause,' Hope said, without thinking. And that was the problem. She did not dare think. She was afraid to.

'I have been to the manor with you,' he said, walking her through the steps to the truth. 'A single chair from the dining room would be worth more than all the things we have recovered. Can you not see what she has done?'

'She stole things that did not belong to her,' Hope said, stubbornly. But there was something in her eyes that flitted on the edges of awareness, crying to her that something was not right. He had but to get her to listen to it.

'She did not take a chair because to do so would devalue the set. Instead, she sold rubbish. Dented candlesticks. Paintings too ugly to hang. Broken vases.' He waved his hand. 'And that abomination in the box. Comstock was right. It is a wonder that we common folk do not rise up like the Americans did and wrest power away from the nobles, for no sane family would want to preserve such detritus, much less punish one who disposes of them.'

'You have spoken to my cousin,' she said, taking the wrong message from his last words.

'Because I wished to confirm that what I suspected was true,' he said. 'It was and he has my sympathies. The poor fellow has only just begun to realise the misfortune that has befallen him.'

'He is heir to an earldom,' she said, shaking her head against what she must know was the truth.

'And head of a family that cannot pay their bills,' Gregory said, making no effort to blunt his tone.

'If Grandmother had not taken the diamonds, he would not have reason to worry,' she snapped.

'If you search your heart, you will know that that cannot be true,' he said. 'One of the smaller stones in the tiara would have been enough to run the estate for a year. The lavalier would have been enough for a decade. If she had sold off the diamonds, why have you been scraping by with half a staff? Why has the Dowager resorted to pawning small things that no one would miss so there might be food on the table?'

She was shaking her head, as if she still did not want to believe. He could see the truth rising in her mind like a bubble in stagnant water.

Before she could speak, he did, so she did not have to say the truth aloud. 'There were no diamonds. There never have been. If ever they existed, they were sold off generations ago to support a decaying system that is finally about to fail. God help Miles Strickland, who has traded a perfectly good life in America for ruin and heartache with a family who refuses to admit to themselves or the rest of the world that they are poor.'

'Poor.' She said it very softly as if the word itself were the problem and by speaking it the situation would be made real.

'You have kept hope alive by thinking that it was temporary,' he said. 'That all problems would be solved when the heir arrived. That as long as he was happy with the three of you, he would set things right and you need never worry again. But what good will it do you to marry the Earl of Comstock if there is no money at all to unencumber?'

'We are poor,' Hope repeated, as if still trying to grasp the thought.

He nodded encouragement. 'I have the proof of it here.' He pulled a piece of paper from his pocket and handed it to her. 'My job was not finished until I kept my promise to you and settled the matter of the diamonds. You know I would not leave you without keeping my promise.'

'You have found them?' He could see the hope coming back into her face like rising colour.

It broke his heart to have to dash it again. 'I found an explanation for their absence. I know nearly as many jewellers in London as I do pawnshops. I made enquiries after we returned to London.'

'You gave away our secret to strangers,' she said, dazed.

He shrugged. 'The ones I deal with tend to have a certain flexibility of morality. I know far too much about them for them to speak of what they know of me.'

'Dealers in stolen goods,' she said.

'And those skilled at the duplication of entailed family jewellery,' he said. 'Many families come forward at some time or other with a need for paste copies to thwart highwaymen. My friends do not care whether the reasons they give are true or not.'

'It is not just Comstock?' she said, still stunned.

'Lord, no. Half the families in London are lying to the other half about how much money they have.'

He should not have told her this way, without any warning at all. Her eyes had grown round and her brow was furrowed in confusion. She looked like a child on an unmoored boat, watching the world she knew slipping away, with no idea how to save herself.

'But back to the matter of the diamonds,' he reminded her. 'When we returned to London, I set about tracing them. The shop I visited has been in business for generations and makes almost as much money for their forgeries as they do with real gems.' He tapped the letter again and pressed it into her hand. 'They also keep excellent records.'

She stared down at the paper in front of her. 'Someone requested stones exactly like the ones in the family jewels.'

'And you can see, from the date referenced that it was during the Civil War.'

'They have been gone since 1645,' she said, staring at the paper.

'Perhaps they hid the real stones from the government. Or perhaps from the rebels. Or they sold them to cover some age-old debt. I am sorry I cannot produce them for you.' He reached out to take her hand. 'But this should be sufficient documentation to prove to anyone who cares that the loss of them was an old family secret and not improper management by your grandparents.'

'I have been worrying about a problem that did not exist,' she said.

'You have done what you have done because of lies that have been told to you for your entire life,' he said, trying to keep the anger from his voice, lest she think it was directed at her. 'If you had told me the truth earlier, I could have saved you much pain. Now that you know it, you must see that you cannot bring back the past, as you remember it. It is gone.'

'But if there is no money, what is to become of us?' she said, still stunned.

'That is up to you,' he said. 'I have no title. But I have money and a house, and on my worst day I can provide a better future than Comstock ever will. Let me do that for you, Hope. Let me care for you. Let me love you.'

After all her talk earlier in the day about starting anew, now that the moment had come, she said nothing.

They had arrived at the town house and it seemed foolish to wait in the carriage once the servants had opened the door. He hopped out and helped her to the ground. But today, she seemed as broken as the

Chinese vase. As her feet touched the pavement she stumbled, unable to support herself.

And as he had before, he caught her before she could fall, putting a hand under her elbow to help her keep her feet. For a moment, things were as they had been, when she had trusted him with her life and her love.

But when she looked up at him, she still seemed as confused as she'd been in the carriage. There was no sign that she had heard the offer he'd made.

With his free hand, he signalled for a footman to take the box of broken china. He helped her into the house, not releasing her until he was sure she was able to stand on her own. 'Shall I call for a servant to bring you a restorative?' he asked. 'Tea, perhaps? Or brandy?'

'No. That will not be necessary,' she said. She was still deathly pale, but she raised her head in a fair imitation of the proud beauty he had met just a week ago.

'You do not have to worry,' he said. 'No matter what happens, you will not be alone.'

'Of course not,' she said, with a faltering smile. 'I have my family and they have me as well. I cannot abandon them when life is at its most difficult, you must see that, Mr Drake.'

'Of course,' he parroted back, fighting the desire to shout the truth back into her white face. Perhaps it was because he had no family, but he did not understand at all.

'I must speak to Grandmama about what you have

told me.' She was glancing absently about the room, as if the Dowager were nothing more than another misplaced item to be found and put in the correct spot. 'And Charity, of course. I do not know if there is anything we might do to ease the burden on our American cousin. But we must try, mustn't we?'

'Of course,' he said again. It should be some comfort that, if she held him to blame for the night at the manor, she had forgiven him as he'd hoped. But she had forgotten him as well. Though he'd offered her the new start she had wanted, only a few streets from where they stood, she could not imagine a life outside this house any more than she could imagine that a trip to China might be more interesting than playing with a vase in the manor hallway.

She had made her choice and it was not him.

Now, it was as it had been on the first day they'd searched. His job was complete and it was time for him to leave. Yet though she had just dismissed him, he was standing there like an idiot, waiting for some signal that he was still welcome. Did he honestly expect her to thank him for turning her life upside down?

So, just as he had on that day, he fell back into his expected role of consummate professional. 'And now, Miss Strickland, we have come to a parting of the ways. As Mr Leggett requested, all the items on your grandmother's list have been found and returned to the estate. I have encouraged you to think of a future that does not include a marriage to your cousin, but I am under no obligation to stand in the way of a match, should the two of you wish to make one. At least, with my research into the history of the Comstock diamonds, I have proved that it is not necessary to offer yourself as some sort of matrimonial sacrifice to appease his anger. Take him the letter and explain all. I am sure he will be as interested in the matter as you are.'

She gave him a hesitant nod.

He continued. 'Given certain things that have occurred between us, I understand that you may not wish to offer a favourable reference for my services. But do not concern yourself that any part of this incident will come back to you as gossip. I was hired for my discretion. No word of it shall ever pass my lips. And if you need them in the future, do not hesitate to call on me.'

The words spooled out of him, as they always did, like the final lines of an actor exiting the stage. With minor variations, it was the same speech he always gave when the job was finished and there was nothing left to do but collect his payment and move on. He delivered them with the same patent smile he had given her on the first day, the one he used on strangers.

This was the moment when his clients often thanked him. The words were almost as gratifying as the money. They would have been even more so today. He needed some small scrap of assurance that what had happened between them was something profound and not the dream it had begun to feel like. But Hope Strickland had mastered the art of ignoring the obvious long before he'd met her. Why should she admit to feelings that would prove inconvenient in the future?

He turned to go, then paused, his hand on the door handle, and turned back to her, unable to resist one more look, one last attempt to repair the damage he had done by falling in love with her. 'Do not believe what you have been told about the fragility of a lady's honour. Any man who deserves your love will not fault you for your past, should you decide to admit to one. You are an extraordinary woman, Miss Strickland. I wish you well.'

Then, he crossed the threshold, closed the door and was alone again.

Chapter Eighteen

Hope sat at the table in the kitchen with a pot of paste and small brush, surrounded by uneven shards of china. It was fortunate that the pieces were large. There did not seem to be any missing. Her makeshift repair would do until the vase could be properly restored.

Of course, if what Gregory said was true, there would never be a time when that could be done. A single failed crop or bad storm could impoverish the tenants and take the estate down with them. Her cousin would have far worse things to worry about than a broken pot.

Still, she could not help trying. That was what the Strickland sisters did, after all. They made the best of what was given to them. They did not give up when things looked hopeless. They soldiered on without cutting corners or breaking rules.

According to Charity that made her tedious and impossible to live with. Was that how she had seemed to Gregory? Perhaps if she had been more reasonable from the beginning he'd have courted her as other gentlemen did, dancing at balls and flirting politely.

And she'd have ignored him. For all she knew, they could have met months ago, if she'd had eyes for anyone but the man coming from America. If she had been honest about the diamonds, with him, or with Charity, she'd have learned the truth earlier and made different choices. She'd made things worse by assuming she could handle everything alone.

Had things been different, she might have accepted his offer. She was sure that was what he had been attempting to do in the carriage. She loved him, of course. But love was not all that mattered.

When she had gone to his room, she'd assumed that the financial problems the family faced would be solved with the appearance of the Earl. The loss of the diamonds would be embarrassing, but not critical. Comstock might be placated and allowances would be restored.

But the family problems were even worse than she had imagined. She could not simply walk away and abandon Charity and Grandmama to poverty. Nor did it seem right to leave Miles Strickland. Whatever he had been expecting when he had crossed the ocean to take his rightful place, it could not have been what he had got. She could not love him, for Hope doubted it was possible to love two men at once. And try as she might, she loved Gregory just as much as she had, that night in the manor. But she owed Mr Strickland some part of her affection, if only because of their shared heritage.

Grandmama had hinted that their American cousin wished to make an offer. He needed someone who knew the details of the estate and understood how to be a countess. She would be that for him, if he needed her to. As long as she kept her heart to herself and did not wear the Comstock diamonds, everything would be fine. Not happy, of course. But she must not let personal happiness stand in the way of the natural order of things.

From the corridor to the muddy back garden came the sound of singing and the happy clopping of the Dowager's pattens on the tile floor.

Hope set the brush aside and listened. She had not heard Grandmama singing since before Grandfather had died. As usual, the woman's mirth was ill timed, but Hope would not begrudge her a moment of it.

The Dowager swept into the room and dropped on to the fireside bench to remove her wooden overshoes. 'My dear Hope, why are you wasting time inside when the robins are singing in the trees and the air is as crisp as a summer apple?' But all movement stopped when she saw the broken vase. 'Good heavens. Whatever are you doing with that?'

'Trying to repair it,' Hope said. Just as she had been trying and failing to fix everything else about the family for the better part of the month. Even though no one had asked her to. Nor had they welcomed her help.

Nor was she appreciated today. 'Do not be silly, Hope. We no longer have to bother with such things.

It is Comstock's vase, now. Let him be the one to mend it.'

'It is not fair that he should be left to solve problems we created,' Hope said, automatically. Did she always sound so tiresome?

'Solving problems created by others is the stock and trade of the peerage,' her grandmother replied. 'If it is not the Crown, it is the tenants. If it is not the tenants, it is the family. It is always something, my dear.' She thought for a moment. 'The new Comstock will have to be rather like your Mr Drake.'

'He is not my Mr Drake,' Hope said hurriedly.

But the Dowager ignored her and continued. 'But I suspect Mr Drake is better paid and sleeps more soundly at night. You chose well.'

'I did not choose him,' she said glumly. Not even when he had given her a second chance to do so.

'Then you should be glad he chose you. If I had picked a different husband, I might have had a much easier life, but it would not have been as happy. I loved your grandfather quite fiercely and he loved me in return. The burden of being Comstock was easier because we shared it.'

'I thought you were happy.' Was nothing as she thought it had been?

Her grandmother touched the locket at her throat that held a tiny braid of her husband's hair. 'I was as happy as it was possible to be given the truth of our circumstances.'

'Gregory... I mean, Mr Drake says that we are

poor.' She'd said it in a whisper, for it seemed as if, spoken aloud, it would suddenly become true.

Her grandmother laughed. 'Poor as church mice, my dear. Albeit, mice that live in a cathedral and not some small country parish. The Comstock earldom has not had two coins to scratch together since your grandfather was a lad. It is why there was no settlement to provide for us, once he died. There was nothing left to give us.'

'Why did you not tell us?' Hope said, shaking her head.

'What could you have done, other than to marry well and escape? Faith has done so already. Soon, you will be gone as well. If I'd told either of you, you'd have thought it necessary to stay together for the good of the family.'

'And for Charity,' Hope reminded her.

'As she has been telling you for years, Charity can manage for herself,' the Dowager replied. 'It is time you listened to her. But you and Faith needed a push to leave the nest and I provided it.'

'You sold these things for us,' Hope said, touching the broken pot in front of her.

'I could not send you to Almack's in a borrowed gown,' the old woman said in a reasonable tone. 'I took the least of what we had to shops where no one would ever see it again. It was just barely enough to launch you all and keep meat on the table.'

Hope reached out and took her hand. 'We never knew.' Or perhaps she did know. She just hadn't understood.

Her grandmother's answering smile said that she had understood for both of them. 'Do not worry about the past. The new Earl has come now and I shall finally be free.'

'Free?' Hope whispered, confused.

'Free of the houses, the debts and the worry. Of trying to make something out of nothing, all the while pretending that we were happy for the honour. And free of the guilt over those ridiculous diamonds.'

'You should not have let me badger you over them. Why could you not tell me the truth of that, at least?'

'Tell you the biggest secret of the Comstocks?' She shook her head and laid a finger on her lips. 'Only the Earl and Countess know the truth and they pass it to the next generation. Of course, that means that each Countess must wear a paste tiara with a smile on her face and pretend that nothing is the matter. I wore select pieces on special occasions in the darkest of venues. But each time I did I was in agony that someone would guess the truth.'

'How will we ever tell Miles Strickland?' she asked.

'We do not have to. I already did. I blurted it out the minute we were alone together.' The Dowager fanned herself with a hand and sighed as a woman did when removing stays that had been laced tight for hours. 'He was very nice about it, all things considered. He arranged for a settlement for me and promised me the use of the dower house, if it can be repaired sufficiently to be habitable.'

'That was very kind of him,' Hope said.

'Too kind, I think.' She smiled sadly. 'He underestimates how much money will be needed to fix the place. It will be far less expensive if I take his allowance and live abroad.' If the old woman had been happy before, now she was overjoyed. 'I shall go to Paris, perhaps. Or Rome. For the first time in years, I shall see something other than a London Season. And no one shall require me to keep up appearances.'

Hope winced and looked down at her stinging hand. She still held a piece of the vase and a drop of blood was forming on the pad of her finger where she'd gripped it along the sharp edge.

Her grandmother reached out and took it from her, offering a handkerchief in its stead. 'You girls will do as you want, for you were never ones to listen. But you will be better off if you do not try to fix things that cannot be mended. Let it all go and you will be happier for it.' She held the piece of vase out over the tiles and released it.

Hope gasped again, as the perfectly mendable scrap shattered to slivers so small there would be no hope of putting them together again.

The Dowager wiped her hands together as if satisfied with a job well done. 'Sometimes it is not the clean break that saves us. Life is messy, Hope. Embrace it.'

'But what about Charity?' she said again.

The Dowager gave another shake of her head. 'I have never met a girl so capable of fending for herself.'

Everything had been done. There were no secrets

to hide from or reveal to Comstock. Grandmama did not need her help. In fact, she was so eager to leave her grown granddaughters to their own devices that she could not contain her excitement. And when it came to being ruled over and lectured by an older sister, Charity had made her opinion quite clear.

Hope was not wanted. She was not needed.

Not in this family, at least. There was still someone who had loved her, had needed her and still might have her if she could unbend enough to ask for his forgiveness. But to go to him, she would have to let go of the past.

Without another word, Hope grabbed a piece of the vase, closed her eyes, dashed it to the ground and listened to it shatter. Then, she fumbled on the table, found another piece and sent it after the first, savouring that crash as well. This time, she opened her eyes, reached out her arm and swept the remaining pieces to the floor. Perhaps she was still not brave enough to look at the disaster at her feet. But the sound echoed in her heart, like the clank of falling shackles.

Her grandmother was right. Freedom was sweet.

Chapter Nineteen

Now that she was decided, Hope did not bother with pattens or cloak and bonnet. She did not even bother to clean up the mess she'd made by throwing china on the floor. Instead, she shouted an apology to the maids in the kitchen and rushed out the door.

Once outside, she did not walk sedately, as a lady should when strolling through the streets of London. Instead, she lifted her skirts to an immodest but efficient level for running and tore down Harley Street, turned at the next corner and ran the three streets to the Wimpole Street address that Gregory had given her.

There she stopped to stare up at the house, momentarily afraid to go further. It was not proper to visit a gentleman unescorted. But if she considered the things she had done with Gregory, she was probably no longer a lady. Her desire to be bound by convention had kept her from doing things she actually wanted to do for too long. She could not waste another minute. She took a deep breath to settle her nerves and grabbed the knocker, letting it drop.

She was still out of breath from running when a butler answered, staring down at her with the sort of distant confusion that one got from servants confronting the unexpected.

In his moment of hesitation, she could not resist craning her neck to gaze past him at the hall. Everything within sight was new, clean and elegant, just as she had imagined a house owned by Gregory Drake would be.

It did not give off the sense of inherited wealth and power that Comstock Manor did. Nor was it cosy, as she remembered the vicarage being. But it did not smell musty and it did not leak and when things broke Gregory could afford to have them mended or replaced. That she could be mistress of a house was yet another revelation.

The butler cleared his throat. 'May I help you, miss?'

She smiled up at him. No. She beamed, for he was just one more example of the efficient household in her future. 'Is Mr Drake in?'

'I am sorry, miss. The master is currently away from town.'

For a moment, she had trouble comprehending the words. When they had parted this morning he had promised that he would be there if she needed him. And yet he was already gone. Had it been nothing more than the sort of empty courtesy that he offered in parting to all his clients?

If she had learned anything from the last week, it was that she must make an effort to understand others rather than demanding a perfection that even she was not capable of maintaining. He had promised he would be there for her. If he was not at home, there would be an explanation for whatever happened. She simply had to find him and ask.

'Where did he go?' she demanded, leaning to the side to peer around the servant, half-expecting that Gregory would appear out of nowhere as he always seemed to when she wanted him.

This time, the butler moved to block her view. 'I am not at liberty to say, miss.'

'Then when will he be back?'

'He did not say, miss. If you wish to leave a card, he will be informed of your visit when he returns.'

'No.' She backed away from the door. 'No, thank you. I will find him myself.'

The butler was looking at her as though she might run mad in the street. Since that was how she had arrived at the house, she should not be surprised.

'It is all right,' she assured him, still backing away. 'Perfectly all right.'

He closed the door slowly. She was sure, as she turned and hurried back down the street, that he watched her from the window. But was the butler the only one to do so? Gregory might be waiting behind a curtain as well, having informed his staff that, should Miss Strickland appear, he was not at home to her.

She could not believe that. He had promised if she

came to him he would not turn her away. He would not have said it if he had not meant it. But that left the question of where he might have gone in less than a day and how she might find him if he had given no one permission to tell her.

She smiled. To find Gregory Drake, she would have to think like Gregory Drake. If he wanted to find a person, he would search systematically using whatever clues he could find. Of course, he had a well-developed network of contacts all over London. She had not as much as a mutual friend to ask.

She knew his last employer. She could write to her sister and tell her to ask Mr Leggett to divulge anything he might know about the man he had hired. But that would take weeks, at a minimum. And since Gregory had completed the job for her family, he was likely to be working for someone else, already.

Of course, I offered my services…

And suddenly she knew.

The trip to the Clarendon was but a short ride through the city. But today, it seemed like the longest journey of Hope's life. She took the time to return to the town house and let Polly comb the tangles from her hair. She put on her best visiting gown, bonnet, coat and gloves. Beyond that, she took no more care than she would for any other visit. She had spent weeks preparing herself for the man she was about to meet. Now that the moment had arrived, it was not as much anticlimactic as totally unrelated to the things that truly mattered to her.

All the same, she was nervous. Once she arrived at the hotel, she gave her calling card to a porter and asked him to deliver it to her cousin with her wish to speak to him in the dining room. Then, she sat down to wait.

A short time later, a gentleman appeared in the doorway, scanning the room as if searching for her. If she had been expecting a family resemblance, she was disappointed. He was taller than her grandfather had been and thinner as well. His hair was dark. It seemed almost black against his skin which was unnaturally pale. His eyes were a not particularly vibrant green.

Her grandmother had called him handsome. While she did not disagree, his appearance left her strangely unmoved. Her head was too full of another man to appreciate him. Once he had recovered his health, her cousin would devastate the maidens of Almack's. She wished them luck.

But of one thing she was sure: he did not look as she expected an earl to look. There was some undefinable thing missing from him that she'd taken for granted in her grandfather and his peers. Was it arrogance? Pride? Or merely the confidence of a man who controlled the world around him for further than his eye could reach. Miles Strickland did not appear to be a master of his universe. He looked as though he was not sure where he belonged.

All the same, he intimidated her. Now that the opportunity had finally come to meet the heir, all her practising was for naught. She rose as he drew near, and dropped into a wobbly curtsy. 'My Lord Comstock.'

When she raised her eyes to smile at him, he looked thoroughly uncomfortable with both her deference and greeting. 'Please,' he said wincing. 'Sit down, Miss Strickland. We are family, are we not? Surely the formality of a title is not necessary.'

'As you wish, my lord.' She resumed her seat.

'And the honorific is not necessary, either,' he said, wincing again before sitting in the chair opposite her. 'I am not totally sure it is even appropriate yet. There must be some papers to be signed. They cannot just expect…' His voice trailed off, confused again. 'To call me Mr Strickland would be rather confusing. Would it be too inappropriate for you to call me Miles?'

Probably. But if it was what he wished she would accede. She smiled again, though she could still not manage the dazzler she had planned for him. 'If you wish, I shall call you Miles. And you must call me Hope.'

He nodded, relieved. 'Very well, Hope. It is good to meet you. If you have come to welcome me, I am surprised that you did not bring your sister with you. I looked forward to meeting both of you.'

'Actually, I had not planned to impose myself on you, until invited,' she said.

'I see,' he replied, disappointed. 'And what changed your mind on the subject?'

'My friend, Mr Gregory Drake, mentioned that he had seen you,' she said. 'I went to visit him today and found he has travelled from town without leaving notice of where he was going. I wondered if, perhaps, he might have mentioned his destination to you.'

And now he was surely wondering about the manners of English women and whether it was normal for them to ask impertinent questions of people they had just met. But, if she had shocked him, he hid it well. 'Yes, Mr Drake. We dined together the day before yesterday and again this afternoon.' He gave her an appraising look. 'He speaks most highly of you.'

'He does?' She had given him no reason to, but it was nice to know.

'Yes. Especially after a few glasses of brandy. When he left me today, he was somewhat the worse for drink and under the impression that I was likely to marry you. In fact, he strongly advised it. He says you are a capital choice and that it makes a great deal of sense for us to wed, for the sake of family solidarity.'

'Oh.' As usual, Gregory Drake was working very hard behind the scenes, like Cupid's own stage hand, to see to it that she got the things he thought she wanted.

'Your grandmother seemed to like the idea as well. When she met me in Bristol she took great pains to remind me that you and Miss Charity are not married and it is my responsibility, as head of the family, to see that you do so. But not just any man will do. Nearly everyone I have spoken to since I arrived seems to assume that it would be for the best if I stepped up and offered.'

'I see,' she said, even though she did not want to. Had it been just a few hours ago that she was prepared to accept? Now, she would have to find a polite way to refuse.

'You wouldn't happen to be in love with Mr Drake, would you?' Miles said with a sympathetic smile.

'Yes?' she said. Her voice quavered, making it sound almost like a question. 'Yes,' she said, more firmly, and smiled as her strength returned.

He sighed. 'That is good to know. Because, you see, while everyone thinks it is a good plan for us to wed, I can't say that I'm sold on the idea. You seem very nice, of course. And you are very pretty. But we do not know each other at all and what kind of a marriage would be made of that?'

'That is true,' she said, amazed at the flood of relief she felt to be rejected by the man she'd waited for for months.

'If you should happen to marry someone else before I've had a chance to court you, I would find that most convenient.'

'I am not sure he still wants to,' she said. 'He asked me, but I refused him.'

Miles sighed. 'What is wrong with the pair of you? You seem quite besotted with each other. Make sure he offers again. By week's end, if that would be possible. That damn Prince is after me to declare myself and I need a reason to say no.'

'The Regent,' she said, horrified.

'Solidarity of the state. Heirs. Something like

that,' Miles Strickland said, shaking his head. 'He wants to make sure I marry the right sort of girl and not an opera dancer or an American.' His lip curled in distaste. 'Back home, we do not have to worry about the government meddling in our personal affairs. James Madison does not know me from Adam's off ox and that is just the way I like it.'

'The Regent expects us to marry,' she said again, pointing between the two of them.

'But we are not going to,' he reminded her, smiling. 'You are going to marry Greg Drake, as soon as possible.'

'But I do not know where he is,' she said, helpless.

'Is that all?' The Earl let out a relieved puff of air. 'I sent him down to Berkshire. Or up. I am not sure where it is, exactly. But I have a house there.'

'To the manor,' she said, shocked.

'I had requested an audit of the entail. But though everyone in this country has been telling me what they expect of me since the day I arrived, no one actually listens to what I want. Except for Greg Drake, that is. He seems to be a dead useful fellow, able to write in a clear hand and smart enough to count the sheep, or whatever it is I have.'

'He is at the manor,' she repeated.

'I'm told it's not far. But I haven't seen it myself. Feel free to take my carriage. Apparently, I have several of them,' he said.

She was gone from the table before he could finish the sentence.

Chapter Twenty

Hope rode the whole way to Berkshire on the edge of the forward-facing seat, as if it was possible to arrive sooner just by wishing it so. She did not bother to look out the windows to chart their progress for it was nearing sunset when they'd set out and would be full dark by the time they arrived.

Nor had she bothered to pack, or even to stop at the town house to tell her grandmother where she was going. She suspected that, when she did not appear at dinner, the family would guess who she had run to. In any case, it was too late for them to object to the thing they had been encouraging her to do all along.

When the carriage arrived at the manor, she was out of it the moment it came to a full stop and hurrying into the house. The servants looked at her in alarm, embarrassed to be unprepared for her late visit and ready to find who or what she was searching for. She held a finger to her lips and shook her head. 'It is a surprise for Mr Drake.'

If it concerned them that she had arrived unchaperoned at bedtime to surprise a man who was supposed to be there as an agent of the Earl, they said nothing. But then, there must have been gossip after her last visit. They had to suspect by now that he was more than just another family employee.

To silence any doubts, she added, 'I was sent by the new Earl with a confidential message for him.' She tried not to smile, remembering what the message was. But the statement brought her the privacy she wanted for the staff would not dare risk intruding in case she had told them the truth. 'Do not bother to direct me. I will find him myself,' she added to send the last curious footman back to his business.

Of course, that left her with the task of locating him. She paused at the foot of the stairs to listen for the sounds of business on the main floor. She heard none, but that was hardly unusual. It was a large house with thick doors. She was used to the sound of silence echoing in the high-ceilinged halls. She also knew that there were forty rooms to search.

She smiled. It was not the first game of hide and seek she had played here, but it was certainly the most gratifying one. To catch him, she would have to think like Gregory, again. If she was completing an inventory, a systematic approach would be the best. Would he work from cellar to attic, or attic to cellar?

Neither, she decided. For while he might proceed in an orderly fashion in someone else's house, Gregory Drake was a romantic. There was only one place he would be, if he had just arrived.

She went to the first floor, walking down the hall to the bedrooms. It made sense that he would be given the same room he had occupied on the last visit. And it was even more likely that he would be overcome by memories once he entered it. That was where she would find him.

The door was open and she looked in to find him sitting on the edge of the bed, facing away from her, staring out the window. He had placed the candlesticks that belonged in the dining room on the side table next to the crystal inkwell from the study. Between them was a ledger with the beginning of a list detailing the contents of the room. The last item he'd recorded was an Aubusson rug, crimson with gold border, seventeen by eighteen feet.

'You might add that the weave is exceptionally good,' she said, glancing down at the tidy lines written without break or blot. 'One can walk on it and you will not hear a footstep.' She had proved the fact. By the time he turned to her, she was practically at his side.

He sprang to his feet and spun to face her, before regaining control and giving her the same polite smile he'd worn when they parted. 'Miss Strickland.' He bowed. 'I did not expect you.'

'I gave you no reason to,' she reminded him. 'When we parted this morning, I doubt you thought you'd ever see me again.'

'That will be at the discretion of Lord Comstock,' he said, the consummate professional he had been on the first day they'd met. 'Is there something I might assist you with?' The mask slipped and his brow furrowed. 'Do you need my help?'

She nodded. 'I went to your home to find you, but you were not there.'

'I did not think you would need me so soon,' he said, his frozen smile returning. 'As you can see, I took another position with your family.'

'And you have removed the candlesticks from the place I put them,' she said, running a finger down the length of one.

'I needed the light,' he said, then added, 'And they reminded me of you.'

'Cold and unbending?' she asked with a smile.

He shook his head. 'When we found them. The look on your face that day. I think that was the moment I fell in love with you.' He stared at her for a moment and she felt the heat of it touching her skin. 'Now will you tell me what brings you here? If it is some task left uncompleted, I will discuss it with you anywhere but in this room.'

'I broke the vase,' she said.

'That was long ago,' he reminded her. 'You know where to find a better one. Should you wish to buy it you do not need my help.'

'No. Today. This morning. On purpose. I threw the pieces on the floor and smashed them to bits. I suspect they are in the dustbin by now, for there was nothing left of them worth saving.'

'I told you so when we found them.' He sounded faintly annoyed. But there was something else there, too. Something encouraging.

'I have decided you are right,' she said. 'We can go back and buy the one we saw that had no cracks in it. No one will know the difference.'

'How will you keep the secret from Lord Comstock?' he asked.

'Very poorly, I suspect,' she said. 'If he asks me, I will admit I broke it and that there was nothing more that could be done.'

'That is surprisingly sensible of you,' he said, his eyes widening. 'And what do you mean to do about the matter of the diamonds?'

'He already knows,' she said. 'Grandmother told him immediately upon his arrival. She has decided to leave him to his fate.' Though it was probably not ladylike to gloat over someone else's misfortune, she could not seem to stop grinning. 'And though he seems very nice, I do not think there is anything I can do to help him.'

'You have spoken to him?' he said, embarrassed.

'To find you,' she reminded him. 'He said you told him he should marry me.'

'I thought it was what you wanted,' Gregory said.

'I know what I said. I want to know why you said it.'

He rubbed his forehead, feigning confusion. 'I am still feeling the effects of the brandy I drank after we parted. By the time I spoke to Comstock, I was in no condition to speak to a future employer. It was an act of mercy on his part to send me here. But I seem to recall informing him that you were hoping for a proposal.'

'I have been hoping for that for some time,' she said, giving him a significant look. 'A decent one that has nothing to do with honour or duty.'

Apparently, the hint was lost on him. 'By God, if you prefer the man, take him. But I will not say another word on the subject of marriage until I am sure you've had the offer you were expecting when we met. Accept him or refuse him, then notify me of the results so I might know if my heart will ever be my own again.'

She sat down on the bed. 'Do you think I would be here, if I'd accepted the offer of another man.'

'Where you are concerned, I have no idea what to think any more,' he said, sitting down on the bed beside her. 'Now tell me what I want to know. Did he offer, or not?'

'He does not wish to offer. I do not want to accept.' She smiled at him. 'I do not want to settle for a man as ordinary as an earl. I would much prefer a man who is truly exceptional.'

'You deserve nothing less,' he agreed. 'As I said before you are an exceptional woman. But what does any of that have to do with me?'

'I think you know,' she said.

'Please reassure me.'

'Comstock was relieved to find that I loved you. You are his employee now and I am to tell you that you must marry me within the week so that everyone will stop bothering him about me.'

The corners of Gregory's mouth twitched. 'I am, am I? And how much will he pay me to do it? For

I do not recall marrying you as being part of our original agreement.'

'You said before that you were too foxed to remember what was said,' she replied. 'But we all know that he has nothing to offer you. If you still want me, I am afraid you will have to take me without a dowry. I am poor, you know.'

'If I still want you?' The smile he gave her as he said it was the same one he had worn the last time they'd been alone in this room, as if she was the most wonderful thing he had ever seen. 'I have never stopped.'

Without another word, he slid from the bed and dropped to one knee. 'But if you will not have me, Hope Strickland, I don't know what I shall do, for I cannot manage to let you go.'

'Nor I you,' she said, smiling back and taking the hand he held out to her and kissing it.

With his free hand, he reached into his pocket and produced a ring, captured her hand and slipped it on to her finger. 'It is not as big as the Comstock diamond, but unlike them it is genuine.'

She spread her fingers, admiring it. 'It would not matter if it were real or not, as long as we can be honest about it. How long have you had it?'

'I found it in one of the shops I visited, when searching for your family jewels.' He shrugged. 'I had meant to offer it to you yesterday morning. But things did not go as planned.'

'Things are going much better now, I think,' she said, standing and pulling him to his feet.

'I agree.' He pulled her forward and wrapped his arms around her waist. 'So Comstock wishes us to wed within a week? That is very close to the amount of time your grandmother allowed me to secure your hand.'

'And when you promise to do a thing you never fail,' she reminded him. 'Since I do not want to spoil your perfect record, I think it best that we abide by their wishes.'

'It is too late to marry you tonight,' he said, with a yawn. 'And I have not completed nearly as much of the inventory as I had hoped to.'

'Then I will help you,' she said with a smile. 'We have already done the rug. I think, next, we must inventory the bed.'

Chapter Twenty-One

Charity Strickland sat comfortably in her favourite chair in the Comstock town-house library. The rest of the family insisted that it was more pleasant than the one in the manor. But that was precisely the problem she had with it. She liked her privacy and she could not seem to get any here.

She could hear footsteps coming down the hall and Hope paused in the open doorway. As she had since the morning after she'd seduced Mr Drake, she looked so radiant that the room seemed to grow brighter when she smiled. Charity set aside the journal she had been readying and gestured her to enter. 'Have you come to scold me about my plans to return to the manor again?'

'You know I have not,' Hope replied. 'Grandmama says that you are worried about the Earl's dog.'

'The poor thing is used to company,' Charity replied. 'And it is a very large house for such a small animal.'

'Your argument will be more convincing if you allow him in the library with you,' Hope replied. 'Be sure you have prepared a bed for him there by the time the Earl arrives.'

'As long as he does not chew on the books, he can have his choice of any chair in the room.' She gave Hope an encouraging smile. 'But never mind that. You have come to tell me about your impending marriage to Mr Drake.'

Hope laughed. 'Why is it impossible to surprise you?'

'Because as I have told you before, you are easier to read than these journals. Our ancestors had atrocious penmanship. Now tell me about the wedding, and I promise I will not try to guess the details.'

'We are eloping,' Hope whispered, taking both her hands and squeezing them. 'Running away to Scotland this very afternoon. Of course, it is not exactly a proper elopement, since we have Grandmama's blessing and the Earl's as well.'

'Only you would try to find a way to elope properly,' Charity said with a shake of her head.

'But it is possible that Faith and her husband might object.' She sounded almost hopeful of the idea. 'I do not know what Mr Leggett will think when the man he hired to help us runs off with me.'

In Charity's opinion, if James Leggett had a problem with this, then he should have had better sense than to send the perfect man for Hope. 'I do not think it is any of their business who you marry, as long as you are happy.'

'It will be even less so if we are properly married by the time they return,' Hope said with an evil grin.

'You are displaying an impressive level of rebellion, Hope Strickland,' Charity said. 'I applaud Mr Drake's corruption of your high standards and hope that it continues after your marriage.'

Hope bent to kiss her on the cheek. 'Even if it does not, I will not have as much time to bother you about your future as I did. If Grandmama intends to travel, it will be up to the Earl to find you a husband.'

'Or I shall have to find one for myself,' Charity said.

'And for that you insist you shall need money.' Hope pulled a paper from the pocket of her gown and handed it to her. 'And that is why I am giving you a wedding gift, in advance.'

Charity unfolded the paper, and read the letter from the jeweller, describing the purchase of the paste stones. 'How very interesting. Wherever did you get it?'

'I asked Gregory to search for the jewels and he found the information in just one day.' Hope was beaming again. 'Isn't he amazing?'

'Indeed,' Charity agreed.

'And the most fascinating thing is he can find no evidence that the stones were sold. They must still be in the house somewhere.'

'What wonderful news!' Charity said. 'The next Countess will not have to parade around in paste if the Earl can find them and replace them in their settings.'

'I have an even better idea,' Hope said, then went to check the hall lest they be overheard. When she saw no one, she returned to Charity's side and whispered, 'You must go back to the manor and hunt for them yourself. You know the house better than any of us. Find the stones and keep one or two of the smaller ones for yourself, just as you joked of doing before. Use them for a dowry, or travel as Grandmama is going to do. There will be little hope for you if you remain in the country. And I know you do not want to live with your sisters.'

'Keep stones for myself? That is a positively wicked idea, Hope. Those stones belong to the entail and I would never think of doing such a thing. I am going to pretend that you never said it.'

'Suit yourself,' Hope said, raising her arms in surrender. 'But I have learned from experience that there is such a thing as being too moral.'

'It's about time,' Charity muttered, then smiled at her sister to prove that there were no hard feelings.

Hope smiled back and for the first time in ages she did not seem the least bit upset that she did not obey.

'Enjoy your elopement,' Charity said. 'And everything that comes after.'

Hope's eyes went wide. 'When we return, I shall go to the manor and tell you all about it.' She giggled. 'Scotland, that is.'

'Or you can write to me,' Charity said, glancing towards the door. 'I hope that Mr Drake means to take you on a honeymoon of some sort. Do not delay it for my sake.'

'I am sure Gregory would not mind,' Hope said. But from the faraway look in her eye, the offer to return had been nothing more than courtesy.

'Do not let me keep you,' Charity said, making shooing motions towards the door. 'It is a long way to Gretna Green.'

Once Hope was finally gone, Charity sat down with a sigh of relief and rang for tea. It was good to see both sisters properly settled and to be left alone to bask in the glow of her grandmother's loving neglect.

Some girls might have been bothered by the lack of attention. But as the youngest of three, Charity had been waiting a lifetime for it.

She glanced down at the letter Hope had brought her, still on the table next to the sofa. It was kind of Mr Drake to have gone searching on his own and very clever of him to have got this far without her help.

She had needed to give him so many clues to the winning of Hope that she had begun to worry he might be a touch slow. But then Hope had needed help as well. But his success in this and his eagerness to help boded well for her sister's future. Charity had wanted her second brother-in-law to be both smart and kind, just as Mr Leggett was.

Of course, she also wanted him out of the way. The longer his inventory could be prevented, the more time she would have to look for the stones. She'd spent months reading old journals, making pages upon pages of notes, measuring walls and comparing architect's notes with old floor plans. As soon as Hope was gone, she could pack up her books and return to the country so that her search could begin in earnest.

Though Hope had suggested she keep a diamond

or two, by Charity's calculations it would take four of them to catch a husband, but five if she wished to remain unmarried. It begged the question if the gowns and folderol that were deemed necessary to attract the masculine sex were an effective use of the money.

She smiled. It did not really matter as of yet. She need not make a decision until after she had her hands on the diamonds and had found a man worth marrying. But of one thing she was sure: she would not spend a minute of her life sitting on the edge of a dance floor waiting for the future to come to her. After all, the Lord helped those who helped themselves.

* * * * *

HOW NOT TO
MARRY AN EARL

To Caffeine, without whom this book could not have been written.

Don't ever leave me again.

Chapter One

It seemed as if Miles Strickland had been running for ages. First, it had been from Prudence in Philadelphia, to avoid the plans she had made for them. Then the Shawnee, during his brief idea to go West and seek his fortune.

He had run from the Iroquois on the way back.

He had been two steps from the altar and one step away from debtors' prison when the letter had arrived from England and convinced him that his luck had finally turned. His kin had been American far longer than that country had existed and in none of that time had they mentioned the noble family tree they had sprouted from. But now, the British branches had died, leaving him heir to lands and a title.

Visions of wealth and comfort filled his head as he boarded the ship to cross the Atlantic. And then, he'd spoiled it all by actually becoming the Earl of Comstock. Apparently, the English Stricklands were no better off than the Americans. His family's debts had been minuscule compared to the ones attached to his new title. And there was no hope in clearing them, since a lord was not supposed to work. Instead, he was expected to collect rent from tenants even poorer than he was and take a seat in a government he knew nothing about. His brother, Edward, had been lucky that the English navy had got to him first. If he'd lived, he would have been press-ganged into Parliament, as Miles had been.

He had no patriotic loyalty to the government he was expected to join and even less faith in this antiquated inheritance of power without money. There was to be no magical solution to his previous problems. Instead, everyone expected he would sort out the mess left to him by his distant relatives.

Worse yet, there had been a stack of tear-stained letters from Prudence that had beaten him across the Atlantic on a faster ship. The situation was dire. He was her last and only hope. He must return home to Philadelphia immediately.

But would he be allowed to do so? He did not think that the Prince who was currently running things would drag him back to the House of Lords in leg irons. But after what had happened to Ed, he could not be sure. His brother had gone to Barbados in an attempt to turn the family fortunes by investing in sugar. The next any of them had heard, he'd been impressed into the British navy. In his last letter home, he had begged Miles to watch over Prudence until he could return to her.

Shortly after that Pru had got the news that she was an impoverished widow. And now, the moment Miles was not there to watch her, she had made things worse. She was an exceptionally foolish girl and probably deserved what she got. But she was his responsibility, more so than these English strangers were. She needed him. What could he do but run back to Philadelphia, as fast as he had run from it?

It did not seem likely that Miles could leave from any of the ports around London, without someone noticing. So, he'd left the city making a vague reference to visiting the Comstock property while omitting the rest of his plan, which was to keep going until the entire country was no more than a distant memory.

He'd set off at a gallop and the fine blood he was riding was eager to carry him at full speed. It was the best horse he'd ever sat, much less owned. He'd had no trouble buying it on credit, since earls did not bother using actual money.

He must find a way to return it to its previous owners. In England, peers who could not pay for the things they bought suffered nothing more than embarrassment. But in America, he'd have been hung as a horse thief. His guilt when he looked at the bill to Tattersall's was almost too much to stand.

What did bother him even more than the debts was having strangers scraping and bowing and calling him my Lord Comstock. He wanted to shout, 'You don't know me.' If they did, they would realise that they had made a mistake in thinking a common ancestry qualified him to do the job they had foisted upon him.

After half a day's journey, he passed the marker that indicated the edge of the Comstock holdings. There was no denying that the land he'd inherited was pretty, with rolling farmland and a village full of thatched-roof cottages. The view was spoiled when he paused to realise that he was responsible for keeping those roofs from leaking. But at least the tavern served a decent ale and did not enquire about his past, despite his accent. The last thing he needed was to be identified as their new lord and master before he could finish his drink.

After a light lunch he rode on towards the estate. But as he came around a turn in the gravel drive he saw two houses: the great house on the hill and a second house, large by normal standards, but dwarfed by the manor beyond it.

The smaller one must be the dower house that he'd been told of. It had been described as almost beyond repair, which meant it was unoccupied and unattended. If there was a couch, or at least a dry patch of floor to lay out his bedroll, he might stay there unnoticed. It would save him the trouble of making excuses to the servants at the great house about his sudden arrival and equally sudden departure.

And if there happened to be a set of silver left in a sideboard, he might still see some profit from this unfortunate trip. When pawned, a saddlebag full of second-best decorations would at least be enough to buy a ticket for home.

He dismounted, looped the reins over a nearby tree branch and approached the house. But before he'd got within ten feet of the door he heard a familiar angry bark and felt a fifteen-pound projectile strike his calf.

He stared down at the little black-and-white head, with the equally small fangs sunk ineffectually into his boot leather, and resisted the urge to kick.

Instead, he reached down, grabbed the dog by the scruff of the neck and tugged it free, then lifted it to eye level, glaring at it.

The dog returned the sort of look normally reserved for cats and creditors.

'I do not know what possessed me to rescue you at the docks, since this is all the thanks I've got for it. If this is how you treated your previous owner, I understand why he was trying to drown you.' It had been instinct that made him drop his luggage and grab for the burlap sack that the boy had been trying to fling off the gangplank of the *Mary Beth*, assuming that the child's father had told him, harshly but sensibly, that a sea voyage was no place for a dog. By the time he'd turned to assure the little attempted murderer his pup would be safe, the boy had vanished and Miles had been the owner of the most ungrateful cur in the New World.

'Grrr…' The animal made a snap at the empty air, trying to reach him. Miles had told himself for weeks that the dog's bad temper was caused by close confinement and the constant rocking of the ship. But he appeared to be no happier on the dry land of England than he had been in America.

'When I sent you on ahead with the Dowager, I hoped we might never see each other again. Have you managed to get yourself banished from the main house already?'

The dog squirmed in his hands, taking another snap

before wriggling free and jumping to the ground. Then, he turned towards the dower house and leapt through a broken window, still barking.

Miles sighed. 'I am not climbing in after you. There is a perfectly good door.' He walked to the front of the house, reaching into his pocket for the ring of keys, before noticing that it already stood open a crack.

'You can come out on your own,' he called. 'You have four good legs on you and no longer need my help.' He listened for a scrabbling of paws or any other sign that the dog had heard and meant to obey him. If he planned to stay here, it might be handy to have the little beast chasing down rodents for him. With the door left ajar, the place was probably crawling with them. But since the dog loathed him and tried to bite each chance it got, he was probably safer putting it outside and trying to befriend the rats.

As he stepped into the house, it surprised him that there was no sign of the dog, nor the sound of barking from deeper inside. Was there a chance that it had fallen through a weak floorboard, or injured itself on broken glass? He was a fool to care for a thing that wanted no part of him. But at least there was no one around to witness his softness. He advanced into the house. 'Where are you, you little bastard?' With luck, he could lead it back towards the open door without incurring any damage to boot or hand. Then, he could block the window and lock the door against it until it gave up harassing him and found its way back to wherever it was being kept.

Miles looked around him at the entryway to the

dower house. Except for the dog, the place would not be a bad one to hole up in, until he decided what to do with himself. The Dowager had spoken of repairs too expensive to render the place liveable. But she was a great lady, used to comfort and entertaining. To a man used to sleeping rough, it was near to a castle. It was damp, of course. But a fire would help that. And the furniture had been covered to protect it against time and the elements, which would likely enter through the leaks in the roof. He would not trust the mattresses to be dry, but in the rooms he passed on the way to the dog, there were no end of tables and chairs, and probably a few long benches and sofas that would make a decent bed if one was tired enough. It would do nicely, even if he couldn't find any silver worth selling.

A streak of black-and-white fur passed by the doorway ahead of him. There was another familiar bark as the dog came to the end of whatever course it had set for itself. Then a moment's pause before it pelted back across the opening in the opposite direction. The creature had played a similar game on the ship, running back and forth down the companionway, dodging curses and kicks from angry sailors and passengers before racing back into his cabin and falling into an exhausted heap at the end of his bunk.

It had been amusing the first time. Now it was just annoying. But before he could shout at it, someone else said, 'Pepper! Be still.'

He froze. Though it had the strength of a general, the voice was definitely female. Was it the empty house that gave it such an unusual tone? It seemed to echo, yet was strangely muffled. He approached the room in front of him with caution, not sure if it was better to confront her, or sneak away unnoticed.

When he passed the threshold, the explanation was obvious. The dog had halted his insane racing and was sitting on the hearth, sniffing at the pair of women's boots standing on the andirons. As he watched, one of them lifted as the woman wearing them stretched her body upwards, reaching for something in the chimney.

There was a shower of soot and a muffled 'Damnation.'

The dog retreated with a sneeze, waiting for the ash to settle. Then, as helpful as ever, he lurched forward and grabbed a mouthful of skirts, swinging on them to further unbalance their wearer.

Miles could not help it. He laughed.

Slowly, the boot lowered, seeking footing on the grate. 'Whoever you are, if you mean to harass me, I have a poker and am not afraid to use it on you.' If her arm held the same resolve that her tone did, any blow delivered would likely be strong enough to make him think twice.

'And I have a pistol,' he countered. 'But I don't think either of us need worry, because neither of us wishes to resort to violence. At least until we know each other better,' he added. In the past, there had been more than one woman ready to crown him with cast iron. As yet he had given this one no reason.

The dog skittered away as the boots hopped off the grate. After some shifting and more falling soot, the rest of the woman appeared in the opening of the fireplace. The rest of the girl, rather. Though she could not have been more than twenty, she was fully, and quite nicely, grown. Her bespectacled face was rather plain, though he doubted the smudges of ash on it helped her appearance. But one would have to be a fool to call a woman with such finely turned ankles homely.

She had nice calves, as well, even under the thick stockings she was wearing. He'd caught a glimpse of them as the dog had tugged at her skirts. And though the sensible gown she wore made no effort to flatter her figure, it could not manage to hide a slim waist and a fine bosom. He was not normally given to debauchery, probably because he had never been able to afford it. But if the village girls in Comstock were all as comely as this one, it might be tempting to play lord of the manor.

As if the dog could sense what he was thinking, its hackles rose and it faced off between him and the girl, baring teeth and offering a warning growl.

Miles braced himself for impact.

'Pepper. Sit.'

As if by miracle, the dog responded to her command and dropped to its tiny haunches, still staring at him.

'If you try anything, I will set my dog on you,' she said, giving him a look as fierce as the terrier's.

'Your dog?' he said, surprised.

She hesitated. 'The Earl's dog, then. But since he is not here and I am a member of his family, Pepper's responsibility and affection have transferred to me.'

He opened his mouth, ready to argue that the owner of the ungrateful cur was right in front of her, should the animal choose to acknowledge him. But since Pepper was incapable of loyalty, obedience, or any other canine virtue, it refused to claim him.

Then he remembered that if his goal had been to slip on to the Comstock property and off again, unnoticed, he should not announce himself to the first person he saw, especially if he had been fortunate enough to meet a family member who did not immediately recognise him.

She was staring at him with narrowed eyes. 'And now that I can look at you, it is apparent that you are not the common tramp I was fearing.' She tipped her head. 'By your accent, you are American. I'd think you were a member of the Earl's party, but I was told he travelled alone.'

'We came on separate ships,' he said, falling easily into the first lie that came to mind. 'I was to arrive first, but the seas were rough.'

'You are the auditor, then,' she said. There was no triumph in her voice, just a flat acknowledgement of the assumed fact.

He nodded, relieved to have his work done for him. But the auditor from America needed a name. 'Potts,' he said, automatically. He must look like the name suited him, for Greg Drake had mistaken him for just such a fellow when they'd met. 'Augustus Potts, at your service, ma'am.' He bowed to hide his wince at the Christian name that had popped into his head. Hopefully, the lie would not be needed for long. Who in their right mind would want to spend any length of time as Augie Potts?

'Mr Potts,' the girl replied, in the tone of one used to ordering servants about.

'And who do I have the honour of addressing?' he said, already suspecting that he knew the truth.

'Miss Charity Strickland. Your employer's distant cousin.'

He nodded in acknowledgement. He'd met her sister Hope, already. With some effort, he could see a resemblance. They shared the same wide brow and pointed chin.

But where Hope was uncommonly pretty, Charity was not currently so blessed. There was something too grave in her expression and the look in her eye was too discerning for one so young. Though she was not a lovely girl, he suspected she would age into her beauty and become a rather handsome woman.

'Were you sent to inventory the main house?' she said, in a matter-of-fact way to remind him that it was not his job to be standing here, staring at her.

'And the dower house, as well,' he said.

'There is nothing of value here.'

In a pig's eye. Her response had been a trifle too quick and too specific for his taste. She had come here to retrieve something or to hide it. And people did not normally take the time to hide things that were worthless. 'If the house is empty, it makes me wonder what you were doing here, halfway up the chimney.' He gave her a subservient smile. 'Is there something I can assist you with?'

'Birds have been coming down it and into the house. I was attempting to close the flue.'

'I see.' That was an even bigger lie than her last words had been. But if he was claiming to be Augie Potts, he could hardly point fingers. Instead, he stripped off his coat and rolled up his sleeves. 'Give me the poker, then. My arms are longer.'

'That is all right,' she said hurriedly.

She was far too eager to handle the matter herself. 'Then, at least let me go up to the house and find a footman. A member of the family should not be doing servants' work.'

'That will not be necessary,' she said, not bothering to try to charm him with a smile. 'I think I have managed the matter well enough.'

He raised an eyebrow. 'I did not interrupt you before you could complete what you were attempting?'

Her lips tightened ever so slightly with annoyance. 'Certainly not.'

'Then, allow me to give you a ride back to the main house.'

'That will not be necessary, either,' she snapped.

'But we are both going the same way,' he reminded her. 'Since I have never been to the manor, I would appreciate a guide.'

'It is not possible to get lost,' she said. 'The house is barely a mile away and you are on the drive already.'

She was trying to get rid of him. He had no reason to care why, for he was as eager to be gone as she was to have him so. Yet for some reason, he could not resist annoying her. 'That is likely true. But it would be helpful if you could introduce me to the rest of the staff.' He glanced out the window. 'And a storm seems to be gathering. It has grown darker as we have been talking. I would not want to leave you here in the rain.'

'I can wait inside until it passes,' she countered.

So she had not finished what she had come to do. Since there was nothing in her hands, it seemed likely that she was searching for something rather than secreting something she'd brought with her. In either case, there must be some hidey-hole in the bricks worth investigating, once he had got her safely out of the way.

He smiled at her. 'I am sure the Earl would have my head if I left you here in the rain.' Then he stepped to the room's doorway and waited for her exasperated huff of defeat.

It did not come. Other than a slight narrowing of her eyes, she gave no sign that his attempts to thwart her were annoying her. 'If the Earl wishes it, then very well, Mr Potts. I would never go against his wishes.'

Then she walked past him towards the front door, the terrier following obediently at her heels.

Chapter Two

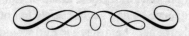

Charity Strickland's day was not going to plan.

It had been bad enough to climb into the chimney and realise the niche she was looking for was just out of reach. To be discovered doing so had been even worse. Mr Potts was proving to be annoyingly clever, giving no indication that he believed her story about an open flue. He had pretended to, of course. But she suspected he was only toying with her, hoping to worm some piece of information out of her that could be reported to his master.

So far, it appeared that the new Earl meant to do just as she hoped he would, remain in London to perform his duties in Parliament. Should he suddenly decide to take an interest in her welfare, there was no telling what he might consider suitable for her future.

Whatever it was, she doubted it had anything to do with what she preferred for herself. As the youngest of three sisters, she was fed up with being dictated to by people who assumed they knew what was best for her. It had taken months to get the rest of the family out of the way so she might have peace to work. The last thing she needed was a stranger asserting his God-given right to control her because his fortunate birth had made him head of the family.

The season did not end until July and it was barely March. It would take only a few more weeks to accomplish her own plan. If the new Earl of Comstock kept to the business of governing, as he ought to do, she'd be gone long before he arrived, with enough money to set herself up for life in a manner that suited her.

But Mr Potts might prove to be just as annoying as the man who'd hired him. Though he had no right to order her around, so far he was proving to be a first-rate sneak. One had only to look at the dog's reaction to him to know that he was not to be trusted. Pepper's hackles had been raised from the moment that the auditor arrived. As they left the dower house, he was dancing along between them, biting at the man's boot heels as if hoping to scare him away.

To Mr Pott's credit, he had not given in to impulse and kicked at the dog. Perhaps he was not irredeemable. Or perhaps he had better sense than to abuse a pet belonging to a peer in full sight of a member of the family.

When they arrived at his horse, he stepped clear of the little black and white dog and mounted, offering a hand to her to help her into the saddle in front of him.

She smiled at him, wishing for not the first time that she'd inherited any of her sisters' natural charm.

'I could not possibly go without Pepper. I would not want him to become lost.'

Potts looked down at the little dog with obvious disgust. 'In my experience, animals like this are surprisingly hard to lose.'

'But what if this time is the exception? He might be set upon by some wild beast.'

'You have wolves roaming so close to the house?'

'No,' she admitted.

'And I am told there are no bears left in England. What else can there be?'

'A hawk. Or perhaps an eagle.'

He sighed. 'Next you will be telling me England has daylight owls.' He held out a hand. 'Give him to me.'

She scooped the dog up and offered him.

Potts took him by the scruff of the neck, nimbly dodging the snapping jaws and dropped him into the leather bag at the side of his saddle. The dog disappeared for a moment, like a swimmer beneath a wave. Then his head poked out from under the flap, offering something that looked rather like a canine grin.

'There.' Potts held out a hand. 'And now, you.'

Gingerly, she offered her own hand and he pulled her up. He seemed to exert no strength at all, settling her on to the saddle in front of him, to sit on one hip. Then his arms took the reins on either side of her waist, holding her in place as they set off.

Though he showed no signs of noticing it, it was a surprisingly intimate arrangement. Perhaps such behaviour was common in America. Or perhaps she was not pretty enough to move him. He handled the horse as easily as if he was riding alone.

But for her, it was strangely disquieting. Though she did not normally dwell on the appearances of the men around her, it was hard not to notice this one. The arms that wrapped around her were long, as were the legs that brushed against her skirts. He must be well over six feet. He was not precisely gaunt, but there was an angular quality about his frame that seemed to carry to his face. The planes of his cheeks were sharp, as was the line of his jaw. His pale skin might have given another man an aristocratic air, but on him it seemed more scholarly than aloof, as if his studies kept him from the sun.

This attracted her more than his fine features or the shock of dark hair shading his brow. He looked like someone who might be content to hole up in a library. Though the muscles she could feel in the limbs surrounding her did not come from inactivity, he looked like a kindred spirit.

But it did not really matter what he looked like, or how he had come to be so. Men, especially ones that looked the way this one did, never gave such scrutiny to her. She turned her head and looked resolutely forward at the house they were approaching.

'Comstock Manor,' he said, stating the obvious. But there was a tone beneath the words that sounded not so much impressed as stunned.

'You did not think it would be so large,' she said.

'I was told. But I could not believe it was true.'

'It represents everything that is wrong with the family,' she said. 'Something that started as a good idea but grew out of hand until it was no longer possible to manage or afford.'

'No wonder there has been trouble finding someone to record the contents. Who would want to take on such a job?'

'We have lost more valuables than most people own,' she said, speaking quite close to the truth. 'Though most of them are not actually gone. They are just sitting in one of the forty rooms, waiting to be rediscovered.'

She felt something quicken in him at the mention of this surplus of material wealth, a faint, covetous quivering of his nerves. Then he relaxed again, as if afraid that she might have noticed his interest. 'As a member of the family, I would think that you would be in a position to know where some of those things are.'

'I might be,' she said, turning back to blink at him in what she hoped was an innocent way. 'The Earl will never be able to have an accurate accounting of them if I do not help. And I doubt you will be able to learn the lay of the place in whatever time he has allotted for the job.'

The horse pulled up short.

'How would I...? I mean, you are right that there is no way for me to do this job without help. But the Earl would not know one way or the other, if I got it wrong, would he?'

He had not even crossed the threshold and he was already giving up. Or did he mean to collect full pay for a slapdash job? His reasons did not matter. Carelessness, laziness or moral flexibility would all suit equally well as a reason for his departure.

'He will not know if the inventory is not complete unless we tell him,' she said, choosing her words carefully. 'But I have no intention of spreading tales to a man I never met, just because other men I have never met decided he is the heir.'

'I see,' he said, in an equally careful tone.

'I am sure he is depending on your friendship for an accurate accounting,' she added.

'My friendship.' Mr Potts laughed. 'I can tell you in all truth that six months ago, I knew nothing of Comstock, his title or his property.'

This was even more interesting. If the Earl had hired a stranger to see to his interests abroad, he was likely to get the results he deserved. 'The property is not technically his,' she reminded him. 'It belongs to the Crown.' She smiled again. 'But, as an American, you have no real loyalty there, do you?' She had opened the door to conspiracy. Now they would see if Mr Potts walked through it.

'Loyalty?' He laughed again. 'The whole point of my country was to escape this one. And yet, here I am, surrounded by riches that do not belong to the Earl and debts that do.'

'That is a pity,' she said with a shake of her head. 'In my opinion, the task set for you is a hopeless one. If you chose to resign from it, you could be long gone from here before anyone noticed your absence.'

Behind her, he started in surprise. 'Miss Strickland, I was thinking just such a thing when you arrived.' His eyes narrowed. 'But then, I would not be paid, would I? And an urgent need for funds was the only reason I even considered the job.'

Then she made the most daring move at all. 'The house is not lacking for ornaments. If you chose to take something to compensate for your lost time, who would know?'

There was a long pause as he considered her words. But just as she was sure he would succumb, he baulked. 'Stealing from the Earl would be wrong. Both a breach of the Commandments and the law.'

'Of course,' she added hurriedly, annoyed. If morality was seriously a concern, she might never get rid of the man. The next temptation would have to be far more subtle. 'But there is no need for us to be discussing such things in the middle of the drive. As you said before, a storm is approaching. Come into the house and we will get you settled.'

And then she could go to work on him. Once he had seen the house and his place in it, he might be gone by morning.

When his ancestral home had been described to him, Miles had got a vague impression of a large but dilapidated manor in the country. But there was no way he could have imagined the thing that stood before him now. It appeared to be two or three large houses built cheek by jowl, as if the owners could not quite decide what they'd wanted and simply kept building on to it until the money had run out.

Having seen the accounts, that seemed to be exactly

what had happened. When he'd set out from America, he'd assumed that all English lords had to be rich. But his family had run through their money generations ago. The rents from the tenants barely kept pace with the cost of maintaining the property. All that was left beyond them was the house and its contents. And the most valuable items were things he was not supposed to sell. He was expected to hold them in trust for future generations that might never be born if he could not manage to settle his business now.

But the caution to respect the entail had not impressed his ancestors. After greeting him on his arrival, the widow of his predecessor had barely taken a breath before announcing that the diamonds in the Comstock family jewels had been replaced with paste long before she became Countess. The Earls and Countesses of Comstock had been telling lies about their value for so long that it might as well be declared a family tradition.

On hearing this, he had assumed that there was nothing left of value. But though the collection of silver-framed miniatures on the hall table was not enough to save an earl from a life of ruin, the humble Miles Strickland could sell a sack full of them and have enough to live modestly for a good long time.

'What do you think of it?' He had almost forgotten Cousin Charity, who had led him in through the front doors and introduced him to the butler, Chilson, who had signalled for a footman to take his valise and another to remove the snapping dog from the saddle bag.

'I do not know where to begin,' he said, peering

down the hall at what seemed to be an endless line of doorways, then staring back at Charity.

'Do not worry. I will help you.' There was no flirtation in the smile she gave him, only a sly twinkle in her eye that made him think any aid he received would benefit her more than him. Her companionable self-interest was an improvement on recent interactions with the fair sex.

When they realised he had a title, the women of London were friendly to the point of predation. He could hardly blame them for it, since they took their cues from the mamas and papas who were practically throwing their daughters into his path. Even the damned Prince who was currently running the country said that an earl without a countess was not doing his duty. He was supposed to marry, soon and well, for the sake of the title's succession.

Apparently, he was to be bred like livestock. If the activity hadn't involved marriage, he would have been all for it. But since a legitimate child was required, it took much of the fun out of his newfound popularity.

Since this distant cousin didn't know who he was, she was currently treating him with the same indifference as women had before his sudden elevation. But since Charity was also the last unmarried girl in the family, the condition was likely temporary. Once she guessed his identity, she would chase him like a hound after a coon.

'Thank you for the offer of aid,' he replied. 'And I assume this help will be in exchange for everything I can tell you about the new Earl?'

'I think I know all I need to on that front,' she said, with a frown that surprised him. It looked almost like a grimace of distaste.

'Has he done something to put you off?' Miles said.

'He has done nothing so far,' she said. 'That suits me well, but I doubt it will continue. And the last thing I need is for him to arrive on my doorstep with a proposal.'

'Your doorstep?' He glanced around him.

'Metaphorically speaking,' she replied. 'It is technically his house. I plan to be out of it before he arrives. But I am not quite ready to go yet, hence my hope that he will stay in London until Parliament ends its session.'

'And you do not want to marry him,' Miles said, strangely annoyed.

She shrugged. 'It is not logical to expect instant compatibility, based on the convenience of a family connection. It is not as if I believe in something so foolish as the need for romantic love when marrying. But I do not want to rope myself to him or any other man for a lifetime without bothering to learn if we are temperamentally similar.' She glanced down her nose at him, in frank and unladylike appraisal. 'So far, I have not found many available men to my taste. I have exceptionally high standards, Mr Potts.'

He stared back at her, just as rudely, ready to say that plain girls were not usually so particular. Then he remembered her fine ankles and bit his tongue. 'And so you should, Miss Strickland. If you meet him, you will find that the new Earl is not a bad fellow.' Not totally bad, at least. 'But you are right not to expect a marriage from him, sight unseen.'

She smiled at him in earnest now. The brightness of it transformed her face into something that was not beautiful, but held a certain allure that her frowns did not. 'You are the first person to say that to me, Mr Potts. It is quite a novelty to hear such frankness.'

'There is no reason for me to be anything else,' he said, ignoring a stab of guilt. He had not been in any way frank. Worse yet, he had been talking about himself in the third person.

He cleared his throat. 'And now, where would you recommend I begin my search—that is, my inventory?'

'I suggest you begin by settling into your room and washing for dinner,' she said with another shrug and an innocent blink. 'If the accounting of Comstock's possessions has waited for years, there is no reason to begin them this minute. You will find the job less daunting after a good night's sleep and a decent meal.' She walked up the stairs in front of him, casting a look over her shoulder to see if he followed. 'Well?'

He paused. In any other woman, he might have thought it flirtatious, should she lead him straight to his bedchamber. But even on such a brief acquaintance, it was clear that Miss Charity did not flirt.

She likely did not know any better. He started up the stairs after her. 'Surely it is not necessary for you to show me to my room.'

'I shall be showing you a lot more than that before we are done with each other,' she said.

He started in surprise.

Now her look was faintly exasperated. 'You want to know the house, don't you?'

'Well…' He did, of course. But was she really so unaware of him that her words held no hidden meanings at all?

'Then you might as well enjoy the best of it.' At the top of the stairs she marched briskly to the far end of one hall, waving at the corridor behind her. 'The family stays in that wing. Grandmama is at the end, as is the Earl's suite. The corridor to our right leads to the old part of the house. This side is for guests.' She had reached a door at the very end. 'And this is the Tudor room.' She threw open the door and stood in front of it, gesturing inside. 'It is said that Henry Tudor himself stayed here.'

He racked his brain for a moment, to attach significance to the name. 'The King with all the wives.'

'Six,' she said with a deadpan look that announced her opinion of his limited knowledge of local history.

He held up his hands in surrender. 'I can tell you everything you might wish to know about George Washington, if that makes a difference.'

'I can tell you about him, as well,' she said, arching an eyebrow. 'There are books in England, you see.'

'In America, as well.' Damn few of them in his past, of course. But that was no fault of his. He looked ahead at the room in front of him. 'So a king stayed here.'

'And now, you shall.'

He supposed he should be honoured. He rarely cared about the previous occupants of the room, as long as the bed was soft and the sheets were clean. This would be luxurious, though not quite as good as the master suite he was entitled to. But he could hardly ask for that. Then he stopped to wonder. 'Why would you give an auditor the best room in the house?'

By the time he'd turned to hear her response, her face was pleasant, passive and hospitable. But before that, had he seen a flash of something else? Alarm, perhaps?

If so, it was gone and she appeared to be the perfect hostess. 'I want you to be happy. You are the Earl's friend, after all. I can hardly treat you like staff.'

He glanced into the room, filled with any number of items worth taking when he went on his way. 'How very kind of you, Miss Strickland.'

She gave a concluding nod. 'Now, I will leave you to refresh yourself. Dinner is in the dining room at eight, Mr Potts. Do not be late.'

He hesitated for a moment, at the sound of the unfamiliar name, before getting his story straight and responding with an equally polite nod. 'As you wish, Miss Strickland.'

Then she was gone down the hall, leaving him alone in the bedchamber of a dead king. He shut the door quietly behind her and turned to the matter at hand, his private appraisal of the room's worth. What was there in this room that was worth selling? The furniture was valuable, the canopied bed hung with slightly dusty velvet on brass rings as thick as his thumb. Interesting, but not worth the effort of dragging down the drapery. The crossed swords over the mantelpiece gave the room a distinctly masculine air. If they were a relic of the room's namesake they might be priceless. But to get them away he'd have to march through the entire house with a sword on his shoulder. The bedchamber he occupied was as far from the front door as it was possible to get.

His train of thought ground to a halt, then circled back, trying to think why that statement seemed so important. She'd said she'd put him in this room because of his supposed friendship to the Earl. But he had just told her that he had no real acquaintance with Comstock. Had she forgotten?

There was something about Miss Strickland that made him think she did not often lose track of the details. Which meant she'd simply told the first lie that had come to mind to explain her choice. There was something strange going on and he meant to find out what it was.

Chapter Three

Once she had put Mr Potts in his room and Pepper in her own, Charity headed back down the main stairs and out the front door, hurrying down the drive towards the dower house. He had been right. It was about to rain. The clouds had darkened considerably since their departure from the house, an hour ago. As she ran the last steps down the drive towards the front door, she felt the first drops striking the hood of her cloak.

She ignored them. She was so close to the truth that she could not let a little weather prevent her from finishing what she'd begun when he'd interrupted her. Of course, she needed an umbrella more than a ladder. She had been able to feel the edge of the niche when she had stood on the grate, but had not been able to reach the depth of it.

But with the arrival of an auditor, the day of reckoning had come and there was not a minute to spare for further preparation. She would find a stool in the kitchen of the other house and make do. Either the box was there, or it was not. She had to know.

She pushed through the dower-house door and slammed it behind her, allowing herself a moment of unfeminine pique now that there was no one around to hear. Then, she hurried to the sitting room, where the chimney was.

'I was beginning to wonder if you were coming.'

Charity gasped and clutched the door frame, startled out of her breath at the words. Mr Potts had removed the holland covers from one of the chairs by the hearth and was sitting comfortably, his long legs stretched out before him.

It took a moment to think of an appropriate response. The cold, rational part of her brain, the part that she could not seem to keep silent, commented that it was rare to be at a loss for words. Or at a loss for breath. It was rare that she was surprised at all. She was accustomed to outthinking the people around her with ease. Yet this stranger had bested her on her home turf.

'You seem to be winded.' He leaned forward and pulled the cover off the chair opposite him with a flick of his wrist. 'Why don't you sit, as well.' Then, he smiled. 'Perhaps I should light a fire for us to chase away the damp of the room.'

He was expecting her to cry out *No!* and confirm his suspicions that there was something up the chimney. She had no intention of obliging him. 'How did you know I would come here? And how did you arrive before I did?'

'What other reason would you have for putting me in a room that faced the back of the house and not the drive?' He held up a hand. 'Do not tell me it is because

I am an honoured guest. I got the distinct impression before that you wished I would go to perdition.'

'Not to hell. Just back to America. Or London, at least. Even after much preparation, the house is in a frightful state and not ready to be inventoried.' She smiled and fiddled with her glasses, doing her best to appear young and out of her depth. 'My sisters are both just married and Grandmama is travelling on the Continent. It is only just me now.'

'But none of that explains why you would put me in the best room in the house,' he said. 'I assumed you wanted to finish what you were doing without my noticing your departure from the house. You did not come all the way here to close a flue. You were searching for something.'

She touched her hand to her chest, feigning outrage. 'What reason would I have to lie about such a thing?'

'I have no idea,' he replied. 'But I wanted to find out. It would have been impolite to ask you. It is one thing to accuse a woman you've just met of lying and quite another to catch her in said lie.' He stretched his arms, lacing his fingers and cracking his knuckles. 'So I shimmied down the drainpipe running beside the window of my room and came back here to see if you would return.'

'If I hadn't?'

'Then I'd have said nothing more of my suspicions.'

Her heart was still beating faster than normal, probably from the shock he had given her when she'd come into the room. And once again, the rational voice spoke in her mind. Or rather, it laughed derisively. Now she was unsure what she should say next. It was a new feeling to be unsure of herself. She did not think she liked it.

But he seemed to be enjoying it immensely. 'It will save us both some time if you simply admit that I am right. Then I will help you look for whatever it is you are hunting for and we can return to the main house.'

'I might not be searching for anything,' she said. 'I might have been hiding something.'

'I interrupted you before you could complete what you were doing. You had nothing in your hand when you came out of the chimney and I felt no bulges in your skirt that might indicate you'd concealed an item in your pocket. And the minute you could get rid of me, you came back to finish your search. It is far more likely you were looking for something than leaving something.'

His logic was not perfect, but it was better than she usually encountered. And he had let slip something far more important than a demonstration of deductive reasoning. He had all but announced that, while they had been riding, he had not just been supporting her to keep her from falling. He had held her tight enough to discern the contents of her pockets. Her heart was thumping in her chest, both from the memory of his hands on her and the subtlety of his reason for it.

He had searched her. And she had let him to it, behaving like a foolish school girl, excited to be in the arms of a handsome man. If she was not careful, he would run her like a greyhound after a hare, destroying her plans for an independent future. She must be much more careful.

'Suppose you are correct in your assumptions,' she

said. 'Why would you offer to help me?' She watched for a slight change in expression that might tell her what he was really thinking.

'I assume that what you are seeking is a part of the estate. We both want it to be found and returned. Don't we?' He steepled his fingers and stared at her as though daring her to deny it.

She should lie and tell him that, of course, that was what she'd been doing. To tell the truth was to surrender before he had a chance to attack. If he had the slightest inkling of what was in the chimney, he'd have the whole works under lock and key before she could save even the smallest portion for herself.

'If there is something missing from the entail, it is only right that it should be returned,' she said, choosing the hypothetical middle ground, watching for his reaction.

'Or, I could help you find the thing you are looking for and look the other way,' he added, his expression pleasant but opaque. 'I could decide that it was none of my business.' Now he was the one waiting for her response.

She gave the one that most suited the situation and pretended to be shocked. 'Why would you do such a thing?'

'For compensation, of course. It is time for us to lay our cards on the table, Miss Strickland. Whatever you are doing here, I suspect it is something you shouldn't. I will keep your secret, if you pay me to do so.'

'You will keep my secret for now,' she corrected.

'Until you decide I have not paid you enough and come back for more. That is how blackmail works, is it not?'

He laughed. 'Very true.' Then he said, in a conspiratorial whisper, 'I am new at it and have not had the time to think through all the ramifications.'

'Then how about this one,' she said. 'I run back to the house and announce that the auditor is threatening me and I do not think he is an honest man. The servants believe me and contact the Earl. Since he barely knows you, he takes the word of family over anything you might say and fires you immediately.'

Mr Potts gave a brief start of surprise, then clapped his hands. 'Bravo, Miss Charity. Bravo.'

He should be calling her Miss Strickland. Though as he had been patting her hips before, he probably thought he was entitled to some familiarity. 'I did not give you permission to use my Christian name, Potts,' she said, dropping the honorific from his to remind him he was little better than a servant.

He gave an apologetic incline of his head. 'My apologies, Miss Strickland. But my rudeness aside, we seem to have arrived at an impasse. What are we to do?' Then he looked at her for the answer.

She considered. It did not really matter if he was a paragon of virtue, or a total villain. The typical masculine response to a situation like this was usually much the same: to go to the chimney and take what was in it. She was smaller and weaker, and she could not stop him. But Potts was confusing her. He was tailoring his actions to hers and at least pretending that she could decide what would happen next.

To flatter your pride, announced the voice in her head. *This one is a charmer. Be on your guard.*

She touched her finger to her chin, pretending indecision, and scuffed the floor with the toe of her boot. Then she stared at him and spoke without irony. '*We* are going to allow me to get on with what I was doing, Potts. It may still amount to nothing. But if I do not do what I came here for, you will do it yourself as soon as my back is turned and abscond with anything you find.'

He nodded. 'You have a surprisingly bleak view of my character, Miss Strickland. Not inaccurate, mind you. Simply bleak. But if the thing you are searching for can be split easily between us, I will be out of your hair and your life before cock's crow.'

She clutched at her heart, feigning ecstasy at the thought of his absence. 'Will you really, Potts?'

'My plan on coming here was exactly what you suggested when we first met. I have urgent business back in America and no money for a return passage. I should not have to count every last part of the Comstock entail to get it. If I can find something of value that won't be missed, I will take it, sell it and get a ticket on the first ship bound for Philadelphia.' He pointed to the fireplace. 'If there is such a thing hidden up that chimney, then go to, Miss Strickland. Go to.'

'Very well, Potts,' she said, with another insincere smile. If they found what she was looking for, there was no way he could take half of it, any more than she could. But he had planned to take something that would not be missed. She must hope that he could be steered towards discretion and not greed. Then she remembered that there were other issues to be dealt with. 'I have but one problem. I was too short to reach it on the last visit.'

'I am taller,' he said, standing up, ready to take her place.

'And wider,' she reminded him. 'It was a snug fit, even for me.'

'There is nothing for it then,' he said, went to the fireplace, hauled the grate out of its place and went down on one knee, patting the level plain of his opposite thigh. 'Up you go.'

'I was thinking more of finding a ladder,' she said.

'Have you brought one with you?'

'Do not ask me facetious questions,' she snapped.

He patted his knee again. 'Come along, Miss Strickland. Let us settle the mystery in the chimney and then you will have time to berate me on my character.'

She sighed. She did not need her sisters to tell her that what he had suggested was improper. It would take only a minute or two to find something else to stand on. But she wanted an answer to the mystery, not in two minutes, but *now*.

Everyone said that impatience was a major flaw in her character. And she would address it later.

She stepped forward, crouched to move past him in the fireplace opening, braced herself on the walls of the chimney and raised a foot.

Before she could fumble, he had grabbed her boot and guided it to a place on his thigh. Then he reached beneath her skirts and tapped the back of her other knee as one might do to a horse to make him raise a hoof.

She lifted the foot that was still on the ground and he made a stirrup with his hands, boosting it to join the other one so she could stand on his leg.

He was right. She was several inches higher than she had been when standing on the grate. She felt the bricks surrounding her for the expected niche.

'Anything?' he asked.

'No,' she admitted through gritted teeth. She stretched her fingers upwards and brushed a ridge and empty air where there should be brick, but nothing else. 'I can feel it above me, but I am still too short.'

'Step on to my shoulders, then.' Before she could argue, his fingers were around one of her calves, firmly guiding her leg upwards.

For a moment, her normally agile mind went blank. His head and shoulders were under her skirt. This was the first, and possibly the last, time that a man would see her legs, much less touch them. She must pray that it was dark under there. If he looked up, he would see far more than her legs. He would be inches from everything she had to offer.

It was...

She shepherded her thoughts, trying to analyse the sensations running through her. The feel of his hand on her ankle was different to any touch she'd felt before, though it was not even skin to skin. The flesh under her wool stocking felt cold, but the blood beneath was racing hot, back towards her heart. And above it all, she was sure she felt the gentle stirring of his breath.

The world seemed to spin and waver around her, unsteady, as if she'd had too much wine. Then she realised that the feeling was not imagination. Her body trembled, trying to find balance as he guided it to stand on his shoulders like a Vauxhall Gardens acrobat. She could stop it by bracing herself against the brick walls around her.

She did so. But she didn't like being steady. She wanted to feel strange and unsure, laughing as the whole world dropped from under her and she fell to land breathless in his lap.

'Miss Strickland?' The voice coming from under her skirts was muffled, but unemotional.

'Uhh, yes,' she said, hurriedly feeling for the niche in the wall that was now on a level with her face. Her heart gave another sudden swoop as her fingers encountered a box. 'I have found something.'

'Excellent.' Both hands transferred to her left ankle as he began the delicate process of helping her down. By the time her feet were back on the hearthstones, she had regained control of her senses and could emerge, sooty but fully rational, from the fireplace. Then she held out the thing she had found: a wooden box about eight inches square.

'It is not very large,' he said, staring down at it.

'It does not need to be,' she said, fumbling with the catch. But she had thought it would be bigger than this. She had imagined a rectangular, leather case similar to the one that held the duplicates, with an easily found latch and hinges. But the wood under her fingers was completely smooth. Nor did there seem to be a separate top that could be lifted off. If she had not felt the lightness and heard a faint rattle from within, she'd have assumed that it was a solid block and not a box at all.

'Hand it here for a moment,' he said, fishing in his pocket for a handkerchief. Once he had hold of it, he buffed enthusiastically to remove the accumulated ash and grime. Then he handed it back to her to admire.

She adjusted her spectacles, wiping the grime from them to get a clear look. What had seemed to be plain mahogany was at least three colours of wood, inlaid in elaborate marquetry, no two sides alike. But though it was lovely to look at, the way into it was not more apparent now that it was clean than it had been fresh from the chimney. She stared back at him. 'Do you have a penknife I might borrow?'

'And spoil the fun?'

'I am supposed to enjoy this?' she asked, giving it a frustrated shake.

'You are holding a Chinese puzzle box,' he said patiently. 'Perhaps you are not familiar with them, but I have seen them brought from the Orient by sailors.' He held a hand out for the box.

She hesitated. She had spent half a day up a chimney, rooting around in the dirt. She had run back and forth from the house, twice. All she wanted was a cup of tea and a wash and some sign that this quest was nearing its end. Instead, this clean and poised stranger stood ready to take it away and finish it for her.

She pulled it back. 'Thank you, Potts, but that will not be necessary.'

'I thought we agreed to share,' he said, giving her a smile that could melt the snow off a roof.

She shook the box again, hearing only the faint rattle of the trick marquetry that hid the latches. 'As you can hear, there is nothing inside. And, even if the box is rare enough to be valuable, it will no longer be so if you try to take half.'

'Are you sure it is empty?' he asked with a raised eyebrow. 'Perhaps something you do not wish me to see?'

She shook her head and gave him a pitying smile. 'Even full to the brim, a box this size could not hold very much. If you wish the money to return to America, I am afraid you will have to get it by doing what the Earl expected: an inventory of the entail.'

'Well, I must say, Miss Strickland, what got off to a promising start has been a most disappointing afternoon.'

'That could be said of most afternoons at Comstock Manor,' she said. 'But there is no point in spending any more time here. Let us return to the main house. Dinner at eight, Potts. And tomorrow, we will begin the inventory.'

Chapter Four

If her sisters had been here, they would have known how to handle this.

Charity had never needed their advice before. It might seem immodest to think so, but wisdom usually flowed from her in their direction and not from them to her. Though she was youngest, she was better read and better educated than either of them. In matters that truly mattered, she was better at observing and understanding the world and the people in it. It was how she had known, before either of them, which men they were likely to marry. One had simply to watch dispassionately and draw conclusions from the data collected.

But that was not required at the moment. Tonight, she needed to be a polite and gracious hostess to a male stranger. She had never before had to deal single-handedly with a man in a social setting. On the rare times she had been forced from the house to go through the motions of the London Season, Faith and Hope had been there to chaperon and guide her, preventing a merely uncomfortable situation from turning into a fiasco.

But they were not here tonight and she had never felt so alone in her life.

Her first instinct had been to announce that Mr Potts could have dinner served on a tray in the location of his choosing. She would eat in the library, as she usually did, and go to bed after she had managed to solve the puzzle they had found in the chimney.

Now that she was in her room, she had taken the time to examine it. She'd run her hands over the inlaid wood panels, giving it a shake and weighing it with her hands. There was nothing about the sounds it made to indicate that they came from shifting contents and not the puzzle mechanisms themselves. Perhaps the things she'd hoped to find were packed tight in cotton wool, but she would have expected there to be more weight.

The problem deserved several hours' study in the privacy of the library. But she had announced earlier that dinner was a formal arrangement and that he was expected to attend it. To cancel it and devote herself to solving the puzzle would announce to this interloper just how important a matter it was. When she had thought success was imminent, she'd felt that there was no choice but to accept his help. Instead, she had been given a locked box and a small reprieve. If she could make it through supper, she could plead exhaustion and retire to her room to open the box. There was a chance she might still complete her task without his even knowing.

But it was a slim chance, at best. The auditor was

not like the rest of her family, who had long ago given up trying to understand her. When she had tried to outwit Potts, he had not just been able to keep pace with her, he had got one step ahead.

Perhaps it had been mere luck on his part. She prayed that when she came down to dinner she would find him as easy to gull as the rest of her acquaintance. But the little voice at the back of her mind whispered that her true wish was just the opposite. She wanted him to be just as clever at supper as he had seemed this afternoon. She wanted to spend more time with him, not less.

That alone was reason enough to avoid him. She was not thinking sensibly and it was all his fault. If she was not sure that she could best him in a battle of wits, what other weapons did she have?

At times like these, her sisters could fall back on their looks and flirt their way out of trouble. A flutter of eyelashes, a few shy smiles, and even the smartest of men around them tended to forget whatever it was that had been troubling them.

Charity sighed. Flirting required that she pretend to be someone she was not: sweet, biddable and somewhat in awe of the men around her. Even if she could manage those things, she was not pretty enough to dazzle a gentleman, especially not one that could dazzle in his own right.

Potts was astoundingly good looking for an auditor. The men in her family were handsome enough, in a refined sort of way, with brown hair and eyes. But looking at Potts was a study in the contrast of light and shadow. His eyes were so dark that it was a challenge to see where irises ended and pupils began, but they seemed almost black against his pale skin. And though he had smiled often, she'd got only glimpses of his teeth, which were very white and very straight.

Perhaps it was not that he was smarter than she. Perhaps her wits were slowed by the sight of him. The thought was cheering, but highly unlikely. She had yet to meet a man so handsome that she was rendered stupid in his presence. If anything, her mind had been working even faster than usual, now that he had arrived, gathering all the information it could about the man before deciding on a course of action concerning him. Dinner would be an excellent time to learn more, pretending that her interrogation was nothing more than polite chatter over the meal.

Charity went to the bell pull in the corner of her room and gave the single sharp yank that would summon her maid. Then she sat on the bed to wait, idly scratching the ears of Pepper, who was already sleeping there. No other female in her family had to go the bother of waiting for a servant. Her sister's maids seemed to be always under foot, often one step ahead of their mistresses when it came to choosing the perfect gown for every occasion. But since Charity rarely bothered with her appearance, she had no right to be surprised that the maid was not pressing ribbons and starching petticoats.

After nearly twenty minutes, the door opened a crack and Dill appeared, staring at her mistress in silence.

Charity stared back at the maid, raising an eyebrow expectantly.

'You rang, miss?'

'Yes, Dill. I wish to dress for dinner.'

'You do?'

Surely the request was not so very odd. 'Yes, Dill. That is why I summoned you.'

'You never dress for dinner, miss. Especially not when we are alone.'

'We are not alone,' Charity reminded her. 'The auditor has arrived.'

'And he will be dining with you?'

'Yes, Dill.'

'In the dining room?'

'That is where we dine, Dill.'

'You usually dine in the library,' the maid said, still confused.

'Not tonight, Dill.'

'And servants dine below stairs,' the maid said, stubbornly. 'An auditor is a sort of a servant, isn't it?'

'He, Dill.' The maid had a point. But employees occupied a place between servants and family. The way they were to be treated was likely situational and better decided by Grandmama, who was absent, just like her sisters.

In the end, Charity decided to lie. 'Mr Potts is a friend of the Earl as well as his auditor. He will be eating in the dining room, like a member of the family.'

'Oh.' Dill stared at her for a moment. 'You don't dress for family, either.'

'But I am dressing tonight.'

'Oh.' Dill gave a nod and a grin that announced she had seen Mr Potts and had a theory about Miss Charity's sudden interest in looking her best.

'Grandmama would expect me to treat a representative of the new Earl with proper respect,' Charity added. When the maid did not move from the doorway, Charity cocked her head in the direction of the wardrobe. 'That is why I have summoned you to help me dress.'

'Ah.' The girl ambled towards the gowns and pulled two from their pegs. Both of them were brand new and with décolletage that Charity found slightly intimidating. Dill grinned again. 'How much respect do you want to show 'im?'

Charity took a deep breath, then pointed to the more modest of the two. 'That one. And a shawl, I think.'

Dill shook her head. 'A shawl defeats the purpose. I will have the footmen build up the fire in the dining room. That and some pepper in the soup and you'll be nice and warm.'

'I suppose you are right,' she said with a sigh. Though the dress would make her feel uncomfortably exposed, it was no worse than what the other girls in London were wearing.

Of course, Mr Potts was not from London. America had been settled by Puritans. Perhaps he would be shocked by her. Or perhaps he would see through her ridiculous attempt to behave as other, normal girls did. Then he would laugh and dismiss her entirely. It would be a disaster, just as it had been in London, on those times she had followed her sisters' advice and tried to mix in society.

She sat quietly as Dill worked over her, afraid to look in the mirror, not wanting proof that she looked as awkward as she felt. It was not as if she needed to impress him. He worked for her family and would have to be polite, no matter how she acted. But whether he voiced it or not, he would have an opinion.

She had escaped to the country because she could not abide the critical gazes and snide comments of the marriage mart, where men treated girls and horseflesh much the same. In both cases, they wanted an animal that was attractive, high-spirited. Then they put a bit in the mouth or a ring on the finger so that it could never think for itself again.

'There, miss. All done.' Dill stepped away, her hands falling to her sides, and added without a trace of irony, 'And do not worry so. You will be the prettiest woman in the room.'

'I will be the only woman in the room, Dill,' she said, putting on her glasses and staring at her reflection. The results were…

Passable. She looked as well as she ever did. She was displaying an unusual amount of skin, which men generally liked. But there seemed to be too much. A gown like this required jewels and she had none.

Then a thought hit her and she smiled. 'Dill, go to Grandmama's room and bring back the case with the Comstock diamonds.'

A decent maid might have questioned her right to wear the things, since they were reserved for the use of the Countess. But Dill was merely adequate and did not bat an eye. She simply returned with the box and placed them on the vanity. Then she pulled a set of ear-bobs from their place and hooked them into the ears that had been exposed by Charity's carefully styled hair.

'The necklace, as well, I think,' Charity said, feeling oddly like she was a little girl again, playing dress up with Grandmama's jewellery.

'In for a penny, in for a pound,' Dill answered, draping the heavy chain over her head until the teardrop-shaped lavalier fell in the hollow between her breasts.

It was an excellent choice. But not for the reason her maid thought. It would give Potts something to look at, other than her. With a three-carat stone in front of him, he would have no reason to care whether the woman wearing it was pretty or not.

And there could be no better way to assure the auditor that the entail was intact than to bring the Comstock diamonds out at the first opportunity. Once he had seen it, she could assure him that the rest of the parure was safe and accounted for. This, the most important item to be inventoried, could be checked off his list. And if he noticed that the stones she was wearing were paste?

She would claim to be just as surprised as he was. Either way, she would be able to draw conclusions about his intelligence and observational abilities. It was information she could use against him later.

She felt somewhat more confident about herself now that she had a plan. But it would not make the dinner any easier. Her stomach filled with nervous butterflies as she walked towards the stairs, only to see him coming down the hall on the opposite side of them.

'Miss Strickland,' he called. 'Ahoy! Or perhaps, avast. I am not sure which is more appropriate in this case.' He walked towards her with a cockeyed grin on his face, looking more appealing than she cared to notice.

She smiled back at him. 'Ahoy is meant to call my attention. Avast is a request that I stop. Which did you want?'

His eyes swept her from head to toe, pausing for the briefest of instants to register the presence of the necklace. Then his gaze returned to her face, still smiling. 'Both. I need an escort to the dining room. This house is not precisely a maze, but it is a long jaunt from end to end. I am likely to starve before the meal if left to my own devices.' Then he held his arm out to her, as if he was about to lead her to the dining room.

But not really. At dinners and balls, the men who took her arm were either assigned to the task by some sympathetic hostess or volunteered because they hoped to make a good impression on one of her sisters. As she walked with them, they did not pay attention to her, but glanced over their shoulders to be sure that someone else was observing their gallantry.

But tonight, the man in front of her was focused solely on her, as if she was the prettiest girl in the room, just as Dill had said. Because they were alone. He was looking at her because there was nowhere else to look. There was nothing personal about it.

'Miss Strickland?' Now he was wondering at her hesitation.

'Just thinking,' she said, trying and failing to duplicate the light, flirtatious smile that her sisters used at times like this. But it was all wrong. She could not manage to look empty-headed while claiming to think. And now she could not decide how she was supposed to look, which must make her seem more dim-witted than thoughtful.

If her shifting expression seemed odd to him, he did not indicate it. He simply continued to smile and guided her down the stairs.

Chapter Five

When they arrived in the dining room, Charity Strickland chose a seat halfway down the table and indicated the place opposite that was set for him. It seemed that the staff had ignored her change in rank as the only family member present and put her in her usual place instead of moving her closer to the head of the table. Even when they were not here, empty places had been left for her sisters.

And for him, as well. The head of the table, where the Earl should be seated, had a place setting, but no chair. He could not help a small shiver of dread at the sight of it and the weird, undeserved respect that was offered to a supposed lord and saviour that none of them could recognise even when he was in the house with them.

'My maid promised that a fire would be lit,' she said, mistaking the reason for his shiver.

'I am fine,' he assured her. 'If you are comfortable, do not concern yourself.' He tried not to glance down at the expanse of ivory skin on display above the neckline of her gown, or to look even lower, searching for her body's reaction to the cold room. Perhaps English gentlemen did not have such thoughts, but the crass American that he was thanked God for the superior view afforded a lowly visitor who was placed opposite Miss Charity instead of at the head of the table.

Her long neck had looked ridiculous in the high-collared dress she had worn this afternoon. But in a dinner gown, her exposed throat swept gracefully down to the swell of her fine, full breasts. Though there had been little light beneath her skirts when he had boosted her up the chimney, he had been holding a fine pair of ankles and felt delightfully rounded calves pressed on either side of his head.

And though her hands moved with masculine efficiency as they sliced the lamb on her plate, the fingers were long and tapered to fine, almond-shaped nails.

There was much to enjoy in the young lady that everyone had been insisting he marry, for duty's sake and the good of the Empire. But there was also one thing he did not like at all. Dangling between those perfect breasts was what had to be the crowning glory of family jewels. The excessively large teardrop pendant would have dazzled him, had he not known it was a worthless copy. Now it merely depressed him.

Did she know? he wondered. Of course she did. The truth was supposed to be a secret passed from Earl and Countess to Earl and Countess. The Dowager had blurted it out to him the first time they'd met, then sighed with relief as if she'd transferred a back-breaking burden on to his unsuspecting shoulders.

As the youngest granddaughter, Miss Charity should know absolutely nothing about it. But she struck Miles as the sort of woman who was exceptionally good at ferreting out secrets. Which begged the question as to why she would flaunt it in front of him at the first available moment.

Because she wanted to convince him that nothing was amiss. Despite himself, he smiled. It was a pleasure to be in the company of a female whose actions had purpose.

She smiled back and the effect on her features was transformative. And for a moment, he forgot himself, grinning back, smitten.

Then she looked at him with a gaze as sharp as an eagle's and said, 'So, Mr Potts, tell me about yourself.'

He could feel the smile freezing on his face, as his brain struggled for an answer. At last, he replied, 'There is not much to tell.' It was true. He had not bothered to invent a past to go with his *nom de guerre*, so what could he possibly say?

She set down her knife and steepled her fingers. 'Tell me anyway. I am fascinated.' She did not look totally sincere, but she did look persistent. 'I have never met an American before.'

He breathed a sigh of relief and a silent prayer of thanks for the topic. 'I am from Philadelphia, in the state of Pennsylvania.'

'Where the Earl is from,' she said.

'It was where we met.' That was metaphorically true, at least.

'And what did you do, in Philadelphia?'

'A bit of this and that,' he said, for it was near to the truth.

'Auditing?'

'Never before. But I have a decent hand and feel qualified to take accurate notes on what is right before my eyes,' he said, deliberately staring down at the counterfeit diamond.

His suspicions on her knowledge of the false diamonds was confirmed. As if she feared the topic of conversation was about to turn to the necklace, she lost interest in talking and concentrated on the strawberry compote that had arrived for dessert.

Which meant it was his turn to question her. He speared a berry on the end of his fork and bit into it with relish before asking, 'Have you had a chance to open the puzzle box we discovered this afternoon?'

'It is not your business whether I have or not, Potts,' she said, not bothering with an honorific as if she sought to put him in his place.

'On the contrary. The box and whatever is inside it are likely to be valuable, or else why would they be hidden? If they are part of the entailed property, I must record them.'

'I doubt they are,' she said, smiling sweetly and trying to put him off his guard, again.

It was badly done. She could not expect to command him one moment and play the fool the next. In response, he gave her a firm smile and a sceptical stare. 'I think you had best let me be the judge, Miss Strickland. It is my job, after all.'

'If there is anything of interest inside, you shall be

the first to know,' she said, not even bothering to look sincere.

'So you have not opened it, yet,' he pressed.

'There has been little time to do so,' she snapped, touching her hair. 'These dratted curls take hours.' Then, as if realising that ladies were not supposed to consider it a waste of time to beautify themselves, she shut her mouth in another forced smile.

'They were well worth it,' he assured her. 'The effect is quite charming.' He paused to see if the compliment had registered.

It had not.

He continued. 'Puzzle boxes can be devilishly tricky things. Some have more than forty steps and secret compartments beyond that. I have done several of them. If you should need help...'

'You think I should come to you?' she said, narrowing her eyes in suspicion.

'Who else is there?' He gave an innocent shrug, then held out his hands to show he meant no harm.

'You are shamelessly angling for an invitation,' she said, both exasperated and surprised.

'I love a mystery,' he said.

'Well, I have no intention of involving you with it, no matter how curious you are,' she said with a sigh, tossing her napkin aside and rising from her seat. 'There are some things that are just too private to share with people outside the family. And as I said before, if it involves the entail...'

'You promise to tell me,' he finished her sentence.

'You have my word.'

Since she had lied to him several times already, he held little hope that she would turn over any valuables she found, no matter how much he might need them. He gave her another disarming smile. 'If not cracking open your mysterious box, how are we to pass the evening?'

'We?' Apparently, she had not planned to entertain him after the meal. She had probably hoped to abandon him and work on the puzzle box. If she did, it would leave him free to stuff his pockets with knick-knacks and take to the road.

And it might leave her with a box holding thousands of dollars of loose stones, any one of which might set him up for life.

'We, Miss Strickland,' he repeated. 'Surely you do not mean to leave me all alone on my first night here? What do you normally do for fun in this mausoleum, after the sun has set?'

'I enjoy a good game of chess,' she admitted, through gritted teeth.

'An excellent suggestion.' In fact, it was almost too good to be true. 'I like nothing better. I will spot you three pieces of your choice.'

'You will what?' she said, narrowing her eyes.

'It is called a handicap,' he said, with excessive patience. 'It gives a weaker player a chance to win.'

Apparently, she did not think she needed one for he could see fury rising in her like water about to boil over a kettle.

'I know what a handicap is, Potts. I have never needed one before and I do not mean to start tonight.'

'Are you sure?' he said, giving her a chance to change her mind.

'I have been the best chess player in this county since I was thirteen,' she said, glaring at him. Then she batted her eyes as if she was some simple female. 'But by all means give my feeble feminine brain the advantage of three pieces. If you can manage a draw, I will let you help me with the puzzle box you are so eager to see inside of.'

'Really?' The secret to her character revealed itself, before he could even suggest the wager. Flattery might get him nowhere. But if he dared to condescend to her, she would not just hand him the keys to the kingdom, she would throw them with all her might.

'Really,' she said, her smile replaced by a deter-mined nod.

'Fair enough,' he said and let the lamb lead him to the slaughterhouse.

The last time Charity had played chess, it had been with Mr Drake, who had been waiting for the opportunity to sneak into Hope's room. He had been so distracted by the thought of her sister it had taken considerable effort on her part to make him feel that he had a chance to win. There was no fun in blunting her play and throwing games to weaker players. But she had not had the heart to punish that poor man when he was already having a difficult time winning Hope.

Tonight would be different. The exceptionally ar-rogant Mr Potts deserved no mercy. She would take his three pieces. And then she would take the rest, as quickly and painfully as possible.

She set up the game and glanced at his side for only a moment before removing his queen and both bishops from the board.

'Ho-ho,' he said, clapping his hands in approval. 'You mean to make me work for my reward. Very well, then. Let's begin.'

She had underestimated him. After so many years of people doing the same to her, she should have known better. Potts was a cautious player, but relentless, taking her pieces one by one and dodging the traps she set for him, even without the help of his stronger pieces. When she managed to claim a piece, it usually came with the sacrifice of one of her own. And, indignity of indignities, when he took her king, it was done with a clever arrangement of pawns.

She stared at the table in amazement. 'I have never played a game like that before.'

'Then you have led an exceptionally sheltered life, Miss Strickland.'

While that was quite true, it had nothing to do with her abilities at the chessboard. Nor had it anything to do with the quality of his play, which had been masterful.

Now he was staring at her expectantly. And for the first time in her life, she felt in awe of a man and at a loss for words.

'Well?' he said, with an encouraging tip of his head. When she did not respond, he added, 'Have you forgotten our bet?'

She found her tongue again, clearing her throat and

saying gruffly, 'It can hardly be called a bet. You offered me no reward, if you lost.'

'Since I did not lose, that is immaterial.' He gave her a pitying smile. 'Perhaps it would have been kinder of me if I had been more specific when you asked what I did, while in America.' He cocked his head to the side, as if reliving the conversation in his mind. 'I told you a bit of this and a bit of that. But when I was between this and that, and low on funds, I played chess for money.'

And she had fallen right into his hands.

'Before we played, you promised that I could aid you with the puzzle box. May I see it, please?' He was still smiling. Still maddeningly polite.

'Of course,' she said, rising and leading him from the room.

Chapter Six

If nothing else, he had found a way to stop Charity Strickland from questioning him about his non-existent past. Since her loss at the chessboard, she had barely spoken to him and put up almost no fight when he had requested a chance to see the contents of the box.

If it had been another woman, he might have feared that this was a sign of impending storm. But he sensed nothing from this one that hinted at petty tantrums or poor sportsmanship. Though she was clearly not accustomed to it, she responded to the trouncing he had given her with the sangfroid of an English gentleman.

It was rather confusing.

Perhaps it had unhinged her mind. That was why she showed no sign of modesty as she led him to her bedroom, instead of bringing the box to the parlour. Once there, she walked into the room without a second thought, took up the puzzle from her dressing table and sat on the edge of the bed, holding it out to him and gesturing that he join her.

He paused in the doorway, tempted to explain to

her that the situation was totally inappropriate. Even Pepper knew it was wrong, for the detestable little cur looked up from where he had been napping on the pillow and gave a threatening growl.

Charity gave a single snap of her fingers and pointed to a chair on the opposite side of the room.

The dog stood, gave an apologetic wag of his tail, then obeyed, giving Miles a half-hearted glare as he passed.

That left him with no reason to refuse her, other than good manners and common sense. There was also the chance that, if he waited too long, the effect of the chess game might wear off and she would remember that she did not want his help. So he smiled, walked into the room and sat down beside her as if there was nothing odd about it.

She barely seemed to notice him, turning the box over in her hands, caressing the wood and feeling for loose panels and trim. A few moments passed. Then she smiled as the bottom panel slid a half an inch to the left. 'I had no time to examine it before supper. It does not seem so very difficult.' She handed it to him, to find the next step.

'Perhaps not,' he replied, running his fingers along the side before finding the wooden latch that had been exposed and pulling it up with his thumbnail. 'But you agreed to my terms when we sat down to play chess.' He handed it back to her.

'But it does not take a genius, does it?' she said, pivoting the front panel to reveal a keyhole and added, 'Even if that is what you are.'

It was delivered as a statement rather than a compliment and he saw no reason to deny it. 'Perhaps I am. But intelligence does little good for the individual when the people in power are foolish.' For example, when one discovered that one's family had already done irreparable damage to the inheritance. He glanced down at her. 'I suspect you are familiar with that feeling, are you not?' She must be. It was her family, as well. He worked a fingernail into the left side panel until he heard a click.

She opened the little door he'd unlatched and admired the tracery of inlaid metal revealed before prying a bit of it loose and fitting it into the keyhole. 'It is worse for women,' she said. 'Men do not like it when we are too clever. They especially do not like being corrected when they are wrong.' Her forehead creased as she turned the key and heard another click as the top panel popped up to reveal a second, seemingly blank surface beneath.

Despite the small success, she continued to frown and cast a quick look in his direction, as if wondering if she would be expected to apologise for her abilities should she find the solutions faster than he did.

Someone had taken great pains to put her in her place. He suspected that it was the last Comstock, since she had made a point of remarking on jealous men. Until recently, there had been none of them in her family but her grandfather, the Earl. But if today was any indication, the old man had failed to break her spirit.

'My father was the same way, when I was young,' he said, watching her reaction as he took the box and pressed down on the smooth panel until it lifted a fraction of an inch, then gave it back. 'He was quick to cut a switch to correct me when I was wrong, which he defined as being out of agreement with him. But a smart man would have left his sons more than debt when he died.'

'Young ladies are not corrected with physical punishment,' she said softly, staring at the box in her hands. The silence that followed her words made him suspect that it had not been necessary to strike her to leave a scar.

'All his beatings managed to teach me was what sort of man I did not want to be when I grew up. As for my opinion on clever young ladies?' He gave her an encouraging smile. 'If you think I am in error, do not spare my feelings over it. There is nothing worse than being allowed to blunder on in the wrong direction when there is someone right at hand that could set me straight.'

Their conversation appeared to have affected her for she fumbled with the box, unable to complete the next move. She held it out to him with a pleading look, asking for rescue.

He shook his head, smiled and waited.

Encouraged, she took a breath, applied herself and had figured it out in a moment's time, sliding the sides away and lifting out a smaller box, hidden inside the first one.

'Bravo,' he said, clapping his hands. 'Now open it and show me what we have found.'

Some time during the course of the evening she had

lost the guarded manner she'd had at dinner. She did not hesitate or try to shield the truth from him as she undid the last latch.

He held his breath as she slowly lifted the lid to reveal…

'Nothing?' She turned it upside down and shook it, then tapped the sides, searching for another trick.

She passed it to him and he did the same and found nothing. 'Some sort of family joke, perhaps?'

She frowned. 'If so, it is not funny.'

'What is it that you were hoping to find?' he asked, though he was sure he knew.

'Nothing,' she said, shaking her head. 'Nothing at all.'

He had known her less than a day. She had no reason to trust him. But the lie annoyed him more than it should have. He picked up the pieces of the box, fitting them back together, sliding panels and latching latches until it was back as it had been, when they'd found it. 'Then, congratulations, Miss Strickland. If you were searching for nothing, you seem to have found it. And now, if you will excuse me, I must retire. The audit will begin tomorrow and we must hope that it is more productive than tonight.'

Chapter Seven

When Charity bothered to imagine her future, it had always included marriage. Though her sisters feared that her lack of interest in society indicated that she meant to remain a spinster by choice, it had never been her intent to spend her life sequestered in the solitude of the family library. She wanted a husband and children and a home of her own, just as her sisters did.

Judging by the besotted way they looked at their husbands, Charity suspected she would be an aunt by the end of the year. The loneliness that had begun creeping into her life since their absence increased at the thought of dandling someone else's baby on her knee. It reinforced her desire for a husband of her own and the children he was likely to give her.

But because something was wanted, that did not mean it would be easy to get. As the years passed, and her sisters grew ever lovelier, Charity had grown more plain. She had only to look in the mirror to realise that it was unlikely that the suitors she might have would be of the handsome and dashing variety.

There were probably any number of quiet, scholarly, not particularly attractive gentlemen that might do. Since such men enjoyed libraries far more than ballrooms, they were surprisingly elusive. When she'd happened upon them thus far, they thought themselves so intelligent that they deserved a wife who would listen more than she talked. She had not expected that they would be even more averse to outspoken women than her grandfather had been.

It was clear that something would be needed to sweeten the pot. Since there was no dowry to be had from the Comstock fortunes, she would have to find one for herself. Thus, she had begun her search for the missing diamonds and the plan to keep just enough of them to make herself attractive to men more poor than particular.

But none of her plans had ever included falling in love. Though her sisters might be convinced that they had married for love, Charity was not even sure the emotion existed in the sense that most girls understood it. She loved her sisters, of course. And her grandmother. She had even loved her grandfather in some hard-to-define way.

But to expect some grand, lifelong passion from marriage was far too impractical. Contentment would be sufficient. She sought a companionable union with a like-minded gentleman who would allow her autonomy in the running of the household and a decently stocked bookshelf. In exchange, she would make no real demands on her husband, allowing him to come and go as he pleased free of tantrums, megrims and excessive millinery bills.

Thus, when love came to Charity Strickland, it struck like an ambush from behind. One minute, she had been slightly annoyed at the condescension of her attractive visitor in thinking that he could best her at a game she knew well. Then, they had begun to play and she'd realised that Augustus Potts was the man of her dreams.

He had lulled her into a false security with a two-knights defence, which was just the sort of primitive, aggressive move that a man might rely on. But once he'd recognised her skill, his game had grown increasingly subtle to accommodate her. While she had initially thought his offer of a handicap was an insult, she learned that it was an attempt to keep the game fair. He'd shown no mercy, simply because she was a female.

By the time he'd put her in check, her pulse had fluttered with excitement. And when he'd declared 'mate in three moves', she had been ready to hand him her heart, as well.

Being in love with Potts had been the worst ten minutes of her life. Why did the object of her adoration have to be a god walking the earth and not an average man who might return her feelings? Why couldn't he at least be willing to stay in England? Why must she break her heart over someone who was brilliant, beautiful and totally unattainable?

Then she had realised that the questions were, in

fact, the answer. She did not love him because he was perfect. She did not love him at all. What she felt was lust. To desire a man like Potts was not just normal, it was sensible. If she was longing to be seduced, the fact that he did not plan to remain in her life or her country was actually an advantage and not an inconvenience.

One question still remained. What did she intend to do about these new feelings?

It had come as a shock to find herself inviting him not just into her bedroom, but on to her bed, so that they might solve the puzzle box. When Grandmama had taught them the basics of etiquette, she had explained that one never brought a man to one's room as one might a woman. When presented with a nearby bed, men were unable to contain their base urges.

Some men, perhaps, but not this one. Potts had simply given her an odd look and sat down beside her on the mattress, more interested in the puzzle and its contents than he was in her.

So she did something that she had never done in her life. It had taken years of practice to not simply blurt out corrections when she knew better than the people around her. After years of scolding from her sisters and grandmother, she had learned that it was one thing to be the smartest person in the room and quite another to rub the fact in the faces of everyone around her.

But tonight, she had looked at the man sitting next to her on her bed and for the first time in her life she had feigned ignorance. She fumbled with a perfectly obvious clue in the puzzle box, handing it to him to solve, hoping to make him like her better.

Instead of being flattered by her need for help, he had raised an eyebrow and handed it back to her, waiting patiently until she had solved it herself. If she had not already wanted him to the last fibre of her being, she had after that.

His adding that he liked being corrected when wrong was like the straw that broke the camel, or the last shot to sink a battleship. Wanting him in secret would not do. She must find a way to have him, or be had by him, even if only for a night. Action must be taken now, or he would be gone and she would not even have a memory.

She lay awake most of the night, putting her prodigious intelligence to work on a plan of attack that would be more successful than her chess game had been. But even as she had lost it, she had won knowledge of her adversary that could be used to her advantage.

He had played the game to get access to the box, only to learn that it was empty. She had been disappointed, but only mildly so. It had been the last in a long line of clues from letters and journals and diaries, and not the first blind alley she had wandered down. She would backtrack and find her way again.

But if he was eager to help her? She smiled. She could invite him on the treasure hunt, offering him information she had already discovered and discounted. He would be just as consumed by the mystery as she had been and willing to do anything to learn more, even if it meant seducing an innocent virgin to steal her secrets.

She gave an involuntary shudder of delight. If she handled him carefully, he might leave Comstock Manor knowing no more than when he came. And she would have a beautiful memory and the treasure all to herself.

Before going down to breakfast the next morning, she summoned Dill again, perplexing the girl by asking for help two days in a row. The end result was a primrose day gown that Charity had always rejected as being too likely to show the dirt and a hairstyle that was not as elaborate as last evening's curls, but softer than her usual tightly pinned braids.

As an afterthought, Dill gave Pepper a good brushing and tied a yellow ribbon about his neck, saying, 'If he means to follow you everywhere, he should learn to look like a lapdog and not a rat-catcher.'

It was probably a mistake, for the little dog seemed to loathe Potts and the feeling was returned in kind. But as usual, the little dog was staring at her, pathetically eager to follow wherever she went.

Charity stared down at him. 'If I must pretend to be tame, so should you. You may come downstairs with me. But one snap and it is off to the stables for the day.'

Pepper wagged his tail, as if he understood and agreed, but it was more likely an attempt to rearrange his fleas. Then he trotted happily at her side as she went down the stairs to the ground floor.

When she arrived in the breakfast room, she found it empty. There was evidence that Potts had been there before her: a footman was clearing away an empty plate and brushing toast crumbs from the table. She glanced at the mantel clock and saw that it was barely nine. When she touched the empty teacup sitting beside his place it was stone cold.

The servant clearing away guessed her question before she could ask and murmured, 'Half past six, miss. He was done well before seven.'

Without bothering to sit, she helped herself to a rasher of bacon from a covered plate. 'Did he say where he was going, after?'

'To work, miss.'

She chewed thoughtfully. Unless the job was to gather eggs while the chickens still slept, she could not imagine the need to rise before nine to do it. Since he was auditing a property that had been collecting dust for centuries, he had got a ridiculously early start. He must be somewhere in the house, but with forty rooms to account for, she could be searching for hours.

She looked down at the dog sitting patiently at her feet, and tossed him a scrap of bacon for incentive. Then she held out another piece, then pulled it away and offered the rumpled napkin sitting beside his place. 'Find him.'

The dog gave a single, long sniff and ran out into the hall.

Charity helped herself to a bun and followed the sound of his barks.

When she caught up to Pepper, he was outside the closed door of her grandfather's study. She hissed at the dog to distract him from scratching at the woodwork and tossed him his reward. Then she reached for the door handle and paused, unable to bring herself to open it. The Earl had been dead for over two years. There was no rule, written or unwritten, that said the room was out of bounds until Comstock arrived. She had been in the study many times herself, even using it to write letters and read.

But on those occasions, the door had been left wide open.

'Doors are closed for a reason, Charity. If you cannot respect that, we will have to find a way to teach you.'

Perhaps that was true. But there was no reason for this one to be closed today. Before she could question the action, she grabbed the handle and yanked it open.

Potts sat in the Earl's chair, his feet up on the desk, reading her grandfather's appointment book. At the sound of the opening door, he looked up slowly and smiled, but made no move to adjust his posture.

For a moment, the sight of a man in that chair at all froze her to immobility on the doorstep. There had been too many arguments here, so many lectures and punishments that she could see a worn spot on the carpet where she stood to receive them. Her fear of the room had dwindled to close to nothing in the two years since Comstock's death. But a new Comstock was coming, like a storm on the horizon. If she did not find a way to escape this house, it would all begin again.

Then she reminded herself that it was only Potts, young, handsome and smiling, and as different from an earl as it was possible to be.

With a snarl, Pepper launched himself from the doorway, making a desperate lunge for his coat sleeve.

He was up and out of the chair in a flash, causing the dog to miss by inches and fall back to the floor with a snap of his jaws.

His action brought a fresh flood of emotion to chase away her fear, as she watched male thighs encased in tight britches uncrossing and swinging clear of the desk, the curve of his hip revealed as he leapt clear and snatched his coat-tails away from the dog. She had to fight the urge to grin stupidly or perhaps to drool, as Pepper had at the sight of her bacon, for her mouth seemed to be hanging open at the sight of him. She closed it and forced her lips into a cool smile. 'Are you afraid of dogs, Potts?'

He returned her smile, probably unaware of the tumult inside her for his eyes never left the dog. 'I normally get along quite well with them.'

'But not this one, apparently.'

He stared down at Pepper with obvious loathing. 'Because there is something wrong with it. Damage to the brain, perhaps. He was rescued from a burlap sack, just as he was to be thrown into the Delaware by a despicable little boy. He came out of the bag, an ungrateful cur who would, quite literally, bite the hand that feeds him.'

Charity produced another morsel of breakfast from a napkin in her pocket and whistled.

The dog sat up on his haunches, wagged and received his treat, taking great care to touch her fingers with nothing more than a grateful swipe of his tongue.

She looked back at Potts. 'I see no such problem.' She looked back to the dog. 'Run along now, Pepper.

The nasty man and I must discuss why he is lounging in the Earl's study, for I see no sign of an inventory in progress.'

'Because I have been busy,' he said, his smile never faltering as he watched the dog trot from the room.

'You have but one job in this house,' she reminded him. 'If not that, what can you be busy with?'

'This,' he said, pulling a folded sheet of parchment from his pocket and handing it to her.

She felt a weird prickling on her skin at the sight of it. Surprise. Excitement. No. It was amazement. She thought she'd known the house well and the secrets contained in it. Her plan had been to tantalise Potts with them, to seduce or control him. But he had produced, seemingly out of thin air, a clue she had never seen before.

The largish rectangle of paper had been folded carefully into fourths and had not a wrinkle in it beyond the creases that had caused. She turned it over, then held it to the light and saw no sign of printing on either side. The only irregularity was a series of small, rectangular holes spaced about the page at random intervals. In some spots the paper was almost intact, in others, perforated so often that it reminded her of lace.

She looked back to Potts. 'Where did you find this?'

He pointed to the puzzle box, which was now resting on the corner of her grandfather's desk and shut up again to be the impervious block of wood that it had been when they'd found it. Without another word, he picked it up and began to solve it, his fingers flying through the steps to reach the inner container. Then he opened that, as well, tapping each side like a conjurer doing a trick.

He set it aside and picked up the case again, completing several more steps until a tray slid out from the bottom of it. Though now empty, it was just deep enough to contain a single sheet of carefully folded paper. *'Voila!'* He gave a little bow and looked at her as though expecting applause.

She resisted the temptation to offer it.

He responded with a slightly hurt expression and offered more information, as if trying to impress her with his cleverness. 'It is a key code of some kind, is it not? The paper should fit over a page in a book or journal and reveal a message. But it is none of the books in this room, for I have checked them all.'

He was right, of course. And the study was one of the places a logical person would search. The wrong one, but a logical choice. It did not explain, however, why he would be reading a diary that was far smaller than the page the key must fit on. That behaviour hinted that, though he was interested in the treasure, he might be searching for something else that she knew nothing about. She filed the fact in her mind and returned to the matter at hand.

'If you are looking for a book, have you considered looking in the library?'

For a moment, his face went blank. Then, his expressionless face split in a dazzling grin. 'There is a library.' From his tone of wonder, she might as well have told him they kept a dragon in the cellar. Surely they had libraries in America.

'I do not know my way around the house or perhaps I'd have stumbled upon it before coming here,' he added. 'Lead me to it.' He paused again. 'Please.'

She smiled to herself, surprised. Had anyone ever expressed an eagerness to see that particular room of the house? If they had, they had certainly not done it twice. Even the family used words like 'gloomy' and 'uncomfortable' when they spoke of it. It was why the space had been abandoned to her. 'It is not surprising that you did not find it, for it is rather out of the common way. Follow me.'

She led him out of the study, making a point to leave the door ajar so it would not disturb her again. Then she took him back past the common rooms, down a hall and then another until they were nearly as far away from the Earl's study as it was possible to be.

Finally, they stood in front of the last door at the end of the furthest wing. Since the key had been safely in her possession since Grandfather's death, she had no worries about keeping this one closed, especially if it preserved her privacy.

Then she opened the door and waited for the reaction that visitors to the manor generally had. He would take one look at the forbidding corner room, shiver in the cold draught, squint into the gloom and ask if it were possible to remove the books they need to somewhere more pleasant.

He stood, frozen on the threshold, amazed.

'This is your library,' he said, undisguised awe in his voice.

'As my family continues to remind me, it is not technically mine. It belongs to the Earl,' she reminded him. 'But previous Comstock heirs seldom availed themselves of this room. Perhaps the estate might not be in chaos if they had.'

'They did not come here?' He stepped into the room, staring up at the packed shelves reaching from floor to ceiling. 'What was wrong with them?'

'The family has always found the room too grim,' she said, then added, 'I am the only one who uses it.'

He gave an indifferent shrug, unable to look away from the shelves. 'A little dark, perhaps. But I would hardly call it grim.' Without thinking, he brought his hand up to caress the nearest leather spine.

He liked books.

It was not such an uncommon thing, really. She understood that a large portion of the population was illiterate. But though some of the people she knew did it grudgingly, all her acquaintances could read.

But she had never seen any of them look at the Comstock library with avarice instead of dismay. Though she did not mind it for research, the room needed light, airing and perhaps a complete redecoration to make it habitable for casual readers. There had been no money for frivolous redecoration in quite some time. Until there was, when the family needed a book they collected it and went elsewhere to read.

But Potts looked as if he had found heaven on earth. Her heart beat faster, as it had on the previous evening, while they'd played chess. The man was almost too perfect. In fact, he was too perfect. At any moment, he would say something disappointingly ordinary. It would break the spell he had cast on her, bringing her back to her senses and saving her from the embarrassment of having to ask for what she really wanted of him.

'The furniture is uncomfortable,' she announced, waiting for him to agree as everyone always did and suggest that they adjourn to the sitting room.

He pulled the book he had been touching off the shelf and dropped into the nearest chair, thumbing through the pages before finding a passage that interested him. 'One could grow used to it, I'm sure,' he said without looking up.

'You are the first to think so.'

He barely seemed to hear, already engrossed in the book on his lap. His fingers spreading on the leather cover like a lover's caress, toying with the cords on the spine, running a nail down the joint. She was unable to contain a shiver of desire and a flush of embarrassment at being jealous of an inanimate object.

'It gets cold in the winter,' she said to disguise her reaction, desperate for proof that he was mortal and disappointing, just like everyone else.

'There is a fireplace,' he replied, then glanced up at her with a frown as if annoyed at her continual insults to the room. Then he set his book aside and rose to pace down the shelves, forgetting her again. 'Where would one even start?'

'To look for the book that matches your key?' she asked, trailing behind him.

He threw his arms wide and turned suddenly to face her, grinning again. 'To read them. There are so many.'

'I recommend, here.' She took his hand and dragged him towards a set of shelves near one of the library tables. 'Perhaps it is not the best method of organisation, but I keep my favourites close. There is Shakespeare, Scott, the poetry of Blake. There are novels, as well,' she said. 'I will admit to the guilty pleasure of reading them. *The Castle of Otranto* is an excellent way to pass a stormy evening.'

'I agree.' He was smiling at her choices, nodding in approval. 'But Thomas Paine?' he said, surprised to find it at the end of the row.

'I told you before that we had books in England,' she reminded him. 'I am sure there are other works by Americans, if that is all you want to read.'

'No. I want…' He did not finish the sentence, but she could guess the rest. He wanted to read it all. He looked back at her, breathless with anticipation. 'My family in America was not exactly opposed to the written word. Though they liked books, there was seldom time or money to enjoy them.'

'You were poor?' she said, surprised.

'Not always,' he allowed. 'Sometimes we had money. Sometimes we did not. A rootless plant cannot be expected to thrive. And a rootless man?' He shrugged again. 'There is no point in accumulating possessions when one does not plan to stay in one place.'

'You will have all the time in the world to read, while you are here,' she coaxed.

He blinked, shocked back to reality. 'I do not plan to stay for ever. And that is how long it would take to enjoy what is collected here. In fact…' He swallowed.

'I do not mean to be here very long at all. The situation here is hopeless. And I have promised…' He stopped speaking aloud. But by the look in his eyes, a conversation that she was not privy to continued in his mind.

Then, as if coming to a decision, he turned his back on the books and looked at her instead. 'I cannot allow myself to become distracted, when there are more pressing matters to deal with. It is time that we are honest with each other, Miss Strickland. I know what you are looking for and wish to help you.'

'You do?' she asked, putting a hand to her breast as another shiver went through her. It did no credit to him if he thought her a frustrated spinster who would be easily seduced. But since it was true, she had no right to complain.

'The necklace you were wearing last night was paste, as is the rest of the set it belongs to. You think the Comstock diamonds exist somewhere in this house and you have been looking for them.'

'The diamonds,' she repeated. For a moment, she had forgotten all about them. It was as if they were playing chess again and she had just lost another piece.

'The Earl suspected they were missing,' he said, voicing her worst fears. 'It is why he asked for an audit.'

Her sister Hope had spent months worrying about what might happen when the Earl arrived and learned that the most precious piece of the entail was missing. But Charity had made much progress in searching for them and assured her that all would be well by the time their American relative arrived at the house.

Now it appeared Comstock had known all along. She had no fears of his being angry, for she knew the stones were somewhere in the house. She could produce them, given a little more time.

But she had not anticipated that a handsome man would arrive out of the blue, smart enough to best her with her own plans but morally conflicted and eager to make a hasty departure afterwards, just as it became inconvenient for him to stay.

'Please, Miss Strickland. Let me help you.' He was smiling at her in a way that was not quite innocent. His eyes held the same glint of avarice she had seen when he had boosted her up the chimney thinking he would split the prize they found.

If he had known about the paste copies, then the only reason he was paying attention to her was in hopes of learning the location of the real stones. It was a good thing she had not actually fallen in love with him, or this revelation would be devastating.

At this, the rational voice in her head offered nothing more than derisive laughter. Apparently, she would not be allowed to lie to herself and claim she felt nothing. The flame of desire at the sight of him had not abated on learning the truth. But it had kindled a second fire of rage that was almost its equal. She had been doing fine with her search until he had arrived and would do just as well without him.

He was the one who needed her.

'You want to help me find the diamonds,' she said, returning the same knowing smile he had offered her. 'And I assume that there is a price for your help, Potts?'

He gave a half-hearted shrug, as if to say talking money with a lady was normally beneath him. But since there was no man about, what else could be done?

There would be a price for her help, as well. She gestured to the chair he'd occupied before.

'Please, sit. Let us discuss.'

Chapter Eight

He had a library.

He also had problems and no time to be distracted from solving them. But it was hard not to be. Shelves around him stretched from floor to ceiling. There was a wheeled ladder attached to them, currently tucked into a corner, but able to run around the perimeter of the room on brass rails, to make it easy to reach to the very top.

And every single one of those shelves was packed with books. Some were in Latin, French and Greek. He did not know any of those languages. But if there were primers, he might learn enough to read.

If he had time.

Which he did not.

He had gone from assuming wealth to assuming poverty. Now that he had seen the house, the truth was somewhere in between. But auctioning the contents of this building would be embarrassing and time-consuming. What he needed was a handful of portable wealth, the sort that could be carried back to America in his vest pocket.

He needed those diamonds. And sitting across from him now was the exceptionally clever Charity Strickland, ready to talk terms.

He sat down and leaned forward with a respectful nod. 'I am at your command, Miss Strickland.'

'First, I must have your word that you do not mean to run off with everything we find,' she said. 'I was not planning to take more than four or five of the smaller stones for myself...'

'You were planning to take them,' he said, surprised. It was odd to be possessive of things he had not even known about a year ago. For some reason, it made him indignant to think of a family member pilfering from the estate. And it was an odd reason indeed, since he wished to do the same thing.

'Only a few,' she reminded him. 'The whole parure has been absent for half a century, I think it only fair that I receive a fee for the finding of them.'

'And what will the Earl say to that?' he asked.

'I have no intention of being here to find out,' she replied.

'You mean to run away from home?'

She laughed. 'You make me sound like a wayward child, Potts. I am a woman, fully grown.'

A vision flashed into his mind of the flesh above her bodice on the previous evening and the calves he had seen before that. 'My apologies, Miss Strickland. But I would have thought, since you are still unmarried, the bosom of your family is still the best place for you.'

'And how long do you suppose it will be so, once the Earl arrives?' she said. 'There is a good chance that

I will be forced into an exceptionally awkward marriage with him, for the sake of the family. I have no illusions about his fidelity, or even his affection. He is like to forget about me the moment the knot is tied. If he does not forget? He will want to mould me into the sort of woman he expects—quiet, co-operative and subservient to him in all things.'

'He is not such a bad fellow as all that,' Miles argued, annoyed that she had formed such an opinion without even meeting him.

'It does not matter if he is good or bad,' she said with a dismissive wave of her hand. 'He is male. In my experience, all men want the same thing.'

'They do?' he said, thinking of the obvious.

'Dominion over women,' she stated. 'Earls are even worse, for they feel it is their right to control everyone on their property. If Comstock does not wish to marry me, then I will be forced into a similarly uncomfortable union with one of his friends.'

'Why would he do that?' Miles said, for it had never occurred to him to do so.

'There will be any number of men eager to curry favour with him, now that he has a title. If he does not know it already, he will soon learn that the family coffers are empty and the land unprofitable. He will find a rich man who is willing to trade that wealth for a family connection and they will work my future out between themselves.'

It was an accurate assessment of the men he'd met in London and their sudden eagerness to help him once they had learned his identity. He had been smart enough to see that such aid came with a price tag that did not always involve money. Some had even mentioned his cousin in Berkshire and her need for a husband. But it had never occurred to him what he might gain in marrying her off to a stranger.

'You think that…the Earl is going to sell you to the highest bidder,' he said, appalled.

'My sisters and I were all destined for such matches, while Grandfather lived,' she replied. 'I overheard him making the plans before Faith had her come out. I was not yet seventeen, but was promised to a baronet of five and fifty.' She snapped her fingers. 'And then he was gone. With no money and no guarantee that an heir could be found, our value on the marriage mart fell precipitously and the suitors did not appear.'

'But your sisters have both married,' he said.

'They have found both love and money,' she said. 'But their first instinct was to find the former, not the latter. When you are told from childhood on that the family exists to preserve the estate, eventually it is almost impossible to separate your wants and needs from whatever Comstock requires of you.'

'But you wish autonomy,' he replied. 'And I suppose there is someone you favour who has nothing of value to offer an earl.'

She gave another short bark of laughter. 'You think I need money for an elopement? You flatter me, Potts. I am a poor relation and a plain one. No man wants me for myself, nor is that likely to change.'

'You are too hard on yourself,' he insisted.

'No harder than society has been, thus far. Before

they found husbands, Faith and Hope refused several suitors for making comments about their "quiz of a sister". It got so bad that I stopped going out with them, lest they reject a gentleman who was perfect in all ways but his assessment of me.'

If this was how she had been treated thus far, her low opinion of men made perfect sense. It made his blood boil to think of the men who had dared to insult her, a woman who had no fault other than a quick mind and an unguarded manner. Then he remembered that it was in his power to right any wrongs that had been done to her and see to it that she had the happiness she deserved.

'Perhaps society has treated you unfairly thus far. But I am sure the new Earl will want to know of your concerns for your future,' Miles insisted. 'If you put it reasonably to him, as you just did to me…'

'You are not an earl, Potts,' she said, with an exasperated sigh. 'You do not have the full weight of generations of nobility, reminding you that it is not your place to accommodate the wishes of others, it is theirs to accommodate yours.'

'True,' he said. At least, he did not feel like an earl. As an American, he found the idea that strangers were obligated to bend and scrape to him disconcerting at best and annoying at worst. He wanted to be long gone from this place before it started to seem normal. 'But suppose that I was. If I had the power to give you anything you wished, what would you ask of me?'

For a moment, her eyes went wide, as though either the question or its answer had shocked her. Then, her control returned. 'You mean to know what I would ask of the Earl. I would not *ask* anything, Potts. I would *tell* him and you that I deserve the right to set up my own household and to keep it should I decide to remain unmarried. If I do decide to wed, I need a dowry that is tempting, but not large enough to attract fortune hunters. And money that is not controlled by the Earl of Comstock, so that I can choose the course of my future without risk of my allowance vanishing the moment I displease him.'

What she sought was perfectly reasonable. Even as little as he had in the bank, he could arrange for her future with the stroke of a pen. Or Comstock could, at least. Augustus Potts could do little but offer her commiserations. 'I respect your right to choose your own future,' he said at last, 'even if I disagree with you on several points concerning the Earl and his plans for you.'

'How kind of you to do so, Potts,' she said, her mouth puckering like a tart cherry. 'But I have no intention of waiting patiently for him to arrive, just so we can see which of us is right,' she said. 'My plan has always been to find the missing diamonds and sell a few of the smaller ones to establish myself. But enough of me. You wish to stake your own future, as well, don't you?'

'That is very true,' he said.

'Then before we go a step further, you must agree to take only a reasonable share. A few missing stones can be excused as loss. But if you think to walk away with too much, I will put my reservations aside and tell the Earl what you have done and he will see you hang for it.'

'Fair enough,' he said, shocked at the vehemence of her threats. 'I will take no more than what you wish for yourself.'

She shook her head in disappointment. 'You surprise me, Potts. I have been poring through journals and diaries for several years and have taken the quest almost to its completion. And yet, after finding one clue, you think you deserve an equal share.'

He had a good mind to tell her that, as the Earl whom she so obviously despised, he deserved as much as he wished to take and she deserved as much as he wished to give her. But that meant that her fears about him had been justified. The money was not even in his hands and he was already thinking of ways to control her with it.

He cleared his throat and made an effort to think as Potts would and be grateful for her generosity. 'You have clearly given the matter some thought. How much do you think is fair?'

Now, for the first time since he had met her, she looked nervous. She rose from the chair and paced towards the bookshelves, then wiped her palms on her skirts as if to hide the fact that nerves had rendered them clammy. Then she turned back to him and blurted, 'I believe you have ways at your disposal that would persuade me to give you as much as you wish to take.'

His first impulse was to laugh and tell her that she must choose her words more carefully, lest he think she was hinting at something she did not understand. But she said nothing more, leaving him to fill in the blanks of her suggestion for himself. And try as he might, he could not find anything else that would fit.

At last he said, 'You cannot possibly be suggesting that I seduce you in exchange for a larger share of the diamonds.'

'I do not think seduction would be necessary,' she said. 'If I am already willing, you will not have to waste time in persuading me.'

He shook his head. 'You cannot begin to know what you are asking.'

'I believe I do,' she replied. 'I want you to lie with me, as a man does with a woman. I believe the Bible calls it fornication.'

'Certainly not,' he snapped and instantly regretted it as he saw the stricken look on her face. Before speaking again, he took care to moderate his tone to kindness. 'That was not meant as a censure of your character or appearance. But, Miss Strickland, you have shocked me to the core. Are you telling me that you have done such a thing before?'

She smiled, as if surprised that he would even consider it. 'Of course not. My knowledge is purely academic.'

'An academic knowledge,' he said amazed. 'Is England so much different than America that they would teach such things in schools?'

She gave him an odd look. 'In my country, they seem to take great pains to teach young ladies as little as possible about all subjects. That is why I am self-educated.' She glanced around her at the shelves surrounding them. 'There are books on the subject, you know.'

'*I* know,' he said, 'because I have spent the last few months in the company of sailors on the passage from America. But how did you learn of such things?'

She walked him to a corner of the library and got down a stack of books that seemed less dusty than the others. Then she set them on the table beside him.

'*Memoirs of a Lady of Pleasure*?' he said, flipping it open to a random page, then slamming it shut again.

'And this.' She held another book out to him.

He glanced at the curling letters across the cover. 'What good is it to you? It appears to be written in Hindi.'

'Sanskrit,' she corrected. 'I learned enough of the language to get the gist of the important bits. The illustrations are self-explanatory.'

Unable to stop himself, he opened it to an elaborate colour plate showing two incredibly acrobatic Indians. He riffled through some more pages, then took a steadying breath. 'If this is what you are using to educate yourself on the subject, I hope you understand that the models exhibit a degree of flexibility not found in most people.'

She snorted. 'Of course. But there are far less intimidating poses in some of the other books.' Her eyes blinked behind her spectacles. 'Would you like to see them?'

'That will not be necessary,' he said hastily, closing the book he held and making a mental note to return to the library and seek out the others when she was not there to observe him. 'So you have no practical knowledge of the thing you are asking of me.'

'That is why I need to ask for your help,' she said, as if her request was simply another leg up to reach a high shelf.

'You are asking me to deflower you.'

'You needn't use such a polite euphemism for it,' she said. 'When I first heard that term, I put a mirror between my legs and was quite disappointed to find that it did not look anything like a flower.'

As if the graphic pictures and frank discussion had not been enough to arouse him, he was now left to imagine Charity Strickland, naked and in curious self-exploration. He took a deep breath to clear his head. 'You do not need to explain that to me. I am familiar with the female anatomy.'

She nodded in approval. 'I hoped you were.'

He felt the beginnings of cold sweat on his brow as his blood rushed south. 'It was not meant to encourage you. What you are asking…' He threw up his hands in frustration. 'It is just not done.'

She arched an eyebrow. 'Really? Then how does the species continue?'

'It is not done outside the sanctity of marriage,' he corrected. 'We are not married, nor are we going to be so.' Especially since she had made it quite clear that she wanted nothing to do with him in his role as Comstock.

'Marriage is not actually a requirement for the act,' she said. 'It is a social convention, having more to do with the man's desire for legitimate children and the transfer of property than it does with what might be pleasant or practical for the women involved.'

'As such, it is a perfectly sensible convention,' he replied. 'Unmarried women are discouraged from engaging in...' he simply could not say the word to a girl he had just met '...in that act, because of the risk of pregnancy.'

She gave him another pitying look. 'There are ways to prevent that, you know.'

He sighed. 'I suppose you have read books on that subject, as well.'

'The library can provide a surprisingly complete education, if one cares to look,' she said.

'Obviously,' he said, then cautioned, 'but some things are not as they are in books.'

'That is another reason I am eager to experience the reality of it,' she said with an earnest expression. 'For academic interest.'

'But why choose me for your partner in this experiment?' he said, still not sure whether to be flattered or appalled.

She stared at him, amazed. 'Why you? Have you never looked in a mirror, Potts? You are quite handsome, you know.'

'I do not give it much thought,' he said.

'That is what pretty people often say,' she said with a sigh.

'Because it is not much of a recommendation,' he said. 'It is a single opinion of exterior appearance.'

'It may be superficial to you,' she said with an angry huff, 'but it is very difficult for me to ignore. When I look at you, I quite forget your willingness to steal your employer's property and abandon your job.'

'Aha!' He pointed at her in accusation. 'You admit that I have obvious flaws. My lack of sound morals should be enough to put you off considering me for...' he gave a wave of his hand '...certain things.'

'Things like marriage, perhaps,' she said, giving him an equally dismissive wave. 'But I am not asking for marriage. I am not even requiring seduction. We can simply have sexual intercourse. Then you may take your portion of the diamonds and return to whatever plans you have made for your life.'

'And abandon you,' he said, shaking his head.

'You speak as if your absence will create a hardship,' she said, confused.

'And you speak as if you will not miss me at all,' he countered. 'You make it sound as if you will lie with me and not give a second thought to it after I am gone.'

'That is not what I am saying at all,' she said. 'Of course I shall miss you, when you go. That is likely to be the case whether we lie together or not. But if we do, I will have sweet memories when I think of you, which will be often.' For a moment, her tone softened in a way that almost made him believe that she had some deeper feeling for him than curiosity.

Then she gritted her teeth in frustration. 'But you are going no matter how I feel or what we do. And I refuse to let you speak of my life as if it will be some great hardship, unbearable without the presence of a man. You are not leaving me in the desert or chaining me to a dungeon wall. Once you are gone, I will be right here, where I have always been, and alone, as I have always been. You will go to where ever you wish to be. Things will be almost as they were before.'

'But you will no longer be a maiden. What are you going to say to your husband, when he finds you experienced on your wedding night?' he said, hoping to frighten her.

'I expect I shall lie,' she said. 'Since you are leaving, soon, our time together is likely to be brief. But I have nineteen years of virginity to draw on. Since whoever I marry is not likely to be as smart as you, it should not be too hard to trick him.'

He wanted to argue against her logic, but she was quite likely right. If she claimed innocence, the gentleman she married would believe her. If he did not, he was no gentleman and she should not be marrying him. Unless she announced it to the world, whatever they did together would remain secret and harm no one. And though he could argue with her and himself that what she wanted was improper, she was a rational being who had argued the subject in her own head and made up her mind on it before coming to him with her request.

Once they were done, he could move on, just as he had countless times before, from jobs, from women and from anything that had ceased to hold his interest. Then he remembered what lay before him and the fact that, for the first time in his life, he was supposed to be running towards something and not away.

'Are you ready to concede the point, Potts?' Charity said, putting her hands on her hips. The gesture outlined her body under her skirt and made her argument almost more persuasively than her words had done.

'No, Miss Strickland, I am not.' He glanced at her for a moment and said a silent farewell to the body under the muslin before giving her a smile that was polite, firm and distant. 'I regret that I will be unable to seduce you, today or any other day. I am flattered by your request, of course.'

'Of course,' she repeated in a mocking tone. 'But you are unable. I have read about that, as well.'

'Not in that way,' he said sharply and reached into his pocket to produce the miniature of Prudence he carried there, holding it out for her to see.

'Mrs Potts, I presume,' Charity said, in a monotone.

'In a sense,' he said, equally expressionless. 'She is my brother's widow. Her name is Prudence. I have promised to take care of her.'

'And by that, I assume you mean you intend to marry her.'

'Yes,' he said softly.

Charity pulled a handkerchief from her sleeve and removed her spectacles, dabbing each eye once, before busying herself with cleaning the lenses. 'She is very beautiful.' There was a resignation in the words that announced this was exactly the sort of woman she had expected to find him associating with.

'She is,' he agreed. She was also monumentally stupid and more than a little greedy. He would not say that aloud, even with thousands of miles of water between them, but that made it no less true. 'Her looks have nothing to do with my decision,' he added.

'Of course not,' she said, turning towards the door as if she meant to run from him, only to turn back in anger. 'You may claim that physical appearance is superficial and unimportant, Potts. But when men who look like you decide to marry, it is to women like that.'

'I have a responsibility—' he began to say.

She cut him off. 'But when one is not pretty and has a manner that has been described as rude, intrusive and abrasive by all who know them, one learns otherwise. Thus far offers of marriage have been non-existent, as have flirtations and courtship. Even social courtesies from gentlemen have been thin on the ground. At nineteen, I am already a wallflower.'

Her lip trembled, just once. Then her iron, almost masculine control over her emotions returned. 'That is why I mean to take my happiness into my own hands. No one wants me, Potts. It should not be so very hard to believe, since you do not want me, either.'

Someone needed to tell her that there was nothing wrong with her face or her personality that time would not cure. Even now, there was much good about her. If men did not acknowledge that fact, then they were fools and not worth her consideration.

But she did not need words, for she had heard them already and did not believe them. She needed something more. Then, as if it had a will of its own, his hand rose to touch her hair. It was the sort that could not seem to hold a curl, but ran through a man's fingers like silk and lay sleek on the pillow when he took it down at night. It smelled of violets. And her lips…

Her lips were warm and soft as he kissed them, barely parted so that her breath feathered against his cheek before rushing away in a gasp as he wrapped his arm around her waist and gathered her close. Then he touched her tongue with his, gently, and her hands, which had been balled into fists at her side, relaxed and stroked his coat sleeves.

If he had an intention at all when beginning this, he'd have said that it was an act of possibility more than passion. What was the harm in a single kiss if it erased some of the doubts she had about herself? But now that he had started, one did not seem like enough.

He traced her jaw with his teeth before returning to her mouth and entering it more boldly, thrusting more deeply and smoothing her body against his to feel curves that were wasted on a virgin.

Would there be anything so wrong in doing the thing that everyone had urged him towards since the moment he had set foot on shore? He could take her in secret now, as she asked him. Then take her again with the blessings of the church. And she would take his side here, in this house for the rest of his life.

Not his house. It was Comstock's: a man he did not want to be and one that she did not want to marry.

So he broke the kiss and set her away from him as gently as possible. She was staring up at him, the picture of temptation with her hazel eyes wide behind her fogged spectacles, mouth still open as if asking for another kiss. The quickest way to stop this madness before it went any further would be to announce his true identity. She would be rinsing her mouth with spirits and locking her bedroom door before he could finish his apology.

But revealing himself would ruin this moment for both of them. Seeing her like this, with soft lips and eyes full of wonder, he could not manage to do it.

Unfortunately for him, there were more than enough unpleasant truths that he did not need to tell her that one. She was leaning towards him now for another kiss and he put his hand on her shoulder to hold her back. 'That was to assure you that there is nothing about you that prevents me from acceding to your request. If my refusal means you no longer wish to share the diamonds we are searching for, then so be it. I cannot make love to you for reasons that have nothing to do with you and everything to do with me.'

'Then tell me what they are,' she said.

'If you knew me better, you would find that I am a feckless layabout who is not worthy of your attentions. But I am not so bad that I would risk leaving a child here when I must go home to give a name to the one Prudence is carrying.'

'She is pregnant?' Charity said.

He nodded. 'You must see that what you suggested would be quite impossible for me.' But even as he said it, his mind was arguing that the kiss they'd just shared had endless possibilities. 'And now, if you will excuse me, I have business for the Earl.' And, though he hated to admit it, he ran away from a nineteen-year-old girl.

Chapter Nine

He had kissed her.

Before and after, he had said a lot of things, some of which were likely important. But all of it paled beside the fact that he had kissed her. On the mouth. The open mouth. He had done a thing with his tongue that she could not remember reading about in any of the books of the library, which were far more focused on other parts of the anatomy. And, now that he was well-rested and clean-shaven, he had been even more beautiful than yesterday.

When James Leggett had arrived, she had admired him physically, of course. But she had seen that he was instantly drawn to her sister Faith and she had done everything in her power to encourage the bond. The same was true of Mr Drake and Hope. They were both very handsome gentlemen and she liked them as brothers.

But Potts was something else entirely. Talking with him was like she imagined fencing might be. Not the clumsy whacking of swords that she and her sisters used to manage when playing with the weapons that decorated the walls of the manor. Trying to convince him to lie with her had been like the rapier battle she had seen at the end of *Hamlet* when they had gone to Haymarket. Fast but totally in control, each thrust met with parry and riposte.

And then his control had slipped. She touched her lip, feeling the smile forming on a mouth that felt ever so slightly swollen.

It should not have surprised her that he had a beautiful and pregnant fiancée waiting for him in America. Though he claimed to be flawed, she doubted that any of those imperfections was enough to prevent women from flocking to him, nor was he likely to resist temptation when it had been offered by a woman like that.

The thought of the miniature hidden in his pocket made her heart ache at the hopelessness of the task she had set for herself. Did the fair Prudence play chess? she wondered. Did they have anything in common other than beauty, or was he marrying her solely out of concern for her welfare? When he had spoken of his plans for the future he had mentioned responsibility and obligation. But nothing had been said of love. There had been no desire in his eyes when he had looked at the little painting.

For that matter, was levirate marriage allowed in America? Though English men sometimes married their widowed sisters-in-law, it was not legal or approved of by the church.

Charity had a momentary fantasy of charging down

the aisle of some distant church and announcing that there was a just cause that such a union could not be performed. It more than likely proved just how far out of society she had fallen that she imagined making a didactic lecture on marital law. A normal young woman would stop a wedding by announcing her inability to live another moment without her beloved.

It did not matter. All her protests would be moot against the sight of Prudence's swelling belly. If he had got her with child it was right that he should marry her.

If…

Before she could finish her thought, there was a soft knock on the library door.

'Enter,' she called, turning to see the butler standing stiffly on the threshold. 'What is it, Chilson?'

'Will you be taking luncheon in the library as usual, Miss Charity?'

She smiled up at him. 'In the dining room. And supper, as well.'

'Mr Potts has requested that a tray be sent to his room,' the butler said with a nod of approval.

'Has he, now?' He had run away from the kiss and now he meant to hide from her at mealtimes. 'He should not be inconveniencing the staff,' she said, smiling to herself. 'Take him his lunch. But when I see him next, I will inform him that all further meals will be taken in the dining room.'

'He is also welcome at the staff table in the kitchen,' Chilson replied, after a significant pause.

'But he is not staff,' she said, firmly. 'He will eat at the table with the family.'

'But when the family is not in residence—'

'I am the family,' she said, to cut off any further discussion.

Chilson did not sigh in frustration, but she had the feeling that he sorely wished to. 'I will see to it that there are two footmen assigned to the dining room, and another to accompany him, should he need assistance with the audit. And perhaps a maid to sit with you, in the evening.'

For a moment, she could not believe what she was hearing. She had waited fifteen years for the moment when there was not a grandparent or a sister telling her that everything she wanted to do was wrong. Now that she was finally alone and could make her own decisions, the servants had suggestions on how she should behave.

It was all the more annoying that they were right to be worried. But they did not understand that it was Pott's honour that needed protecting.

She gave the butler a firm smile. 'Footmen and maids will not be necessary, Chilson. I do not want or need a chaperon.'

There was another pause that could have contained a sigh, had Chilson been any less disciplined. 'Very good, Miss Charity.'

'You may go,' she said and watched him retreat in silence.

The servants would stop pestering, for the moment, at least. But after lunch, she would have to lure Potts out of his room. That was what the diamonds were good for. Although the kiss he had given her was worth at least one of them, he could not have any until they were found. And to find them, she must pretend to need his help.

It had taken Miles less than a day at Comstock Manor to completely lose sight of his plan. He had come to find something to sell so he might leave the country. Though he'd not been eager to return home empty-handed, he had found nothing in England for him but more trouble. He had most assuredly not wanted to marry some distant cousin, who was a total stranger to him, just because everyone here thought it the expedient thing to do.

One day later, he had been tempted with the prospect of lost diamonds, even one of which might save him from debtors' prison. And he had kissed the very same woman he had been meaning to avoid, as a way to deflect her desire for a full-blown affair.

Worse yet, he had liked it. He was not about to seduce and abandon a virgin, even if she had asked him to do so. But then, he had not thought he was going to kiss her, either. If he meant to do right by Pru, he should not be thinking about doing it again.

There was also the fact that Charity disliked the new Earl of Comstock, on principle. It was a point in her favour, since Miles didn't like being him. Still, should she discover that he and Potts were one in the same, she would not be happy with either of them.

Better to go back to his original plan, find a portable treasure and leave. The best place to find such a thing was in one of the older, closed wings where an absence might never be missed. He took the main stairs at a trot, then chose the middle hall, between the family bedchambers and those reserved for guests.

The corridor was narrower than either of the other wings, and darker, as well, with matched pairs of doors on either side. At the end, there was a change in the plaster of the wall to indicate yet another, older wing. There, the passage widened to reveal more halls spreading out in opposite directions.

He reached into his pocket, retrieved the silver dollar he kept there and flipped it. Heads. Left it was. He walked down the left hall, trying and failing to imagine where he might be in the building as a whole.

The first storey of the house seemed to be in the shape of a large H. But the ground floor was a straight line that widened in the middle like a snake that had eaten an egg. If the lower portion of this wing had not been destroyed, he could not think where he might access it, except from the public rooms of the newest wings.

There was a curved stairway at the end of this hall that might enlighten him, but it was unlit and appeared to end in a brick wall before reaching the ground level. He retraced his steps, pulled a ring from his pocket and began fitting keys into door locks.

The majority of the rooms that he was able to open were sparsely furnished with uncurtained, mattressless bedframes, empty cupboards and rickety benches. But halfway down one side, he opened on the sort of room he was looking for.

It was fully furnished and decorated in a garish combination of red and gold with painted Chinese silk on the walls and heavy velvet curtains on the windows and bed. There were no ornaments on the dresser and no jewellery forgotten in the drawers. The cupboard contained gowns and coats that were at least fifty years out of style and of no use to him unless he meant to waste time picking off the brass buttons and tarnished lace.

But on the other side of the room, there was a rosewood cabinet fitted in brass and inlaid with what appeared to be jade. It was also locked. What could be so valuable that it would be locked inside a chest like this, yet left in a back room and all but forgotten?

There was nothing on his key ring that might open this door. But what was the point of being an earl if one could not take liberties in one's own home? He reached into another pocket, got his penknife and jabbed it into the opening, jiggling the latch.

There was a squeak and the doors popped open. He stared in horrified fascination at the contents of the cabinet. The shelves inside were filled with row upon row of carved ivory ornaments, most no bigger than his fist. The front row was made up of well-rendered animals and fish. But the further back he searched, the more surprising they became. There were fewer animals and more people: couples and sometimes groups of three or more. And they were all as acrobatically flexible as the Indians in the book he had seen earlier.

He closed the cupboard again, wiggling the popped latch until it caught. It was just his luck that the first pawnable items he found were the sorts of things he would be embarrassed to carry around in his pocket.

'Grrr...'

He turned to find his evil, little dog standing in the doorway as if it meant to block his exit.

'Do not growl at me. I saved your life once and have seen to it that you will end it in luxury, fattened on table scraps and sleeping on a lady's pillow.'

The dog plopped into a sit, as if considering.

Since the fight seemed to have gone out of it, Miles walked towards the door so he might leave the room.

At the last minute, the dog jumped to its feet, bared its little fangs and charged.

Miles leapt over it, grabbing the door handle as he passed, closing the door with a slam and trapping the dog inside. He fumbled for the key that would lock it in, then thought the better of it. It had been hard enough to explain to Charity that he would not be making love to her. He did not want to admit that he had sealed her dog in an abandoned room without food or water.

He opened the door cautiously, preparing for another attack. When none came, he called into the room, 'Come out, you miserable beggar. Do not think I have gone soft. I am freeing you for her sake.'

There was no sound from inside.

He opened the door cautiously to reveal...

Nothing.

There was no sign of the dog that had been there only a moment ago. For a moment, he thought of searching for it. But only a moment. It was probably lying in wait behind a curtain or under the bed, ready to bite him when he got close. 'Suit yourself, Pepper.

The door is open. You found your way this far. You can come out when you are hungry, or starve, for all I care.'

He went back into the hall and retraced his steps to the main floor and back to the library. He opened the door slowly and paused on the threshold, as he had above for the dog. But this time he wanted to make sure that Charity Strickland was not currently in residence. After the tumultuous meeting earlier, he was not ready to see her again, certainly not during his current errand.

Once he was sure he was alone, he shut the door and returned to the shelf where she had pulled the books she had described as 'educational'. The word proved accurate for, despite a varied tutelage in the ways of the world, there were things here that he had not seen before.

He had heard of the Cleland book, while in America. Who had not? But he had never actually seen a copy of it. It appeared that the library had both the first edition and several even less reputable copies. There was the Sanskrit manual of love and another book in equally unreadable French, but with a trove of illustrations that left nothing to the imagination. The next books, in Latin and German, were not illustrated. But Charity was clearly fluent in both for she had taken the trouble to bookmark the most interesting pages with neatly written translations. He could not decide which shocked him more, the subject matter, or the scholarly care she had taken in writing words that no innocent girl should know.

It was no real surprise that the rest of the row was made up of art from the Orient, albums of paintings on silk depicting all manner of copulation. After what he had found upstairs, it seemed that one of his predecessors had an obsession with all things Asian. If he had travelled extensively to find such collectables, it likely explained where much of the family money had gone.

But other items might have had been here even longer. The shelf beneath held heavy leather tomes with metal loops set into the bindings showing where they had once been chained to a monastery shelf. On seeing the illuminations, he understood the reason for such security. The monks who had done the work seemed possessed to draw phalluses into even the most innocent pictures.

He closed the books again, taking care to return them to the shelves in the same order he had removed them, to give their curator no indication of his examination. The last thing he needed was for her to realise he had been looking at them again and thinking that he needed inspiration.

But that was hardly the case. While it was certainly titillating, he preferred the actual activity to looking at pictures thereof. He doubted that anywhere in the entail documents, he would find that he was required to preserve and display the extensive Comstock pornography collection for future generations.

But the presence of the things put ideas into his head that had nothing to do with bedding Miss Charity. The problem remained that he had no idea how to carry it out. But that did not mean he did not know a fellow to help him.

When they had met, Gregory Drake had introduced

himself as a solver of problems and seemed to specialise in getting the nobility out of just the sort of jams that he had fallen into. Drake had been willing to take on the daunting project of inventorying Comstock Manor, even after he'd seen the place and known what he was up against.

Then he'd quit the task in the middle and run off to Scotland with Charity's older sister. Miles had found it annoying, but only faintly so. He could not blame Drake so very much. He was beginning to see how persuasive the Strickland sisters could be, when they got bees in their bonnets. But it had been several weeks and the man had not sent any kind of resignation from employment. The honeymoon had gone on long enough. It was time for him to return to work.

Miles quit the library, but could not help looking both ways on exiting, lest Miss Charity was lying in wait to spring on him and demand that they copulate in the hallway. This was the problem with pornography. It gave one ridiculous ideas about what was likely to happen in moments of passion and not nearly enough information about what actually did. Then he climbed the stairs to his room.

Luncheon was waiting there, as he had requested, as was a writing desk well stocked with quills and ink, and paper. It took several pages to outline his requests, but the end effect looked quite impressive on stationery embossed with the Comstock family crest. Then he addressed it to Drake's London address.

He hesitated for a moment before going to the bureau drawer that held his fresh linen and fishing around under a pile of neckcloths to find the signet he had hidden there. Then he took it back to the desk along with the tinder box from the fireplace to melt the sealing wax. He'd vowed, once he'd left London, that he would never use the Comstock seal again. He'd felt like an imposter when signing documents before and was eager to be free of it.

But in this case, it was appropriate. This project was less about what he needed and more about what was necessary to the estate. If the finances could be stabilised, perhaps he could persuade Charity to take on the running of it, even though she had been dead set on escaping the house and having her own life.

But her desire to leave home seemed to have much to do with avoiding the Earl of Comstock. If she learned that the Earl wanted to avoid his responsibilities in just the same way, she might think differently about leaving home.

Now that it was finished, he stared at the properly sealed letter in his hand. If he wished to remain anonymous to the staff here, he could not exactly toss it into the morning's post with the Earl's mark pressed on to the back of it. At last, he tucked it into a coat pocket and made an excuse to the butler about the need to exercise his horse. Then he went down to the stables, mounted and rode to the inn he had passed in the village the day before. Once there, he drank a glass of ale, posted the letter and returned to the house in time for supper.

Chapter Ten

Though she had known him for just over a day, Charity had changed significantly since Potts had come into her life. This evening, when Dill held out a choice of dinner gowns, she chose the more revealing of the two without another thought. Then she sat patiently as her too-straight hair was piled high on her head and secured with pearl-headed pins.

When the maid held out the Comstock necklace to her, she shook her head. Since they both knew it was false, it seemed a pointless addition to the ensemble. Instead, she polished her spectacles and glanced in the mirror. She looked well enough, she supposed. She was still nothing like her sisters, but an effort had been made. Then she gave Pepper a good-luck pat on the head before going down to the dining room.

Potts was already at the table and gave her a sullen expression as he rose to greet her. 'At your service, Miss Strickland.'

She gave him a sour smile in return. 'You have no

reason to be cross with me. Despite our financial difficulties, Comstock Manor has an excellent cook.'

'I could enjoy the food just as well in my room,' he said, staring deliberately down at his plate.

'To avoid me,' she concluded, trying not to sound hurt. 'Do not be ridiculous. Though I made my position plain this morning, it is not as if I mean to spring on you like a wild beast now that you have refused me.'

He started in surprise.

'And in case you have forgotten, we have not yet found the diamonds. Since we parted, the situation has grown much more urgent.'

'In half a day?' he said doubtfully. 'They have been lost for a century or more. What difference will a few hours make?'

'Your employer has been seen in the village. It is only a matter of time before he arrives.'

'Seen, by whom?' he said, glancing around him. 'No one here, surely.'

'He was at the inn, this afternoon. He did not announce himself,' she added. 'But the ostler saw the Comstock stamp on the letter he posted. He told the baker, who told the greengrocer, who informed the kitchen maid who went to place the order for this week's vegetables.'

'Who returned here to tell the cook, who told the housekeeper, who informed you,' he said.

'She told my maid, actually. And then Dill told me. Do not underestimate the speed of local gossip,' she said. 'It is not always accurate, but it is very fast.'

'Apparently,' he agreed with a weak laugh and emptied his glass in a single swallow as if he was no more eager for the arrival of the Earl than she was. 'But can you trust any story that has passed through so many tellers?'

'Even if it is not true, I mean to take it as so and re-double my efforts. I meant to be away from here before he arrived.' Though the prospect of that now seemed as hopeless as seducing Potts. 'But if his appearance is imminent, I suppose I shall have to settle for depart-ing soon after.'

'You have no reason to have formed such an aver-sion to a man you do not know.' He gave her a scepti-cal look. 'If it is because you had problems with your grandfather, you will find that they are nothing alike. And though you seem to brood on him, when I spoke to him, Comstock did not mention you at all. He does not give two figs for your behaviour…other than to wish you well with it, of course.'

It was a strangely passionate defence of a man Potts claimed to barely know. But she was having none of it. 'The idea that he does not care about me is almost worse than that he does,' she said. 'Much damage can be done in ignorance, you know.'

'Then when you meet him, you must take the time to tell him what you want.' He tapped his forehead. 'You cannot expect him to read your mind like one of the books in your library.'

'Because speaking my mind worked so well with you,' she said and watched him start again.

'You have made it plain that you do not wish to

marry him,' Potts reminded her. 'What can you have to say that would be more shocking than that?'

'I have ideas on the running of the estate that might not be in line with what he wishes to do.'

His beautiful lips pursed in a thoughtful pout, forcing her to take a cooling sip of wine so that she could concentrate on what he might say with them. 'I suspect he will listen to your opinions, request further information and proceed on them, if he finds them wise.' He gave her a thoughtful look. 'Which he probably will, since he has heard that you are a very intelligent young lady.'

She snorted and took another sip of wine. 'You have not met many earls, have you?'

'Until recently? No, I have not.'

'And you are new to this country, as well. You are still enamoured of the American idea that men can be self-made and rise to great heights based solely on their ability.'

'They can,' he said with an earnest sincerity that made him all the more charming.

She finished her wine and stared morosely at the empty crystal, knowing it was unwise to take more, lest she be seen as intemperate. 'What you believe to be true has nothing to do with the way things actually are. Comstock is Comstock because of who his father was. Or, in this case, his grandfather. He is the last flower at the end of the last branch of the family tree. And I?' Perhaps she had already had too much wine, for she was not sure of how to end the metaphor to account for the fact that women were not part of the tree at all and girls were even less than that. 'Let us simply say that he will not take to my suggestions any better than the last one did.'

'You did not get along with your grandfather?'

'We managed well enough,' she replied. 'He adored me when I was a child. And as I grew he was still quite fond of me. At least he was when I behaved as my sisters did. They obeyed him in all things. In return, he doted on them.'

'And you were not so obedient?' he said.

'He said I read too much and that it affected my mind.' She gave up the struggle to moderate herself and reached for the carafe.

He was on his feet, refilling her glass before her arm was fully extended.

She gave him a nod of thanks. 'Girls are not supposed to think too hard. Women even less so. We are expected to be obedient to our parents and subservient to our husbands.'

He smiled. 'I have already noted that subservience is not your strong suit.'

'It makes no sense to follow a man who is going in the wrong direction,' she said, staring at him. The candlelight made him even more handsome than he was in daylight, softening some features and throwing others into sharper relief. She wanted to stare at him, to drink in every last detail so that she could remember him before he disappeared from her life.

She wanted to. But that would be rude. Instead, she removed her spectacles, pretending to clean them with her napkin and letting her poor eyes render him a pleasant blur.

'And what direction was your grandfather taking that you did not want to follow?'

'The same way his father and grandfather took. The path of least resistance,' she said. 'He sought to preserve the house and the things in it as it has always been. His successor is likely to do the same, since he will be taking the advice of other men who are all doing exactly that.'

'And what would you do, in their stead?'

'If I was the Earl?' She smiled. 'I would get a proper inspection of the house to see if the far wing is even worth saving. It makes no sense to have the rooms if they are falling to ruin and never used.'

'And once that was done?'

'Do the same with the dower house. Grandmama must be provided for. But she should not be expected to live in a house with dry rot and loose bricks. If that house does not suit, perhaps he can rent her rooms in London and designate a suite of the manor for her use when she visits.'

'And then?'

'Then he should sell everything that is not nailed down. What is the point of keeping things that are never seen and never used, just for the sake of posterity?'

'An excellent question,' he agreed.

'And if that is still not enough, he should sell the rest of the diamonds, should we manage to find them. It will be somewhat more difficult to give up such a prominent part of the entail. But we have been managing on paste for so long, I see no reason we should not continue to do so.'

'Those are all excellent suggestions and much in line with what I would have said.' He added an approving nod.

'And there are likely other sources of income that have not been considered,' she added. 'But when I made even the smallest suggestion, Grandfather banished me from the library.'

'He locked you in,' Potts said, horrified.

'He locked me out,' she corrected. 'And out of his study, as well. He denied me admittance to the things I loved and refused to speak to me until I promised to be quiet again.' He had filled her glass again and she drank deeply. 'But I refused to be silent, so the doors stayed locked. That was how things ended between us, for he died later that year.'

'I am very sorry,' he said, in a quiet voice.

She sighed. 'My sisters had no problems with him. But then, they never bothered Comstock with anything more taxing than the colour of the sky and whether it might be wise to take a coat when he rode out.' She stared down at her plate, no longer hungry for the food on it. 'But he taught me that it was better to be alone than to feel alone.' She looked up at Potts. 'The day he died, I stole his keys and unlocked the doors. But I do not mean to stay and see them locked again. I will not be ignored in my own home, or bartered off to marry a stranger, or any of the other things that might happen to me should I stay. I want a say in my own future.'

She was becoming overwrought with the memories, for when he answered her, it was with the calming tone one used on small children and horses. 'I will speak to him. It will be all right.'

'Because you are good at solving other people's problems, aren't you, Potts?' she said, and watched him start in surprise.

'What makes you say that?' He seemed honestly puzzled.

'This afternoon, you said that your dear Prudence was with child,' she said and watched to see if he squirmed.

'Yes,' he said, his face as blank and unreadable as it had been when they'd played chess.

'Not your brother's child, for you mentioned that it was fatherless. But I doubt you'd have left her, had you thought it might be yours.'

'Perhaps you give me too much credit,' he said, admitting nothing.

'I do not think so.' She stared at him, losing herself in his bottomless dark eyes. 'You are not the sort to scatter your seed unheeding of the consequences. If you were, you'd have had no second thoughts on my offer this afternoon.'

'The identity of the child's father does not matter,' he said, filling his own glass again. 'I promised my brother before he died that I would take care of her. I would not be doing so if I let the world call her a whore and her child a bastard.'

'You do not sound very happy about it,' she said.

'My happiness does not factor into the equation.'

He drained his glass, refilled it and drained it again. 'When I make a promise, I do not break it. I told my brother he need not worry and I will tell you the same. You will have nothing to fear from Comstock. You have my word.'

Then he pushed away from the table as if that was all it would take to leave his problems behind. 'But let us speak no more of the future. It will come fast enough without our worrying about it. Let us forget the Earl, the diamonds and everything else. Would you fancy chess? Or perhaps some other game that you stand a better chance of winning?'

He was taunting her. And despite herself, she smiled. 'How are you at billiards?'

'Abominable,' he said, smiling back.

'And you will be even worse on a warped table. This bodes well for me. Come, let me show you the billiard room.'

Chapter Eleven

The Comstock billiard room was everything he could have hoped for. Though it must have been empty for some time, there was a faint smell of tobacco still hanging in the air. The walls were hung with trophy mounts and paintings that alternated between hunting scenes and pretty women showing an excessive amount of flesh.

It was a testament to the diligence of the servants that though the house was practically empty, the crystal decanters on the sideboard were kept well stocked with brandy. He poured a glass for himself and, after a moment's thought, a smaller glass for her. They'd both had too much wine at dinner, but to be sober was to remember his duty and his future, and he did not want to do either. He set his glass on the edge of the table and turned to select the straightest of the cues from a rack along a wall.

Charity poked at the fire and surveyed the table. 'There should be an iron around somewhere, so we can get the worst of the wrinkles out of the felt. Try the little Chinese cabinet behind you.'

He turned to the corner she'd indicated and was alarmed to discover a mate to the one that he had seen in the bedroom above. Knowing the sense of humour that gentlemen exhibited when ladies were not present, it was probably not wise to open it in front of her. 'It is locked,' he said, then waited to hear her announce that it never had been before.

'I believe the key is on one of the ledges,' she said, now pointing above his head. 'When we girls wished to play, we usually had Chilson prepare the table for us. But I have dismissed the servants for the evening.'

'I see.' She seemed occupied with choosing her mace, so he turned quickly, snatched the key from its place and bent down to unlock the doors, blocking the sight with his body.

The shelves of this one held an array of erotic *objets d'art* rather like the things he had seen some of the sailors carving from walrus tusks to pass the time on the crossing. 'No iron,' he said, wincing and slamming the cupboard shut again.

'Oh, well. I suppose we shall have to make the best of it, then.' She gave him a wicked smile. 'Shall I set up the game?'

'If you would,' he replied, eager for the distraction.

She removed the balls from a tray on a side table and leaned across the breadth to put them in their proper place.

He took a long sip of his brandy. As she'd sat across from him at dinner, he'd noticed that her gown was pleasantly low-cut. Even lower than on the previous evening, in fact. Without the depressing distraction of a false diamond, he had been able to enjoy the sight of her. But his admiration had been well within the bounds of gentlemanly good taste.

Now, as she bent low over the table, he could see all the way to Delaware. And an excellent view it was. He turned his head, only to find himself staring at a painting of randy cherubs. The opposite way was the Chinese cabinet, which he did not want to think of, much less look at.

As she stood up straight again, he gathered his wits and forced himself to look her in the eyes.

'Now, what shall you give me if I beat you?'

'Eh?'

'Last night, you tricked me into letting you help with the puzzle box. Tonight, I shall name the stakes.'

He took a gulp of brandy, preparing himself.

'I think I should like another kiss, please.'

'No!'

'It is not so much to ask, is it? The one you gave me this morning was very nice and it has not changed anything between us.'

After all he had seen today, he was in a much different mood than he had been this morning. But to tell her so would reveal far more than he wanted her to know about the contents of his mind and, perhaps, his breeches.

'A kiss,' he repeated, to buy time to think. He was quite handy with a cue and she was just a girl who could not be trusted to keep the felt intact without using a mace. He would beat her, just as he had last night. 'I think that can be arranged,' he said at last. 'And if I win, you will stop pestering me about such things.' One game and he would have his peace of mind back, intact, just as it had been before he'd met her.

'Of course,' she agreed. She was staring at him again. 'Well, don't just stand there holding your stick. You may take the first shot.'

He managed to break the balls without scratching, but just barely.

'A terrible shot, Potts,' she said, smiling sweetly at him. 'For you, at least.' She twirled the mace in her hands, holding the tail end of it forward to shoot, unencumbered by the weighted end behind her. Then she leaned forward again. As he was staring at her breasts, there was a snick of the cue meeting the balls. Then, some magic he had never seen before sent them spinning wildly around the table, caroming off banks and each other to end just where she needed them to be.

Over the next few minutes, she avenged herself of every British loss from Bunker Hill to the Battle of New Orleans. Her skill was staggering, her smile sweet and her breasts nonpareil.

Her grandfather's brandy was also exceptionally potent and he'd had too much of it. Why else would he be thinking the things he was thinking about her?

Love.

He smirked at the idea. He had known her for only a day. He admired her intellect, of course. Her good sense, as well. She was a wickedly smart chess player. If she would school him at billiards, he might make his living on it back home. But if he loved anything, he loved her breasts, which were almost falling out on to the table as she sunk the shot that finished him.

Then, she stood up again and her bodice gave a friendly bounce of encouragement. 'Another game? But remember, you will owe me even more kisses, should you lose.'

'What would be the point?' he said with a happy sigh. 'You have mastered me.'

'I seriously doubt that,' she said, placing her mace into the rack and walking around the table towards him. 'Now, if you would be so kind as to give me my reward?' She smiled and held out her arms to him.

And, God help him, he finished the last of his brandy and stopped resisting.

This kiss was different from the last one.

That had been soft and gentle and a little exciting. It had been everything she had hoped for in a first kiss.

She'd had no doubt she would beat him and had known that this kiss would be coming almost as soon as they had started to play. Still, it took her by surprise. It happened a split second sooner than she'd planned, for he had eagerly closed the distance between them as she'd approached. Since he was sure of her consent, he did not bother to hesitate, sealing their lips and taking her open mouth with a sudden, challenging thrust of his tongue. Then he gripped her waist and lifted, balancing her on the edge of the billiard table and stepping between her spread legs.

It seemed that the last few seconds were but a preamble. Now he was kissing her as if she were food and drink and air, as if he could not survive if they were parted. It was glorious. She kissed him back as best she could, matching the movements of his tongue and trying to return the pleasure he was giving her, afraid that at any moment he would stop and she would be alone again.

But when he did stop, it was only to whisper, 'Just one? Or do you want more?'

'More,' she murmured. 'More.'

'You do not know what you are asking,' he whispered into her ear and ran a finger along the top of her bodice, then back up her throat. 'I want to bite you. Here. Here. Here.' His finger tapped the pillow of her breast, the side of her neck and the place where her pulse hammered in her throat. 'I want to suck on your skin like a juicy peach and mark you so the world will know I've done it.'

This was the point where she was supposed to object. But she could imagine his teeth on her throat and every muscle in her body seemed to tighten in eager anticipation. He stared into her eyes and, when he was sure she would not cry off, his hands cupped her breasts and squeezed them possessively, then more slowly, massaging them through the fabric of her gown. 'But anything that happens between us will need to be secret. There are places that I can kiss you that will not show. Would you like that?'

He meant in places that were always covered by clothing. She tried to take a breath to show that she was calm and not the least bit frightened by what she had suggested, but it came out as a wordless gasp. So she looked into his eyes and nodded.

'Before we continue, I must know something.' He touched the tip of her nose with his finger. 'Did you know what was in the cabinet when you brought me here?'

Her reason returned with a thump at the *non sequitur*. 'What?'

He stepped to the side, turned the key and opened the cabinet doors.

She stared in silence at the contents. Grandmama had frequently hinted that her generation was not confined by the current morality and enjoyed themselves without guilt. Charity had to admit that her views towards Potts might have been coloured by the suggestions. But she had not thought that her grandparents were quite so free as this.

Considering that this collection had been locked up tight in a room normally occupied by men, it was possible that Grandmama would be just as shocked as she was to see them. But unless she wanted to risk hearing stories about her grandparents that were even more hair-raising than usual, it would be best not to ask.

She glanced to the man at her side, trying to guess if he wished her to be curious or horrified. At last, she decided to attempt to bluff. 'I have no idea what these are,' she said quickly. 'But if you wish to enter them into the inventory...'

'You have no idea,' he said, giving her a dubious look. 'If you admit to not knowing something, it will be the first time in history. It will also be a lie. I doubt, after the books you have been reading, that there is a gap in your education the size of this.' He picked up one of the smaller pieces and weighed it in his hands.

She was supposed to be shocked. But it was overcome by her curiosity as to the accuracy of the carving, and the size, which still seemed overly large compared to pictures she had seen.

When she did not answer him, he continued. 'Far be it from me to allow you to continue in ignorance, especially after what you have requested from me. The thing I am holding is what the French call a *consolateur*. I have also heard the euphemism, widow's comforter. In New England, the whalers call it a "he's at home". They give them to their wives to keep them from having just the sort of ideas you have been having about me.'

'Really,' she said faintly.

'Indeed,' he said, then glanced at the contents of the cabinet and gestured towards the back row. 'Though the man who carved that one on the left either had a very high opinion of himself or a problem with carving to scale.'

'Of course,' she said, dropping her gaze so as not to be caught staring at the thing. 'That is what I suspected.'

'My question for you would be—have you considered putting such an item to its intended use?'

'You should not…'

'Ask you such a personal question,' he said, finishing her sentence with a knowing smile. 'Proof that I should not take your maidenhead. If I were to ask such a thing, our spirits should be so closely aligned that there is nothing left that we cannot speak of.'

'But we hardly know each other,' she whispered.

'And that is precisely the problem, my pet. You are actively seeking a lover who is a virtual stranger to you and who will leave you soon after. And I do not understand the reason for it.'

He stepped closer, until his lips were barely inches from hers, as if readying for another kiss. 'You deserve a man who will stay with you because he cannot imagine being happy anywhere else but in your arms.'

Perhaps it was true. But she did not want that man. She wanted the one standing before her now. 'But what if no such man exists?' she said. 'Am I to go my entire life without ever knowing physical love?'

'If that is your concern, we must satisfy your curiosity in a way that does not make me—how did you describe it?—scatter my seed unheeding of the consequences.' He gripped the carved ivory in one hand and stroked it with the other before drawing it across her bare shoulder until it settled into the cleft of her bosom. Then he stroked.

She gasped as her nipples tightened at the feel of it, hard, smooth and cool against her skin.

He spoke as he continued to move it, dipping deeper and deeper into her bodice. 'There are advantages for both of us, should you be interested in seeking relief this way. The need for contraceptives, and the fear of their unreliability, would be rendered nil. And when I go, it will lessen my guilt at taking something that should not belong to me.'

'If you mean my body, it is mine to give or deny and not something that belongs to the first man who enters me,' she said, trying to think past the tight feeling in her belly and the wetness spreading between her legs.

'A true statement,' he agreed. 'But men have developed curious ideas on the matter and I find it hard to cast them off just because one woman wants to be reasonable. If I bed you and leave, I will feel guilty.'

'You don't—'

He stopped her argument with a kiss on the mouth. When it ended, she was too breathless to speak.

He had no such problem and continued. 'There is also the very real possibility that I will make a mess of it. I have a history of doing so in other parts of my life. And though I know perfectly well how to satisfy a woman, I have no experience with virgins. There can be only one first time. If yours is horrible, there will be no one to blame for that but me.'

'That could be true of any man I lie with,' she argued. 'Should I wait until marriage and the first time be unpleasant, I doubt my husband will be driven by guilt to a lifetime of abstention. If I decide I do not like it, I will be instructed to make the best of it and that will be that.' She was speaking faster than normal, driven by some strange sense of urgency to arrive at wherever it was he was trying to take her.

'True,' he agreed, sensing her need and speaking slower. 'But that does not make it right. And we are not talking of some hypothetical fellow you have not

yet met. We are speaking of me. If you do not enjoy
what happens, it would trouble me.'

'If that is how you feel, then I am sorry that I asked
it of you.' If he did decide against making love to her,
he could at least stop teasing her and leave her alone,
before she burst into tears of frustration. 'Forget I suggested it. Do not give it another thought.' She pinched
her lips together to keep herself from begging for release and readied herself to jump down from the table.

Before she could escape, he caught her by the hips,
pinning her in place, and dragged the phallus down
the outside of her thigh. 'Stop thinking of it? Since you
asked, I have been able to think of little else. But I have
not been able to convince myself that it is a good idea.'
She felt hard ivory sliding down her leg and something
else, almost as hard, pressing between her legs, where
their bodies touched.

'This, however?' He rubbed her ankle, below the
hem of her gown. 'Harmless pleasure.'

'I have no intention of using that thing on myself,'
she said, trying to squirm away from him.

'I do not expect you to,' he said, leaning forward and
kissing the shell of her ear. He let out a breath, slow
and hot, blowing down the side of her neck. His teeth
brushing the spot he had threatened before.

She gave an involuntary whimper of pleasure as
her body readied itself for the sudden release she felt
when she touched herself in the privacy of her room,
late at night.

He recognised it for what it was and lowered his
head to run his tongue over the tops of her breasts

as the ivory dipped under her petticoat, dragging her skirts up to her knees.

His fingers were tugging on her bodice, pulling it down. Cool air touched her nipples, followed by hot breath and then the teeth he had promised. 'Magnificent.' The word was murmured against her flesh and followed by a nip and a long, slow draw. Her back arched and her hand cupped the back of his neck, holding his mouth against her.

The sensation was indescribable. Perhaps he was right and they did not need to lie together after all. Surely this was as wonderful as it was possible to feel. Then, the comforter in his hand was pushing her skirts up to her waist. The smooth ivory shaft traced a line up the inside of her leg, pausing when it reached the top of her stocking to rub the naked skin above it.

Her legs twitched to squeeze his hips, ready to close on anything that was between them. He gave her a knowing smile and stepped closer. She could feel his arousal pressing against her, faintly amazed that she had caused it. The world could not be as grim as she thought it if a man like this wanted her, even a little.

He continued to smile, staring into her eyes as the hard thing in his hand continued its progress up her thigh, pushing between her legs, the tip sliding in the wetness pooling there, touching her as she touched herself. She could feel the tension building in her and the nearness of release. He'd had no need to worry about pleasing her. It would be good.

He spoke, in a strange, husky whisper, as if sharing

a secret. 'My only regret will be that I cannot look into your eyes as it happens.'

Her brow furrowed. There was no need for regret. If he waited as he was for just a moment, it would all be over.

Then he dropped to his knees and kissed her.

As his tongue touched the sensitive bud at her core, she felt pressure against the opening to her body, the pain of stretched skin and then the inexorable slide of cold and hard against the soft, hot, wet insides of her.

She screamed.

She could not help herself. After, there was a flash of fear that he might think it was from pain and stop to ask if she was all right. He must not stop, not ever, lest she die of disappointment. Or perhaps it was the pleasure that would kill her, for she was shattering under the onslaught of his kiss and the strokes of unyielding ivory against her quivering flesh.

She panted. She moaned. Her hands tore at her clothing, palms rubbing against her breasts, hips thrusting against his mouth. Was she trying to help, or trying to fight what was happening? She was not sure. But his hand pinned her to hold her still, his teeth grazed her skin and he thrust harder, faster and deeper.

She cried out again as she broke, mind empty of all but him, body conquered, yet triumphant.

His mouth stilled. He withdrew. She felt the stubble of his cheek against the skin of her thigh as he pressed a final kiss, just above her garter.

She stared up at the ceiling, too weak to lift her head, which was heavy and yet so light that it could have been full of sunshine. She could hear him rock back on his heels and the rustle of satin as he pulled her skirts down to cover her legs, stroking her knee though the fabric.

'I must leave you now.'

She sat up so quickly that the room spun around her, as if, in the few minutes they had been together, it had come unhinged from its axis and wobbled loose in the firmament. 'Leave? No!'

'If the servants come in answer to your cry, we must not be found together.' He turned his face from her, as if afraid a single glance might change his mind. 'I will see you at breakfast.' He took a deep breath. 'But right now…I have to go.'

Without another word, he hurried from the room.

Chapter Twelve

The next morning, she was still shaken by what had happened. Potts had been right. Chilson appeared shortly after he had gone, to assure himself that nothing was the matter. She had made some lie about a mouse running across her slipper, which, of course, explained why she was still sitting on the billiards table in shock.

The always discreet Chilson accepted the explanation as gospel. Both of them ignored the fact that she had never screamed at a mouse in her life. If she had seen one, she was far more likely to summon him requesting a small cage, a bit of seed bun and a thimbleful of water. Since his gaze never left her face, she was reasonably sure he had not seen the thing that had actually made her cry out, which had been dropped on the floor when her lover had run away.

Her lover.

Even if she did not say the words, the thought put a giddy grin on her face. She was quite sure she and Potts were lovers now. The lack of conventional coitus was a mere technicality. It was also one that might be rectified with just a bit more encouragement. Potts had proved a most inventive and unselfish partner. It was only polite that she return the favour he had done her.

He wanted her.

This was also unexpected. When she had first asked him to relieve her of her virginity, she had imagined that copulation for men was an instinctive act that would not be refused when offered. His immediate rejection made her suspect that the choice of partner mattered. If he had no taste for her, it was not surprising. She had not expected him to. She had assumed that the act of lying with her would be done out of pity and a masculine desire for release.

But the things he had done last night had been done solely for her pleasure. The thing that Shakespeare had called a dildo was now tucked between the ropes of her mattress and the rest of its fellows were locked away in their cabinet. She was still not sure that she could use such a thing again without embarrassment. But she had done several things that night that she had not thought herself capable of and did not feel the least bit ashamed this morning.

He had not only put her needs ahead of his own, he had taken some time in contemplating how best they could be met and worried about whether he would hurt or disappoint her if he failed. And in doing what he had done in the way he had done it, he had opened the door to what was probably a wide range of activities he would have deemed 'harmless pleasure'.

But he had denied these things for himself to pre-

serve her reputation. He had hurried away to avoid
possible repercussions afterwards, even though she
suspected that there were things he might have liked
for her to do for him. The matter required discussion,
education and, hopefully, a great deal of practical ex-
perimentation.

When Dill arrived, they chose a pale rose day gown
that was positively frivolous. The long white sleeves
were caught up with ribbons at multiple points on her
arms and the bodice was finished with a sheer chem-
isette that did little to conceal the bosom he had called
magnificent. Pepper accepted his matching bow with
a proud lift of his head and a vigorously wagging tail.
Then, they went down to the breakfast room to find
Potts.

And, as he had on the previous day, he disappointed
her. There was nothing but a small pile of crumbs by
the place she'd hoped to find him. Today, she took the
time to fill her plate and eat before searching for him.
The activities of the previous evening had left her with
a ravenous appetite. Perhaps it had done the same for
him. If he was an early riser, he might have been too
hungry to wait for her appearance.

When she had finished and given Pepper a hearty
meal of the scraps, they set off in search of him. He
had returned to the study again and was sprawled in
the chair behind the big desk with her grandfather's
recent journals spread in front of him.

And at the sight, her throat closed and her mind
went blank. In part, it was for the same reason as yesterday. There was a man sitting in Comstock's chair

who in no way belonged there. The man in that chair was not supposed to be young and carefree, nor was he supposed to look up at her and smile in a welcoming way, pushing aside the book he had been reading as if eager to see her.

It was perplexing. She had been prepared to find the new Comstock intimidating because of the power he had acquired. Potts made no bones about the fact that he was a no one come from nothing. But he had put his head between her legs and teased her until she'd screamed. Now, even though she had a hundred questions for him, she could not seem to think of any of them.

'Good morning, Miss Strickland.' His smile was innocuous, his tone polite. It was as if nothing had changed. And yet, everything had changed.

She cleared her throat. 'Good morning, Potts.'

Pepper jumped to the desktop and stood between them, staring at Potts with hackles raised.

He sat up slowly and, without breaking eye contact with the dog, said, 'Your help would be appreciated, Miss Strickland.'

She snapped her fingers. 'Pepper.' She pointed to a divan by the window. 'Sit.'

As quickly as it had come, his protectiveness disappeared and Pepper hopped off the desk and trotted to his place without another thought for Potts.

She tossed him the last of her breakfast. 'Good dog.'

Potts shook his head. 'Amazing.'

She shrugged. 'Hardly so. He is a smart little fellow. I am sure, when you get to know him…'

Potts shuddered. 'Hopefully, I will be gone before that is necessary.'

He was leaving. Even though he had spoken of little else since arriving, she had forgotten the fact. She had also forgotten her promise that things would not change after they'd made love. It was time to prove that she had meant what she'd said and get back to business.

She pointed to the journals lying on the desk in front of him. 'I thought I told you that there could be no clues in the recent books.'

He raised his eyebrows in surprise. Then he, too, continued as if nothing had changed. 'There aren't. But on coming here, I was given no restrictions in where I could not go and what I must not see. Since you voiced strong opinions on the folly of the previous Comstock's methods, I was interested in how the estate was being run.'

'And what is your verdict?' she asked, surprised to have been taken seriously over comments that had been fuelled by too much wine.

He dropped the book he had been reading and slammed it shut in front of him. 'His management was disastrous. The estate has been in debt for decades and yet it continues to spend. Each year, the farmers produce less only to see their rents raised. This drives them to poach the deer and rabbits that are eating their failing crops. And those animals are reproducing at a breakneck pace since a family of daughters cannot hunt them fast enough to control their numbers.'

It was an astute assessment for only two days' reading and raised points she had not considered. 'What would you do to bring matters in line again?'

'I would begin by forgiving the poachers for trying to feed their children. It makes no sense to hang or imprison the men who pay the rents. In fact, I would open the land to hunting parties, at least until the deer stop coming directly to the front door and eating the shrubbery. Then, there is the question of the failing crops.'

He leaned forward in his chair, obviously excited by the subject. 'Did you know that foodstuffs grow better when the roots are nourished? The Indians in America had a habit of planting a dead fish with their seeds to make the plants thrive. Perhaps there is some substance we might add that would improve the harvest. At the very least the midden piles and manure should be buried, since it is unhealthy to leave them too near the villages.'

'You seem to have given the matter some thought,' she said, dazzled by the sudden rush of ideas.

'In another life, I might have been a gentleman farmer,' he said with a thoughtful smile. 'I was told my grandfather did quite well planting tobacco. The land was the envy of the county.'

'In Philadelphia?' she said.

He shook his head. 'Maryland. Our house was not so great as this, of course. But from what I was told, it was large and beautiful.'

'You do not know?'

'That was before the revolution. Your army came and burned it to the ground. The money that was left was spent in the cause of patriotism.'

'And I assume your family was rewarded for its loyalty?' she said.

He laughed. 'On the contrary. My father was orphaned and embittered. He had plenty of tales to tell about the time when life was better, but he did little to improve the situation that had been left to him.'

'And what were you doing with yourself?' she asked, remembering that he called himself a feckless layabout. Perhaps he was, for playing chess for money did not sound like much of a job.

He shrugged. 'Since I had no family money to begin with and could not afford to go to university, there were many paths that were closed to me. But I am not a fool and have made out the best I could. I have written and read things for the illiterate and set type for a printer. I wrote articles for the *Daily Gazette*. I tried my hand at soldiering, but that can hardly be called a job. When my country was invaded by yours, all men took up arms.' He thought for a moment. 'I played a banjo in a tavern. But not well. And travelled about for a bit with my chess set.'

Perhaps he was a wastrel. Though the jobs he had chosen sounded interesting, they were not what she'd expected from a man of such intelligence. 'You aspired no further than that?'

He shrugged. 'I am much better at finding things I do not enjoy than things I do. Thus far, it has not really mattered. I had no wife. No children to support. I have enjoyed my freedom. I always knew that the time would come when I needed to settle. But thus far?' He shuddered. 'I do not like to be tied to one place and am easily bored. When the challenge is gone, so am I.'

'But that must change now that you mean to marry,' she reminded him.

'It had changed even before I left America,' he said. 'When my brother was alive, we pooled what money we had saved and borrowed more, planning to invest in sugar. My brother took our funds and travelled to the Caribbean. But before the plan could come to fruition, my brother was lost to us.'

'Leaving you with the debts and his family to care for,' she completed for him.

He nodded. 'My family is not what you would call lucky.'

'So you came to England to change your fortune,' she said, oddly proud of his plans.

'And found someone who has even more debts than I do,' he added.

'There are other jobs in England,' she reminded him. 'If you wish, I will help you forge what letters and references you might need to appear formally educated.'

'You think I should lie about my past?'

She gave a dismissive wave of her hand. 'When people are so easily deceived, it can be hard not to take advantage of them.'

He gave her an odd look. 'Some day you will be the one who has been fooled. It will be interesting to see if you are still so forgiving.'

'Should it happen, we shall see. But so far, it has not.' She smiled and continued to plan his life to her own advantage.

'And there is still Prudence to consider,' he reminded her.

'You could use the money you are seeking to bring her here, instead of returning to her,' she said. 'Now, with your understanding of the Earl's current difficulties and your progressive ideas, you might make an excellent estate manager. Comstock Manor certainly needs one.'

If his plan was to marry another, he could never truly be hers. But it would be some consolation to have him close by, where they could see each other occasionally to play chess or discuss books. Because at some point in the last twenty-four hours, the idea that he might leave and never return had become unbearable.

'There are several reasons that your plan will not work,' he said in a gentle voice that made her think he knew far more about her feelings than she cared to admit. 'The least of them is the time involved in arranging her passage. She is unmarried and increasing. Even if I could send her a ticket with a snap of my fingers, she is in no condition for a sea voyage.'

'Of course,' Charity said, trying to pretend sympathy for this stranger who had trapped her Potts into marriage.

'And, of course, there will be certain complications involved in raising another man's child.'

'I should not think so,' she said, considering. 'It is not as if you have a great inheritance to consider or are worried about succession.'

'I am discussing my feelings on the matter,' he interrupted. 'The situation will not be an easy one and

I prefer to deal with it at home, rather than starting a new life and a family simultaneously.'

It did not matter that he might do well here, or that she wanted to keep him near. He wanted to return to America. Staying had never been part of his plan. 'Of course,' she said, smiling all the harder and pretending that it had been nothing more than an idle suggestion. 'But if you truly want to go back home, you will need your share of the diamonds. Have you given any thought to how we might find the book we are looking for?'

He was watching her carefully. 'Very little. I was rather distracted yesterday.'

He had not forgotten. He was being so casual this morning that she had begun to wonder if it had been some sort of wild dream. At the very least it must have been far less important to him than it had to her. But now that she was thinking of it, her nervousness had returned and she could hardly look him in the eye. Was she actually blushing? She could not remember ever doing it before, but her cheeks had grown so hot at the vague reference to what had occurred that she was sure they must be bright red.

'I have not thought on the matter of the diamonds,' he repeated, ignoring her flustered reaction. 'But something tells me that you have.' He looked even closer, as if he could read her like the book they searched for. 'I think you know perfectly well where we should be looking and are keeping secrets from me.' He made a coaxing gesture with one of his fingers. 'Do, tell.'

They were fencing again, matching wits for their

own amusement. Instantly, life became easier. She smiled and pinched her lips together, then shook her head. 'Let us see if you can come to the same conclusion without my help. Come with me. We must visit the Blue Earl and see if he can tell you anything.'

Chapter Thirteen

Apparently, they had decided to pretend that nothing had happened between them. It was just as well, since he had no idea what to say to her that would not make parting from her more difficult.

Did you like it?

Of course she had. Women did not normally scream in that way without there being extreme pleasure or extreme pain. Had it been pain, she'd have asked him to stop. Instead, she had thrown back her head and bitten her lip in a way that made her mouth even more kissable.

But while she had been over the moon in ecstasy, the pain he had experienced was excruciating. He should have locked the door, wrapped her legs around his waist and spent himself where she had asked him to be. Instead, he had run, just as he'd run every other time that his life had not gone to plan. He had grabbed a candle from a hall sconce and walked the endless hallways of Comstock Manor until he was too tired to do anything but sleep.

But she looked well-rested and glowing with vitality. The pinched expression she'd worn when he'd met her had disappeared, as had her dowdy gowns and her brisk manner. The gown she was wearing today was quite fetching and bordered on frivolous. She smiled more easily. She blushed. He had obviously done her good.

She had also decided to meddle in his future plans, which were immutable and not part of their bargain. The quicker they returned to treasure hunting, the sooner he could be away. But now she was talking nonsense to him, weighting her words as if there were some hidden meaning in them that any fool should be able to understand. 'The Blue Earl,' he said, then waited patiently for illumination.

'I discovered that the diamonds were missing when I was a child,' she said. 'But I have only been looking for them for the last year or so.'

'You began after your grandfather died,' he said, cutting to the truth before she could tell him.

'It was one of many things he did not want me meddling in,' she replied.

'The missing diamonds were supposed to be a secret between the Earl and his Countess,' he said, then remembered that he could not possibly know something that Comstock had been told by the widow of his predecessor. 'Or so I would assume.'

'Very true,' she said. 'And you were right to begin your search in the study for the book that might hold answers. Until he died, he kept the materials I needed to find the truth in a locked cabinet in this room.' Her smile turned smug. 'Once he was gone, I picked the lock and moved it all to the library.'

'Well done,' he said.

'I have been reading the diaries of the previous Comstocks and believe that the stones were hidden in the tenure of the Blue Earl, during the Wars of the Three Kingdoms. Which means that the book that fits the code key you found must have been in the house at the time of his death in 1648.'

'The Blue Earl?' he said, still confused. 'Would you care to elaborate, for those of us who have arrived late?'

'It is easier if I show you,' she said. 'Come with me to the portrait gallery.' She led him out of the study and to the huge hall that held the family portraits.

'I have not been here since my sister rearranged the portraits,' she admitted. 'The one we will be examining has been gone from the house for several years.'

'Gone where?' he asked.

'To a pawn shop in London,' she admitted. 'Grandmama sold it to pay the butcher's bill. But my sister Hope got it back so the new Comstock will have all his ancestors to greet him, when he arrives.'

'I am sure he will be grateful for that,' Miles replied, feeling guilty again.

'Reserve your opinion until after you have seen the picture,' she said, opening the tall double doors to the gallery. The room they entered was at least forty feet long and lined on either side with full-length portraits of his predecessors, some wearing the ridiculous coronet that had been plopped on his head when he had been dragged to court to meet the Prince.

'Let us work our way backwards, shall we?' She looked up at the newest painting, of a middle-aged man in powdered wig and wide-cuffed coat. He had posed with eyes slightly downcast and seemed to be staring down from the wall in disapproval.

'My grandfather.' Charity gestured to a portrait at the end of the row. 'He did not always look so stern. Unless he was looking at me, of course.' She smiled as if it had not bothered her.

If that had been true, she would not mention it so often.

'There is a painting of my grandmother in the town house in London. But since it is a nude, I have no intention of showing you.'

'Thank you.' He had met the Dowager in Bristol when he'd arrived. Though she was a handsome woman for her age, he had no desire to see so much of her.

There was a glass-topped table beneath the Earl's portrait that contained a row of miniatures. 'My father,' Charity said, stroking a likeness of a man in a clergyman's black coat and high collar. 'That is my mother beside him. And Father's two brothers. All lost.'

'I am sorry,' he said, remembering the diaries he had read in the study and the last Comstock's account of the typhus epidemic that had taken his youngest son and orphaned three little girls.

'It was a long time ago.' She frowned. 'I was barely out of leading strings when we were brought here after my parents died. I remember my uncles. But not them.'

'It must have been very hard for you,' he said.

'I was not alone. I had my sisters,' she said, touching the next little paintings, which were of two stunning young ladies with a passing resemblance to the woman beside him.

'And where is yours?' he asked. If he wished for a remembrance from a lady, he'd have much preferred carrying Charity about in his pocket than Prudence.

'I do not need a portrait to remind me of my appearance,' she said, not looking up. 'I have a mirror.'

'You do not sit for a painting for yourself,' he said. 'You sit for the pleasure of others. Did your grandmother not wish you to do so?'

'I refused,' she said through tightened lips and walked down the row of pictures.

Though she did not like to speak of herself or explain her aversion to being painted, she was a font of family history, able to share anecdotes about each earl as she passed them.

Her words registered with him on a superficial level, names and dates, children and notable achievements. It appeared that the avid collector of erotic art was the brother of her great-grandfather, who had posed for his portrait in odd silk robes and a turban.

Miles stared at the faces in silence, looking for any similarity to himself. His looks must have come from his mother's side of the family for he could find no trace of the Strickland features in his own. If his hope had been to feel a part of this family after seeing it all together, he was not to get his wish.

But he was painfully conscious of the blank wall beside the most recent Comstock. The family had left a place for his portrait there. Some day, if they managed to find an heir to take his place, that man's progeny would be walking strangers down the row, pointing to the Eighth Earl, the one who had taken one look at the job before him and hightailed it back to America.

But what else could he do? If it had been the goal to reclaim his branch of the family tree and keep the Stricklands alive, it had been hopeless from the first. There was no way he could fulfil his promise to Ed and his obligations to an earldom. He was only marrying Pru to acknowledge her child as his. That meant that the next Comstock stood a fifty-fifty chance of being an American stranger with no ties to the family at all.

A man could not serve two masters. Deciding between a brother he'd loved and his recently sworn loyalty to the Crown had been no choice at all.

Without his realising it, they had come to a stop and she was staring at him expectantly. It took a moment to realise that she was awaiting his reaction to the portrait in front of them and not expecting the full confession that was on the tip of his tongue.

He turned and looked up at it.

'My God.'

She was smiling. 'It tends to have that effect on people. I should have warned you.'

'Very true,' he said faintly. The man in the picture looked more like a Shakespearean villain than a member of a noble family. It was difficult to estimate his height against the objects in the background, but he appeared to be shorter than average, a homunculus beside the tall and noble men around him. His wrists were thin where they protruded from his lace cuffs and his calves were bony in the silk hose beneath his breeches. His face was no better, decidedly lopsided so that one eye squinted and the other bulged. His red hair was sparse on his scalp, which was the same pale blue as the rest of his face.

'Cyril Strickland. The Blue Earl.'

'Aptly named,' Miles replied, unable to look away.

'If the family has a black sheep, it was him. Ugly, weak and not long for the world.' She pulled the perforated sheet of paper that they'd found from a pocket in her skirts. 'And, apparently, a duplicitous trickster who wished for his family to suffer in poverty. But that was mostly omitted from the family record.'

He thought for a moment. 'What was included in the aforementioned record? Anything that might give us a hint as to what he meant in leaving that key?'

'Practically nothing was written about him,' Charity said. 'He inherited the title on the death of his older brother. A suspicious death, I might add. Averill Strickland was everything an earl ought to be: brave, handsome and beloved by tenants and servants alike.'

'But not by his brother,' Miles supplied.

'One night, Averill went to bed healthy and woke up dead,' Charity said.

'And Cyril became the Earl of Comstock.'

'But not for long,' she supplied. 'He was a sickly child and grew no stronger in adulthood. He was prone to megrims and fits, and had thinning hair…'

'And the blue skin we see in the painting,' he finished for her.

She nodded. 'He died unmarried, within a year of

taking the title. But I think he used what time he had to hide the family jewels and spite us all. There was much turmoil in the fighting between the Roundheads and the Royalists. If he thought that invasion was imminent, it probably made sense to keep the most valuable possessions hidden.'

'Bastard,' Miles said.

'If he had been, we would not have had to deal with him,' she replied.

'Figuratively speaking,' he added. 'And you know nothing more of him?'

She shook her head. 'There was no immediate family left to write his memorial or to retrieve what he had hidden. They had to hunt far afield to find an heir, just as they have done with the current Comstock.'

She stared thoughtfully at the picture. 'Grandmama claimed to be impressed with the American. But she said he had been ill.'

'Seasick,' Miles said hurriedly. 'It was a difficult crossing.'

She glanced sharply at him. 'I thought you arrived separately.'

'We travelled the same ocean,' he insisted. 'There is nothing delicate about Comstock's constitution, if that is what you were implying.'

She gave him another searching look and he regretted making such a strident defence of a man who he'd claimed he barely knew. 'Even if he is the picture of health, it makes no sense to haul him from the other side of the globe and drop him into a seat in Parliament,' she said. 'If there is no one nearer, then perhaps it is time to admit that the Stricklands have had a good run but are ended.' Then, she smiled at him. 'Of course, you would not have come here, had they done that.'

'Very true,' he said. Truer than she knew. A few days ago, he would have told her how heartily he had wished he'd never heard of the Earl of Comstock. Now? He was not quite so sure.

To distract her, he pointed at the painting. 'Where is he standing, do you think?' In the shadowy background of the painting, they could see what appeared to be stone walls and some sort of statue, perhaps a saint or an angel, and a greenish tinge to the light, as though it were filtered through coloured glass. 'Could it be a church?'

'None I am familiar with,' she said. 'It does not look like the one in the village.'

'It was a bit late for repentance, if he committed fratricide,' he replied, then stared at the picture's background. 'Help me take it down.'

One on each side, they reached up and lifted the portrait down from its hook, then struggled it to the floor. Then he reached into his pocket for a handkerchief and spat into it.

'What are you doing?' she asked, startled.

'Some necessary cleaning,' he said, dabbing at the paint with the dampened cloth. 'It will do no harm. But there is something I must see.'

'I don't suppose you can make it worse,' she said and pulled a smaller, lace-trimmed hanky from her own pocket, spat in a most unladylike way and offered it to him.

Between the two linens, he managed to remove the grime from the area of the canvas that most interested him. Behind the murderous Earl there appeared to be a raised dais and a long marble altar. In the centre sat a large book, lying open on a metal stand. 'Do the Stricklands have a family Bible?'

'In the parlour,' she said.

'I think it is time that we pay it a visit,' he said.

Chapter Fourteen

She had been right about him.

Although he did not have her depth of knowledge about the family's past, it had had taken only one nudge from her and he had found his way to the next step in the puzzle. Nor had she known that it was possible to clean an oil painting by expectorating on it. Or that it was a good thing to nourish plants with dead fish.

The depth of his understanding was awe-inspiring.

Now he stood before the family Bible, staring down at the handwritten record of births and deaths at the front, as if searching for some key there. His finger traced names, pausing now and again as if they held some meaning for him and were not just an extension of the history lesson she had given him in the portrait gallery. Then he began flipping pages, as if suddenly remembering his reason for being here. 'May I see the key, please?' He held out his hand for the paper and she retrieved it from her pocket.

He set it against a single page and looked through

the windows. 'Not the printed text, then. The spacing is all wrong.'

Then he flipped to the back and the empty signature that had been sewn in after The Revelation. He glanced up at her. 'Sermons?'

She shrugged. 'More than one earl has fancied himself as a bearer of the Lord's truth. Having read some of their work, I have my doubts. But there is one in particular that will interest you.'

He read through some of the pages, making occasional faces of disgust or disbelief. Then he came to the one she had thought of. 'Averill Strickland?'

'The Blue Earl's brother,' she confirmed.

'Have you already read it?'

She shook her head. 'I decided it might be nicer to do it together.' The thought surprised her. Her sisters often chided her for her need to be right, to be first, to be the cleverest one in the room. But with Potts, it had not seemed so important.

He glanced at the writing desk, then said, 'I doubt we will need to write the message down, for we are both likely to remember it verbatim.'

She nodded, surprised again at how ready he was to put confidence in her and how easily they understood each other. Then, very deliberately, she remembered the face of the woman in the picture that was resting in the breast pocket of his coat. It did not matter that they were perfectly suited. He was a man of honour and had promised himself to another. For his sake, she hoped that Prudence was as smart as she was beautiful and worthy of his loyalty.

He had fitted the paper key over the handwritten sermon and began to read. 'To the right and noble man who finds my message.' He paused to glance at her with a smile. 'Let greed not be your guide in looking for what is left of the things right and fully left to you. Seek ye first the kingdom of God.' He looked up again, waiting for her opinion.

'That is all?'

'There are some windows that do not align,' he said.

'Turn it over and read again.'

He flipped the page. 'Three. For. Too. One.'

She glanced over his shoulder. 'They are meant to be numbers.'

'So it would appear.' He turned the key over again. 'And on this side, we have right, left, right and left, hidden amongst the text.'

'It is a pattern of some sort,' she said. 'Doors or windows.'

'Rooms,' he suggested.

'Bricks in a wall.'

'Stairs,' he added. 'There are so many possibilities that it will be difficult to choose one without some sort of starting place.

They both sat, thinking in silence.

'How much of the house existed, while he was alive?' he asked.

'None of the parts we are inhabiting,' she replied.

'So whatever this pertains to would be happening in an older, unfamiliar part of the house,' he concluded. 'And you did not recognise the statue that was in the background of the portrait.'

'It is nothing I have seen here,' she said. 'And my sisters and I explored every room we had access to.'

'Were any of them fitted out as a chapel? Because Cyril has suggested that we seek first the Kingdom of God. I can think of nothing else that would fit the bill.'

She had been hoping that he would arrive at any other conclusion than that one. But it was the logical answer. 'There was a chapel in the oldest part of the house. It would have still have existed when Cyril was alive.'

He frowned at her. 'That does not sound very encouraging.'

'Come with me and I will show you the next problem we face.' She led him out of the parlour, up the main stairs and back into the central wing. At the end of it she paused to get her bearings, then turned right. And then, to the end of the hall and down what had been a main staircase, some time long before she was born.

Potts trailed behind her, gaping in amazement at the high ceilings and many doors. 'Did the family need all this space?'

'My family gives little thought to what it needs,' she said. 'There used to be many of us. Enough to occupy a castle. Then a manor would have sufficed. Then a large house would have been enough. Now we could manage with a few rooms in London.'

She had led him down the stairs and through a ballroom that might have been useful if they'd had enough money for lavish entertainments. Now it stood as a sad and empty testament to a once-great family.

She escorted him to the end of the room, beneath the musicians' gallery, to a stone wall that did not match the other three, and a Gothic archway. 'The Stricklands no longer need so much space. But we never throw anything away. Not a button, not a book, not a room.'

She put her hand on the stones that filled the arch, which were just as dark and heavy as the rest of the wall. 'We do, however, occasionally brick them up.'

'This is the chapel?' he said, pressing his hands against the wall as if he expected it to move.

'I believe so. I have no proof, of course. But that is what we always imagined it must be.'

'You closed it off.'

'My ancestor,' she reminded him.

'Of course,' he agreed.

'As a country, England has sometimes disagreed as to whether we should be Catholic or Protestant. One of the Earls of Comstock decided it was best that we be neither.'

'How refreshingly humanist,' he said, slapping his palm against the wall in frustration. 'Shall I find a hammer and get to work?' He slipped out of his coat and prepared to roll up his sleeves.

She opened her mouth to object, then closed it again, overcome with a sudden desire to see his arms bared and taking physical action. Then she shook her head both to clear it and to indicate the negative. 'Let us not be so drastic until we are sure of what we are doing. I am not even positive that this was the chapel. For all we know, knocking a hole here will lead us directly out into the garden.'

He gave her a sheepish smile and slipped back into his coat. 'Or into another room that was built over the remnants of what had been here. Forgive my impetuous nature. We Americans pride ourselves on being men of action. But I must not carry the behaviour to excess.'

A man of action with the heart of a scholar and the instincts of a chess player. She swallowed, thinking of the easy way he had lifted her up into the chimney and on to the billiard table the night before. He was staring at the wall, giving her an excellent view of his flawless profile and running his long, deft fingers over the seams in the joinery. Now he turned to pace off the length of the room, frowning as he calculated the dimensions in his head.

If he'd thought that he had escaped by giving her the tools to her own pleasure last night, he had been utterly wrong. Though she knew it was unwise, she still wanted him every bit as much as she had before.

He looked back at her now, totally unaware of the thoughts that were foremost in her mind. 'Are there architectural plans for the house and its additions? I doubt such grand work could be done without them. And for the life of me, I cannot manage to envision how the parts of this house that I have seen of it can connect to make the whole.'

'It is very confusing,' she agreed. 'If plans exist, they are likely to be in the library with everything else of value.'

'Let us go and look,' he said, glaring a challenge at the sealed doorway. 'I refuse to give up when we are so close.'

* * *

As they retraced their steps back through the baffling labyrinth that he'd inherited, Miles tried not to look at the swaying hips of the woman in front of him. She had still made no mention of what had happened in the billiard room. But he, at least, was thinking of it more and more, as time passed.

The search for the diamonds should be paramount in his mind. His trip into the village yesterday had aroused far more curiosity than expected. It was only a matter of time before someone described the Earl to one of the servants and the whole house realised who he was. If they could manage to find the stones today, he might be gone by morning without being forced to reveal any difficult truths.

And that would give him one last night with Charity Strickland. Like the search for the missing jewels, he had uncovered far too much of her to walk away unsuccessful. If the point of last night's experiment had been to bring matters to a satisfactory conclusion, it had failed. Judging by her screams, she had been satisfied. He had not. His desire for her had not been blunted by sleeplessness or exercise, though a few hours spent reading the accounts of the Comstock finances had done much to depress his spirits.

Of course, it had also given him ideas. With a progressive peer in control of the land, it might be possible to turn the tide of failure and salvage some of what had been built. Though he could not stay to do it himself, it might take some time for his replacement to be found. Until then, he might give Charity the power to implement her own ideas in his absence. At the very least, he could write her a formal letter from Comstock, assuring her that she had nothing to fear from him. Her future would not be some bargaining chip to refund the estate.

They had come back to the front of the house and she was talking to the butler and ordering that tea and sandwiches be brought to the library so that they could continue their research. They would be alone together in a room full of erotica, at the far end of the house in a location that was more remote than the rather risky choice the billiard room had been.

Disaster was inevitable. And yet he could not manage to be bothered by it. They would be together all afternoon, either in the library, or investigating corners of the house that no one visited without a reason. What happened would happen and he would deal with the consequences afterwards. Whatever it was that he felt for her, it was futile to resist. He would follow her to his own damnation, if that was what she wanted. For today, at least. Tomorrow, he might be gone.

She had completed her orders and started down the hall to the library. But before he could follow her, Chilson stepped into his way. 'A moment, Mr Potts?' The butler managed to phrase the words in a way that was both a question and a demand.

'Of course,' he said, smiling at the servant as Charity went on towards the library, oblivious.

'Last evening, there was a commotion that disturbed the staff. It sounded rather like a woman's scream.'

'Perhaps it was after I retired,' Miles said, trying to look innocent.

'When I went to investigate, Miss Charity informed me of a difficulty in the billiard room,' Chilson said, his face expressionless. 'She had been startled by a rodent.'

'How surprising,' Miles responded. 'Are rodents often a problem at Comstock Manor?'

'We have mice, occasionally,' the butler admitted. 'But she is not normally bothered by them. Therefore, I suspect it was a rat.'

'Really,' Miles said.

'A rather large one, I should think. One that has recently found its way into the house and is unaware of how hard the staff work to keep the family safe from vermin.' There was a slight constriction of distaste around his mouth as he looked at Miles. It did not bode well.

'That is most commendable of you,' Miles said, feeling much less confident than he had before.

'The footmen have been equipped with large hammers. I have informed them that, should the rat alarm her again, they are to hit it with all their might and evict it from the house,' he said, with a final nod.

'An excellent idea,' Miles said, trying not to imagine the feel of a hammer blow, delivered without warning. Then he added, 'We all want what is best for Miss Strickland, I am sure.'

'It gratifies me to hear it, Mr Potts,' Chilson said with a smile, stepping aside to let him pass. 'Please inform Miss Strickland that the tea tray will be there directly.'

'Thank you, Chilson.' Then Miles turned his back on the servant. After waiting a moment to see if he was struck down where he stood, he walked down the hall to the library.

Chapter Fifteen

'More tea, Potts?' Charity smiled as she filled his cup, trying to catch his eye.

'Thank you,' Potts said without looking up. He had spread the plans she had found for him out on the library table and was trying to fit them together, one on top of each other like overlapping pieces of a puzzle. 'I thought I was clever, but I can make little sense of this.'

She put down the teapot and picked up a pencil. 'We are here. Here are the main stairs.' She found another page and slid it part way under the first. 'This is the old house and fits here.' She pulled it out again and crossed out several of the rooms. 'So these have been torn down, replaced or repurposed.'

She looked up to see if he agreed with her assessment and found his attention remained resolutely on the papers in front of them.

Had something happened in the last few hours? She would not have described him as overly familiar, over the course of the morning, but there had been an easy camaraderie between them that was lacking now. Since coming to the library, his manners had been perfect and his behaviour unexceptional.

Too perfect. Too unexceptional.

She had not expected to be swept from her feet the moment the door had closed. But she had hoped that there might at least be a smile to prove that he still enjoyed her company.

She reached across the table for another plan, brushing her arm against his coat sleeve. As she did so, she was sure she felt him flinch.

She dropped the paper on top of the others. 'This is the second floor. Where the bedrooms are.' She made a large X over the Tudor Room. 'You are here.' Then, she tapped the pencil repeatedly on the paper and stared at him. 'This is my room.'

He looked up slowly, his eyes smouldering. 'I realise that.'

'And what do you mean to do with this knowledge?' she asked.

'Absolutely nothing,' he said, looking away from her again.

'After last night?'

'Last night, we were careless,' he said, through gritted teeth. 'The servants are aware of what is happening between us.'

'And they know better than to question me on it,' she said.

'So they questioned me, instead,' he replied.

'Are you afraid of them? If so, I will tell them to leave you alone.'

By the fierce look he gave her, she knew that she had spoken wrong. 'I am not afraid of the servants. I am in agreement with them. You deserve better than a man who has nothing to offer you and does not mean to stay longer than one more night.'

'One night?' Did he really mean to leave so soon? 'Are you not even going to attempt an audit?'

'I see no point in it,' he said. 'Even if I could account for every silver spoon and stick of furniture, it would take months to arrange for the sale of them. I do not have that kind of time.'

'Prudence,' she said, hating the word.

'I wrote to her as soon as I received her letter and promised her that it would not be long until I returned.' He shook his head. 'She was fine when I left. But that was nearly four months ago. She is running out of time. And since we cannot find the diamonds…'

There was no reason for him to stay. They both knew it was true, but she did not want to hear him say so. 'There might still be hope. There are a few journals I have not read.'

'We know where they are. But short of tearing down a wall of the ballroom, I don't know what good the knowledge will do us,' he said. 'I will write to Comstock and make certain recommendations that will provide for your future. But as for mine?' He gave her a sad smile. 'It would be best if I fill my valise with the second-best silver and be on my way.'

'You cannot…' But she had no idea how to end the sentence. She could not tell him that she would die without him. She had never believed in such melodramatic displays. She had promised that she would let him go without argument when the time came. She had been sure that she had no heart to break.

'We are not finished,' she said, at last. 'We have not…'

He touched a finger to her lips to stop her from speaking. 'I am afraid we are,' he said. 'I am ashamed that I had to be reminded of the fact by Chilson. But what I said yesterday evening is still true. I cannot do more than I have done already because I am not the sort of man who would lie down with a virgin who has only the most superficial interest in me, to satisfy her curiosity and my personal desires.'

'But you want to,' she said, remembering how he had been in the billiard room. 'And so do I.'

'And we both know that it is dangerous in more ways than one to be governed by fleeting desires,' he said. 'We have but to look at the trouble caused by Prudence and a long string of Comstocks to see that.' Then, he leaned forward and kissed her, quickly and with lips firmly closed so she would not take the wrong meaning from it. 'And now, if you will excuse me? I need to find myself a sideboard to pillage.'

Charity sat silent, as Dill combed out her hair and prepared her for bed, ignoring the maid's attempts to chat. If she had not managed to speak today, when the words might have made a difference to Potts, she did not want to begin talking now that he had gone to his room. After he had left, she had pored over house plans and journals for the better part of the day, not bothering to change for dinner and asking for a tray to be brought to the library. Chilson was probably disappointed to find that there was no need at all for a chaperon. The man he'd feared had decided she was not worth the effort.

She had hoped to find some scrap of information that might change his mind and convince him to search a little longer, but in the end, it had come to naught. The house as she remembered it had little to do with what it had been when any of the parts had been built. The combined plans showed a tangle of rooms that had been demolished and built over, or repurposed, or sealed. Doorways and stairs had been added or removed on the whim of the current occupants. Very few of them had kept proper records of what they'd done and when they'd done it.

At any time in those long disappointing hours, she could have given up and found him so that she might tell him the truth. What had started as physical desire on her part was growing into something far more complicated. It did not matter that what she felt for him could have no future. The thought of him disappearing from her life tomorrow was almost too much to bear.

If she had given him some indication of a deeper attraction than physical desire, then he might have been more receptive to her overtures. Instead, she had let him continue to think that what she wanted was nothing more than lust. He had rejected her not because he did not like or want her. He had rejected her because he thought she was as shallow and easily seduced as the woman he meant to marry.

Now Dill had left her and Pepper was sound asleep on the end of her bed, unaware that she had not joined him. The house was quiet. But Charity felt as if she would never sleep again, unless the gulf she had created between herself and Potts had been breached. It might not change the way he felt about her, but she doubted it would make things any worse.

She rose from the dressing table and left her room, creeping nightgowned and barefooted down the length of the family wing and then down the even longer guest wing, until she arrived at the door of the Tudor Room.

Then she paused, realising how foolish and impulsive her plan was. She could see no light coming from the crack under the door. He might already be asleep. Even if he was awake, he might feign sleep and refuse to answer the door when she knocked. Since he had not even bothered to wish her goodnight, she had no reason to think he would welcome her company, once the lights were out.

But if he was taken unawares, he could not refuse her. She had but to open the door. If he was asleep, she would sneak away again. And if not?

She knocked once, then opened before her nerve failed her.

Though the room was lit only by moonlight and the banked fire, he was not asleep. He stood at the window, his back towards her, staring out into the garden. And he was naked. She had wanted to tell him that it was not just his appearance that she admired. But good Lord above, he looked like Michelangelo's *David* must look from the rear.

But much angrier. For when he turned to see who had interrupted his privacy, his face turned from pensive to irate. 'Miss Strickland, avert your eyes!'

She did as she was ordered, but not before she caught a glimpse of him grabbing for the shirt that hung on the back of a chair and throwing it over his head. Then he was stalking across the room, hand already outstretched to grab her and put her out.

She dodged to the side before he could reach her, closing the door as she did so. 'Please. Wait. I need to talk to you.'

'Whatever it is can wait until morning,' he snapped, reaching for the door handle.

She moved in front of him, pressing her shoulders into the closed door and hiding the handle behind her body. 'What point is there in waiting? You are an early riser and I will no doubt wake to find that you have already gone.'

By the stricken look he gave her, it was clear that she had guessed the truth.

'Before you go, I must speak. I was not totally honest with you. And I cannot let another minute pass without correcting the mistake I have made.'

Now that the moment had come, she was afraid to meet his gaze, lest it show that her feelings were not reciprocated. But it did not help to look down, either. That only made her aware of the bare feet and legs beneath his shirt and the curious way the front of the hem seemed to jut out, away from his body.

'Speak, then.' The words came in a low growl, as if he was more animal than gentleman.

'This afternoon, you seemed to think that my reasons for wanting you as I do were trivial. You seemed to think that it was nothing more than your good looks that attracted me. You thought my desire was some passing fancy and I did nothing to correct you. But that is not the truth.'

'Then what is?' he snapped. 'Are you attracted to my fortune? My good name?'

'You are the most brilliant man I have ever met.'

When he did not respond, she gathered her courage and looked up. He was frowning, but from confusion rather than anger.

'The way you outsmarted me at the dower house. The way you beat me at chess. The puzzle box. Everything,' she said, holding her hands out to him in a gesture of defeat. 'I have never met anyone who could do those things. And when you did…' She dropped her hands to her side. 'I do not know how to talk to men. And your looking the way you do should make it impossible to speak to you at all. But somehow, when I am with you, everything seems easier.'

'Everything?' he said and she saw the beginning of a smile.

'Almost everything,' she corrected, suddenly very conscious of the lateness of the hour and the thinness of her nightclothes.

'I wish I could say the same of you,' he said with a sigh. 'You have the quickest mind that I have encountered, male or female, though you are only a slip of a girl. And you are excellent company.' He took a step closer. 'But when I am with you, nothing is easy. I cannot seem to think straight and my common sense all but disappears.'

'Is that bad?' she whispered.

'We will decide tomorrow, when I have to leave,' he whispered back. 'But I would like to spend tonight with you.' Then he leaned forward and kissed her. His lips moved to her cheeks, her eyes and her hair, before returning to her mouth, settling there, coming home.

It was even better than it had been in the billiard room, for there were not so many troublesome clothes in the way as he held her. His bare legs were touching hers, the hairs on them tickling her. She could feel each muscle in the arms that held her. And it took only a tug of his fingers to open her nightgown and push it down her shoulders. She gasped as the cloth slid away, leaving her breasts uncovered.

At any moment, he would explain why what she wanted more than anything in the world could not possibly happen. Then he would send her back to her room. She had prepared an argument to counter his rejection, but it did not come. Instead, he was staring down at her breasts in silence. Then his hand reached to touch them, a featherlight brush of his fingers that made her gasp. He smiled at her response and covered one of them, then nodded with satisfaction at the way it seemed to fit perfectly in the palm of his hand.

He was not stopping. Perhaps it was her imagination, but when she stared down, the prominence beneath his shirt seemed to be increasing. And he did not seem to mind her curiosity, nor order her to look away as he had a few moments ago. She forced herself to look up, into his eyes. 'Does this mean…?'

Potts was smiling at her now. 'Having second thoughts? It is not too late to turn coward, you know.'

No,' she said hurriedly. 'But thus far, you have been adamant that we must not do what I think we are about to.'

He sighed. 'That was before you flattered my intelligence. You are the first woman to do so and I find it difficult to resist.'

'Only difficult?' she said in a voice made breathless by his touch.

His hand rubbed her nipple as he shrugged. 'There is also the fact that you have surprised me at bedtime and we have very little clothing between us.' He kissed the side of her throat before continuing. 'It has left me fully aroused and incapable of begging you to think of your future.'

'And after last night, there is probably not much of my innocence left to preserve.'

'You would be surprised,' he said. Then his mouth took her breast and she decided she had been wrong. He drew her nipple into his mouth and as he suckled, one of his hands lifted her skirt and touched her, entered her and thrust in time with his pulls. The climax that resulted was sudden and short, and she had to cling to his shoulders to keep from collapsing to the floor.

He raised his head and kissed her mouth again. 'No scream tonight? I must try harder.'

'You have not yet given me what I asked for,' she said, trying to be glib.

'And what is that?' he said. His finger moved inside her again.

'More,' she said, at last, still unable to say the necessary words, though she knew them well enough.

He took her hand from his shoulder and dragged it down his body, wrapping it around his erect manhood through the linen of his shirt.

She nodded. 'Inside me.' Then she released him and reached under his shirt to hold him properly.

He sucked a breath in through his teeth and released her to yank the shirt over his head and throw it to the floor. Then he put a hand over hers, guiding her exploration. She stroked, amazed. He was not as hard as the thing that he had used on her in the billiard room. But he was warm and alive, large and still growing in her hand as she touched him.

She had said that how he looked did not matter. But that was not totally true. 'May I look at you?' she whispered.

'If you return the favour,' he said. He moved out of her grasp and pulled her nightgown over her head, leaving her as naked as he was. Then he took her by the hand and led her to his bed, opening the curtains so the moonlight might stream in and touch their skin. He climbed in, lying on his side and patting the mattress beside him.

He was looking at her. For a moment, she forgot to indulge her own curiosity. He opened his mouth to speak and she put a finger to his lips to stop the words. If he said them, she might not believe. But the look in his eyes right now said that, for tonight at least, she was beautiful and he loved her.

Only then did she allow herself to enjoy him, with her eyes and her hands. His hard, flat nipples were almost hidden in the cloud of dark hair on his chest and a line of it trailed down his stomach to the place she had touched him. Now she traced it with her fingers, wrapping one hand around him, cupping the sack beneath with the other.

He gasped again.

'I am not hurting you?' she asked, prepared to withdraw.

'Please, continue,' he said through clenched teeth. 'I will tell you if it becomes too much.'

'Too much,' she repeated, trying to imagine what it would be like to push him beyond his limits.

'If you continue touching me, I will lose control.' He took a shaky breath as her hands moved on him. 'But it might be for the best. I should not spend inside you.'

'Because of the risk of making a child,' she said. She felt a bead of moisture forming at the tip. 'But I am not afraid.' She stroked him again, slowly. Then she moved her hips to press against his.

He closed his eyes and touched her breasts, rubbing the nipples with his thumbs as she held him between her legs, letting him feel how wet she was becoming. Then she teased herself with the head of his penis.

As she brought herself near to breaking again, his hands pressed harder on her breasts. Then he gave a sudden buck of his hips and pulled away from her hands, grabbing her by the waist, rolling her on to her back, pushing her legs apart. He was on top of her now, spreading the lips of her body and pushing inside her.

Without him having to urge her, she wrapped her legs around his waist, wanting to be even closer to him as he moved, lifting her head and begging for the kiss that would smother her cries.

He shook his head. 'I want to watch.' Then he raised himself on his hands to free his hips as he thrust.

She cried out as she had last night, and again, moaning as he moved faster. Then he slowed. 'Touch yourself,' he commanded. 'You know where.'

She slipped her hands between them, touching the place where they were joined before moving forward and giving herself up to pleasures that only increased at his answering thrusts. Then she reached her peak, tumbling down the other side of it, as his body tightened and then collapsed, limp on top of her.

He lay still for a moment. Then, he whispered, 'Why did I ever fight this? You are sublime.'

'I don't know,' she whispered back. 'You are usually so intelligent.'

He laughed and rolled off her. 'Now that it has been done, I do not think we will make matters any worse by doing it again. After a little rest, of course.'

'How little?' she asked.

He laughed again, rolled her on her side and gathered her to him, her back against his chest, grinding his hips against her. 'You will feel when I am ready, you wicked girl.' Then he kissed the side of her neck. 'But there is no reason to rush. We have all night.'

'Yes.' She sighed, smiling into the darkness ahead of her.

And the darkness smiled back. As she stared at the bedside table a foot from her face, she saw the outline of the little miniature propped against the candle stand and the perfect white smile of the lovely Prudence.

She stiffened in his arms.

'Cold?' he murmured. 'Let me keep you warm.'

'Yes,' she replied, shivering. Then she turned in his arms until she could see nothing but him.

Chapter Sixteen

A man could get used to this.

Miles stretched his feet to their fullest length, enjoying the way his toes did not poke out from under the covers or extend past the edge of the mattress. Then he threw his arms wide and did the same.

It was likely no bigger than the bed he'd rented at the Clarendon in London. That had been soft and clean, as well.

But here, the bed was exceptional. Not just clean, but pristine, pressed flat as paper and just as white. The hangings were purple velvet, the coverlet silk brocade. He felt like the King that had given the suite its name.

At the movement of his body, the heavy linen of the sheets rubbed his naked skin in a way that was as decadent as the kisses he had received last night. If he had not taken the lady back to her room, she'd be waking beside him and they'd have made love again. Then he'd have called for the servants to bring breakfast on a tray, so they could refresh themselves and make love once more.

Since this was his fantasy, he substituted the shirred eggs, fish, muffins and strong, black tea that they'd been feeding him for johnnycakes with maple syrup, black coffee and Kentucky corn whisky. He could imagine the taste of them, heavy sweetness and the grit of cornmeal. The taste of the liquor, both sharp and smooth. The smell of pine forests and the gulls screaming over the Delaware. There was so much about home that he missed: the newness of it all, the rough edges and the feeling of a world to conquer, just a few miles to the west.

But what use had he for the frontier? He forced himself to get out of the bed, stretching in the chill bedroom air and glancing out the window. The phrase, 'master of all he surveyed', popped into his head. Until this week, it had been nothing more than an expression. Suddenly, it was true. He had been reminded by the Prince Regent himself that though, technically, the land belonged to the Crown, he was responsible for the care of every inch of the property he could see, all the way to the horizon.

The staggering weight of the responsibility hit him again, as it did almost every morning, spoiling the glow of happiness. He wanted to crawl back between those delightful-smelling sheets, pull them over his head and refuse to come out. The men who had slept here before him had been birthed on clean white sheets, swaddled in silk and lace, and walked every step of their lives in well-heeled, bespoke boots until their inert body was arrayed on the satin pillow of their casket. And yet, when it had come to taking care of this place, they had failed.

Of course, they did not have his sense of vision. And they had not had Charity Strickland to help them. He grinned. She had called him brilliant. He did not like to think of himself as such. But Charity had been quite adamant about it. She had grown misty-eyed talking, listing his accomplishments in a way she had not when complimenting his looks.

That had been either his making or his undoing. She had not said she loved him in so many words. But she must have felt something very like that. She had looked at him last night as if he was the finest man on earth.

Then she had let him love her. And at some point, the room they'd shared had become the paradise he'd awakened in. Her perfume on the rumpled sheets had scented his dreams. Her kisses had filled his heart with uncontainable joy.

He had told her they would know in the morning if it had been a mistake. It was not. With such a woman at his side, the future might not be hopeless after all. He could share his life with her, his failures as well as his successes, and have no fear that she would turn from him, looking for a man who offered more.

It was not until he had walked to the basin for a wash and a shave that he looked in the mirror and remembered that he had shared nothing with her. She did not even know his name. What had possessed him to let the lie go on so long? Why had he come here in the first place? If he'd meant to hide, he'd done it in the first place anyone would look.

It had been because he had not really wanted to go. It was too late to call back the letter he'd sent to Pru, promising that he would return to marry her. Nor could Ed return from beyond to release him from the promise he had made to care for her. But if he was as smart as Charity seemed to think, he should be able to free himself from the trap Pru had set.

She had been quick enough to call him aimless when Ed had been alive, continually reminding him that he was a ne'er-do-well and not half the man his older brother was.

Her tune had changed immediately after the letter from England had arrived. It was some comfort to know that he had been clever enough to resist, when she had tried to seduce him before he'd left. Then, she had called his sense of honour naïve. In getting herself with child, she had found a way to use it to her advantage.

Perhaps he was naïve. He had offered to return and marry her because it was the right thing to do, comforting himself that he would be walking away from a world of trouble here in England. Perhaps he would not be lord of the manor, but he had barely begun to see what he might make of himself in America, where a man might count himself rich if he had a little money and a pretty wife.

He glanced at the miniature that was lying on the night table where he had dropped it on undressing the night before. Then he opened the drawer of the table and swept it out of sight. The little ivory oval had felt heavy as a millstone for some time. It was as lovely to look at as the woman who'd posed for it. But neither it nor she made him feel the way he did when he looked at Charity Strickland.

She was what he needed now. He needed her wisdom as well as her love. He did not like being Comstock any more than she wanted to be his Countess, but he could not help who he was. He would tell her everything that had happened, from the moment he had received the life-changing letter telling him he must come to England. He would apologise for lying to her. He would tell her of his love.

Then he would let her choose his fate. He would stay or go on her command. If she thought it right that he should marry Pru, he would do so. If not?

He grinned. He would offer for her. For her, he would be Comstock or plain, old Miles Strickland, or spend the rest of his life as Augustus Potts, if that was what she preferred. And he would do it all on the continent of her choosing. He would be and do whoever and whatever it took to give her the life she deserved.

By the way he felt after making it, he was sure that his decision was the right one. He was still poor, of course. And his life was still a disaster. But with the love of a good woman and a decent breakfast in him, he was one step closer to conquering the world.

He grinned at the servant coming down the hall towards him, full of the bonhomie that came the morning after the best night of his life. As the fellow drew

closer, Miles had only a moment to wonder at the fact
that he had not seen the man since the first day, when
he'd taken the reins of the big black horse that had
brought him here and walked it towards the stables.
What was a groom doing in the guest wing of the main
house?

The groom smiled back at him in reassurance, revealing a set of huge teeth that would have been worthy of his charges. Then, without a word of greeting, he
pulled back his fist and drove it into Miles's stomach.

All the wind in his body left in one woof and there
was an agonising moment where he was convinced that
it would never return. But through his distress, he felt
the big hand of the groom cupped around the back of
his neck, keeping him from collapse.

'There, there, Mr Potts. It will pass.' He added a
thunderous clap on the back, which sent the air rushing back into his lungs.

Miles looked up at the man through streaming eyes,
still unable to speak.

The groom grinned. 'I was sent by the rest of the
staff to give you that message.'

'Huh?' He attempted a response, but could manage
nothing more than a wheeze.

'Perhaps things are different in America. But when
you are in service, it is never wise to give yourself airs
and behave like a member of the family, eating in the
dining room and swanning about the house as if it is
yer own.'

He could feel the first flame of anger, kindling behind the pain in his gut. He was the first to admit to

his faults. But he had never *swanned* in his life. When he got his breath back, he was going to fill his gloves with scrap iron and give this fellow a lesson behind the stables on what was and was not *swanning.* But at the moment, all he could do was look up at him, eyes streaming from the pain.

The man allowed a few moments of silence to let his words sink in before continuing. 'Perhaps an auditor is a different kind of animal from a common servant, so we will let it pass.'

Miles opened his mouth to bellow that he was no kind of servant at all. He was the Eighth Earl of Comstock. And though he had not yet had time to investigate the cellars of his new home, there had been something on one of the older house plans that had looked rather like a dungeon. Unless this lout wanted to find himself locked in it, he had best return to the stables, where he belonged.

And then he stopped. He was still Potts until he had spoken to Charity. This was even worse than the gossip spreading after his visit to the village. The only thing that would be worse than lying to her would be having her hear the truth from someone else. So he closed his mouth and took the punishment he deserved.

The groom stooped to look him in the eye, his breath smelling of this morning's sausage and last night's sour ale. 'Whatever the Earl intends for you, I doubt it is to take liberties with his hospitality. I am sure he would not approve of anyone who would do harm to Miss Charity. Neither would we. We have known her since she was a wee girl, ya see?'

Miles's nod turned into a wince as the meaty hand on his shoulder tightened to pinch a nerve.

'And if a stranger should court her without honourable intentions?' He shrugged and gave a sad look. 'I would not want to be that fellow. And that is all I will say.'

'I understand,' Miles wheezed. 'No harm will come to her, on my life.'

'That is an excellent thing to swear on,' the groom said, with another smile, giving him a slap on the back that nearly sent him through the plaster on the opposite wall. 'For that is exactly what is at risk. Do you understand me?'

Miles nodded again.

'And if I was you I'd pack my bags right smartish and be on my way before something unfortunate happened.'

Probably something involving a hammer. Miles nodded again.

The groom nodded back to signify a bargain, then continued down the hall, whistling as if nothing had occurred.

Now that he was not being held upright, Miles slumped against the wall, taking shallow breaths until the pain began to ease. This was what came of telling lies and not appreciating rank, even when it was forced upon a fellow. An earl could get up to whatever dubious behaviour he chose and face no consequences. But the fictional Augustus Potts had no such magic shield and he had best watch his back until Charity had accepted his suit.

He dragged himself to his feet and wobbled down the stairs towards breakfast. Ready or not, the time had come to explain everything to Charity and throw himself on her mercy. Her anger was formidable, but a small thing when weighted against the risk that his own servants would beat him senseless to protect her.

But when he arrived at the ground floor, he changed his mind. Gregory Drake stood in the doorway, offering his coat to the butler. At the sight of Miles on the stairs, he smiled. Then his mouth opened, ready to speak.

Still too soon.

Could he not at least make it to the breakfast table before all hell broke loose?

'My...' Drake's greeting had already begun. In another second, the title would be out of his mouth and the shocked butler would be running to the basement to tell the staff. The whole house would know in the time it took him to find Charity and explain.

Miles jumped the last few steps to the floor, reaching for the fellow's arm as he spoke. 'Mr Drake! There is an urgent matter I must speak to you about concerning the entail.' He continued forward, pushing Charity's brother-in-law back through the open door, shutting it behind them and leaving them both coatless in the early-morning air.

'What the devil...?' Greg Drake stopped, probably remembering that, no matter how mad he appeared, one did not speak disrespectfully to a member of the peerage. 'My Lord Comstock—'

'Until I tell you otherwise, I am no such thing,' Miles interrupted. 'Not to you, or to anyone who might be with you.'

'I am alone,' Drake replied in confusion. 'For the moment, at least. I was in the mood for a gallop and set off on horseback at dawn. But Faith's husband, James Leggett, is just behind me. Our wives will be arriving by carriage later this morning with the servants and the luggage. When the girls heard that you'd left London, they insisted that we come to the country to welcome the heir.'

'God's teeth.' Miles cast a quick look at the closed door, hoping his outburst could not be heard though it. 'You must intercept them immediately. There is a problem.'

'Not with Miss Charity,' Drake said in alarm. 'Tell me she had not fallen ill.'

'Her health is excellent,' Miles replied. 'But… There has been a misunderstanding.'

'Charity misunderstood something?' A slow grin spread across the other man's face. 'That cannot be possible. Charity Strickland does not make mistakes. She knows more than the rest of the family put together.'

'Well, my identity is the one thing she is not aware of,' Miles snapped. 'She thinks I am an auditor named Augustus Potts.'

Drake was staring at him as though he had suddenly gone mad, which was quite possibly the case. 'Where did she get such a ridiculous idea?'

'From me.' There was no way he could imagine to explain the pass that he had come to, but he did his best. 'Things between Charity and myself are at a rather delicate juncture,' he said, carefully.

'A juncture.' He watched as his former auditor and future brother-in-law jumped to the logical conclusion. 'With Charity.' His expression changed from amused to incredulous.

'That should not be a surprise.' Miles gave him a warning glare. 'It is what everyone in this country, from the Prince on down, has expected of me. But Charity does not expect it. In fact, she would be four-square against marrying me if she knew I was Comstock.'

'Would she consider marrying Mr Potts?' Drake said with raised eyebrows.

'It doesn't matter whether she would or not,' Miles said. 'Mr Potts does not exist.'

'And which of you sent me this letter?' Drake asked, pulling the note Miles had sent him from a coat pocket.

'Let us say that it was from both of me,' Miles replied.

Drake nodded. 'Then I think it is wise that we blame it on Mr Potts. I have come to tell him that it is not legal to distribute pornography in England and the Earl of Comstock wants nothing to do with it.'

'It is not legal in America, either,' Miles answered. 'But I did not ask about the legality. I asked how it could be done. The items in question were obviously meant for someone's private enjoyment and were never intended to be part of the Comstock estate. They are too valuable to destroy. And I...or rather, Mr Potts cannot exactly hawk them on a street corner.'

'Then, tell Mr Potts that I have the necessary contacts to make it happen and an estimate of the amount of money he is likely to receive should a discreet sale take place. I am ready to act, at your convenience.'

Miles glanced at the numbers on the paper and smiled. 'That is exactly what I'd hoped to hear. We will begin this afternoon.'

The ever-efficient Drake reached into another pocket and produced a stack of letters and handed them to Miles. 'I have brought your mail from London, as well. You received letters on the last two ships from America.' He turned to look, as a horse and rider came galloping up the drive. 'And this is James Leggett, just arriving. Since I am not sure which name you wish to use, let us spare you the awkwardness of an introduction. If you go back into the house, Mr Potts, I will explain matters to him, so he might ride back and inform the ladies.'

'And I will go and talk to Charity,' Miles said, with a sigh of relief. 'The matter will most likely be settled by the time you arrive at the house. Even so, proceed with caution and give nothing away until I tell you to.'

'Very good.' Drake strode out to meet his approaching brother-in-law and Miles returned to the house, walking past the surprised butler, who was watching him with suspicion.

'Confidential business for Lord Comstock,' Miles

said, giving him an arch look in return that dared him to enquire further.

Then he went off to find Charity, before the fellow could summon a pair of stout footmen to beat an explanation out of him.

Chapter Seventeen

Charity awoke the next morning in her own bed, unsure of how she had got there. A vague memory surfaced of being wrapped in her dressing gown and carried down the hall, then tucked safely into her own bed with a final kiss. As he had walked, he'd whispered in her ear of the importance of being found where she was expected when her maid arrived.

She had nodded sleepily and pressed kisses on to his bare chest, still not ready to let him go.

In response, he had groaned and muttered something about her need to recognise that even a virile man needed his rest and that virgins were supposed to be easily satisfied, not insatiable.

She smiled. After last night, the word did not apply to her. Then the smile faded.

When she had gone to his room, she had thought that what they were doing was to be an isolated incident. It would be a final goodbye and the memory of it would act as bulwark against an uncertain future. Now that it had happened, she could not stop imagining a repeat of last night's activities, as soon as she felt sufficiently refreshed.

Then she remembered all the reasons she should not. Potts had made it clear from the first that he wanted to return to America and had not wavered on that point in any of their conversations. He had a fiancée and slept with her picture beside his bed. Even now, he might be waking to see Prudence smiling back at him from that miniature and regretting his weakness of last night.

Worse yet, he might already be gone. The fact that Charity was in love with him made no difference. She had found him too late.

But at least she had found him. The idea that he might love her in return had been a foolish one, of course. He was far too perfect for that. But if she had wanted to experience the kind of passionate affair normally denied to proper young ladies, he had been a perfect choice. He had taken her to paradise. Now he meant to disappear. She need never fear seeing him walking on Bond Street with another woman's children or be forced to make nice to his lovely wife at some inescapable social gathering. She would have perfect memories, nothing more.

It was what she'd told him she wanted. But what if she'd changed her mind? As she'd slept, when her mind was unfettered from common sense, she had dreamed of a long sea voyage and a ship pulling into a strange harbour. It had looked as she'd imagined his country looked, roughhewn, bustling with strangers and Red Indians. But there had been a familiar face waiting for her in the crowd on the dock. Potts had waved and smiled, and held his arms out to her as she had walked down the gangplank.

Her dream might have been more accurate had she imagined the lady from the miniature standing at his side. For it was probable that he would marry Prudence the moment he returned.

It did not matter what Charity might want or dream. She could not have him. In truth, she would not know what to do with him, even if she caught him. She had always assumed that a plain woman would end up with a plain husband. But seeing Potts disrobed last night had done nothing to dissuade her opinion that he was a god walking the earth. He was handsome, intelligent and when they were alone, he demonstrated skills that had nothing to do with auditing.

When Dill entered, to prepare her for the day, the maid took one look at her and her mouth fell open in amazement. Then it snapped closed in a catlike grin. 'A bath this morning, miss? They can be very sooth-ing on the muscles.' It seemed she had found one thing that her normally obtuse maid understood completely.

'Why would I…?' Charity said slowly. She glanced in the mirror. Then pulled on her spectacles and looked again. Of course, Dill had guessed what had happened. She had felt beautiful last night. Though she had not thought it to be true, emotions must have a profound effect on physical appearance.

She was still not as pretty as her sisters. They had been exceptionally beautiful, even before falling in love. But she could not deny that, this morning, she was radiant. She looked like Hope had been after a week with Mr Drake. She looked as Faith had when Mr Leggett had changed her life. She had promised that nothing would change after.

But clearly, she had fallen in love.

She looked back at her maid, unrepentant, mind racing to find a course of action. 'No bath, Dill. There will not be time to heat the water. Mr Potts plans to leave today. I need to speak with him while he is still here. How quickly can you dress me?'

Dill looked at her, considering. 'An hour, at least.' She pulled a confection of ribbons and lace from the wardrobe, draping it over her hand.

Suddenly, there was a knock on the door and what sounded like the housekeeper, trying to console an increasingly emotional parlour maid.

'Come in,' Charity called, baffled at what would have them up in arms so early in the morning.

'Miss Charity.' The woman bobbed a nervous curtsy, while the maid cowered behind her. 'We have just come from the dining room.'

'Yes, Mrs Till?' The information was not surprising in the least.

'It is Millie's job to polish the silver. When she opened the sideboard, she discovered a significant absence.'

Charity's mind returned to Potts's threat of the previous day. 'Indeed.'

'A dozen spoons, fifteen forks and two pair of short candlesticks,' Mrs Till affirmed.

'It wasn't me, miss. I told her as soon as I found them missing. It wasn't me.'

'Of course not, Millie,' Charity said, smiling at the girl to calm her. 'I do not suspect you or any of the servants.'

'Thank you, miss.' The girl sagged with relief.

Charity turned back to Mrs Till. 'Do not worry about the matter. I will settle it all when I come down to breakfast.'

'Very good, miss.'

Charity thought for a moment, and then smiled. 'And do you happen to know if Mr Potts has gone, yet?'

'I saw him in the main hall a few moments ago,' the housekeeper said.

'Speak to Chilson for me. Tell him that Potts is not to leave until I have spoken to him.'

'Of course, miss.' With another curtsy, the housekeeper turned, shooing the maid back out of the bedroom and closing the door behind them.

Then Charity turned back to her maid. 'I have changed my mind, Dill. I would definitely enjoy a bath. Take all the care you wish with my hair and leave no ribbon unpressed. This morning, I need to be as close to perfection as you can bring me.'

'Yes, miss.' If Dill was surprised at the Herculean task set for her, she gave no indication. But Charity saw no other way forward. If one meant to stop the man one loved from marrying the wrong woman, one needed to look one's best.

When Miles could not find Charity in the library, he tried the breakfast room. But though it was almost half past nine, there was no indication that she had eaten so much as a slice of toast. Nor was she in the study, the morning room, or several other sitting rooms that he had discovered while searching the ground floor.

She was likely still in her bedroom.

Since a gentleman should not even know where that was, he was none too eager to search her out there. The warning he had got from the groom was still fresh in his memory and the bruise from it was still blossoming on his stomach. He did not want to risk a second lesson before the staff learned his identity. But they might never know if he did not find Charity to tell her. There was nowhere left to look but her room.

As he started towards the stairs, he heard a scrabbling in the upper hallway and saw Pepper appear above him. If possible, the dog looked even angrier than usual, possibly because of the offence done to his canine dignity. His collar had been decked with more ribbons than a maypole. After a single bark of warning he then pelted down the stairs straight for him and used the advantage of his elevation to leap from the fifth step, firing himself like a furry bullet at Miles's face.

He reached out and caught the dog in mid-air, leaving him suspended by the scruff of his neck in a cloud of rage and women's cologne. Then he brought the dog to eye level, staring into its little black eyes. 'Are we finished?'

There was no answer, of course, other than some angry squirming at being bested, again.

'I think we are. Like it or not, dog, if your mistress can abide me, I mean to stay and there is nothing you can do about it. But there will be some advantages.'

He reached out and untied the ribbons, dropping them to the floor. Then he set the dog back on the ground, where it gave a shake of relief, followed by a prodigious sneeze.

He stared down at it. 'You are right. It smells much better on her than it does on you. I recommend you find something foul to roll in. You will feel worlds better, afterwards.' He reached in his pocket for the muffin he had filched on his recent pass through the breakfast room and dropped it on the floor. 'You need this more than I do. And I need to find Charity. If you still hate me, do not bother to attack again until this afternoon.'

He started up the stairs again. He had almost gained the landing when he heard the sound of footsteps, thundering up the flight behind him. It took effort to prevent himself from running and to remind himself that the best way to appear innocent was to make an effort not to look guilty. Instead of panicking, he stepped to the side and gripped the banister, preparing to let the person or persons pass him.

His plan failed, utterly. A pair of hands hit him square between the shoulders, dislodging his grip on the rail and pushing him forward. Before he could fall he was caught again by two sets of hands, one on each bicep. The men who had him lifted him easily to his feet and further, carrying him the rest of the way up the stairs with his suspended feet slapping helplessly against the risers.

He glanced to one side and saw the groom that had accosted him earlier. 'You again.' On his other side was an equally large footman. 'And this time, you have brought a friend. It has only been a few minutes since our last meeting. What is it that you think I have done between now and then?'

'Pinched m'lord's spoons,' the groom replied with a toothy grin as if he had been waiting his whole life for an opportunity like this one.

'Now, see here.' Then he realised that he had no idea how to answer a charge that was, technically, true. 'I am sure, if we find Miss Strickland and discuss the matter, she will tell you that this is an honest mistake. Drastic action is not necessary.'

'She knows,' the footman grunted. 'We were told that we were to detain you.'

'I do not think that is what she meant,' he said, only to realise that he had no idea what her intentions had been. If she had discovered he was Comstock, it was exactly the sort of thing she might do, only to offer a false apology and claim that she'd had no idea since he had not bothered to tell the truth. In fact, the longer he thought of it, the more likely it was that this was exactly what had happened.

He struggled in their grip, trying and failing to break free. 'Now, see here, fellows. You are making a terrible mistake.'

'It's you what made the mistake,' said the groom. 'But you can't say you weren't warned.'

They had reached the top of the stairs now and were hauling him forward into the old wing, towards places that were all but abandoned.

'You would not be doing this if you knew who I was,' he insisted.

'Yer Mr Potts.'

'That is who I claimed to be,' he admitted. 'But my real name is Miles Strickland.'

The footman's hands tightened on his arm and the groom let out a braying laugh.

'Truly,' he insisted. 'I am the heir to the title, the Earl of Comstock come from America.'

'And I'm the Queen of Spain,' the footman announced, making the groom laugh again.

'If you let me go, I will prove it. I have the Earl's signet in my room.'

'Next to the soup spoons,' the footman replied.

'Probably stole the signet, too,' the groom agreed. 'Cannot trust Americans. My uncle was at the Battle of Trenton.'

'Do not think you can hold me responsible for that,' Miles argued. 'It happened before I was born.'

They had reached the end of the first old hallway and his captors turned right, continuing down the next hall until they were far out of earshot from anyone in the main part of the house. At the end of the hall, a door was standing open, as if waiting for him. Miles swung his legs forward, trying to find purchase against rug, or wall, or anything that might stop their progress. 'This is all an honest mistake and I do not mean to punish you for what you have done to me.'

This was greeted with even more laughter.

'I am sure, if you take me to Charity, this will be sorted out in no time.'

'Charity, is it?' Without warning, the groom released his arm and he dropped to the rug, barely able to keep his feet. This unsteadiness worked to his advantage, for the blow that struck his chin did not land with the catastrophic force the groom had intended. But it was more than enough to daze him as he was pushed into an empty bedroom whose only distinguishing feature was the size of the lock on the door. Before he could rouse himself sufficiently to argue, the door had slammed and he heard the bolt hit home, trapping him inside.

Chapter Eighteen

When Dill had finished with her ministrations, Charity examined herself in the mirror. She had never considered herself a vain creature. But today, she had to admit that she had never looked better. The spectacles rather spoiled her attempt at conventional beauty. But so would squinting, which she would most certainly do if she tried to do without her glasses.

Since she had never been at a loss for words before, it was most unexpected that her near-complete transformation into a proper young lady had been easier than coming up with an argument that would convince Potts to stay. Far too much of her position seemed to hinge on the fact that he should not go because she could not bear to part with him. Since this was exactly the opposite of what she had promised, she was not even sure if she should announce the fact.

Other points in her favour included the fact that Prudence was a conniving hussy who was in no way worthy of him. Until he arrived in Philadelphia, he could not even be sure that she had told the truth about her pregnancy. Should it be a lie, he might be trapped there by finances and unable to return even though he wanted to.

Unless he could definitively demonstrate the existence of the afterlife, there was no proof that his brother would know whether he had kept the promise or not. Nor could they be sure that his brother would expect him to abide by it in the current circumstances.

Only after she had made these points did she want to resort to the fact that she loved him. The rational voice in her head insisted that it was the lowest form of debate to appeal to emotion if there were facts to support the argument. But for the first time in her life, there was another voice demanding that she follow her heart and do it quickly before she lost the chance.

That was assuming it was not too late already. When she reached the ground floor, there was no sign of Potts in the breakfast room, the study, the library or any of the other rooms she could think to check. With growing trepidation, she rushed back up the stairs to the Tudor room.

It was empty. The bed was still rumpled from last night's activities. But the wardrobe was open and empty, as were the drawers. There was no sign of the leather satchel she had noticed on a chair, last night. Like a coward, she had taken too long in preparing to meet him. Or perhaps the staff had not got her message to prevent him from leaving.

Maybe it had been too late from the start. He was an early riser who could have been gone at first light.

But she had refused to believe that he would go without at least saying farewell.

There was only one place left to look. If his horse was no longer in the stable, she would know that it was too late. She should hurry, since there might still be a chance to stop him. But as she left his room to head to the door, it felt as if she was slogging through mud. Each step grew more difficult because she was afraid of what she would find.

But as she came down the main stairs, she heard the sound of people talking and laughing in the hall, and Pepper running in circles on the parquet and barking furiously at visitors.

'Charity!' Hope was waiting in the entrance hall, arms out to embrace her. Right behind was her oldest sister, Faith. Beside them in an animated conversation with each other were their two husbands.

'I have missed you,' she said, coming down the stairs to hug them both. The words were true. Though she had been waiting a lifetime for them to leave home and stop pestering her, their actual departure had left her lonelier than she'd expected. But now, when she assumed she would be joyful at their return, she felt nothing but numb. Since they'd been gone, her entire life had changed and she had no idea what to say about it. 'It has been so long.'

'Only a few weeks,' Faith said, kissing her on the cheek.

'And now that the Earl is here, we do not have to worry that you will be alone,' Hope said with a smile.

Charity looked past them at the open door, but saw

no sign of the peer. 'I have been told he was in the village, yesterday. But I have seen no sign of him as yet. Is he arriving after you?'

'He is not here yet?' Faith said, giving their sister an odd look.

'My mistake,' Hope said, quickly.

'He is not here yet,' Faith repeated somewhat more loudly, to catch the attention of her husband.

'How strange,' Mr Leggett replied, frowning at Mr Drake.

'Truly,' Hope repeated. Then she glanced at her husband, as well. 'You said he was going to settle things before we arrived.'

James Leggett glared at him, as well. 'You said matters would be settled by the time we arrived.'

'I thought they would.' Gregory Drake's brow furrowed. 'But obviously not.' Then he looked to Charity. 'Perhaps Mr Potts can explain matters to us.'

'You know about Potts?' she said, surprised.

'The Earl told Gregory all about him,' Hope supplied. 'We thought one of them would be here to meet us.' She frowned again. 'We hoped it would be the Earl.'

The assembled party was looking at her now, as if expecting her to produce one man or the other from under her skirts.

'I believe you have just missed Potts,' she said, forcing herself to smile as if his departure did not matter to her at all.

This was met by a sea of blank faces and more expectant silence.

'He left early this morning,' she added. 'He was already gone when I came down for breakfast.' It was surprisingly difficult to voice her fears aloud. Her tone sounded rather like she was about to cry.

'Where did he go?' Faith asked, arms crossed.

'He has spoken more than once of returning to America when he was through here. I believe his home is in Philadelphia.' She blinked at them, waiting for them to lose interest and go back to worrying about the Earl, as they had been for the last three months. It was not as if she would be able to forget Potts. But perhaps if there was something to distract her, it might not be quite so painful to remember him.

Her sisters shot cryptic glances at their husbands. Then, Faith said, 'Perhaps there is a servant who can give us more information on his plans.'

All the servants would want to talk about was the missing silver. The whole family would have the wrong opinion of him if she did not make it clear to Chilson that the auditor had got her permission to remove the items. 'You are right. Asking the servants is an excellent idea,' Charity said. 'I will go and talk to them immediately.'

'Oh, darling, do not bother yourself,' Hope said, standing between her and escape. 'Gregory and James will make the necessary enquiries.'

Before she could think of another excuse, her sisters had linked their arms in hers and were leading her towards the stairs. 'Come along, dearest,' Faith said. 'It has been ages since we have talked. You must tell us how you have been managing.' Then, under the guise of devotion, they dragged her up the stairs and towards her bedchamber.

'It has not been so very long,' Charity said, trying to struggle free. 'And nothing at all has happened here. Nothing at all.' If she meant to put them off the scent, her denial had been far too strenuous. She changed the subject. 'How was your honeymoon? Tell me all about Italy.'

'Never mind that. Tell us all about Mr Potts,' Hope said, with a feline smile.

'He is the auditor sent by the Earl,' Charity said.

'And?' Faith added.

This was very strange. The pair of them were acting as if they knew something they could not possibly know. Was the truth still plain on her face? Or was this just sisterly revenge, for the way she had tortured Hope when she had fallen in love with Mr Drake?

If so, it was unfair. Mr Drake was an Englishman and had lived just down the street from them. It was clear that they were meant for each other. It was not as if Hope had fallen in love with an engaged American.

She disengaged her arms from theirs, pushed her spectacles up the bridge of her nose and gave them her sternest look. 'There is nothing more to tell about Potts.'

They ignored her, pushing her into her bedroom and shutting the door.

'If there is nothing to tell, how do you explain your hair?' Faith said, snatching at a curl.

Charity slapped her hand away. 'Leave it be. There is nothing wrong with it.'

'Has Dill forgotten how to braid it in that ghastly coronet you favoured?'

Ghastly? Had it really been so bad? 'I requested a change,' Charity said.

'Curls,' Hope said with an ecstatic sigh. 'I always knew you would look better with them.'

'Indeed,' Faith agreed. 'The mysterious Mr Potts has put a curl in our little sister's hair.'

'And colour in her cheeks,' Hope agreed. 'Not to mention the ruffles and lace on the rest of her. Mr Potts is a worker of miracles.'

'There is nothing miraculous about him,' she replied. 'Was nothing miraculous, I mean. He was an American hired by the Earl. And now he is gone.'

'Is he, really?' Hope said, raising her eyebrows.

Faith gestured to another gown still lying on the bed. 'Have you taken to changing for tea when you are in the house alone?'

'So what if I have?' Charity snapped. 'There is nothing unusual about it. Nor is there anything strange about the gown I am wearing. Hope chose them for me when we were in London.'

'And you refused to wear any of them,' Faith reminded her. 'But while we were gone, you have gone all ruffles and curls.'

Hope was rummaging through the wardrobe. 'Her dinner gowns smell of perfume. She has been wearing them.'

'Now that you have finally left me alone, I have been doing the things you've been badgering me to do all year.'

'For Mr Potts,' Faith said.

'He is a very interesting man,' she allowed.

'And very handsome,' Hope added.

'Not really,' Charity lied.

Hope looked at Faith and repeated, 'Very handsome.'

'You do not know him at all, so you cannot possibly make that assumption,' Charity said.

Faith ignored her logic and stared back at her. 'Never mind how much we know about him. How well do you know Mr Potts?'

Biblically.

The temptation to announce the fact was almost irresistible. Instead, she answered, 'He was here for several days. I was helping him with the audit.'

'And is it going well?' Hope asked. The question was innocent enough, but the meaning was something deeper.

'Of course,' Charity replied.

'Show it to us,' Faith said, arms folded.

'There is nothing written down,' she said, giving up the pretence.

'Then what have you been doing, all this time?' Hope said, smiling as if she knew.

'We have been searching for the missing Comstock diamonds,' she admitted.

'And?' Faith asked.

'Playing chess,' she added.

'And?' Hope asked.

'Billiards,' she concluded through gritted teeth.

Her sisters shared a look of sympathetic frustration. Then Faith said, 'If you were going to play games, I could recommend several that are even better than that.'

'We are not supposed to be encouraging her,' Hope reminded her.

'But I cannot think of a better match than...Mr Potts,' Faith said.

'But chess?' Hope shook her head. 'Gentlemen do not like to be bested by ladies.'

'He beat me,' Charity said, unable to keep from smiling at the memory.

Faith dropped into the chair by the vanity table, overcome with shock.

'He gave up three pieces, to start, and still he beat me.'

Hope sat on the edge of the bed, stunned to silence.

'And he has been willing to listen to my ideas about the estate,' she added. 'Not that it matters. I doubt he will have any influence at all over Comstock.'

'I would not be so sure,' Hope said faintly and received a quelling glare from Faith.

'Do not contradict your sister,' Faith said, as if either of them had ever cared what Charity thought. Then she turned with an overly bright smile. 'Suppose he decided to stay. If there was a position here on the estate and we could get him to return, would that please you?'

More than anything in the world. She should have run to find him the moment she awoke. 'What I want does not figure in the equation,' she said at last, a lump rising in her throat.

Hope clapped her hands together, as if a miracle

had occurred. 'You do want him to stay. Do not bother to deny it. And it is because you have fallen in love with him.'

At the suggestion, Faith looked equally overjoyed. 'I cannot think of a more perfect situation.'

'Then you are not thinking hard enough,' Charity snapped. 'England is probably full of men who would be more suitable than Potts.' And she did not want a single one of them.

'It is normal to have doubts,' Hope said.

Faith nodded in agreement. 'But the important thing is how he feels about you.'

'If she has been dressing for dinner, I am sure he is favourably disposed,' Hope said. 'Her gowns are scandalously low-cut.'

'Because you chose them for me,' Charity said, exasperated.

'Your bosom is your best feature,' Hope said and Faith nodded in agreement.

'My bosom is neither here nor there,' Charity concluded.

'To you, perhaps,' Hope said. 'But I dare say the gentleman you dined with has noticed it.'

'She is blushing,' Faith said, eyes narrowed as if it helped her see the truth.

'One might even say you are glowing,' Hope added.

'Has he offered yet?' Faith said.

'Not to me.'

'I am sure it is only a matter of time,' Hope said. 'He was probably waiting until the family arrived so he might surprise us.'

'I think we have had surprises enough already,' Faith reminded her. 'We are all familiar with the mischief that happens when men and women in love are left alone together, but I never expected it of Charity.'

'We are not in love,' Charity insisted. Of course, she knew what she felt for him. But she had not managed to say it out loud and he had done nothing to make her think the statement would be reciprocated.

'If you do not think that is what has happened here, then you are more naïve than I thought possible,' Faith said, with the superior air of an older sister. 'Mr Potts will be staying, whether you expect him to or not. And, after what has happened between you, we all expect an offer to be forthcoming.'

'Do not make us summon Grandmama,' Hope said. 'She talks a good game when it comes to liberal behaviour. But that will change immediately once she has seen the two of you together.'

'We are not likely to be together, ever again,' Charity insisted. 'Even if we were, I do not want my family forcing him into an offer that he does not wish to make.'

For a moment, her sisters stared at her in silence. Then both tried to talk at once. 'Why ever not? Is there another gentleman? Are you waiting for someone? What possessed you?'

The questions were coming faster than she could answer. She held up a hand to halt them.

'We discussed the matter between us, before we began. We had agreement.' And yet she had been ready to break it as soon as it was time for him to go.

'An agreement not to marry?' Faith practically shouted at her. 'Then we have been misled. The man is no gentleman.'

Hope reached out quickly, glancing towards the hall as if afraid that someone might hear. 'Now, Sister. Let us not jump to conclusions on his motives. He is not here to question.'

Then she smiled at Charity with false brilliance. 'But since Charity is involved, I am sure that there is a perfectly logical explanation as to why we should not start gathering orange blossoms. Is there another man involved? Are you waiting to meet the Earl of Comstock, perhaps?'

At this, Charity laughed aloud. 'Whatever gave you such a daft idea?'

'There is nothing daft about the notion of marrying our American cousin,' Hope said.

'Of course you would say so. You wished to marry him yourself,' Charity reminded her.

'And then I met Mr Drake,' Hope said. 'But if there had not been Gregory, I would not have minded overly, settling for Miles Strickland.'

'And he is the last man on earth I would want to marry.'

'It is unfair of you to judge the man before you have even met him,' Faith said.

'He might be just the sort of fellow to suit you,' Hope added.

'Or he might be exactly like our grandfather was,' Charity reminded her.

'Grandfather was not so very bad,' Faith demurred.

'To you, perhaps. But that was because you agreed with him. He locked me out of the library and threatened to give the books away, since they made me unmanageable.'

'They were only threats,' Hope reminded her. 'The library is as complete as it ever was.'

'You were lucky that he was not the sort to result to violence,' Faith said. 'Since he was the head of the family, he had a right to discipline the children in his house however he saw fit.'

'He could have whipped me from now until judgement. But that would not have changed the fact that I was right and he was wrong,' Charity declared. 'If he had listened to any of my suggestions, we might not be in the mess we are in.'

'You must be sure to inform the new Earl of the fact, when we manage to find him,' Hope said, smiling.

There was a sharp rap on the door and the sound of muttering male voices in the hall.

Without waiting for Charity's permission, Faith opened it and let her husband and Mr Drake into the room.

'There is no sign of him,' Mr Leggett said. 'His horse is still in the stable and the stable boys know nothing about any proposed trip.'

'I spoke to Chilson, who is beside himself with worry,' Drake supplied. 'Apparently, there was an altercation in the hall today.'

'That is nonsense,' Charity insisted. The house had been quiet until her family had arrived, expecting to find the Earl. She and Potts had parted in silence, at dawn. The joyful noise made before that had been done in a wing empty of servants.

'A groom struck him,' Drake said, ignoring her interruption.

'For what reason?'

'It was at Chilson's instruction.' Mr Drake glanced at her and then back at her sisters. 'Since he cannot be found, the butler fears that the matter may have got out of hand. The groom has been summoned back to the house to explain what happened to him, after the attack.'

'Good Lord,' Leggett said, wiping his brow. 'He will have all of our heads.'

'If he is alive to do so,' Drake said glumly.

'Who are you talking about?' Charity interrupted.

'Comstock,' the two men said in unison.

'What reason would they have to strike the Earl?' she said, now truly baffled.

Mr Drake looked past her, to her sisters. 'Apparently, it was a matter of honour, involving Charity.'

Everyone stared at her, waiting for an explanation.

She stared back. 'I have no idea what could have given him such an idea. I have never met the new Comstock and he has done nothing to me that would result in the servants springing to my defence.'

There was another significant silence as the entire family stared at her.

Then Faith said, 'You have never met the Earl.'

'No,' she said again. 'I have not.' She had met another American instead. One who came from the same city and arrived at the same time that the villagers reported seeing the Earl. A man who had been as interested in finding the diamonds as he had been in understanding the running of the estate.

A man who had sat at her grandfather's desk as though he belonged there even though he did not look like an earl, or talk like an earl, or act like an earl. He had been far too reasonable to be a member of the peerage. Nor did he look anything like a member of the family. They had been through the portrait gallery from one end to the other and she had not seen a single part of him that looked as if his picture would end up hanging with the rest of them.

'Potts,' she said, still unable to believe it.

There was a knock on the door and Mr Leggett opened it and stepped out into the hall to question Hoover, the groom.

Faith shook her head in pity. 'It is Comstock's business why he would tell such an outlandish story. Or why he would involve us in deceiving you. But really, Charity, I have no idea why you would be so foolish as to believe him.'

He had lied to her from the very first moment he'd met her. If he could lie about a thing like his name, then there was no telling what the truth of the rest might be.

'Never mind that now, dear,' Hope said in a gentle tone. 'Can you tell us what has happened to him?'

'I have no idea.' Other than that the new Earl of Comstock might have run away to America leaving them all to fend for themselves.

'He is in a bedroom in the old wing,' Leggett said

from the doorway. 'The servants are under the impression that you wanted him detained until the magistrate could be called, for stealing the dining-room silver.'

'I said no such thing,' she insisted, feeling sorry for the mistake until she remembered the horrible trick that he had played on her. 'But if that is what happened to him, then I am glad of it. I do not care if he never gets out.'

'Are you forgetting that he is not some American nobody? He is the Earl of Comstock.' Mr Leggett appeared ready to shout at her for the utter stupidity of her behaviour. But his wife threw up a hand of warning and he fell silent.

'Show us,' Faith said to the groom.

'Oh, yes, Hoover,' Charity agreed. 'Take us to him so that I can say to his face what I said to you all, right now.'

As she walked, she heard the worried murmurs from her sisters as they dissected the story of her first love, creating a far more interesting version of it than the truth had been.

'Broken heart…'

'Poor dear…'

'Should have known better…'

She had a good mind to turn on them and give them a taste of what lay in store for Potts. Perhaps she should have been smart enough to see the truth. But she was sure that her heart had not been broken since she could hear the blood pounding in her ears with each step. He had made a fool of her. The whole family had, for they'd arrived at the house knowing exactly who he was, fully aware that she had no clue. Then, rather than telling her the truth, they had allowed her to go on in ignorance while they'd laughed at her.

Her sisters' whispers were far off the mark. But Mr Leggett had a far more accurate assessment. She distinctly heard him say something that ended with '...safer where he is.'

When she arrived at the place where the servants had imprisoned the perfidious Miles Strickland, she gave the door handle a rattle. 'Comstock!' She rattled again, but it did not want to give way. 'I have come back to give you what you deserve.'

When he did not answer, she shouted again, 'Comstock! You liar, open this door.'

Mr Drake put her gently to the side and tried the handle himself. When it did not give to his touch, he pulled a penknife from his pocket and thrust it into the gap between the door and frame. After a few moments' patient jiggling, there was a click as the bolt slid back and the door could be opened.

She lunged forward, ready to confront the Earl, only to be brought up short by her sisters grabbing her arms and pulling her back.

'Now, now, Charity,' Hope said softly. 'You must give the man a chance to recover.'

'He has nothing to recover from,' she said. The groom shuffled nervously from side to side as she struggled to break free. 'But he will once I get hold of him. He's had three days of chances to tell me the truth and has not taken any of them.'

Mr Drake opened the door, stuck his head into the

room and called, 'My lord?' Then he threw it wide and stepped into the room, coming out a moment later.

He looked at Hoover. 'Are you sure this was the room?'

The white-faced groom gave a solemn nod.

She yanked her arms free of sisterly restraint and went into the room. 'Do not try my patience further, Comstock. You owe me an explanation.' But there was no point in lecturing him.

She was talking to an empty room.

Chapter Nineteen

She had managed to lose the Earl of Comstock.

Actually, the servants had. But since everyone was convinced that they had done it at her behest, she was the one likely to be blamed for it.

Charity did not overly mind the fact. If hell had opened and swallowed him whole, he would have wholeheartedly deserved it. She could not exactly blame him for seducing her. That had been totally her idea. But she'd never have suggested it had she known who he was.

There was no reason to lie to her. Yet he had done it from the first moment to the last. If he had told her who he was and said he wanted to leave, she would have packed his bags and helped him go. Instead, he had lied.

The servants were searching the house, top to bottom, but had found no sign of him. She had told them of his habit of climbing down drainpipes, but the window of his prison had not had so much as a scrap of ivy to cling to. The door had been locked from the outside, just as the servants had left it. There was no obvious way out of the room.

Where had he gone?

'How could you?' Faith was still trying to scold her, as if it was somehow her fault that he was missing.

'It was not my idea,' she replied. 'I only wished to speak to him before he left. The blame lies with him. If he had done a better job of concealing his theft, then the staff would not have discovered it and assumed the worst. If he had waited where he was until someone came to let him out, we would have nothing to worry about now. And if he has come to some misadventure?' She shrugged, smiling.

She was sure he had not. He was not an idiot. He would turn up when he was ready. If she had cared to find him, she might have applied herself to the problem, for it was an interesting question. If they did not find him in a day or so, perhaps she would look.

'You are incorrigible,' Faith whispered.

'Quite possibly,' Charity said, feeling somewhat better. There might be curls in her hair and she was developing a penchant for frilly dresses, but it was a relief to know that three days with Potts had not improved her personality. 'I am going to the library,' she said with a smile. 'Call me when they find the body.'

But when she arrived in her favourite room of the house, it was already occupied. Mr Drake had set two large wooden crates on the biggest of the library tables and was staring at the shelves as if trying to find the best place to start.

'What are you doing?' She stood in the doorway, frozen in shock.

Mr Drake looked up at her with the professional smile he had used when solving other people's problems. 'Business for Comstock.'

'What sort of business, precisely?'

'Nothing you need worry about,' he said, still smiling.

'Indulge me,' she said, her throat tightening in panic.

'Comstock has decided to sell off part of the collection to make up the deficiency in his finances.'

'No.' Where she had felt hot with rage on learning of his lies, this final betrayal left her feeling ice cold inside.

'He did not tell you?' Mr Drake's smile flickered for a moment and his eyes were sympathetic.

She shook her head.

'If you ask him when he returns, I am sure he will explain it to you,' he said. 'However, it is not really my place to do so.'

'Because you work for him,' she said. It was as she had feared from the first. He had barely arrived, and yet, Comstock had already begun to turn the family against her.

'He wants what is best for you, I'm sure.'

'So did my grandfather,' she said. Just as she'd always feared, though Miles Strickland was young and handsome, at heart he was no different than the last Earl.

She needed an intercessor. Someone to stop this until she could find a way to protect the books. 'Hope!'

She turned and ran back to the front hall where her sisters and Mr Leggett were conferring with the servant. 'Hope!' She grabbed her sister by the arm, tugging on her sleeve as she had when she was a little girl, unable to control the panic she felt at the changes that had taken place in their lives. 'Hope.'

Her sister stopped. 'What do you need, Charity?'

If anyone could reason with Mr Drake on the disposition of the books, it was his wife. 'Your husband is crating up the library,' she said. 'My library,' she added. 'Make him stop.'

Mr Drake had followed her back from the library and gave his wife a helpless shrug. 'I am acting on the instruction of Comstock. We discussed the disposal of certain items.'

Hope looked back at her sister. 'As we have been trying to tell you for years, Charity, it is not your library. It is Comstock's. He can do what he wants with it. If you have a problem with that, you must take it up with him.'

'But to do that, we must find him,' Faith reminded her. 'And since you have caused the problem…'

'For the last time—'

Suddenly, there was a clattering in the wall as if several pounds of stones had been dropped from a great height.

The family turned in every direction. Looking about them for the source of the sound.

In the quiet that followed, they heard a man's moan.

'This house is not haunted, is it?' Mr Leggett said doubtfully.

'Do not be ridiculous,' Charity snapped. 'There are no such things as spirits.'

'If any place has ghosts, I would expect it would be this one,' Mr Drake said. 'It is large enough to hold several.'

Now there came a strange, syncopated scrabbling that grew louder as if it was approaching, though nothing could be seen in either of the halls.

And then there was a bark.

'It is just Pepper,' she said with an annoyed sigh. 'He is chasing something through the walls. Although how he found his way inside them, I have no idea.'

'The more important question should be how we will get him out again,' Hope said, alarmed. 'We cannot let the poor thing die in the woodwork.'

'Perhaps a hole could be created,' Mr Drake said. 'Shall I tell Chilson to find a footman and a stout hammer?'

Hope looked at him in horror. 'I did not mean that we should pound holes in a building that does not belong to us.'

'We could bait him out, perhaps,' her husband countered.

'Or we can simply show some patience,' Charity said, exasperated with all of them. 'He is not stupid, you know. He will come out on his own, given time.'

'Because of you, we do not have time,' Faith snapped at her. 'The Earl is already angry with us. What will he say when he discovers that we have lost his dog?'

'He will probably shout for joy,' Charity said, annoyed. 'Now stop talking as if he is Grandfather and you must all walk on eggs to please him. You have married out of the family. If he is cross with you, you can simply turn and walk out that door, never to see him again.'

They could. But she was in the same state she had always been, utterly dependent on a man who did not respect her and with no rights to plan her own future. Worse yet, she had stripped herself naked for him, both figuratively and literally. She had no idea how to defend against someone who knew her as well as Potts did.

The barking seemed to be getting closer.

Then there was a hollow creaking sound and a shower of paint chips as a panel fell from the wall beside the main stairs and the Earl of Comstock emerged from the opening, hair and coat covered with plaster dust and face crimson with anger.

'Miss Strickland, I have found your damned chapel.'

For a moment, Charity could do nothing but stare at the man in front of them. He had been handsome enough before, but with his reasonable temperament she had never imagined he would amount to anything better than a lifetime as a clerk or secretary. He had looked like the sort of fellow that one saw adjacent to the men of real power. But as a sword might have been tempered by fire, a few hours trapped in the bowels of the house had turned him into a peer. He was in a towering rage worthy of anything her grandfather had managed when she had disobeyed him.

In the face of his ire, the entire family instinctively resorted to formality and respect, bowing and drop-

ping curtsies, and greeting him as 'My lord', although
the words coming out of Hope's mouth sounded more
like a prayer.

They needn't have bothered. By the look in his eyes,
Charity was the only one that he was angry with. But
she was having none of it. She still stood firmly on
the side of the little dog that had rushed out of the wall
after him and would have bristled her hackles, had she
been given any.

He pointed a cobweb-covered finger in a dire gesture worthy of a spectre, then shouted, 'You locked
me in!'

'And you sold off my library,' she shouted back.

He gave a bitter laugh. 'After all your fine talk about
liquidating the estate, you care about a few books? And
it is not your library, it is mine.'

'So that is the way it's to be?' she said, raising her
eyebrows and waving her arms. 'Everything is yours
now, is it?'

'It is,' he said. 'Debts and all. And everyone thinks
I am supposed to manage you, as well.'

'Do not think that means you can dictate my life to
me,' she snapped. 'If you try, I will make you regret
the day you left Philadelphia.'

'I already did regret it,' he countered. 'But I had no
idea that, given the chance, you would try to kill me
as Cyril killed poor Averill.'

'Kill you?' she laughed back at him.

'You might as well have had me thrown in an oubli-
ette. No one could hear me screaming. Had I not found
my way out of that room, I might have starved to death.'

'You missed tea,' she mocked. 'But please, tell me the agonies you suffered.'

'And then you set the dog on me. I was trapped in the walls with him.'

'The dog found you on his own. And you deserved whatever he did to you,' she said. 'You lied to me. From the first breath out of your mouth. You lied.'

'Not in everything,' he said. His voice changed, not quite softening, but displaying some new emotion beyond anger.

'You lied in all the things that matter,' she snapped back. 'How can I trust anything you say, Lord Comstock, or do you still expect me to call you Potts?'

'Miles,' he corrected.

'Ha! You did not even give me your Christian name when we...' she was suddenly conscious of the family about them, watching the argument in rapt fascination '...when we spent so much time together.'

'You were the one who decided I was an auditor,' he said.

'Because I did not believe that there was a man on the planet who was so awful that his own dog would hate him,' she said. 'I should have trusted Pepper's opinion of you and stayed far, far away.'

'He was away from me because I sent him,' the Earl said. 'Just as I should have done with you, instead of thinking that I could reside in the same house with you for a single day without being driven to madness.'

'I drove you mad?' She laughed. 'I made an honest mistake and you ran with it.' Then she turned to glare at the rest of the family. 'And when you all arrived, you all knew. Didn't you? You knew and you continued to allow me to be misled.'

'It was quite funny,' Faith said, unable to contain her smile. 'You have always been so smart. And yet you were so wrong in this.'

'So you took the opportunity to laugh in my face over it,' she said. 'I hope you all feel better for it. But you have proved that there is not a single person in this house I can trust.' She gestured to the dog. 'Come, Pepper, we are going to our room.'

But the dog, who had been her loyal companion only a week ago, ran to Comstock, wagging his tail.

'Very well, then, Judas, I will go alone,' she said, staring down at the dog in disgust. Then she turned and walked, back straight and eyes dry, up the main stairs to her bedroom.

Chapter Twenty

The discreet knock sounded on the Tudor Room door as Miles was attempting to brush the last of the brick dust from his coat.

'Come,' he shouted and immediately regretted it. After the very public argument in the hall below, he did not want to see any member of the Strickland family, ever again.

The door opened and Greg Drake stuck his head in, eyes lowered in deference as one might do when facing an angry lion. 'My lord, I have come to offer the services of my valet to help restore your clothing, after recent events.'

'I am fine on my own,' Miles said, with a vigorous scrub that seemed to be working the grime deeper into the wool.

'And your boots have become scuffed,' Drake added in a tone normally reserved for a death in the family.

'They are fine,' Miles snapped.

'Are you sure? Because Hagstead has a trick with

blacking and champagne that will have the most tired leather shining like a mirror.'

This was Drake's polite way of telling him that an earl was not supposed to take care of his own basic needs. He was supposed to be combed and curried like a show pony, too delicate to do as much as tie his own neckcloth. He had been getting such hints since the moment he'd stepped off the boat and he was damned tired of them.

But today he put down the brush, pinched the bridge of his nose and sighed in defeat. 'Very well. He can come before supper. There is no reason for him to waste his effort sooner since I will be going back into the walls.'

'Going back?' Drake was clearly baffled. 'Perhaps with the help of a servant...'

Miles tried to laugh, then stopped. It hurt. 'No, thank you. I would like to make it back out of the walls in one piece.'

'About that...' Drake gave a nervous cough. 'Chilson is here in the hall and wishes to speak to you.'

'The more the merrier,' Miles said with another sigh and a mockingly beneficent wave of his hand. 'Come in, Chilson. Speak your piece.'

'My lord.' The butler came into the room, knees wobbling and with a face as chalky white as Miles's had been before he'd wiped the dust from it. 'I take full responsibility for the incident that occurred this morning. Hoover would never have come above stairs, much less do what he did, had I not encouraged him. Nor would he and Biggs have locked you in a bedroom had they not assumed that it was what Miss Charity wanted done.'

'She did not ask them to?' It was probably an oversight. Now that she knew his real name, she was more than willing to lock him up and lose the door key.

'They misunderstood an instruction. Hoover is beside himself.'

'Better that than that he is beside me,' Miles said, grimacing.

'He truly is the gentlest of men.'

Miles rubbed his ribs. 'Do tell.'

'And good with the horses.'

'He should be. He is almost as large as one.'

'And kind to children, as well. He has six of his own,' Chilson added with urgency.

'What do his children have to do with this?' Miles asked Drake, annoyed. 'Are they going to hit me, too?'

'You are new to England and to the peerage. Perhaps you are not aware of the laws and etiquette that accompany your title.' Drake gave another quiet cough. 'As an example, should I have a reason to strike you—' he held up a hand of denial '—which I do not, of course. But if I struck you it would be a much more serious matter than brawling with some other gentleman. The punishment would be more severe, as well. And if a man of a lower class should assault you...a servant for example...' Drake stared at him, waiting for him to understand.

'He thinks I am going to have him hanged,' Miles said in disgust. And Chilson had come to plead for mercy and claim the punishment so that there would not be a family of orphans crying in the stables. 'This entire country is mad.'

'Perhaps,' agreed Drake. 'But we must make the best of it, mustn't we?'

Not for much longer, if he had any say in his future. But the current problem could not be solved by running away. Miles grabbed Chilson by the arm and pulled the quaking man into the room to a bench by the window. 'Sit.'

'Yes, my lord.'

Then he reached into his coat-tail and removed the flask he kept hidden there. He uncorked it and handed it to Chilson. 'Drink.'

'My lord?'

Miles tipped it up and poured some courage into the butler. 'Cherry bounce. A favourite of General Washington. Perhaps, you would have won the war had you some of this.'

It was probably not what he should say to a man who'd threatened his life. But at least the colour was returning to the butler's face. Chilson sputtered once, then helped himself to another sip. 'Thank you, Lord Comstock.'

Miles looked wistfully at the flask as the last of his American liquor disappeared into the butler. 'Now there will be no more talk of punishment for Hoover, who was only following orders.'

Chilson gave a relieved nod.

'I cannot fault any of you for decisions made in ignorance of my name and title, especially when I was the one keeping you in the dark.'

'Thank you, my lord,' said the butler, obviously curious but unable to ask him the reason for the deception.

'And you were acting in the best interests of the family and trying to protect Miss Charity.' Miles's throat tightened at the thought of her and the loathing with which she had greeted his true identity. 'I hope you will continue to do so, even when I am not present.'

'Of course, my lord,' the butler said and rose, back as stiff as ever and eyes clear despite the cloud of cherry brandy on his breath.

Miles did not bother to force him down to his chair again. Clearly, it had made the servant uncomfortable to be seated in the presence of a peer and some habits were not worth breaking. 'Very good, Chilson. Share my thanks with the rest of the staff for their hard work. And my apologies to you and to them for my deception.'

There was the faintest look of horror in Chilson's eyes at having to receive an apology, since Miles suspected that peers were never sorry for anything. But the butler accepted it with a 'Thank you, my lord.'

'And tell them to return my luggage from wherever they have taken it.'

The butler winced again. 'The duck pond, my lord.'

'Really?'

'It was thrown there after the silver was removed. The maids are drying your linen as we speak.'

'That is most kind of them,' he said. 'You may go.'

'Thank you, my lord.' At the dismissal, Chilson turned and disappeared in a cloud of subservience.

When Miles turned back, Drake was still in the

room. 'You may go, as well, Drake,' he said with a mocking wave of dismissal. 'I am fine here. Everything is fine.'

'The hell I will,' Drake said, his respect falling away now that he was sure no one was going to die. 'You are planning to go back to America, aren't you?' The man was looking at him as if his intentions were written plain on his forehead.

'What makes you think so?' Miles said, collapsing on the bench the butler had vacated.

'Charity claimed you were, but none of us could believe the fact. I assured them that you were making plans to get the estate in order. I said that it could not possibly be true.'

'So what if I am?' Miles replied. 'I have not learned much about this country, since I arrived. But I know that you have nothing to say in what a peer does or does not do.'

'True,' Drake agreed. 'But I also know that her sisters will not take kindly to finding that you have trifled with Charity's affections and then abandoned her. We will be forced to do something about it.'

After what Drake had just told him about the dangers of threatening an earl, it was an act of impressive bravery. It was also pointless. 'The notion that it is possible to trifle with Charity Strickland proves just how little you know her,' Miles said, shaking the abandoned flask into his mouth, trying to drain the last few drops from it. 'Next you will accuse me of breaking her heart, which is just as unlikely, since it is made of cold iron.'

But her body had been softer than he'd ever imagined. He shook the flask again.

'That is hardly a way to talk about a lady.'

'Perhaps not,' Miles said with a sigh. 'But in her case, it is accurate. Before she knew who I was, she made it quite clear that she wanted me to leave. What might or might not have happened between us meant nothing to her. And after?' He winced, thinking of the scene in the hall. 'I did not see any sign that her opinion has changed.'

'It does not matter what she wants,' Drake reminded him. 'You are the Earl of Comstock. Your place is here. Since you are the head of her family, her place is wherever you say it should be. Tell her to stop behaving like a child and accept your offer.' Drake paused, realising that he'd overstepped his bounds again. 'If you mean to offer, that is.'

It was exactly what she had feared would happen from the first and why she had hated him before she'd ever met him. And why she hated him even more, now that she realised that she had been lied to, manipulated and made to look like a naïve fool in front of the entire family.

'You are right. I am the head of the family and can do just as I please. And what I mean to do is return to America. Charity is quite capable of managing the estate in my absence and I shall leave her to it. If there are papers that must be drawn up to give her the authority, see that it is done. Then book me passage on the next ship to Philadelphia.'

He stood and brought his hands down the front of

his coat in a vicious swipe, to shake the last of the
dust of England from it, along with the memory of the
previous night. 'But before that can happen, she and
I have a matter to settle that cannot wait another day.'

Chapter Twenty-One

It was not the first time that someone had knocked on her bedroom door that afternoon. But this knock was, by far, the most persistent. As she had done with all the others, Charity ignored it, along with all entreaties to 'open the door and listen to reason'.

Though she could not avoid the family for ever, it should not be unreasonable to lick her wounds in private for a little while longer. The mirth at her expense had been bad, but the pity that followed it was likely to be even worse.

And it was totally unneeded. There was no logical reason to mourn the loss of a man who had never existed. She had always known that there would be no future with Potts. The fact that he had been nothing more than a fictional construct made it better, not worse. She could preserve the time they had spent together like dried flowers under glass. As long as she took care to avoid the scoundrel who wore his face, she would be as content with the memory of him as she had expected to be when he had returned to his fiancée in Philadelphia.

'Go away,' she called to the person on the opposite side of the closed door.

The knocking stopped. Then she heard the key turn and the door open.

She glared at the Earl of Comstock as he crossed the threshold and closed the door behind him. 'I did not give you leave to enter.'

'I do not need it,' he said, jingling the ring of keys in his hand.

'I do not wish to see you, or speak with you, ever again.'

'I am endeavouring to make that possible,' he said. 'As you might remember, the Comstock coffers are near to empty. If we do not finish what we have begun, we will be forced to share this house for the sake of economy.'

'I thought you meant to sell my books,' she said, thinking of the empty crates in the library that were probably filled and on their way to London.

'Some of them,' he agreed. 'I have been living amongst Puritans and Quakers the whole of my life. I begin to see why they emigrated. They would have thrown the Comstock pornography collection into the fireplace to keep it out of the hands of impressionable girls.'

'Do not speak of me as if I am an absent child,' she snapped.

'I apologise,' he said, without sincerity. 'You are no longer a child. No one knows that better than I.' The admission was made without passion, but it hung in the air between them like a fog of musk.

Then he continued as if nothing had changed. 'I mean to sell the more prurient works collected on this shelf, along with the scrimshaw in the billiard room and a collection of lurid ivory figurines I discovered in one of the unused bedrooms. The items are barely legal and cannot be displayed in public and I have no interest in keeping them. But there are private collectors who will pay a pretty penny to own them.' He paused. 'Drake had been instructed to leave your shelf of favourite books in the library untouched and it will be quite some time before I need to cull the rest of the collection for valuable works. If you desire to keep any of the ones I wish to sell, all you need do is say so.'

The solution was so reasonable she'd have thought it had come from Potts. Thanks were probably in order, but she could not bring herself to give them.

'But that might be nothing more than a temporary solution,' he said. 'To be sure of the future, it would be better that we go to the chapel and collect the diamonds. If they are still there, that is.'

'I have no reason to search for them, now that you are here,' she said, all but tasting the bitterness as her ruined plans were used against her.

'You do not want your share?' he said.

'Do not taunt me with them,' she said. 'Now that Comstock knows of the plan, he will keep them for himself. There is nothing for me to collect.'

'And now you are speaking of me as if I am not in the room. Nothing has changed in me but my name. You were prepared to take a modest amount of the total. I see no reason to disagree with that.'

Oh, Potts.

It was his reasonable voice and logical solution that had spoken to her from somewhere inside this stranger. No matter what the rest of England thought, the Earl was a pale imitation of the man she had fallen in love with.

'Unless you are no longer interested in the search,' he said, becoming Comstock again. 'Then I will go get them myself and do as I will with them after.'

He was wrong. Something in him *had* changed, more than his name, for this was exactly how she expected an earl to behave. The moment she'd resisted him, he had issued an ultimatum.

When she did not answer, he added, 'You are not the least bit curious to see what I have found? Because what I discovered will fascinate you, even if you find my company intolerable.'

Damn him. He knew just how to pique her interest. She did want to see what he had found. Especially if his assessment of it was accurate.

'Think about it,' he said. 'And if you come to your senses, meet me in the bedroom where I was trapped. Then I will show you the secrets that lie between these walls.'

He had won again. It did not matter that he had lied and in doing so had ruined the happiest week of her life. He had hinted that the diamonds were as good as found and promised her the share that she had meant to take all along.

Still, she might have resisted, if he had not seemed

so very like Potts. But that did not mean she was going to continue to put on airs for him. She returned to her room and changed into her drabbest gown, then covered her hair in a mob cap that Dill claimed was only fit for an old lady.

The end result screamed her lack of interest louder than words could. But to be sure that there could be no doubts as to what she thought of him, she brought his dog.

When she arrived at the room, she found the door already open. By the sound of creaking floorboards she had heard as she approached, the Earl had been pacing. He froze when he saw her, then clasped his hands behind his back as if he could not quite decide what to do with them. 'I feared you would not come.'

He was making it seem like some romantic assignation and not an act of financial necessity. 'Well, I am here now. As is Pepper.' She stood back and waited for the attack that would put him in his place.

Instead, the dog ran forward and sniffed at him, wagging his tail once before losing interest and examining the hem of a nearby curtain.

'He did not try to bite you,' she said, amazed.

'We made our peace earlier today,' the Earl said. 'Later, when he found me wandering in the passages between the walls and he finally had his chance to do me real harm, he led me to an exit.' He stared pensively at the dog. 'He is not such a bad little fellow, I suppose. But if he has decided that I am to be master of this house, he is mistaken. My plans to leave have not changed.'

'The lovely Prudence,' she said, surprised to find that her bitterness on the subject had not abated now that she had learned his identity.

'If you think that her looks have anything to do with this, you are wrong,' he said. 'If you met her, you would say she is thick as two short planks. I proposed to her once, shortly after Ed died. But it was done out of duty to be sure she was looked after. There was nothing more to it than that. She did not like my prospects and refused. I was not good enough for her, you see.' He shook his head, in disgust. 'Her opinion of me changed quick enough when she learned of the title.' He gave her a sad smile. 'You might be surprised to know that not everyone is as set against marrying Comstock as you are.'

Of course they weren't. A single earl was a sought-after commodity on the marriage mart. To find one as young and handsome as the new Comstock would be like planting catnip outside a fish market. 'I do not doubt your attractiveness. To some people,' she added.

'When I refused to renew my suit, she became pregnant with another man's child.'

'Apparently, she is not quite so stupid as you thought.' The trap was so cleverly sprung that she almost felt sorry for him.

'She knows I will not break my promise. But she thinks that she can force me into bringing her to England as my wife. I do not care for monarchy, or inherited government. But I will be damned before I make her a countess and her bastard the next Earl. I decided that it would be better for the family if I went back to where I came from and did not let my problems affect the succession.'

If his description of her was accurate, the logic of his decision was sound. She would rather the family had no head at all than see all they had built placed into the hands of Prudence and her bastard child. 'You planned to disappear,' she said.

'And I would have, had I not run into you at the dower house.'

'And then I mistook you for someone else,' she said.

'I apologise for allowing the mistake to continue,' he said, with an embarrassed dip of his head. 'I did not intend to be here more than a day or two.'

In truth, it had been four. But it felt like she had known Potts for a lifetime. And now he was gone. 'It is over now. Let us speak no more about it.' Perhaps he'd expected some formal acceptance of his apology. But as yet she had no such thing to offer him. The hurt was still too fresh. 'Now, what did you wish to show me?'

'I found a way into the family chapel,' he said. 'And you are well dressed to go there for it is not an easy trip.' He walked across the room and handed her a lit lantern and a cloth sack containing candles, a tinder-box, paper and a pencil, and an assortment of small tools. 'This time, I mean to be better prepared,' he said and added, 'Here, you. Get off,' as Pepper began worrying at the second bag.

In response to the scold, the dog gave a happy yip and darted away from it to disappear under the bed.

The bedstead was already angled away from the wall and, with some effort, he pushed it further, revealing no sign of the dog. But there was a piece of panelling behind the headboard that appeared to be loose.

She hurried to it and pried at the edge, calling for the dog, and starting in after him.

'Not so fast,' he said, catching her arm before she could climb through the hole. 'Pepper has more lives than a cat and knows these passages far better than we do. But it could be rather dangerous. It would be wise to let me lead the way.'

Then he tugged at the panel and it swung away from the wall to widen the gap. He picked up the second bag and lantern with one hand, then stepped into the wall and offered his free hand to her. 'Stay close behind me and hold your lantern high.'

She jumped as the panel swung shut behind them, sealing them into the hallway between the walls. She held the lantern up as he had suggested, examining the space around them. On one side was the stone wall of the old house, on the other, the brick and timbers of the new.

'When I realised that you were not coming to release me, I decided to find my own way out,' he said, as if it were no mean feat to discover hidden passages that were unknown to the family. 'I wandered in the dark for what felt like hours. Then Pepper found me and led me to an exit. I suspect he has been chasing mice through the walls.'

Then he pulled a ball of string from the bag he carried. 'It will be easier by lantern light. But this should help if we lose our way.' Then he walked forward, letting the string spool out behind them as they proceeded.

She did not think his object in bringing her here had been to make her sorry for abandoning him. Even so, he succeeded. The space they were in was overhung with cobwebs and thick with dust. Though it did not overly bother her, a skittish girl would have screamed at the spiders, or run from the bats that sometimes fluttered out of the gloom. More than once, Comstock had been forced to stop short and work his way around missing floorboards that revealed dark, seemingly bottomless gaps.

But his first trip through this maze had been done in complete darkness. No wonder he had shouted at her in the hall. He might have been killed by accident and his body lost for ever.

They'd reached the end of a corridor and he turned to the right, then held up a warning hand. 'Be careful. The steps to the main floor are steep. We are lucky that they bothered with them, instead of leaving us with a ladder.'

When they reached the bottom of the stairs, she looked back. The walls of the next passage rose high on either side of them, twice as high as the last ones had been. 'We are near the old ballroom, I think,' he said.

'How did you know without a lantern?' she said.

'I found the steps by falling down them,' he said. 'And the ballroom by the echo.'

'And the chapel?' she said, baffled, as they turned a corner.

'Because, as you told me before, the Stricklands never throw anything away.'

'Oh.' Her jaw dropped in surprise.

Even a blind man might have known that was what he had found, but it was even more amazing in the dim light of their lanterns. 'I thought that they had blocked it off and torn it down. Or that perhaps it had been turned into a bedroom, or a parlour.'

'Because it makes no sense to subsume one building inside another,' he said, the lantern light wavering as he shook his head. The floor of the passage they stood in was littered with slates from a roof that angled away, a few feet above their heads, the slope ending where the foundations had been nailed for what was probably the musicians' gallery for the ballroom on the left. Stretching in front of them to the right was the outer wall of the chapel, complete with the deep stone sills of the stained-glass windows, the faces of saints in their leaded panes unreadable in the gloom.

'It is even more incredible, now that I can see it,' he said, his reverent voice echoing in the strange space. He tugged her hand and led her to another hallway around the corner that held a pair of iron-bound doors, set with large rings for handles.

'Have you gone inside?' she whispered.

'I was waiting for you,' he said, whispering back. Though they were alone, there was something about the space that demanded respect. He cleared his throat and spoke in a normal tone. 'But I doubt it is locked. What reason would there be for it?'

He reached into his bag again, removing an oil can and a pry bar. Then he went to work, greasing the hinges before taking one of the rings in his hand, twisting and pulling. The door creaked, moved a few inches, then stuck in the rubble on the floor around them.

As he put the pry bar to work, Charity crouched at his feet to clear away the debris. They worked well together, without the need for questions or orders. It was a shame that he had to go.

Then she remembered what she'd forgotten. He was not going anywhere. The man she wanted was already gone. Or perhaps not. As she stared up in the dim light, his features seemed to change from familiar to strange and back again.

Suddenly, the door gave way and he grabbed her hand, pulling her out of its way. He gave the hand he was holding an encouraging squeeze. 'Are you ready, Miss Strickland?'

He was being formal with her again. She'd thought, after last night, that had ended. And now that he was not Potts, what was she to call him?

He raised an eyebrow, waiting for an answer.

'Yes,' she said.

'Ladies first.' Now he held the lantern high, for her.

The space inside had a different kind of stillness, the noise of their breathing amplified by the confines of the room. The lights they carried could not seem to fill the space, leaving the ceiling and corners in darkness. Charity pulled the candles from her own bag, lighting first one, then another off the lantern. 'Let me see if I can find a place for these.'

She walked forward into the room, bumping against a bench before adjusting her course to put the doors at her back and pacing forward to find the altar. When she felt the corner of the table in front of her, she tipped the candle on its side to drip a pool of wax to fix it in, then stopped. Two more paces brought her to a branched candle stand with enough sockets for the rest of the tapers in her bag.

She lit them and fitted them in their places, then looked around her at the room revealed by the retreating darkness.

'Astounding,' Potts said, in a hushed tone. 'And you did not know this was here?'

'No one did,' she said, holding up her hands to indicate the room. Behind her, there was a marble altar, at least six feet long, on a raised dais with the metal stand that they had seen in the Blue Earl's portrait. On either side of her stood three rows of pews, stretching the length of the room towards the doors through which they'd entered.

Above them, the ceiling vaulted up and away into the darkness, the roof still largely complete. The angles gave the illusion that the space was much bigger than it probably was. But still, it was hard to contemplate how the room had been hidden.

They would need to illuminate the hallway, she thought. A series of candles to light them from the outside would make it possible to see the pictures in the windows.

She frowned.

The family had managed without a chapel for generations. There was no need of one now. Even if there was, there was no one left to marry at Comstock Manor. Even if his Prudence talked him into returning, Charity doubted that she would be willing to settle for anything less than St George's in Hanover Square.

'Do you remember the clue?' he asked.

'Right, left, right and left, three, four, two, one.'

'Alternating the two things, we have three to the right, four to the left and so forth.' He stamped his foot on the flagstones at their feet. 'But we must find a starting point.'

Charity retrieved her lantern and swung it low, searching the floor. 'Here.' She scuffed the dust from a brass cross, set in a stone at the base of the dais.

'Do we face towards the Bible, or away?' he wondered.

'Towards, I should think.' She shrugged. 'To be polite.'

'Very well, then.' He counted for her and she paced off the stones, only to stumble as she reached the last one.

Because it was loose.

She stared at him in surprise, then pointed down, too excited to talk.

He came to her side, staring down at it and then back to her again. 'Before I turn over this stone, we must talk.'

'I cannot imagine a thing you might say that is more important than the fate of our future,' she said, pointing down at their feet.

'You might be surprised to know that time will continue to pass even without the presence of the Comstock diamonds.' Perhaps it was a trick of the light, but he looked older than he had when they had left the bedroom. 'Have you thought of what you will do if we turn over the stone and find nothing?'

Just the thought of another failure made her throat tighten. It felt like the beginning of tears. But she refused to cry over disappointments. There had been many of them in her life and crying had not done a single thing to change them.

'What would I do? I would go back to the library and continue to search,' she said. 'They must be here. All the clues we have found point to the spot.'

'But suppose they have already been found,' he said. 'Perhaps they were sold long ago. What will you do if we discover that all there is to the estate is what you know there to be: debt and difficulty?'

'What would I do?' she said, staring at him in the gloom. 'You speak as if there is a decision to be made.'

'There always is,' he said softly.

'For men, perhaps,' she replied. 'My only decision will be whether I should depend on Faith and her husband, or Hope and hers.' In either case, she would become the spinster that her sisters had always expected. After what had happened between them, she could not imagine marrying another man. 'It is not as if I can remain here,' she added.

'You love this house,' he reminded her. 'When you spoke of it before, your only fear was that I would come and dictate your life to you should you remain. I told you then and I tell you now, that will not be the case. You are free to do as you like, whether I am here or not. And can stay here until you die,' he replied.

'To what purpose?' she snapped. 'There is no reason for a Comstock Manor, if you are not here to live in it.'

'You have always known that I would leave,' he said, surprised at her anger.

'I knew that Potts meant to leave.' The thought of that had been painful enough. 'But I had no idea that the Earl meant to abandon…everything.'

Me.

After all she had promised, before they'd made love, she had almost accused him of the very thing she swore she would not mind. But that was when she had assumed that there would be an earl eager to rule over her. She had hated the thought of it, willing to do anything to prevent it. But it had never occurred to her that a time might come when there would be no one at all to rebel against.

It was terrifying. Before she had known he was Comstock, she had been prepared to beg him to stay with her. But he had made his decision based on what was best for the earldom. It was the one area that she was sure she had no right to interfere with. If she did, she would tell him that yoking himself to this beautiful, American schemer was the height of stupidity. 'What will I do when you are gone?' she said at last. 'I can only tell you what I will not do. I will not sit alone, weeping over the loss of you. If you intend to go back to America, you had best get about it. Now lift the stone so we can see if your trip will be financed on diamonds or silverware.'

'Very well,' he said, scuffing the flagstone with the toe of his boot and watching it shift. 'There is nothing more to say.' Then, he walked back to the door and retrieved the pry bar, fit it into the widest open crack and lifted.

For a moment, they stared down into the hole he'd opened, stunned.

Then he said, 'Well, this is unexpected.'

Chapter Twenty-Two

'Chilson!' Miles tried to keep the manic tone from his voice. Earls were not supposed to panic when they located the family fortune hidden under the floorboards. It probably happened all the time in England.

When he had moved the loose flagstone, he had assumed that, with luck, there would be a jewellery box, or perhaps a small sack containing the loose stones. They would have a moment of celebration as he counted out five of the best of them into her hand to show that the new Earl was not the demanding ogre she'd expected, just a perfectly reasonable fellow who honoured his bargains. If they could not be lovers, maybe they could at least be friends again.

But their search for the Comstock jewels had been more successful than they'd ever thought possible. Instead of a single pouch of diamonds, there had been several bags of jewellery, several small boxes of loose stones and a large metal strongbox full of coins. Cyril Strickland had not just hidden the family jewels from looters, he had amassed a dragon's hoard of gold and jewellery, then tucked it up under a stone and bricked off the room for good measure.

And then he had died and the world had moved on without him.

After a single, silent glance of agreement, they'd emptied the sacks they'd been carrying and begun to refill them with loot. But it soon became clear that they could not carry it all, and they'd agreed to take just enough to dazzle the rest of the family at dinner. Then he'd replaced the flagstone and led the stunned Charity out of the netherworld between the walls using the passage that led to the main hall.

Having recovered his composure after their earlier meeting, Chilson was there to greet them, freshly combed and starched, ready to serve.

Miles grinned at him. 'Yesterday you promised me footmen with hammers. Bring them here, please. And Hoover the groom, as well. I need muscle to demolish a wall.' It made no sense to be creeping through the house with a lantern, when there was a direct route available through the blocked archway in the ballroom.

Once he had explained to the butler what was required, Miles retired to his room to explore the damage done to his person and his wardrobe by the day's adventures. After its swim with the ducks, his clothing had been returned to the cupboard and seemed no worse for wear. But when he had stripped to wash, his body was a testament of scrapes and bruises from his run-in with Hoover and the time spent stumbling around in the walls. He would likely need help to get out of bed tomorrow once the stiffness had set in. Today, he was still numb.

He glanced at the stack of letters on the bureau that Drake had given him before everything had gone wrong. Damn Prudence, for introducing him to the idea that failure was even a possibility. He had been perfectly happy with how his life had been progressing until she had declared that he was not fit to marry her.

And now, when he had finally found a woman who was his equal, Pru had ruined it for him again. What had he expected Charity to say when he had questioned her in the chapel? Had he wanted her to proclaim her love for him and beg him to break his promise and stay with her?

It had not been her job to ask, it had been his to offer. He had been either too proud or too weak to say the words without some assurance that his proposal would be accepted. Perhaps it was just as well. Despite her many arguments to the contrary, she had spoken of the house being pointless without Comstock in it. If he had offered to stay and marry her, she might have accepted him against her better judgement, for the sake of the family.

But not for love. And without that, there was no point in remaining. If he wanted a loveless marriage, there was one waiting in Pennsylvania already.

He grabbed the letters, ready to throw them into the fire unread, then thought the better of it. If he truly meant to return home, he had best learn what fresh hell awaited him.

The first one he opened had been written while he

was still at sea. It was full of the same pleas for aid that the last letter had contained, interspersed with reminders of the difficulties she would face if Pru could not find a husband and the fact that her delicate condition grew more difficult to hide with each passing day.

The next letter was far more recent, dated several weeks after the proposal he had sent her on reading of her plight. In his letter, he had promised to help her and offered marriage, but explained there might be difficulties in getting home and the problems with the Comstock finances. He'd urged her to be patient and promised that he was returning as soon as he could gather enough money to clear Edward's debts, but would arrive well before the child would need his name.

Her answer to his three pages of promises took barely half a sheet of paper.

Only you could find a way to ruin an earldom.

There was more. But the gist of it stated that his return would not be necessary. His fancy title was worth nothing compared to cash on the barrelhead. She had dared to hope that the second Strickland might finally equal the first, but he had proved sorely disappointing.

To add insult to injury, the letter had been signed Mrs Prudence Parker, the surname of the banker who held Edward's notes. That man was middling handsome but, since he owned one of the largest houses in Philadelphia, a lack of hair and an excess of belly had made no difference, once Miles had been out of sight of land.

There was a third, somewhat longer letter from the banker Horace Parker, accusing him of abandoning a woman in need, and the child he had fathered. Apparently, Pru had been as thorough in her entrapment of Horace as she had been of him. Parker had dried her tears and settled her debts, and now made it clear that there was no room in Pennsylvania for a turncoat who would renounce his country and serve King George. They were all better off without him. Dire action would be taken should Horace hear that Miles had darkened American shores.

He sat on the bed for a moment, staring at the papers and trying not to grin. She had refused him again. He was free of his promise. Even the ghost of Ed Strickland could not expect him to come back and sort this mess out.

Somewhere deep inside him, there was a desire to return in triumph and prove her wrong. He ignored it. Only a fool would send an answering letter to Pru, announcing that she'd just made the biggest mistake of her life.

But if he was not wanted at home, and he was not wanted here, where did he belong? His plan to turn the estate over Charity was a sound one, but it was so much more complicated now that there was money to give her. Tonight, his mind was as numb as his body. Life was much more complicated than chess. He could not manage to see more than a single move ahead.

As he had not eaten since the night before, his opening gambit would have to begin with food of some sort. He rang for Drake's valet. In no time at all, Hagstead had worked miracles on him, his clothing and, as promised, his boots. Then, with a sigh of resignation, he went to the linen drawer and retrieved his signet again, slipping it on his finger before going down to dinner.

Tonight's menu was mutton, likely the best that the cook could manage when surprised by the arrival of four extra guests. But the ragout was as tender as lamb and Miles had sent word that the meal was to be accompanied by the finest wines in the cellar. Instead of the comfortable place halfway down the table with Charity, he sat at the head.

The family rose in respect as he entered. Even Charity, though she did so with downcast eyes. The sight made him wince. 'Please, sit,' he said, gesturing them back to their chairs. 'And the first one of you to call me "my lord" will be banished from the table.'

'And what are we to call you now? When you can't seem to keep a name from one day to the next, it is difficult to know what to do.' It was Charity, of course, the only one with nerve enough to speak her mind.

He smiled. 'Miles. It is my given name and, since you are my family, I would prefer that you use it.'

'Of course, my lord,' Charity replied.

Apparently, the familiar affection that they'd fallen into as they explored had disappeared at the sight of him sitting in her grandfather's chair. He would have no help from the rest of the family, who sensed the tension between them and began emptying their plates at a speed that made it impossible for them to speak.

'Thank you, Charity,' he said. No longer bound by formality, he could call her by the name he had only whispered as they'd shared a bed. 'Have you told your sisters what it was we discovered this afternoon during our exploration of the house?'

'I was waiting for you, Lord Comstock,' she said, her hands in her lap, her tone subservient and her eyes glaring a challenge.

He raised a hand to signal the footman standing at the door of the dining room and instructed him to go to the study and bring the bag that was sitting on the desk.

When it arrived, Miles rose to take it, then dumped the contents out on to the cloth. Forks dropped as gold coins spilled across the table, clinking against wine glasses. An emerald necklace slithered out after them to lay beside his plate like a snake.

He sat again and took a sip from his wine glass as though nothing unusual had happened.

'My Lord.' It was Leggett who spoke, clearly invoking the deity rather than his host.

'This is just a small portion of what we found,' Miles announced, revelling in the drama of the announcement. 'It was not possible to carry it all away. The servants have begun opening a passage to the chapel where it was hidden.'

Then he turned to Drake. 'This is likely to lead to some complications in the plan I put forth this morning to turn the management of the estate over to your sister-in-law.'

'What?' Charity's voice was sharp as a whip crack in the silence of the room.

Miles gave her a bland look. 'Though you insist that no Earl of Comstock would ever listen to your suggestions, your ideas so far have been as sound as anything I could come up with. When I left, I was planning to leave the running of the estate to you.'

For the first time since he had known her, she seemed too stunned to speak. It was strangely satisfying.

'Of course, there are problems with that now,' he said directly to Drake. 'Though it shall be easier for her to run things if there is enough money to do it, when we total up the booty, I suspect she has just become one of the most eligible heiresses in England. There will be a problem with fortune hunters, of course.'

'I am not an heiress,' she snapped. 'I am a distant relation to the Earl of Comstock. Perhaps you do not understand the principle of primogeniture.'

'I understand it. I simply do not agree with it,' he said, smiling down the table. 'America has been managing well without it for a generation or longer. I do not intend to come here and regress in my thinking. Like it or not, Charity, you and your sisters will receive a substantial share of the family fortune.'

'I don't understand,' she said softly. 'Why would you do such a thing?'

'Since the day I arrived, you have made it quite clear what you wanted from life. You wished for money of your own with which you could set up housekeeping. You wished for a sufficient dowry to attract a husband and to choose him for yourself. Most of all, you wished to be taken seriously by the Earl of Comstock.' He stared at her, willing her to understand what he had no intention of saying in front of the entire family, especially if he was not sure of her response.

'I am giving you everything you asked for. Just as I promised, when I was Potts, I am giving you the freedom to choose your own future. And I hope, the next time you choose a man, you will do a better job of it than you have this week.' Then he threw his napkin aside and left the table.

Chapter Twenty-Three

Once he was gone, the table erupted in conversation and demands that she describe the afternoon in detail, with particular attention to the size of the fortune they'd found. Was it truly as large as he'd said?

'Yes,' Charity said, staring down at her hands, which were folded tightly in her lap.

'How amazing,' Faith said, unable to contain her smile. 'And he means to share it with us. The man is kindness himself.'

'But Gregory told me he is going back to America,' Hope said urgently. 'It is not that we have not always suspected you were capable of running the estate. But you cannot take his seat in Parliament for him. Is there nothing you can do to persuade him to stay?'

'No,' Charity said firmly.

Ask him.

She ignored the perfectly reasonable suggestion in her own head.

'Nothing at all?' Faith said with a pointed expression, as if to hint that, though they did not know what the matter could be, they were sure it was her fault and that an apology might solve everything.

'He is going back to America because his fiancée is there,' Charity announced. It did not matter that he was marrying an unworthy trollop who was likely to make him miserable. He had made the offer and he was a man of his word.

'He is engaged?' Drake said, frowning. 'This is the first I have heard of it and I made some effort to discover his past.'

'Her name is Prudence. She is very beautiful,' Charity said, swallowing a bite of her pudding around the lump in her throat.

'And when did he tell you of her?' Faith said, eyes narrowing.

'From the first,' Charity answered. 'He made no secret of her.' He had lied about his name, but in all other things he had been completely honest with her.

'He was engaged. And yet he...' Hope's voice fell away as if she did not want to accuse him of something that could not be taken back.

'He did nothing,' Charity snapped. 'It was me. It was always me. He did everything in his power to avoid a liaison. But I badgered him until he succumbed.'

There was another profound silence at the table as the family tried to digest that they were not only speaking of something totally inappropriate for mixed company, but that it seemed to involve the youngest and supposedly most naïve member of the family instigating an affair.

At last, Mr Drake spoke. 'Though you may feel you

are to blame, your version of events is not accurate. He concealed his identity from you. If he had been honest, you might have felt differently towards him.'

Of course she would have. She'd have treated him as she had tonight, arguing, snapping and being difficult for no reason. She was as bad as Pepper, who had yapped and nipped, angry at the unfairness of the world and taking it out on the man who had rescued him. And Potts... Comstock...

Miles.

His true name seemed to resonate in her mind like the ringing of a bell. Miles had done nothing to deserve the dog's hatred. But that had not changed the way he behaved towards it. He had never kicked, never shouted, and gone out of his way to keep the dog safe and well, expecting nothing in return. It was the sort of nobility that one imagined for the peerage, but seldom found in real life.

Mr Leggett was unimpressed. 'No matter the provocation, he knew what he was doing was wrong. The onus lies with him to do right by you.' He had been a rake before falling in love with Faith. Apparently, it had taken only two months of marriage to her sister to turn him into a tiresome busybody, eager to spoil the fun for everyone else.

'We will speak to him,' Mr Drake added. 'And remind him that his duty lies with family first.'

'Prudence is his family, as well. She was his late brother's wife.' And she did not need Charity's help in getting or keeping the man she wanted. She had lied and cheated and won.

'A widow,' Mr Leggett said, as if this explained all. Mr Drake nodded.

'None of this matters,' Charity snapped, glaring around the table at him. 'Whatever has happened was between Comstock and myself, and is no business of any of you. You will not speak to him about his supposed obligation to me, nor will you question me about it. Not now. Not ever.'

And then, before she dissolved into the pointless tears that her family was expecting, she fled the room.

One of the advantages of living at Comstock Manor was that when one wanted to run away, one had plenty of space to do it in. She had been no more than four when they had first arrived and Charity had vague memories of wandering the endlessly long corridors, searching for her mother and weeping.

It had been years since she'd got lost. But tonight, she was tempted to try. At the very least, she could find a place to have a good cry in private, to give vent to her frustrations without having her brothers-in-law demanding satisfaction and her sisters forcing her down the aisle when she simply wanted to be left alone.

Since Comstock might have retired to the Tudor Room or the Earl's suite, she did not want to be anywhere near the bedrooms. It would be hard enough sleeping down the hall from him with a wing full of chaperons. She could not trust herself to be alone.

Instead, she ran down the centre wing to the back of the house and was halfway to the ballroom before she had realised what she was doing. Then she slowed. The sound of rhythmic pounding came from somewhere ahead, along with the incessant barking of Pepper, the dog. Perhaps the foolish creature had run back into the walls and was stuck. Though she did not relish the idea of navigating the tunnels in the dark, she could not stand the thought of leaving him for the night.

She walked on in the direction she'd been going, as the volume of the sounds increased. Then, as the back staircase widened to reveal the ballroom, she understood. At the end of the great room, the Earl of Comstock was stripped to his shirt sleeves, swinging an enormous hammer at what was left of the wall that blocked off the chapel. Pepper danced around his feet, barking in approval as he dodged out of the way of falling bricks.

Her beautiful Mr Potts, the American man of action. She could not help smiling as she walked down the room to stand at his side. 'If you think it so important that the job be finished tonight, you can call for servants,' she said, over the pounding of the hammer.

'I do not want help,' he said, scowling. 'Not from you, or anyone else.'

'You will not get more than advice from me,' she said, pulling a delicate gold chair from the stack along one wall and sitting to watch him work. Though she had told herself that she did not want to see him again, the view was hard to resist. His sweat-soaked shirt clung to his back, outlining muscle and sinew as he moved.

'I would prefer that you not give me that, either,' he

said, leaning on the hammer. 'You said that taking liberties with your person would have no permanent effect on either of us. What a load of hogwash that turned out to be. I'm in such a state that I'm breaking rocks after dinner so I can sleep at night.' He pointed an accusing finger at her. 'After the billiard room, you likely slept like an angel. But I ran through the upper halls like a madman until I was too tired to think about you. The night after that, you caught me hanging my hair splitter out the window to cool the thing off. And tonight?' He cocked his thumb at the loose bricks on the wall. 'I am knocking down walls.'

'Because of me,' she repeated.

He looked thoughtful. 'After I return to America, I suspect I will turn to lumberjacking. I have never tried it, but it looks like damned hard work.'

'Do they have forests in Pennsylvania?' she asked.

'They have forests in Maine,' he said. 'I am no longer welcome in Philadelphia.'

'What about Prudence?' she said, almost afraid to ask.

'Once she learned there was not likely to be much money in Earl-ing, she turned around and married a banker.'

'Then you are free,' she said softly.

'If you call this freedom,' he said, gesturing at the house around him.

'Now that there is money to run the place, I do,' she said.

'Then take it with my blessing,' he replied, as if it should make any sense at all.

'You still mean to go to home, though you do not have to?'

'You are here,' he said. The words should have hurt her. But there was a longing in the way he said them that made her heart flutter.

'If my presence bothers you, there is all the rest of England to hide in,' she said.

He shook his head. 'Not big enough. You could drop a dozen Englands into America and still not fill it up.'

The idea amazed her. 'I should rather like to see that.'

'If I am going away so I do not have to see you, your following me there defeats the purpose,' he said.

'You are trying to avoid me?'

'Does it matter? When we were in the chapel, you seemed more concerned about the absence of an earl than you were about losing me. Before that, you wanted me, but not the Earl. You cannot have one without the other, Miss Strickland.'

He had gone back to being proper. But rather than feeling cold and distant, the sound of her surname raised the colour in her cheeks. 'Now that I have met the Earl of Comstock, I think I could grow quite fond of him,' she said, smiling. 'And I will always have a soft spot for my dear Mr Potts, even if that is not his real name.'

'That is good to know. Because the more time I spent with you, the harder it was to imagine how I could ever be happy with someone else.' He let the hammer fall and walked towards her. 'It is rare that I have to exert myself when beating someone at chess. I suspect, once

you have studied my play, it will become even harder.'
Then he smiled. 'And I have never had an opponent
with such distracting cleavage.'

'Was it the chess that decided you?' she asked eagerly. 'Because that was when I knew that I loved you.'

'Probably not,' he admitted. 'When I found you up a
chimney, I was intrigued. Even more so after the chess
game. But when I realised that you came with an entire library...' He shrugged, helpless. 'How could I not
love a woman with so many books?'

'They are actually your books,' she reminded him.

'The family's,' he corrected. 'I still intend to share
them with you. If you want them, that is,' he added.
'You are a rich woman now, Charity Strickland. Once
word gets out that we are flush, you will have your pick
of gentlemen. I will have to fight my way through the
throng just to get to your billiard table.'

'You forget that you are an earl,' she said, smiling.
'I will not even bother talking to barons and misters.
It would be just a few dukes and marquesses ahead of
you in the line.'

'I did not think you were interested in titles,' he
said. 'I'd have told you my name much sooner if I had
not been sure that being Lord Comstock would count
against me.'

'I suppose some earls are all right,' she allowed.
'But in my experience, English lords can be quite full
of themselves.'

'Then it is a good thing I am not really English,' he
said, pulling her into his arms for a kiss.

Epilogue

'Chilson! Where is my wife?' As his Countess had frequently pointed out to him, it was not really necessary to shout when calling the servants. There were bell pulls in every room. Even without a summons, they tended to hover close by, ready to help. Unless he took pains to shut them out of the room, there was usually a maid or footman close enough to hear him if he spoke in a normal voice.

But if he stood in the middle of the entry hall and shouted, there was an echo. It gave him an irrational pleasure to be able to hear how large his new home was, without even having to look at it. It was also an excellent position to admire the greenery that had been brought in to decorate the house for the Christmas season. He had insisted that the holly and ivy, mistletoe and hellebore were supplemented by a proper Christmas tree in the main parlour, decorated with fruits and nuts and gingerbread, and lit with candles just as he'd had back home.

'Lady Comstock is in the library, my lord.' Chilson arrived as he always did, seemingly out of nowhere and as staid and silent as Miles was loud. After almost ten months, the butler had grown used to his habits. Miles suspected that they amused him, if English butlers were allowed a sense of humour. It also seemed to please him that the woman who had arrived here as the smallest of three orphans was now a countess. He repeated her title whenever he could, as if unable to contain his pride. 'Lady Comstock is with the painter.'

Miles grinned. 'Then she will not mind being interrupted.' He bounded down the hall to find her. Even with the sudden influx of money to the estate, the library was as tatty as ever. The Christmas greenery on the mantelpiece could not seem to hold its leaves and the berries fell from the kissing bough in the doorway almost faster than they could pluck them off.

But it was Charity's favourite room and his, as well. He could not think of a better place for her to sit for her portrait.

He leaned forward and kissed his wife on the cheek and was rewarded with a hiss of disapproval from the artist.

'I will not move.' Charity sighed, then returned a rigid smile and muttered, 'He wants me to remove my spectacles.'

'I forbid it,' Miles said, using his earl's voice and enjoying the painter's flinch of subservience.

'And I would like to remove the tiara,' she said, making a face.

'I forbid that, as well,' he said in a much more affectionate tone. 'You may have talked me into waiting for the formal portrait. But if this miniature is to be my Christmas present, I reserve the right to choose your costume.'

'I lack the energy to stand for a full-length painting,' she reminded him. 'Perhaps when I am out of my confinement.'

He grinned at the mention of her delicate condition. 'I will insist on it.'

'And do not puff yourself up about the chances of getting an heir on the first go,' she said, still murmuring through an unwavering smile. 'Though you know much about advising the local farms in the care of their crops and animals, you have done nothing to grow this child.'

'I was there at the start,' he said, feeling quite smug about it. 'And I have been keeping its mother well fed and properly coddled. I have just come from speaking with the workmen. The family chapel will be in fine shape for the christening in spring. The windows are quite lovely, when lit from behind.'

'So there will be no risk of you stepping in holes in the floor, as you did at our wedding?' she asked.

'It is good that we spent the next week in bed,' he replied. 'My ankle was not quite right for some time after.'

'But it was strong enough as you danced last week,' she reminded him.

'When the whole family is gathered for a ball, one cannot sit out the dances,' he said. 'But we must see about cutting another doorway to the ballroom. The guest wings are looking much better, but it is a bother to have to walk through them to get there.'

'Next year,' she said, smiling.

As he dismissed the portrait artist for the day, she pulled off the jewellery she had been wearing, stretching her neck and rolling her shoulders as if the weight of them bothered her. For the first time in several generations, the Countess of Comstock would be wearing real diamonds in her portrait and Miles had requested that she deck herself in as much of the set as she could stand. They did nothing to make her more beautiful or precious to him, but he liked to be reminded of the fun they'd had in searching for them.

He stepped behind her to massage her shoulders, making her sigh in satisfaction. 'So you have enough energy to visit the village? A wagon has been loaded with baskets for the tenants and I am eager to be done before dark.'

She smiled. 'I am never too tired to play Lady Bountiful. It must amuse Faith and Hope to no end that I am finally developing manners and living up to my name.'

'Wise and generous,' he said with a proud smile, then kissed her ear and whispered, 'Beautiful, as well.'

By the way her skin coloured at the words, she still did not fully believe him. But she believed in his love. Believing in herself would come, with time.

'And has your surprise arrived?' she asked, turning to kiss him.

'Several barrels of it,' he assured her. 'Cook has poured it off into bottles. Every family on the property will have maple syrup for their Christmas dinner. And this is for you.' He pulled the napkin from his pocket and offered her the treat he was carrying there.

'Candy?' she said, taking a brittle string of sugar into her mouth.

'You cook the syrup down, then pour it out on to the snow to harden,' he said. 'Since nature will not cooperate and give me proper winter weather, I had to make do with a bowl of shaved ice. But there is plenty left to have over corn pudding with our dinner.'

She laughed and made a face. 'Maize mush for a holiday meal. Lord Comstock, you are an odd man. But I love you dearly and will clean my plate if it keeps you from returning home.'

'It is not my home, darling,' he said, kissing her again. 'America is just the place where I was born. My home is with you.'

* * * * *